CW01240402

HERE AND BEYOND

HERE AND BEYOND

Hal LaCroix

BLOOMSBURY PUBLISHING
LONDON • OXFORD • NEW YORK • NEW DELHI • SYDNEY

BLOOMSBURY PUBLISHING
Bloomsbury Publishing Plc
50 Bedford Square, London, WC1B 3DP, UK
29 Earlsfort Terrace, Dublin 2, Ireland

BLOOMSBURY, BLOOMSBURY PUBLISHING and the Diana logo
are trademarks of Bloomsbury Publishing Plc

First published in Great Britain, 2025

Copyright © Hal LaCroix, 2025

Hal LaCroix is identified as the author of this work in accordance
with the Copyright, Designs and Patents Act 1988

All rights reserved. No part of this publication may be: i) reproduced or transmitted in any form, electronic or mechanical, including photocopying, recording or by means of any information storage or retrieval system without prior permission in writing from the publishers; or ii) used or reproduced in any way for the training, development or operation of artificial intelligence (AI) technologies, including generative AI technologies. The rights holders expressly reserve this publication from the text and data mining exception as per Article 4(3) of the Digital Single Market Directive (EU) 2019/790

A catalogue record for this book is available from the British Library

ISBN: HB: 978-1-5266-7825-6; TPB: 978-1-5266-7827-0;
EBOOK: 978-1-5266-7823-2; EPDF: 978-1-5266-7824-9

2 4 6 8 10 9 7 5 3 1

Typeset by Integra Software Services Pvt. Ltd.
Printed and bound in Great Britain by CPI Group (UK) Ltd, Croydon CR0 4YY

MIX
Paper | Supporting responsible forestry
FSC® C013604

To find out more about our authors and books visit www.bloomsbury.com
and sign up for our newsletters.

For product-safety-related questions contact productsafety@bloomsbury.com

For Elahna

CONTENTS

1	Year 118: End of an Era	1
2	Years 0–12: Excerpts from *The Chronicler's Journal*	65
3	Years 193–196: The Dark Age	107
4	Years 250–252: Out of the Black	147
5	Years 312–321: Excerpts from *The Second Chronicler's Journal*	203
6	Years 359–360: Achieving Orbit	243
7	Planetfall	281
8	Year 1: A New Era Begins	287
	Acknowledgements	309

1

Year 118: End of an Era

Franika Longstem was ready to walk out, to take the leap. To see for herself.

Tomorrow, like everyone on their twenty-fourth birthday, she would finally behold the truth of existence. She would experience the Revelation. And so the doubts that young people invariably entertain – that reality was a tailored fantasy, that the frigid vacuum of space didn't actually exist outside the windows and bulkheads, that the history of Shipworld was a fiction, all of it, the secret construction project, the Constitutional Convention on Iceland, the fateful choice of HD-40307g, the great escape from anarchy and civilisational collapse, the fuelling of the fusion drive at Jupiter and the Oberth manoeuvre that slingshot them around the gas giant to twelve per cent of light speed – tomorrow, all such doubts would be swept away. Franika would know, absolutely, that the testimonies of Revelation spacewalkers were not audacious lies woven into a crisscrossing conspiracy; that Shipworld in Year 118 was not hanging like a bat in an Earthworld cave as part of some strange, sadistic experiment; and that they were, in fact, travelling forty-two light-years across the void to a new home.

✦

Always running late, Brenz Oort-St George improvised a route from his dank, aft-section room to the extravehicular activity (EVA) airlock. Up/down Pictor Boulevard he weaved around shipworldmates who barely turned at his passing. In retort, gangling Brenz executed a series of awkward but effective bounds over storage benches and then ducked around a bamboo screen shielding an algae tank. He raced past a stacked kale and tomato garden gushing colour, climbed onto the southwestern utility catwalk and came out on Carina Way where he wasn't supposed to be except on maintenance duty. But what could be more important to the ceaseless functioning of Shipworld than his role today as Franika's Katan?

Brenz hustled up a stairway, its metal rails two-tone dull and shiny with years of grabbing, and for a moment in his bid to reclaim lost time, he beheld from this high/low point the sweep of Shipworld, of home. Two hundred and one metres long, one hundred and sixty-five metres in diameter at the midpoint. An oblong warehouse tapered at the ends. A corrugated countryside of crops and gardens served by pollinating nano-mists in the absence of birds, insects, wind and water. A gizmo bazaar, sustaining sustainability. Dense neighbourhoods of row houses, apartment buildings, playgrounds, picnic areas and parks designed for tai chi, yoga and kick boxing. Walking paths twisting like Möbius strips. The Olmec Head, ever heedless, the ficus tree on its gentle mound. And ground on the upside down where the sky used to be, so he'd been told, back on Earthworld.

What a waste of space that must have been, he thought, all those kilometres of sky – unless you're an airplane or a bird or one of those misty water-transfer things – what did they call them? Right, clouds. There'd been birds on Shipworld but they'd gone extinct by Year 2, no one knew why, and now it occurred to Brenz that they might have died for lack of limitless sky. Could that be possible? They'd just felt too cramped, their flying confined to an egg-shaped volume of empty space between encircling ground.

Bisecting that space lengthwise, like one of those steel pokers slid through a baking potato, ran the Tube, a transparent, zero-gravity tunnel. If Brenz could have taken it this morning, he'd be there by now, but the passage was reserved for freight shipments, spacewalk training and school field trips. Once a year, on Launch Day, the Tube was opened for general tomfoolery. A favourite phrase of his father's.

Now he scooted down another stairway, stepped on a window – a square of star-streaked black set into the floor – and headed across the lobby adjoining the Mess Hall which, he noticed, was being used for a meeting. A ring of shipworldmates faced each other, maybe vine trainers or Equi-fans or reciters of poems and prayers preserved only in memory, maybe expectant mothers or student teachers or even meeting schedulers, so many meetings about every-last-thing and how that thing might be used, reused, repurposed and, ultimately, vaporised and reborn. It could be an open meeting of the Council, the governing body who mostly mediated disagreements and reallocated resources. And made sure, of course, that rules were followed.

Brenz continued in the direction of the Bridge, which pointed at HD-40307g and so, in a way, he was going faster than the ship. Then he zigzagged through the library's Art Cove where several paintings on easels were covered in red sheets of cloth. Brenz wanted to double back and rip off the sheets, to see what lay beneath – or was that the art exhibit itself, canvases draped in scarlet? – but he didn't. Time flies on melting wings – where did that expression come from? His mother, probably, muttered while crocheting. He latched onto a mechanised zip-line, in the process violating a bunch of safety regulations, and rode it up/down the last fifty metres, then unlatched in Shipworld record time, *click, snap, rip*.

At the EVA airlock, Brenz checked the data/tracking panel implanted in his forearm – late again, damn, by ten seconds. Close enough. He fixed his hair, stroking the defiant cowlick over his right eye, and rapped on the door. Seconds passed. He rapped again, not so hard this time, and the door slid open.

As soon as he stepped inside the small, inner airlock, the door sealed behind him with a gaseous *thunk*. Just metres away stood Franika in navy blue long johns. A rack held the many exfoliated layers of her EVA suit, and her helmet hung on a hook like some kind of magic techno-orb. She offered a trace smile. Brenz began to speak, but she stopped him with an outstretched palm. It was her place to initiate, his to respond.

'Welcome, Brenz. I'll be twenty-four tomorrow and these are my last hours before the Revelation. Will you consent to be my Katan?'

'Yes, I will,' he replied. 'It's a great honour, Franny.'

'The honour is mine, Katan.'

She bowed slightly. He returned a deeper bow – not protocol, but it seemed right. Brenz *was* honoured, and confused. They were friends, sure, but he was three years younger than Franika and hadn't a clue why she'd asked him to be her decompression companion. Traditionally, the Katan functioned as a kind of guide and helper, a source of strength for the spacewalker right before the leap. But he didn't feel strong, and he had no expertise worth sharing, no wisdom to impart. There was, as the saying goes, no gravity about him. Hollow Brenz, floating-above-it-all Brenz, yet to be afflicted with the Fears even though he roughly understood the Occam's razor-what's-more-likely argument behind Shipworld scepticism.

As in, what's more likely, he's one of 600 humans lucky/unlucky enough to be on an intergenerational mission to HD-40307g, a habitable super-Earth hug-orbiting a simmering red dwarf star, that he, dorky, ever-late Brenz with his mediocre grades and ridiculous sexual fantasies, lives inside a spaceship built by a super-rich guy who didn't bother getting aboard, a ship spinning on its axis every twenty-four seconds for the last one hundred and eighteen years, a ship using propulsion and life-support technologies untested beyond the inner planets of the old sol system, a ship in which the population remains level and society functions despite the grave dangers of deep space, the frailty of built things and the homicidal history of humanity. What's more likely: all that, or that this place is just a big building with fancy video screens for windows? Or, if you're hung up on the zero-grav centre of Shipworld, if you can't imagine how that could be simulated, then how about an elaborate but doable experiment in low-Earth orbit?

Be honest, what's more likely?

Over several hours, the room's air pressure ratcheted down from 14.7 psi to 8.3 psi, the atmospheric pressure that Franika would experience inside her EVA suit. She and her Katan breathed pure oxygen, to ease the transition. The first hour was devoted to getting Franika dressed. She knew the procedure, after months of spacewalk training, so he didn't do much except steady her as she wriggled into each component. Periodically, they performed double checks. Protective layer after protective layer went on, thirteen in all, some soft and thin, some bulky, and to Brenz it seemed as if a machine had grown around her body in concentric rings, a machine-habitat for sustaining life functions and warding off ultra-cold temperatures, cosmic radiation and micrometeoroids.

Together, Brenz and Franika confirmed that the primary and secondary oxygen packs were operational, that her electronics worked, and that she could twist her hips and lift her legs without too much strain. The helmet would go on last. They inspected its seals and hinges, tested the sliding neck ring and dusted the inside and outside of its polycarbonate visor with a nano-pen. When they were finished, Brenz cradled the helmet like an egg.

'I didn't expect you to pick me,' he said.

'It's random,' she replied, her surprise bubbling into a laugh. 'I had to submit a list of ten names, and then it's just chance. Didn't you know?'

He hadn't. Sometimes Brenz failed to learn things simply because he didn't want them to be true. Really, why couldn't Franika make the final choice for her Katan? What was the Great Social Good in doing it this way? Except, he thought, to rub it in. To remind them: keep your place. Like at Mess Hall – why couldn't he choose his dinner? Instead, one of four entrees was randomly assigned to each diner. Trading was discouraged, though he'd seen people do it on the sly.

Some rules on Shipworld were ironclad, such as the prohibition against having children until your late fifties. Brenz knew the stated reasons: to allow shipworldmates to fully develop their lives before parenthood and to reduce friction between generations. On Earthworld, the creation of a new generation every twenty to thirty years had led to constant social and political turmoil. But this was Shipworld. Everybody got along, or pretended to. Everybody was committed to the Mission. Just because the Correction lengthened the reproductive window, why couldn't some people choose to start families earlier if they had their acts together? Which he knew he didn't – not by a long shot.

Brenz and Franika stood there, looking at each other, for several seconds. He wondered if she sensed his muddled musings. If she shared a few.

'Do you ever think about Earthworld?' he asked.

'Not really,' she said. 'It was so crazy and violent back there. Nothing worked, not in the long run. I guess I'd rather think about here.'

'I think about it, sometimes,' Brenz admitted. 'You know, all kinds of different things could have happened. We don't know their history anymore.'

'We'll never know – we're going too fast to get a transmission.' A statement of obvious fact, as they were travelling roughly one hundred and twenty thousand times the speed of sound; they would never hear the voices calling them back, or cursing their flight. Then she added: 'The earthworlders are probably all dead. We're it, the last humans.'

'Yeah, maybe,' he said. 'Or they developed faster propulsion and we'll meet them when we get there. I mean our children will. Our descendants.'

Brenz blushed, turned his head. The children of Brenz and Franika. She smiled, reaching out to touch his elbow with the index finger of her outer glove. It was fashioned from a stainless-steel-chromium-silicone composite layered over a thermal inner glove equipped with a water-evaporative cooling system. Brenz had a way of remembering such details, for no apparent reason, to no apparent end.

'Katan, it's time for the Fears.'

And so, it was. Franika waited for her Katan, who took a deep breath of pure oxygen that found its way into uncharted regions of his lungs. He felt buoyed, and without rushing he asked her to speak her Fears in all their ugliness and glory. He promised her that what passed between them would never be repeated, never copied, never violated. And so, she began.

She is terrified, she said, deep in her bones, deeper than the dark spaces between the atoms of the molecules that make up the cells of her bones, that she steps through the EVA airlock and doesn't float. She doesn't emerge into a weightless, starry vacuum. Instead, she falls like a stone dropped down a gravity well. She falls, the tether snaps and she lands, *thud,* in a pit of jagged rubble, her bones smashed, her organs pierced, her screams strangled in her mouth as snarling beasts rip layers from her suit, one after the other until they find the red meat within and devour her alive, for she is not after all a creature flying through space, not a soul seeking transcendence, but a disposable carcass.

Franny's mind, Brenz realised, spun about as wildly as his own. He was not allowed to join her, though; his duty was to stay fixed in opposition, to wave a light in the darkness.

'This will not happen,' he told her. 'So says your Katan.'

She's afraid, too, she declared, that she leaps out and awakens attached to plastic tubes in a hospital bed in a room glaring with light. No one's there, she can't move, and the only sounds are a shrill humming and a faint liquid gurgling coming out of her, moving into her, and she realises that everything she's perceived as her real life until this very moment has been the product of manipulated electrochemical reactions in her brain. Her mother's encircling arms, the cosy blanket, her stuffed animals, the food she gobbled and the playground slides and spinners she conquered, the playmates she bested, the tears, the kisses, the cascading voices, her body growing, morphing, those dazzling moments when she figured something out, yes, that's it, and the new, beguiling questions that bloomed in the soil of those revelations, everything, all of it, just catalysed chemicals, electromagnetic blips, and now a thunderclap of panic engulfs her, the horrid realisation that she's nothing but…

'This will not happen. So says your Katan.'

Another scenario scares her, she told Brenz. She steps from the airlock into yet one more airlock and then into a corridor and a room that she's never seen before, and there she asks shipworldmates who she's never met, 'What's happening to me?' They inform her, as if it's obvious, that a biomimetic copy of herself has been sent back in her stead. An identical copy who's better than her, who's kinder and more generous and doesn't have mocking thoughts about people with obvious weaknesses, who doesn't make excuses to avoid caring for her father. That copy will report her Revelation with great enthusiasm, proclaiming that Shipworld indeed travels through outer space, that it has both inner and outer dimensions, and that she touched its chill skin, an awesome moment beyond description. That she beheld with infinite longing the light of multitudinous, burning suns, one of which holds in orbit HD-40307g…

'This will not happen. So says your Katan.'

And even worse, *this* Fear: Franika jumps awkwardly into outer space and tumbles head over heels, the stars whirling, taunting. She can't control the spin, she can't even remember how she mastered it in Tube training, how she righted her body-ship in VR sims. Her limbs flail, she whirls about on all axes. Even though no one's supposed to be watching, she's deeply embarrassed at her failure, mortified at her inability to perform the basic manoeuvres enabling a proper Revelation, and her mind is shot through with shame. She cries out, sobbing into her helmet, she can't stop crying, can't stop gagging and coughing, struggling not to throw up…

'This will not happen. So says your Katan.'

Franika's afraid, too, that her tether snaps. Outside Shipworld, alone in the void, she becomes unmoored. Perhaps it's an accident, perhaps the cord is cut by an unknown enemy, and wouldn't you know it, her powerpack thrusters have malfunctioned, too – sabotage, punishment, karma – so there's no hope of returning, absolutely none. She just wanders away from the ship, watching it get smaller. No one waves goodbye. It's so sad, Shipworld becoming a pinprick, a pulsing star, and the view is weirdly peaceful until a micrometeoroid tears through her suit – maybe that's why the tether broke, maybe Murphy's Law is galactic in scope – rips through her chest and gouges out the other side. The pain, a dagger plunging, and she hears her own breathing, a storm brewing, and she's sweating, the evaporation controls overwhelmed, she's sloshing in sweat as oxygen levels…

'This will not happen,' said Brenz, his tone slightly agitated this time. 'So says your Katan.' He found the quiet, lonely violence of this Fear more disturbing than the others. And he bowed, requesting forgiveness for his lack of calmness, and Franika returned the gesture.

Even more terrifying, she continued, is the Fear that everything goes well, that she sees Shipworld from the outside, floats with expertise, and marvels at the expanse of interstellar space. And yet it's still not enough to break the illusion, to prove that her helmet's visor is not actually a video screen. She requires absolute proof of the truth behind the apparent truth, so she deactivates safety protocols. With each hand she reaches for the latches and clicks them loose, *snap*, then does the same for the secondary latches, *snap*, and she slides the helmet one-sixteenth of a turn along the neck ring and just like that it pops free. The helmet floats up, she gasps. She feels the cold upon her skin, knows its crushing touch. For a moment she glimpses Shipworld with naked eyes. The Revelation is complete as her head freezes, cracks, fissures into shards…

'This will not happen.' The statement, however, seemed limp, insufficient to ward off such a monumental Fear. 'This will *never* happen. So says your Katan.'

Brenz stared at Franika, at her beautiful, intact head. At her soft mouth and freckles scattered beneath intense, brown eyes that didn't seem to notice him. She had acquired that ten-million-mile, deep-space stare, but without vacancy or amusement. No, she seemed to be watching something in the far, far distance, in the future beyond their lifespans. The future they all lived for. A single tear burst forth, rolled down Brenz's cheek.

Her last Fear, she said, is kind of stupid. She's scared that this experience will change her. Don't get her wrong, it's what she wants. She wants to know Shipworld for herself, wants to witness her place in the cosmos, and wants to become a stronger, more confident person after the Revelation walk. Above all, she wants to be a part of this tradition performed by her parents and someday by her children and their children. But she knows it's going to overpower her. She feels the shock of change coming. And that's really scary.

Brenz said nothing; he wasn't sure how to respond. As Katan, he was supposed to banish her Fears. But this particular Fear, her seventh, would happen. It *should* happen – she should change. And he should change, too, stop being the dreamy goofball coming up short of his potential. Now Franika's eyes refocused on him. She tilted her head, curiously.

'I think,' said Brenz, 'that this Fear isn't stupid. It's the most real Fear of all. It will come true and I will stand by you and be your friend no matter what. So says your Katan.'

And so, it was done. From this point forward, they were supposed to remain silent. Nonetheless, Franika stepped towards him, her boots making echoey *clunks* on the iron floorboards, and she moved her lips just millimetres from one of his ears.

'I hoped it would be you,' she whispered.

Then she stepped back. He offered her the helmet with both hands, as if it contained something of himself, and herself, their very souls, perhaps, and she took it and put it on. Secured the latches. Waited while Brenz performed the last double and triple checks. Opened the door to the outer airlock and entered that space. The door closed and Brenz dutifully certified the seal. Two hours remained in the decompression cycle, during which air would be slowly pumped from the outer airlock until a near vacuum was achieved. He could still see Franika through a small window in the door, as she stood before the final barrier. As she awaited her time to go.

✦

Franika turned away from her Katan.

She hooked up her fifty-metre tether, verified its hold on both ends, and stood, motionless, trying to modulate her breathing and clear her mind. Time slid by, smoothly, minute following minute like water droplets from an irrigation hose, until the decompression cycle was complete. She double-double checked the tether, then pressed a button on the outer airlock wall labelled EGRESS – an odd word. Like egret, a giant, white bird on Earthworld that she'd read about, with long legs and a head held high on a curving neck. Now the door slid open and, consequently, Franika floated up. Her helmet hit the ceiling, yet she barely noticed, for there it was, straight ahead. Space, finally. With the tether coil looped loosely about her right arm, she grabbed the edge of the doorframe with her left hand.

She felt unafraid, and that thrilled her.

Franika pushed off. She leaped, letting the tether fall from her arm, and suddenly she became a straight line seeking infinity, if very, very slowly and on a leash. The parabola that her brain expected her body to travel could not, of course, occur without the demand of gravity – a weird, cause-without-effect sensation that she'd experienced in training, but this was much more intense. It was strange, too, to float within her EVA suit, even as the suit itself floated within its galactic medium.

Then her eyes widened as her optic nerves fully interfaced with her visual cortex and she saw, as never before, stars. My God, she realised, countless stars, innumerable stars, fields of stars sown all the way back to the Big Bang. Stars fixed in space, unspinning. Stars beckoning, stars beyond deadly if you got too close, and she surprised herself in not feeling humbled or insignificant in the vastness, the way other spacewalkers had reported. It was simply beautiful – stupefying, stopping abstract thought – and awesome to behold. All her life, inside, she'd watched stars streaming past windows as Shipworld spun, and she'd had to remind herself that she, Franika, stuck to the spot, was actually the spinning factor – but now she existed outside and there were no frames for measuring motion. No frames to define, diminish or deceive.

As she stretched her arms up/down, Franika heard a gasping, braying laugh: her own laughter, pitched low inside the suit's reduced atmospheric pressure. Nobody else would hear it; the com channel was shut off and would only be activated in an emergency, initiated either by a distressed Franika or the bridge officer observing in the bow. (The Viewing Portal, as well as all smaller windows, were blacked out on Revelation Days, which occurred three or four times every year.) Audio and video recordings of this spacewalk were forbidden. It was for her alone, to be sanctified in private, cherished in her memory. Her father, perhaps, was thinking of her as he tested soil in the Ag Lab or, more likely, sat alone in perpetual low-level mourning for her mother, who had died in an accident in Engineering five years ago, and who, Franika thought for a microsecond, might be watching from a vantage point beyond reckoning.

A soft alarm, *beep-beep*. She checked her suit's panel: she'd travelled fifty metres, far enough. Franika began the slow, twisting, kicking motion she'd rehearsed many times, pulsing the backpack's thrusters to arrest her journey out and keep the tether from snapping tight. She turned about, one hundred and eighty degrees, and what happened next happened suddenly as if she was struck in the face: she saw Shipworld. She saw it for the first time. She saw it hulking through the cosmos, her home, revealed.

And then terror lashed her.

Terror at the sight of the slender tether, a composite wire wrapped in white sheathing, stretched from her hip to the airlock. Terror at the sight of Shipworld, so singular in the universe. And terror, most of all, despite the lecture she'd received about the relative speed of a spacewalker and spacecraft remaining the same barring acceleration or deceleration – terror at the thought that she couldn't actually be travelling at twelve per cent of the speed of light *outside the spacecraft*, that indeed she was just a drop of flesh without propulsive capabilities and therefore Shipworld, fusion engines blasting, would shred the tether and leave her for dead. It was the final unnamed Fear, severed from reason.

Franika breathed in and out. She counted six long breaths and then, according to her training, tailored the terror into a purple, twirling ribbon and let it flow through the top of her head and away. She reminded herself that she was free now, free from the background anxiety, the cognitive dissonance that assailed all those who were expected to trust without verification.

Yes, Shipworld sailed beside her – a real thing, no illusion, no conspiracy, spinning at 2.4 rpm, although she couldn't perceive that motion because she was spinning, too. And it was ugly, reassuringly so, a massive elliptical structure studded with antennas and lumpy with externally mounted equipment racks, high-res telescopes, electromagnetic batteries cooled to −270 °C and scoops sifting the near-vacuum for periodic-table treasures. There it was. She was born there, she lived there and she'd die there – undeniable, unchangeable reality. Unless, that is, they encountered aliens or learned to boost engine power or lifespan. No, stop that, Franika ordered herself. Accept your life. Her descendants in the Seventh Generation might step foot on HD-40307g, might breathe its air, if everything went to plan. But she would not.

Her world, Shipworld. They were tied together. Its history, her history. And yet seeing wasn't quite enough. To be absolutely sure, to achieve everlasting faith in her caretaker role on this great and foolhardy journey, Franika needed to touch it.

She pulsed the thrusters again. As she approached, her umbilical-cord tether waved like a cilium, as if moved by cosmic currents, now forty metres, thirty metres, twenty metres. The bulk of the thing grew before her, eclipsing space, obliterating stars, and at ten metres the EVA suit's proximity alarm made a harsh *beeeep!* She reached out with both hands, five metres, four, three, two, one, and just then in that last moment she wondered if certain things weren't meant to be proven, should remain forever in shadow. What happens after death. Why someone loves you. The truth of Shipworld.

Because momentum cares not for sudden misgivings, she touched the outer shell with her right hand. Through multiple layers of inner and outer gloves, she touched Shipworld. Hard, metallic. Irrefutable. She made a fist and banged on it; no sound could be heard in the vacuum, of course, but she felt the reverberations. Tactile revelations of her strikes travelled up her arm to her shoulder and neck and beyond. The low, braying laugh returned and tears plunged from her eyes, a reservoir undammed.

Twenty minutes later, when the door between inner and outer airlocks opened, there stood Brenz. Vigilant, waiting for her – Brenz Oort-St George with his uncombed sandy hair, his soft brown eyes and slouched shoulders. Franika stepped further inside, the door closed behind her, *shussh*, and she rushed to unclasp her helmet. It clattered to the floor as she reached for her surprised Katan and enveloped him in a hug. The tears flowed again, from her cheeks to his. Oh, if only he could know!

✦

For several days, Brenz couldn't concentrate in his cosmic chemistry class. He shifted in his seat, blinked his eyes and even pinched his cheeks. They were studying dark energy and dark matter, the elusive subatomic soup through which everything ploughs – the Two Darks in the slang of Teacher Varbala – and even though the material was fascinating, he couldn't stop thinking about Franika's tears, and her lips, the mingled taste of salt and flesh, and the dizzying fact that she mumbled his name, Brenz, between the kisses, Brenz, like an incantation. He couldn't stop thinking, too, about how she'd trusted him with her Fears, unreservedly. That trust had gifted Brenz with a measure of confidence, at once alien and joyful, that emboldened his curious nature and challenged him to pose vexing questions.

Foremost in this category: what was the origin of the Revelation?

A family dynamic fuelled his interest: Janelle Oort, his aunt, was the first shipworldmate to experience the Revelation. At one hundred and seventeen years old, Janelle now enjoyed status as the last surviving Pioneer from the group of 600 who began the journey. A toddler at launch, her mother was Cecilia Oort, who later chose to have a second child, in Year 38, by a different father. That child grew up to become Brenz's mother, Lavender, who claimed not to know, not entirely, why the Revelation had started with her peculiar half-sister.

There'd been some kind of trouble, evidently.

'I'm not the one to say. Janelle and I, we've never been close,' Lavender remarked as she and Brenz sat together in the community vegetable garden, he with his cosmology textbook, she with her crocheting. Beside them, a red-streaked spray of rhubarb. A few steps further, the towering ficus tree – the only tree in their existence, a riot of branches bearing inedible figs stuffed with slimy seeds – and the Olmec Head squatting beneath. Thirteen tonnes of sculpted basalt dug from the ground by Earthworld archaeologists, the Head glowered at Brenz as if pained by his presence. It was ancient and rare, the only Earthworld treasure that Thaddeus Parsons, Shipworld's founder, had put aboard. That is, as far as anyone knew. Brenz imagined a storeroom filled with art, jewellery and keepsakes from across human history.

Lavender hummed, a doodling of stray notes, as she manipulated the bamboo crochet hook, yanking at yarn, executing intricate stitches. Brenz hoped she was making him a pair of sleeping socks; his feet got cold at night and he'd lost his other pair. Perhaps they'd been snatched, the occasional fate of homemade things that were beyond the programming of the 3-D printers. Probably his sister, Chive, had taken them out of jealousy. Or spite.

'Janelle, Janelle, Janelle,' said Lavender, embedding the name in the weave. 'You should talk to her, while there's still time. Some people don't make it all the way to one-hundred-and-twenty. And bring your sister.'

'Maybe,' he replied to the first invocation. No way, he thought, to the second. Eighteen-year-old, know-it-all Chive was going through yet another obnoxious phase. What was his mother trying to engineer here? He returned to his textbook, to the apparent invisibility of dark matter, ubiquitous yet unseen, the medium through which they sailed towards HD-40307g, also ubiquitous as the ultimate, unquestioned destination, also never to be seen by current generations, and in doing so the elbows of mother and child brushed, lightly, and her hands slowed their pace, just a bit, and she inclined her head towards her beautiful boy, her firstborn, reading. He pretended not to notice. They worked in silence for a while.

'Mother?'

'Yes, Brenz.'

'Oh, nothing.' And he snapped his book shut and loped away.

Brenz's aunt, Janelle, was an odd, crumbling old lady. He hadn't visited her in several months, which he knew was no way to treat an elder. But the thing was, even though she'd only spent her first year or two on Earthworld, it seemed as if Janelle was from there, not here. Like some extraterrestrial stowaway on a secret mission.

Before visiting Janelle, Brenz decided to learn more about the Revelation. On the fifth day after his duties as Katan – he and Franika had exchanged postcards since the airlock, but met only once, briefly, on a garden bench – he made his way to the library.

Flying down Pictor Boulevard, dodging shipworldmates, he played the game of silent name-saying. Not knowing someone's name was considered rude, a sign of asocial dysfunction syndrome according to the school pysch-evaluator. Hi there *Shameer, bald Ivar, Rhododendron, Thomas, Racine with the flowing red hair*… Then Brenz diverted to the southwestern catwalk, his favourite shortcut. Next onto Carina Way, dive, duck, bound up and around, hello *Veronique, Samson, Burtoq who always gets the last word, Astor*…all staring their deep-space stares… Didn't these people want something to happen today, something epic, amazing, transformative? Something different, at least? Then up the stairs, grab the railing, release, grab, down the other stairs and past the rim of the Mess Hall.

Here, he stopped. One of the red sheets had fallen to the floor in the Art Cove. Brenz approached the exposed easel, which held a painting of a bearded man staring at him. His long, curly hair fell casually over his shoulders. His brown coat was fur-lined, with slashes above the elbows revealing a silk shirt beneath. The man's eyes found Brenz's, confronting him without accusation, but without letting him off the hook, either. He seemed centuries old, certainly not from a Shipworld art class.

Brenz stepped closer. The painting's double frame appeared to be made of wood, the varnish long worn away, jagged and scratched in places. A card on the easel read: *Self-Portrait, Albrecht Dürer, 1500, Oil on Lindenwood.* The year 1500 – created, therefore, six hundred and sixty-seven years ago. Had Parsons put this aboard, too? Was it hidden, until now? He took in the painting, eyes focused and mind ablaze, almost forgetting to breathe. This man, this handsome man with a cowlick not so different from Brenz's, with watchful green eyes and a thick vein coursing north across his forehead, with his strong right hand cupped at his midsection in a gesture of gentleness, with Latin words and the personal mark of the artist floating in gilt letters around the black space that enveloped him, celebrated him – this Albrecht Dürer knew something. He had arrived at a place in his life that Brenz could only faintly imagine.

After a while, he tried to cover the painting, but the sheet slid off again and now Dürer's stare pierced more sharply. 'What?' Brenz said out loud. 'What do you want?' No answer, just those eyes, and he turned away and looked at the other easels, all shrouded in red. Then at his forearm, at the data/tracking panel that recorded information such as his location and vital signs, one of 600 or so panels in 600 or so arms providing a constant stream of public health and efficiency data, all for the Greater Good of Shipworld. Who knows what other kinds of surveillance data and just-for-the-hell-of-it data the gadget relayed; perhaps even his desire for Franika had been calibrated by some nosy algorithm and compared to similar episodes within his demographic.

Suddenly, Brenz realised that the library might close, so he left the sheet on the floor and hurried down a spiral staircase. Inside the small library, at a desk polished to a dark sheen, sat the librarian. She stared down at a large open book. Shelves full of hardcovers, floor to ceiling, rose up behind her. They were available for reading, but only inside this room at a table within the librarian's view. Now she looked up, smiling.

'Hi, Rosemary. I'd like to learn about the Revelation.'

'Hello, Brenz. Aren't you a few years away from that?'

He bristled, struggling not to react. Her remark sounded like 'go away', but maybe she was just being chatty. It was true, he'd made it only one-sixth and a smidge through his lifespan, and he came off even younger. But still.

‘I was Katan last week,’ he said, trying not to sound defensive.

‘Really,’ she replied, trying to sound unsurprised. He appreciated the attempt. Strange, he thought, how so many people in the Second-Gen were named after Earthworld herbs and spices: za’tar, basil, nutmeg, ginger, rosemary. His mom’s name, Lavender, was a plant with a sweet, lemony fragrance. Of course, he didn’t know that first-hand because they’d long ago gone through the spice stores, resigned themselves to plainness, and it was considered a waste of space, even in the vertical farm racks in the bow, to grow non-nutritious plants. Their seeds were preserved for HD-40307g.

‘That’s a great honour,’ said Rosemary, as she placed a woven bookmark between the open pages and closed the book. ‘I was Katan once, in my early years. I still think about it.’ She motioned to a chair and he sat.

‘My aunt was the first person to have a Revelation,’ said Brenz. The librarian waited for him to continue. ‘Janelle. I was wondering, who was her Katan?’

‘Her mother, Cecilia,’ said Rosemary.

‘I’ve never heard of a parent doing it.’

‘There’s no rule against it. Besides, it was a special circumstance.’ Once more the librarian stopped and waited, prompting Brenz to abandon his gradual, probing strategy and state that he wanted to know why the Revelation had started with Janelle, twenty-four years into the journey. The Revelation wasn’t mentioned in the Constitution or the Amendments, and they didn’t teach anything about its history in school. And yes, he planned on speaking with Janelle, but needed background first.

Rosemary rapped the desk with her knuckles. ‘Excellent,’ she said.

Janelle was unique, she explained, the only Pioneer with no conscious memories of Earthworld. The next oldest kids were eight or nine at launch and could remember their homes, schools and pets, as well as the plagues, the disastrous effects of geoengineering and the refugee waves smashing borders. The rioting, the dying. Those kids recalled stepping from Earthworld's bloody ground onto a transfer rocket, then being ferried to their new home in orbit. They looked back at Earthworld, then away. But Janelle lacked that context. At the same time, though, she wasn't like the children who were born soon after on Shipworld. Her body had grown in a womb on Earthworld, her first cry and crawl happened there, and she'd stared up from a stroller at the moon in the sky. That mattered somehow; it made her.

Rosemary stared at Brenz. 'Do you know the term "difficult child"?'

'Someone called me that,' he said.

Rosemary made a barking laugh. 'Well, if I had to guess, you're near the top in IQ and EQ. A somewhat rare and confusing combination – that's why you're difficult.' Brenz started to speak but Rosemary rolled on, relating how Janelle became increasingly erratic and angry as she grew up, impossible to control in school, hitting her mother, leaving bruises. As a teenager she fantasised new versions of Shipworld, proclaiming that it wasn't travelling in space but in orbit around Earthworld, or hung in some cave as a fiendish experiment. The windows were video screens, the Mission a sham, and everyone was lying about everything.

'The Fears,' said Brenz.

'Yes,' continued the librarian, 'it's normal now, part of development. But no one expected it then, and it came from such a wild, furious source. They were worried that other young people would adopt her beliefs, sabotage the ship, lead a rebellion. The social ecosystem of a newly created 600-person society is more fragile than you might think. We seem like a cosy village, but we're also a world near capacity, without room for radical variance.'

'What happened?' asked Brenz.

'It just got worse. For years she was kept secluded, but that didn't stop her decline. Cecilia, I believe, had the idea to send Janelle on a spacewalk, to give her proof that her fears weren't based in reality. The problem was that she didn't want to go. She thought they were trying to exile her, kill her, alter her mind. She started harming herself, wouldn't eat. In the end, they forced her to do it, kicking and screaming. Cecilia was suited up in the outer airlock, to pacify her, and to make sure she did it. Just a horrible time, no wonder it's forgotten – except now you know.'

She let that sink in for a moment. The spacewalk, Rosemary continued, changed Janelle. Her paranoia subsided and she led a normal, quiet life – eighty-plus years in systems maintenance, an expert in sodium regulation. But it was no fairy tale – a separateness afflicted her, growing over time, and she refused to marry or have children. That was concerning, certainly, but the Psych Advisory Panel saw the episode as an opportunity. They established the Revelation as a way to prevent another Janelle. To squash the irrational Id on a communal basis, and here the librarian pointed at a book of Freud essays on the shelf. Ever since, she explained, the Fears that arise naturally or otherwise in children are validated and resolved in a ritualistic manner, in a coming-of-age ceremony that imparts meaning and purpose to life.

'Perhaps,' she added, 'that's what you experienced with Franika.'

Brenz didn't even nod; he had pledged to keep her Revelation between them.

'Good, you shouldn't say anything.' Rosemary stood, revealing herself as a tall person, capable of reaching high bookshelves on her tippy toes. He stood in turn, and they looked at each other, eye to eye, before he glanced away. Her laser gaze lacked the inviting sureness of Albrecht Dürer's.

'Memories are funny things,' she said. 'They have a certain flexibility; they can change over time – you might say evolve. Keep that in mind when you speak to Janelle.'

'But not if they're written down,' said Brenz, tentatively.

'Words on a page,' returned Rosemary, 'can be interpreted differently, depending on the reader, as well as the space and time that reader occupies.'

Her thoughts were so articulate and carefully constructed, observed Brenz. She was either super-sharp or she'd been tailoring these words for a long time, waiting for the right moment with the right person.

'Do you understand why information is restricted?' she asked.

Brenz replied that he had a pretty good idea. In school, they'd studied the deliberations of the Shipworld Constitutional Convention. Delegates agreed that the chaotic and unjust state of Earthworld was in part due to the explosion of information technology. People had become obsessed with their devices, stuck in tribal silos, and addicted to pornography, conspiracy and triviality. Social media pushed them to extreme positions, and they stopped using their own minds to assess situations. Stopped listening to each other, hardly knew their neighbours. So Shipworld's Pioneers decided not to preserve much of Earthworld culture. That's why there's no internet, added Brenz, and no AR or VR or AI companions acting both more and less human. No TV and movies, and no audio or video recording devices – not even for keeping journals, which encourage selfishness and pull folks away from face-to-face and flesh-to-flesh connections. Even paper and pens were severely limited for personal use. The notable exceptions to the ban on Earthworld culture were Parsons' Top 100 songs and this library.

'And it's worked. That and getting rid of money,' said Rosemary. 'Here we are, Year 118, and we haven't had a revolution, social breakdown or tribal calamity. We're at peace. The Council is democratically elected, responsive but not overreaching. The tenders maintain order while keeping a low profile. Our biggest challenge is the sustainability loop. All in all, it's a triumph of perseverance and cooperation. A long, boring space ride, really. What do you think?'

Brenz needed a moment to process her summation. He didn't disagree exactly, but he sure didn't feel as if he was living inside a triumph – unless survival and stability were the only metrics worth considering. And what about Janelle?

'I don't think,' he said to Rosemary, 'that she should have been forced. It's like everything we have is based on a…'

'Sin,' she responded. Then she turned to the shelves behind her. 'You know, people think I have the great works of humanity back here, but that's not the case. There are a few…but mostly it's Thaddeus Parsons' personal collection, a somewhat peculiar mix. Books about salesmanship and minor sports – badminton, curling. Lots of genocide studies, memoirs of suffering, apocalyptic fiction, that kind of thing.' She pointed at the book on the desk. 'This is a journal written under great duress, *From Day to Day* by Odd Nansen. Come in and read it some time, we can talk about it.'

'OK,' said Brenz, not sure if he would.

It was as if she could read his mind. 'What interests you?' she asked.

'Albrecht Dürer,' he replied, surprising himself. A person, dead for several centuries, who he'd first encountered less than an hour ago. Who he knew almost nothing about.

'Ah, the exhibit,' she said. 'I tried something interactive this time, making people hunt for the painting, *discover* it. Dürer means "door" in Hungarian, you know. Open the door.' She smiled at Brenz. 'Anyway, Janelle inherited it from her mother and gave it to the library. A real treasure, we have so few.'

'I want to know more about him,' said Brenz. Most of all, he wanted to know how the young artist had achieved, and then captured, such a moment of personal peace and power merged together. Perhaps he'd gained some special knowledge or possessed a depth of self-awareness that Brenz woefully lacked. Or was it the other way around, that by painting himself, by acting, he'd discovered who he really was?

'Well, I have a book about Dürer,' said Rosemary, who had waited, patiently, for Brenz to finish his thought. 'It has Parsons' signature in it. It'll be here for you.'

'Thank you, Rosemary.'

'Thank you, Brenz.'

✦

Sunday, two days later, was Equilibrium Day. Franika looked up at scores of multi-coloured climbing ropes extended eighty metres from Tube to ground in every direction, reaching to the hinterlands and held in place by grappling joints at each end. Some ropes were pulled taut, others swayed like flexible spokes, beautifully out of sync. According to Equilibrium rules refined over decades, rules which Franika prided herself on knowing in great detail, the ropes were attached to the central segment of the Tube at six-metre intervals. Players, known as Equis, slid along assigned ropes while outfitted in helmets, elbow pads and team colours. They wielded long-handled racquets for whacking birdies and, with free hands, operated servos that adjusted their ropes' tension and propelled them up and down/down and up the airy field of play.

Franika hurried to find Brenz. His team, the Comets, were taking on last year's champions, the Pulsars. She found him on a path between two fields of corn – Shipworld, ultimately, was a floating farm – kneeling over his rope's ground-based grappling joint. She kissed the brown-haired snarl on top of his head: presto, he looked up. 'Hey, Franny.' That sweet, eager smile bloomed. She slid a note into his hand – time and place of their next assignation, tomorrow noon, under the ficus – and left him to his preparations. Looking for a good vantage point near the bow, Franika spied Brenz's father, Jacques St George, and joined him next to the 3-D Printing Nook and an adjacent, glowing algae pipe (the Green Gunk of Life multiplied faster, and tasted better, when kept moving).

'Greetings, Franika,' he said. The eighty-two-year-old man, tall and lean, preserved a jittery spark in his eyes. To her he seemed an older version of Brenz, a glimpse into the future; even the hair, tamped down but escaping on the edges, evoked his son.

'Hello, Jacques.'

'You're in fine fettle today.'

Brenz's father loved arcane phrases that, she guessed, were acquired from library books or passed down within his family. Fine fettle – was that a hint about Brenz and her? Or perhaps he sensed the ecstatic feelings of Revelation that coursed through Franika, like an antibody infusion against doubt and despair.

Indeed, everything seemed different, to a degree she hadn't imagined possible. Her parents, friends, teachers, Brenz, even Jacques right now – they vibrated before her, in resonance with the stars that she'd beheld, in harmony with the quantum components of outer space in which she'd floated – and so what if that sounded crazy! The mysteries of Shipworld no longer oppressed her. She'd banged on its side, *bam, bam, bam!* And now she knew, now she thrived on the reality, *lived on it*, that Franika Longstem and everyone swirling around her were nothing more nor less than a big bucket of human beings traversing the Orion minor spur of the Milky Way Galaxy. Their substance: humble, fragile. But their mission: a glorious adventure.

Presently, the undulating network of Equilibrium ropes knitted everything together, providing strength. Franika witnessed this from both the spot next to the algae pipe and the spacewalker's perspective that she delighted in summoning. Shipworld, inside and out. An intricate assembly of people at play, a gnarled spheroid spinning. And then the ark's metal skin grew translucent in her mind's astonished eye, like the amniotic sac around an embryo, and the two views slid and merged into one, revealing her world's lonely status in the cosmos.

The game began. Thirty-six Equis – half in Comet red, half in Pulsar blue – ascended ropes to various heights. A moment of stillness, of held breath, followed.

'There he is!' Jacques pointed up, towards Brenz.

Cymbals clashed. Around the Tube's midpoint fluttered out a flock of seventy-two blue and red birdies, twice the size of their badminton counterparts, with bulbous rubber noses and flamboyant plumage. Racquets flashed furiously as the Equis whacked at the birdies. They shuttled between the familiarity of .9g on the ground and the rarified world of near-zero gravity at the Tube, operating not only in three spatial dimensions but in a constantly evolving gravitational environment. Since it takes decades to learn the game's nuances and patterns, many of the best players were in their sixties and seventies, the sweet spot before hand-eye coordination declines.

'Whoa!' reacted Franika, as Brenz swerved to avoid the flying body of another player.

The goal of Equilibrium was simple: propel as many of your team's birdies across the scoreline on one end of the Tube, while preventing the other team from smashing its birdies across the scoreline at the other end. Everyone played offence and defence simultaneously, in a grand mélange of rope-sliding, racquet-swinging and strategic readjustment, with every grounded bird replaced by a new one at the Tube's midpoint.

'I've always thought,' said Jacques, in a casual yet oracular tone, 'that Equilibrium evolved because it's a controlled way to express and resolve our most primitive urges. There's nothing like smashing that birdie, letting loose the goose.'

The result, indeed, was orchestrated chaos. From inside the blizzardy cloud of play even the most seasoned players had a hard time knowing which team was ahead. The final score was announced after thirty minutes of frenzied action. No time outs, no halftime: go, go, go!

But from afar, the game's drift was easily apparent. Today the Pulsars were dominant, as the vast majority of red and blue birdies migrated to the Comets' side. Franika watched Brenz as he did his best to stem the tide, ascending to a low-grav position near the Tube and executing a spinning whack that propelled a blue birdie towards the scoreline. Alas, Doctor Tam, a short man in his fifties, whizzed up his rope and flicked the same birdie to a teammate in the southwest quadrant, a young woman who gracefully redirected the birdie around the perimeter to another player, and another, and soon one more point was scored for the Pulsars.

Still, Brenz was good for his age. *Yeah, Brenz!* Franika's cheers expired in the clamour of competing voices, the whirring of servos moving on rope, the *whoosh* and *pop-pop-pop* of racquets smacking birdies.

After several minutes, Franika zoomed out once more, admiring the spectacle of Equilibrium as a singular, electric entity. A mutating organism adapting to stimuli, roiled with patterns evaporating as fast as they appear. There was an elusive beauty to its swarming parts, as well as a sense of struggle that disturbed her. She resisted the urge to manage these impressions – a leftover reflex from before her Revelation – and from their clash and mingling came warm satisfaction. She couldn't remember feeling this unleashed, and at the same time so strongly connected to everyone and everything, certainly not since her mother's death.

'Do you want to talk about it?' Jacques asked. 'The spacewalk, everything you—'

'It was wonderful,' said Franika, but then halted. Jacques was a member of the Psych Advisory Panel, not to mention her boyfriend's dad. 'I'm still processing it.'

'That's healthy, make up your own mind,' he replied.

Jacques continued to stare up at his son, now descending his rope in rapid chase of a birdie that accelerated as it passed through different levels of gravity. Brenz lunged, swung and missed. The birdie fell into thigh-high stalks of corn, and far above, at the Tube, a new birdie was released to compensate for the one that had exited the field of play.

He turned to Franika. 'For me, it was a kind of bonding,' he said. 'Just seeing Shipworld, the sight of it. After the Revelation, the Mission becomes the most important thing in people's lives, and you conceive of yourself as a kind of relay runner across generations.' Here he stopped, perhaps noticing the quizzical expression on Franika's face. 'It was this competition on Earthworld, at these festivals called "Olympics". Each team had multiple runners, and each runner carried a stick which you had to pass to the next one without slowing down, and you couldn't drop it or it was over. That's our *existence* – the job of every runner is absolutely crucial, the first ones, the last ones, and all the ones stuck in the middle.'

Jacques glanced up at the game, now at peak frenzy. 'And then you have kids and all you want is for them to be happy and fufil their potential.'

'In this tin can,' he added.

The cymbals crashed again, signalling match's end, and Franika, Jacques and hundreds of fans clapped as exhausted

Equis, backs arched, hung from their ropes. Franika said goodbye and rushed to her duty rotation in environmental systems, all the while chewing over Jacques' comments. '*In this tin can.*' A note of discontent? Regret? She couldn't relate to that. But bonding, yes. Shipworld loomed within her now, and she felt bonded to everyone living and dead who'd ever undergone the Revelation, including Jacques. Their shared leap, their transcendence multiplied over time, kept the community in peaceful equilibrium. Sustainability achieved, ultimately, through an idea.

He'd also said, 'Make up your own mind.' What was that supposed to mean? She made up her own mind, of course she did. No one told her what to think. OK, her Revelation wasn't unique – get over yourself – but it was her own. In making these assertions, Franika felt a surge of combativeness that pushed back against her newfound, ecstatic outlook. Jacques' primitive urges, she supposed, improperly channelled.

Franika entered Algae Production and, without delay, suited up in white coveralls, booties, gloves and mask. She flashed her card and entered the inner chamber, nicknamed Lake Texcoco after an ancient Earthworld waterway where Aztecs had harvested algae. She nodded at Ynar, a cloying Third-Gen who worked, mercifully, at the other end of the room. From the main reservoir, Franika pipetted a sample. She held the lustrous, emerald-green substance to the light. The algae known as spirulina – a cyanobacteria rich in protein, amino acid and vitamins – crawled along the pipette chamber. The viscosity looked about right.

Ynar, hunched at her station, referred to algae as pond scum, but Franika had never seen a pond – neither had Ynar, she was just repeating stuff – and scum was but a chemical byproduct. Franika, fascinated by algae since childhood, recalled scurrying about with her parents in a scavenger's hunt for every green gunk pipe snaking through fields, behind fences and even under the Head. Algae, her mother had said, is the cornerstone of the closed food system that sustains Shipworld. Indispensable, her father had added, and therefore beautiful.

She supposed that things could work the other way, too. Beautiful, and therefore indispensable.

At a nearby lab bench, Franika began a testing regimen. Contaminants could not only ruin the taste of algae-based foods, but cause digestive and metabolic problems. First, she pipetted a dollop into a spectrophotometer no bigger than her hand, checking for light absorption properties: right down the centre of the normal range. Next, she squirted a bit into the tabletop DNA sequencer and set that machine to running. She filled a mini test tube and ran a pH series. These came back normal, too. Finally, she analysed algae samples on slides, a time-consuming affair. As she calibrated the phase-contrast microscope, Franika thought about kissing Brenz. About the warm, knobby bump on the back of his head, probably born from banging into walls and doorways, careening here and there. She dropped a touch of algae on a slide and set down the coverslip.

Last night she'd eaten a new algae entrée at the Mess Hall, with Ynar and two friends from enviro-systems, Javier and Gulika. Someone in the kitchen had written an archaic and long-winded description of the recipe on the message board:

> *Veggie Galactic Chowder. Put half a dozen onions, in rustic fashion, in bottom of pot; hang high over flame, so onions may not burn; when done brown, place layer of algae chunks, chopped in crisscross pattern, in pot; then layer of crackers, peppers and potatoes sliced as thin as a fourpence, mixed with fried onion pieces; then another layer of algae chunks, and another, don't be shy. Strew salt, if you have it, which we don't. Over the whole pour two bowls of whisked flour and water. A sliced kumquat*

gives flavour. A cup of crushed tomato is excellent. Some cooks add beer, who can blame them. Keep whole shebang covered so not one particle of steam escapes. Do not open to taste until nearly done.

'Shipworld is a kind of chowder, if you think about it,' said Franika.

'Yum,' remarked Javier, with a smirk. 'What's a shebang?'

'How about a fourpence?' asked Ynar. Small and spindly, she rarely spoke more than a few words at a time, and always softly, weakly. Her hair was perpetually tied in a bun. Franika once more felt the urge to whack it, release the strands. An awful impulse, she knew, unworthy of a Revelation spacewalker, and she smiled at Ynar in contrition.

'Fourpence is money,' said Gulika, who tended to speak with an off-handed tone: oh, right, that. Everyone knows that. 'I read this library book about Earthworld economics.'

'Economics based on the constant growth model,' said Javier. 'On the exploitation of planetary resources and the justification of suffering.' Once more he'd one-upped Gulika, and not subtly. 'Fortunately, we're post-economics, a harmonious closed system, so we don't need fourpence. We don't have rich people, poor people, or everyone wanting things they don't need. Earthworld even had this thing called advertising, these messages stuck everywhere to push people to be wasteful.'

'GGPP,' said Gulika, reciting an old study acronym. 'Growth, greed, profit, pollution.'

'Equals pandemonium,' said Javier. That was also the name of a popular card game played by kids and centenarians alike.

Javier was mostly right, thought Franika. But why be so smug about it? She dipped her spoon into the Veggie Galactic Chowder and slurped it down. Not bad, interesting texture. Javier went next, shrugged, and kept eating. Then Ynar and Gulika started on their kale and algae-crouton salads, a common dish, and no one talked for a few minutes – and no one wondered, either, how far Shipworld had just travelled in the silence, one thousand kilometres or so if you did the math – until Ynar, who would be old enough for the Revelation in four months, complimented Franika for completing her spacewalk.

'You look happy,' she said, avoiding eye contact. 'It must have been…'

'You'll see for yourself,' said Franika, and she returned to her chowder, following the unwritten rule not to influence the progression of doubt and fear that shipworldmates experience before their Revelations. She told herself that she'd spoken to Ynar politely, that she'd stopped her transgression in a non-judgemental tone. Again, she flashed a quick smile at her. Ynar, nonetheless, appeared chastened; she bit her lower lip and moved an algae-crouton around her plate. Javier and Gulika, each in their thirties, kept blank faces.

Back at the lab bench, Franika checked for contaminants by dropping stains, one by one, on separate algae samples under the microscope. Normal, normal, wait a second.

Franika peered at the sample, blinked rapidly, peered again. The stain for microcystin toxin looked slightly off-colour. She ran a chem-analysis and found microcystin levels on the high end, but within the approved parameters. An acceptable fluctuation, nothing to be alarmed about. No reason to call Ynar over for confirmation. Nonetheless, she noted the finding in the log, and then let her thoughts again drift to Brenz chasing the birdie down his rope, reaching, missing, but not fading in defeat. Her gallant Equi warrior traversing their great ship-island, and she came to him, floating without a rope, and held him and he kissed her, and she pressed the bump on his skull and he kissed her harder.

✦

In Janelle's final days, they assigned her a nurse with warm hands, like rolls just pulled from the oven. Anat seemed nice enough; she'd lived a little, eighty-odd years, and sometimes she actually listened, but Janelle suspected that she'd rather be elsewhere. Well, too bad, because on Shipworld you can't just do whatever you want. Everyone can't be guitar-strumming or stargazing or psycho-evaluating with no one to maintain the sewage system or lever old ladies out of bed. Personal freedom is a wonderful idea with little place in this sealed-up spheroid. So said the former kid-paranoiac so utterly devoted to her view of the world, her self-delusions and mangled feelings, that they had to lock her away in her room for years and then shove her out an airlock.

How things had changed. Janelle was the living/dying end of an era. Perhaps it was an honour to sponge-bathe the Last Pioneer? Maybe she was supposed to whisper some pearl of wisdom in the nurse's ear – and why pearl, why not rock of wisdom? The profound stuff isn't smooth and shiny; no, it's jagged, crusted with dirt.

Even miracles, she now realised, can be hard to swallow. The Correction, for instance. An amazing therapy, the way it postpones the diseases and frailties of ageing through gene-editing, but it also presents a not-so-minor drawback: old age arrives suddenly, a shock. You're not given decades to ease into its infirmities and indignities, its brain fogginess. For a hundred and fifteen years or so you're fine, more or less, and then, *bam*, what the hell? Off the cliff you go. Now at least she knew, in her aching bones, that there was an endpoint. Moses himself was limited to one hundred and twenty years, she'd learned yesterday from the miniature Old Testament that Rosemary had snuck her. At the end Moses stood on a mountaintop looking over the land of Canaan, the glorious promised land that he'd never walk upon. God's gift, just to see it. And a punishment, too – behold, what you are denied – for breaking arcane rules about water sources and how to show proper respect, isn't that always the way. Anat read the Bible passages to Janelle in a whispery voice.

No one came by, of course – except this afternoon. Her nephew Brenz appeared, Lavender's boy, a jittery creature, all limbs going all ways. She watched him size up the room's little world, from the hairbrush clotted with white, wiry strands to the wee Bible – black cover, gilt-edged pages, visible inside an open drawer – to the stars streaming through her circular floor-window. An observant one; an Oort, after all. Her mother, Cecilia, had been alive when Brenz was born, so maybe she'd held him, combed his hair with her fingers (Janelle remembered that feeling) and whispered a stray secret in his ear. Come to think of it, didn't he have a morose sister who never visited?

'Greetings, Aunt Janelle,' he said, formally. 'I'm sorry it's been so long.'

'You're here now,' she replied, then asked Anat to give them time. The caretaker left the room at light speed.

'How are you feeling?' he asked her.

'Nice weather, outside,' she replied, a lame Shipworld joke that never died. Why, she wondered, had he come?

'Tell me something new,' Janelle demanded.

Brenz hesitated; he was here to ask questions of her. But something amazing and unbelievable had happened this morning, and he burst forth.

'I'm an intern in the Astronomy section,' he said, 'and we just discovered a rogue planet.'

'What's that?' she asked.

'It's this planet that gets spit out of its solar system. There are hundreds of billions of them in the galaxy and they're all iced-over – they wander deep space alone. This is the first one ever observed nearby – in our telescope!'

'So, you discovered it?'

'No, not really, but I was the third person to look at it.'

The young man's ardour enchanted Janelle.

'Rogues are dark, really tough to spot,' Brenz continued, and no one had expected to see one so close. Certainly not travelling in the same direction, almost in parallel. 'It's totally unlikely,' he said, and trailed off. She could sense him calculating the odds.

'I am a rogue planet,' she replied. One purpose of people her age was to say cryptic things to young folk, but she meant it, too. Ever since the day she'd been pushed out of Shipworld, her hands ripped from the airlock doorframe, she'd felt alone in the dark, jettisoned.

He stared at her, as if frozen by her statement.

'Tell me more,' said Janelle.

Beneath the ice-surface of the rogue, he explained, there could be liquid oceans heated by geothermal energy or a moon's tidal power. Life could exist in that ocean, even sentient life. Like on Europa, back in the sol system, there could have been life under the ice, the scans from the orbiter showed a vast ocean, the right salinity, everything, but it remained a mystery after the Earthworld lander crashed. Brenz paused again, eyes roving over Janelle's shrinking form, along the carved-deep, vertical wrinkles of her neck.

'Did you see Jupiter?' he asked. 'During the fuelling?'

'I was very young,' she replied. 'It's more of a dream. What's next with this runaway planet?'

'I guess we're going to study it.'

'But what do you want to do?' Here she surprised herself. The humbled Janelle, the learned-her-lesson Janelle toiling in systems maintenance, would never ask such a question.

Now she invited him to sit on the bed, and she wiggled her feet beneath the blanket so he wouldn't squash them. What do *you* want to do? A very un-Shipworld question, indeed, but there it was off her lips and orbiting between them, between their weak yet persistent personal suns, and the old woman realised, sharply like a pinprick, that she'd stayed alive for no other reason than to speak to Brenz. This boy, unsure and yet untamed.

His fingers touched the ragged edge of the blanket. She'd carried it onboard as a toddler. Clutched it for many years. Chewed it, drooled on it, ran the satin trim along her cheek to comfort herself. Wore it around her neck, a beautiful scarf, and snapped it in anger at her mother, the only person who loved her despite all the trouble she caused.

'I'd like to make a diversion,' said Brenz. 'You know, turn the ship a bit, run alongside the rogue, get a closer look. I know we can't, but I just thought—'

'Why can't you?' she asked.

'Technically, there's no reason. I ran the numbers; it's a minor use of fuel and it'll only add four years to the total voyage. That's not much out of three hundred and sixty.'

She tapped his hand. 'Then do it.'

'I'm not in charge.'

'It's not a dictatorship, either.'

'It would affect people in the future.'

'Everything does. Not acting does.'

Brenz fell quiet; he looked down at the room's window, at the constant, star-streaked reminder that they were spinning, spinning, spinning in circles.

'Good,' said Janelle, as if that rogue business was settled. She tapped his hand again, twice. He looked up. 'What else, young man?'

So much else, it turned out. Brenz said that he wanted to understand the origins of the Revelation, and he told her what he'd learned from the librarian, including how a spacewalk had been used to cure Janelle's Fears. That account, the old woman replied, is essentially correct, and she swayed a little to one side and then back. But what Rosemary didn't know, or wouldn't say, is that Janelle had tried to stay outside until her oxygen ran out.

'I didn't want to return. My mother tried yanking me by the tether, but I clung to the hull with both hands.' Janelle raised her crabbed hands and clutched at something invisible between her and Brenz. Eventually, she explained, Cecilia had to leave the airlock and physically force her daughter inside.

'Why? Didn't you believe it?'

'I did. But it crushed me. You have to understand, I was convinced that we didn't exist in space. It wasn't just a possibility for me, a rite of passage. Crazy or not, I *believed*. I was terrified, and when my own mother threw me into the void…'

Her eyes widened, as if the great hulk of Shipworld reared up before her.

'I'm sorry,' said Brenz. 'She shouldn't have done that.'

'What, save my life?' Suddenly Janelle bent forward at the waist, causing a shear of pain in her left hip. She touched Brenz's face; he didn't flinch. 'It was *my* rebellion, but ever since, they've made it everyone else's. The state-sanctioned rebellion. Is it yours?'

'I don't know,' he said. 'I mean, not yet. I'm told that the Fears grow in the twenty-third year.'

'You're told many things.'

She lay back on the pillows, a gentle collapse, and closed her eyes. For a while there were no sounds in the room except for her breathing, creaky as a garden gate. The boy said, 'Thank you, Aunt Janelle,' and, a long minute later, Brenz Ort-St George pulled his weight from the death bed. The mattress shuddered as if riding an ocean swell, and he departed the room. Anat soon returned and gave her patient a sip of water, her warm hand brushing the old lady's chin. Softly, she whispered a song that Janelle's mother had sung to her at bedtime:

The bear went over the mountain, the bear went over the mountain,
The bear went over the mountain to see what she could see.

But all that she could see, all that she could see,
Was the other side of the mountain, the other side of the mountain…

Over time, Cecilia had added verses, sending the poor little bear over the river and through the woods, then into orbit and across the solar system and through the galaxy, always going farther and farther but never finding anything but the other side. Which was, by definition, the same as staying still, as never voyaging out at all? Ah well, the song soothed Janelle. And she knew this much: ultimately, on Shipworld, everything that could be seen was seen. Every journey ended at its start.

Anat sat at the bedside while the Last Pioneer fell into a painless, final sleep in which she saw herself again as a middle-aged woman, blessedly beyond her youthful madness. She went to work every day, dependable and proud of it. Small tasks, endlessly repeated: clean intake valves, check for tiny imperfections, test seals, take salt samples. Record data in blocky handwriting with sharp diagonals crossing every t. Relieved to be left alone; despondent, at the same time, for settling so irrevocably. Now Janelle's breath grew raspier, as if she was ripping herself open from the inside, and she thought of the father she'd never known, the graduate student on Earthworld. Cecilia claimed not to remember his name, only that he was special. Maybe she didn't, maybe he was. The swirl of family half-stories, of gaps to be leaped over, coalesced, and she descended into deeper sleep and saw Janelle the wobbly child by the Viewing Portal during Jupiter fuelling. One hand held the satin-fringed blanket, the other reached for her mother to keep her from floating away.

And here it comes, gargantuan planet, spinning into view. Monstrous Jupiter, marvellous and raging, a thousand storming, curlicued streaks of orange, brown, red and yellow racing across its body. Gratefully, she—

According to Franika, talking rapidly at Brenz as she paced about the Art Cove, three steps, turn, three steps, turn, it was exactly five weeks ago that she'd recorded the microcystin levels in the computer log and then, the next morning, spoken to Javier about the aberrant finding. Now she stopped in front of the Dürer, shrouded again like the other paintings. 'I followed protocol,' she declared, and, besides, it was only a high-normal reading, nobody should be sick, fifty shipworldmates shouldn't have come down with fatigue and abdominal pain over the past month. Doctor Tam diagnosed the sickest ones with vanishing-duct syndrome, which meant that the bile ducts on their livers were compromised or destroyed.

Brenz nodded. A lot had happened since Janelle's death. Franika continued: maybe the slide medium was wonky or the safety parameters for microcystin toxicity were wrong, but none of that made sense after one hundred and eighteen years of similar fluctuations – she'd checked the historical record, this was nothing special. And wasn't the Correction supposed to prevent organ damage? Still, she felt responsible; she must have missed something in the algae samples.

Brenz nodded again. He wanted to tell her about the plan that he'd set into motion this morning, a decisive action regarding the rogue planet, but he knew better than to interrupt. Not with that look in her eye.

That's not the worst of it, she lamented. Several people had contracted something called phenylketonuria. Ynar had two seizure episodes and could have died! Franika paused – waiting for Brenz to speak? – then asserted that it probably had nothing to do with the microcystin levels because phenylketonuria is a genetic condition, not triggered by toxic exposure. Back on

Earthworld, Doctor Tam told her, one out of twelve thousand babies were born with it. They followed strict diets because their PAH genes were defective, mutated, and they couldn't process all sorts of foods. Now get this: one of those restricted foods is spirulina, the blue-green algae grown here – the same thing poisoning people. So Ynar's gene fritzed for some mysterious reason and then she ate algae croutons in her kale salad – Franika had watched them go in her mouth! – and that's why she's sick.

'Wow,' said Brenz. 'I'm really sorry about Ynar – about everything.'

Franika stared at him, her expression pained. Or annoyed. Had he said the wrong thing? Then she reached for his hand, squeezing it briefly before letting it go. She started pacing again, three steps, turn, three steps, turn.

'It's kind of strange, isn't it,' offered Brenz. 'I mean, both things happening at the same time, the toxin and the gene.'

Franika whirled around. 'Yeah, it is. What are the chances, right? It has to be the same cause.'

'Maybe,' he said. 'Or it's a coincidence.'

He didn't, however, give voice to another thought: when it rains, it pours. An Earthworld saying he got from his dad. Bad stuff clusters together. Again, he thought of Janelle – the terrified child clinging to the hull; the old lady sunk in bed, touching him – and how strange it was that these medical outbreaks happened so soon after the passing of the Last Pioneer. Was that another coincidence? When it rains it pours it floods? She'd died just one hour after Brenz had left her room.

What had Rosemary said? That for all its apparent stability, Shipworld was more fragile than people realised. Even so, he didn't regret the crazy, future-affecting thing he'd done this morning, not at all. But he did feel a gut-deep need to tell Franika about it, to explain everything to her.

'The same cause,' she said, her voice firm. 'The same thing mutating a gene and making people get sick from microcystin at normal levels!'

And the great yawning void of space between them disappeared. Franika kissed him, and he felt her fingers seeking the sore, sweet spot on his head, her lips encompassing his, and then she pulled away. The vast gulf reappeared. She said, 'I gotta go,' and was gone, leaving him alone among the shrouded paintings. A wave of dizziness rolled from neck to skull. Brenz steadied himself, feet planted wide, and looked up at the ever-present Tube, opaque in the morning light, and all around it the patchwork of fields and buildings curling into each other, around and around without end. The ficus tree broke this pattern, its aerial roots a mass of tangled capillaries hovering in partial gravity. As if trying, and failing, to be free.

The dizziness faded. Brenz lowered his gaze to one of the sheet-covered easels, which possibly held the Dürer painting. Recently, at the library, he'd consumed the biography of Dürer that Rosemary had offered, rereading passages about the artist's awakening like a thirsty traveller at a water pump. He'd been relieved to learn that Dürer faltered in earlier self-portraits, painting himself at an angle, shying from the ultimate confrontation. He came up short, just like Brenz, but dared to try again and again 'to pour out new things that had never been in the mind of any other man'. But when Brenz pulled the sheet from the easel before him, he found nothing but a white, empty canvas. He pulled another sheet. Empty canvas. And another – empty. He pulled six sheets from six easels, all holding empty canvases, until one remained. Slowly, he pulled the last sheet and there he was, Albrecht Dürer, rendered in oil on a panel of linden wood. Dürer, staring back. Composed, self-assured. Myself/himself.

The gilt-scrawled Latin words floating over his left shoulder: *I, Albrecht Dürer of Nuremberg, portrayed myself in everlasting colours aged twenty-eight years.*

Was that the ultimate meaning of Rosemary's exhibit? Dürer's bold act – the first eyes-front self-portrait produced by a major artist – was surrounded by blank canvases, by self-portraits never made. Brenz found himself looking at each empty canvas as if it was unique, as if it did not contain the same identical white space, untouched, waiting, as the others. Then his eyes returned to Dürer. He noticed the faint, blue-green veins on the artist's painting hand, veins bulging and branching towards the fingers.

Brenz moved closer, just centimetres from Dürer, and fixed on the signature mark that he'd created for himself:

The A stood like a temple over the smaller D. The individuality of the man, the A, sheltered the history and obligations that were wrapped up in the family D. But the A was more than a dutiful servant. It reigned supreme and proud.

According to the Dürer biography, the rise of the individual in his time – a phenomenon that in hindsight was seen as inevitable – had not only released millions of people from oppression and unquestioning allegiance to corrupt kings and popes, but sparked centuries of achievement in art, philosophy and science. People gained greater freedom to move about the planet, say what they liked, and try things once considered risky, ridiculous and heretical. It was why something as wonderful and complicated as Shipworld could ever be built. And the next stage, considered Brenz, the toxic conversion of healthy individualism into techno-enhanced narcissism that had nearly destroyed Earthworld in the twenty-first century, perhaps that was inevitable, too. As was Shipworld on its journey away. As was Brenz waking inside it.

This morning, before meeting with Franika, he'd gone to the Astro-team head, Reggert, to plead his case for a diversion to the rogue planet. A short, stocky man with a shaved head whose father was on the Council, Reggert invited Brenz to sit on a plastic chair. He leaned against the side of his desk, a tolerant smile playing around his mouth as the young intern made his argument for studying the rogue up close.

'It's a rare opportunity – the opportunity of lifetimes!' said Brenz, spooling out rehearsed words. 'No one's ever approached a rogue. We'd be the first. Plumes of outgassing water, maybe life under the ice! Maybe a whole civilisation! They could be ice-trapped and don't even know that an outside exists.'

He stopped, waited for a response. Reggert waited back.

'I know it's unconventional,' Brenz continued, 'but we could argue that the search for life supersedes other considerations. The extra four years might seem like a lot, but it's just one more year for each upcoming generation. We've got enough fuel for the manoeuvre and, besides, why do we always have to follow our ancestors' plan?'

The supervisor's smile was gone, the feigning of collegiality over. Yet Brenz forged on. 'Think about it, please. We could make a proposal together to the Council.'

'Together?' Reggert laughed. 'Nice try, kid.' A diversion to the rogue was out of the question, he stated. A total daydream, a fantasy. 'The Mission always supersedes scientific ambition and personal desire. Together – you've gotta be kidding.'

'The search for life—'

'Life is right here,' interrupted Reggert. 'Our lives, our descendants' lives. As for following our ancestors' plan, it's written in the Constitution. It's *sacrosanct* – why don't you know that?'

Reggert didn't wait for a response. It's entirely possible, he told Brenz, that the Council wouldn't write his proposal off as an 'enthusiastic outburst of youth'. They'd consider him a troublemaker, even a rebel – a threat to the orderly unfurling of a preordained history – and there's just no room for that kind of deviance. 'Want my advice? Keep your unconventional ideas to yourself.' Then he leaned forward, patted Brenz on the shoulder, and promised to get him some extra telescope time on the rogue, real soon.

That was that, and Brenz couldn't get away from the man fast enough. He needed to think, so he took the long route to Engineering, through a neighbourhood that ran like a thick ring around the centre of the Shipworld. He'd spent his first eighteen years here. The walking paths between three-storey row houses – for families with one or two children – were cluttered with kids tossing balls, playing card games and making towers out of blocks they'd slapped and stretched into myriad shapes. A shriek pierced the voice-babble, more ecstatic than terrified. Everything seemed weirdly normal, given the medical crises, though he noticed that only a few parents and grandparents watched from chairs along the path.

The urge to join in the haphazard play, to build a twisting spire to Tube heaven, tugged at Brenz. He wanted to revert, but kept walking. He forced himself to review events.

Six days ago, a standard gravitational microlensing sweep found the usual batch of rogue planets, between fifty thousand and one hundred thousand light-years distant, distorting the fabric of space-time as they transited stars and quasars. Then, amazingly, another rogue emerged just ninety thousand kilometres away – next door, practically. What's more, the planet appeared to be only 1.5 times the mass of Earth, a rare pocket-sized rogue. Spectrographic analysis suggested a hydrogen-dense atmosphere that hadn't frozen out. Unfortunately, there was little else they could learn from here. But if they flew closer, to within a couple hundred kilometres, then radar and lidar sweeps could penetrate the atmosphere, even pierce the ice shell, and reveal its incredible secrets. Life, possibly – life like Brenz, or completely unlike him. Microscopic, huge, primordial, highly evolved, peaceful, cruel, kind, insignificant, unimaginable life.

So, close the gap. Sidle over, take a look. Reach out and unfurl a little history of your own – who wouldn't want to do that? People like Reggert, obviously. Now the man's patronising voice played on a grinding loop. Enthusiastic outburst of youth, enthusiastic outburst of – so what if it was? What's wrong with youthful enthusiasm, with adventure? Why were people so wedded to written-in-stone, generational dictates? To Brenz that didn't seem like life – not like Dürer facing the canvas, unflinching – but like death. Or worse, a kind of death-life that he'd have to drag within himself across the galaxy.

He picked up his pace to a jog, and the playing children became a colourful blur, their voices like fleeting birdcalls. Brenz had first met Franika on this path, when he was nine. She and a group of older girls sat on the ground playing with a small rubber ball and tiny pieces that looked like wooden flowers. He crept forward, watching, as Franika bounced the ball a metre or so in the air, swept up a pile of flowers, placed them on the back of her other hand and then caught the ball before it came back down.

'Riding the elephant!' she proclaimed.

Brenz had never heard of an elephant. A second girl bounced the ball, gathered flowers in her palm and yelled, 'Frogs in the pond!' Frogs, he'd seen pictures of them. Then Franika turned to Brenz and waved him over. He obeyed, eagerly, while frog girl sourly asserted that he was too young. Franika ignored her, telling Brenz that the game was called knucklebones and had been played by kids on Earthworld for thousands of years. Anyone smart can play, she said, fixing him with a laser look, and as she bounced the ball once more her hands flew, grabbing pieces, arranging them. It was amazing what she accomplished in that brief interlude between the ball's human-powered launch and its gravity descent. She grabbed the moment of opportunity, without hesitation, before the universe regained domination.

Franika didn't cheat or deceive. Then and now, she seemed to go about her life directly, honestly, and so Brenz attempted to be honest with himself, too. He slowed to a fast walk. OK, fine, probably they won't find life on the rogue planet. It's a long shot. Most likely, it's just a flying ice ball – but you can't know without looking. And there's nothing subversive about wondering, about seeking, it's essential, like air and food and love. Shouldn't the Council hear him out? Shouldn't all of Shipworld get a chance to decide?

Shouldn't we have choices?

'Shouldn't I?' Brenz said out loud.

Around the next corner he noticed Tender Beatrice. She waved to him. A tall woman, six centimetres above Brenz and a dozen years older, she stood very straight as if to claim the ideal observational vantage point. She was dressed in a white suit accented with a red scarf and belt. Her mop of blonde hair seemed windblown even though the winds created to strengthen crops weren't blowing today. Like other tenders charged with keeping public order and assisting shipworldmates in distress, she didn't wear a uniform or carry equipment outside her forearm implant. Even so, people knew her and her role.

'Brenz, how are you? How's Lavender and Jacques?'

'I'm fine, Beatrice. I haven't spoken to my parents today, but they were OK last night.'

'Glad to hear it,' she said. 'And your sister?'

'I don't know. She moved to the dorm, doesn't stay in touch much.'

'She'll grow out of it,' replied Beatrice. 'Everything in its own time.' She scanned about, on some automated schedule. 'These medical emergencies, it doesn't make sense after all these years. Your mom's a researcher, right? I'll bet she's working the problem.'

Brenz nodded, catching himself from responding. Tenders presented themselves as trusted mediators, as resources for the community, but Brenz had never liked the way they casually mentioned details about him and his family – as if they were friends. As if they weren't digging for information, pursuing some unspoken agenda.

'The children were inside, taking care of the sick ones,' she said. 'We thought it would be nice if they came out for a few hours. Kids have to play.'

'That's true,' he said, lamely. What do adults have to do?

'The rogue planet – exciting news,' she remarked, not looking at him, once more scanning the path and surrounding houses like a lighthouse. Lighthouse Beatrice, the human panopticon. 'It's almost a shame we can't swerve over and take a closer look. I have to admit, every now and then even I want to do something…unusual.'

Her head didn't revolve back around. Could she have talked to Reggert? Was she trying to bait him?

'The Council would never agree to it,' said Brenz. As he spoke, he realised that Reggert was right about that. They would shut him down, kick him off the rogue project. In fact, he was probably on the way out already, just for suggesting a diversion. He hurriedly added: 'The Mission supersedes everything.'

Tender Beatrice looked into the distance. 'Words to live by,' she said, straightening herself even more, if that was possible. Words to live by – one of his dad's sayings, which often travelled about like a virus. 'Have a good day, Brenz.'

'You too,' he said, and walked away. Who spoke to who, who suspected what – it didn't matter. A minute later, he veered from the old neighbourhood and took a maintenance corridor leading to Engineering. He'd ducked down this route a hundred, no, a thousand times, a corridor of daydreaming and reverie, of snatched solitude on little, churning legs and the long, loping ones they'd grown into. Along the way, he activated a false message on his forearm data/tracking panel, one that situated him in his bed, in his room, deep in sleep, and while doing that he whistled the tune that his mom had improvised for crocheting. That's it: he was putting a knot, a rogue knot, into the fabric of Shipworld.

One might assume that the controls for regulating the thrusters would be highly protected, but that wasn't the case. Perhaps it hadn't occurred to the designers that anyone would try to alter course, or perhaps they'd been focused on preventing sabotage of the fusion engines themselves. Perhaps the Pioneers were too busy, too self-obsessed, to fathom the mind of a person in the far future who might not feel as they feel, believe as they believe. This lack of security would, soon enough, be described as an oversight, a failure of imagination and criminal negligence.

The navigational hack, from a remote console beside a nitrogen processor, was easy for tech-clever Brenz. He worked smoothly, without error, even though he hadn't practised the procedure. It took him only a few minutes, during the eleventh hour of the morning. And so, on this soon-to-be famous day in Year 118, during a monthly maintenance firing of the fusion engines, the constitutionally mandated route of Shipworld on its three-hundred-and-sixty-year journey to HD-40307g was altered, about two degrees to starboard, in order to investigate the possibility of life on a recently discovered rogue planet. The near convergence with the rogue, if allowed, would occur in fifteen days.

Now, alone in the Art Cove, Brenz contemplated his actions. Later that afternoon, when the daily navigation check occurred, the course alteration would be discovered. His plan was to confess. More than anything, Brenz worried about Franika's reaction. Would she understand? Fresh from her Revelation, infused with the glory of the Mission, might she accuse him of heresy? Or even betrayal in the middle of a crisis.

He turned his head and looked at Dürer, Pioneer of Earthworld. And Dürer looked back at him with cool regard. At any rate, it was done. *I, Brenz Oort-St George of Shipworld, portrayed myself in everlasting colours, twenty-one years.* He wiped a tear from his cheek, shook it into the ether, and then covered the easel with a red sheet. He covered the other six easels, too, for the next person who came along, and walked away.

Later, that night, Brenz used his only pencil and a piece of torn paper to sketch a signature mark for himself, an ornate B that protected within its dual heart-chambers the O for Oort and St G for St George. The B reigned supreme and proud.

Franika couldn't believe it, and couldn't stop thinking that it was all her fault. A week into the medical emergency, nine shipworldmates were dead from phenylketonuria and one hundred and five were incapacitated with microcystin poisoning. That was more than one-sixth of the population, with new cases every day. The fatalities had suffered seizures and heart failure brought on by eating spirulina algae, the very product that Franika had spent her days analysing and approving for consumption. Sixteen young people, including Ynar, were gravely ill. The Mess Hall, of course, had stopped serving algae, which normally provided about one-third of the calories and protein ingested onboard. Moreover, as bad news spread – much of it true, some of it exaggerated and doom-laden – the worry grew that the population couldn't sustain genetic diversity in the long run if too many people died before having children. Both the now and the later, the here and the beyond, seemed in peril.

In order to support her theory of a single cause for the two illnesses, Franika interviewed several scientists and doctors. She made some progress when Lavender Oort-St George and colleagues in the Bio Lab confirmed that the victims displayed a mutation on a specific gene – the phenylalanine hydroxylase, or PAH, gene – and that mutation severely impaired an enzyme key to digesting foods, such as algae, that were high in amino acids called phenylanines. But it was just a clue, nothing more.

Hundreds of healthy people, including Franika, extended their work shifts from eight to twelve hours a day to cover for sick colleagues; meanwhile, the families and friends of the deceased reeled with unfathomable grief. Because non-elderly people rarely died on Shipworld, they hadn't the words, rituals or historical context to react with anything but horror. Through their safe, sustainable world roared these weird, fatal conditions, beyond their comprehension or emotional capacity. Several grievers found themselves inconsolable; a few became suicidal and had to be sedated. Franika, in dark moments, was overcome by memories of holding her mother's hand as she'd died years ago, of watching the usually very precise Louisa Longstem struggle to form words at the end. Words of comfort, advice, admonition? They came out garbled, as if rendered in a lost language. For months afterwards, shipworldmates had treated Franika with gentle sympathy, a communal act that helped revive her and for which she was grateful. At the same time, she'd felt as if her grief was an exotic contagion that had to be contained, even purged, for the good of society.

Now and then, as she made her investigations, Franika wondered if those last, unfathomable words had been a warning of disasters to come. A prophecy of catastrophe and ruin. And the daughter found herself fantasising about breaching the barriers of time and asking the mother one simple question: how do we survive?

For patients with microcystin poisoning, anti-necrotic drugs were being employed to stabilise liver function; the extreme fatigue remained, but they were likely to recover. Among the stricken was Jacques Oort-St George. By his side, day and night, sat Brenz, ordered into confinement while the Council discussed his punishment and the ramifications of Shipworld's new trajectory. Given the general chaos, and the fact that they couldn't achieve a quorum with five severely ill members, the Council kept putting off the decision to fire the engines and resume the original course. With each day of inaction, Shipworld moved closer to the rogue planet; with each day, months were added to the duration of the voyage.

Franika's spirits rose, again, when she learned that microcystin levels in patients' tissues were within high-normal ranges. Another key clue. It wasn't high toxin levels per se, Doctor Tam explained over coffee at the community garden. It was *sensitivity* to the toxins that must have changed. He slugged the dregs of his brew, frowned.

'Toxic sensitivity, it's not on the PAH gene?' she asked.

'No,' he replied. 'It's not.'

He looked over at the Olmec Head, and Franika joined his gaze. The ancient one didn't bother to look back, its expression as sour as ever. She noticed, too, that the smooth, grey bark on the nearby ficus tree appeared swollen, riven with bulging veins – or perhaps they were the tree's own vines, strangling and supporting it at the same time. It had always perplexed her, the ficus, the way it enacted seasonal rituals – bearing inedible figs, dropping bright green leaves – in a place without seasons, or with just one. Its genetic programming won out, she supposed. Some shipworldmates called it the Community Tree and believed that it symbolised their world's enduring togetherness. It was nice to sit under, lean your back against. But at this moment, to Franika, the tree seemed very alone, and lonely.

'Are children getting sick?' she asked.

He shook his head. 'The children are fine.'

'We get the Correction when we're eighteen,' responded Franika. 'Maybe their genes aren't mutated because they haven't got the Correction yet.'

'Maybe,' said Doctor Tam, shrugging. 'Or it could be a hundred other things related to paediatric physiology.' He slugged his coffee again. 'Let's not get ahead of ourselves. This isn't some kind of biblical plague.'

'What's that?' asked Franika.

'The Bible, it's in the library,' said Doctor Tam. 'God punished the Egyptians for following a corrupt leader. You might want to read it, when all this is over.'

He departed a few moments later, before Franika could ask more questions about the plagues of Egypt, and before she could share her hypothesis that cosmic radiation – the only dynamic element that entered from outside – could be behind both medical emergencies. Perhaps it was just as well. Tam enacted friendliness and cooperation, even while exhausted, but it was pretty clear that he didn't respect her. A lowly technician, a child getting ahead of herself. Not an expert like him. She'd gotten the same impression last night when she'd met with Reggert, who'd grudgingly agreed to share data from air samples taken inside and outside the craft. He'd also criticised Brenz for his 'immature rebellion', for challenging the ways things had to be. Franika chose not to respond, out of loyalty to Brenz.

But she was angry at him, too.

Her Katan, moving Shipworld! Arrogantly making the decision for everyone – it just didn't make sense. He'd been so caring, so empathetic when he pledged undying friendship during the recitation of the Fears. And he seemed to listen, really listen. She'd convinced herself that he *got* her, that by osmosis he understood her Revelation experience. That he, too, could see Shipworld alone in space and feel the beauty of its inhabitants' devotion. Franika sighed. Obviously, she'd misjudged Brenz in a fundamental way. And fallen victim – wishfully, foolishly – to her own needs, operating in stealth mode just beyond her control.

Many people, however, appeared ready to forgive Brenz's actions. Some, to Franika's surprise, even whispered support. Sure, it wasn't right for him to change course, went a common refrain, but it was cleverly done, and we have worse problems to worry about... Besides, the rogue planet might be amazing... It could be fate... Let the Seventh-Gen wait a few more years for journey's end. Her friends were just as bad. Why, Gulika carped, fret about a little lost time? Everyone alive today will die without arriving, chimed in Javier, as if that banal statement explained anything. Franika suspected that more than a few people harboured unspoken admiration for Brenz's decision to do what he wanted, for his reasons, and to hell with the consequences. It was almost as if he'd done it for them.

She walked down Pictor Boulevard. The way was empty with only a few passers-by, eyes averted, moving fast. Overhead, parallel to her direction, ran the milky-white Tube like a stiff plant tendril. Within it, she glimpsed the shadow of two people carrying a body on a litter. What in the world, she wondered, is happening here? Are we finally coming undone? She sensed an ending to how they'd lived for one hundred and eighteen years. Earthworld, she'd been taught, had fallen apart over centuries from neglect and avarice and, as the crises mounted, a selfish reluctance to make shared sacrifices. And, perhaps, from following corrupt and captivating leaders. But Shipworld was different. People cooperated – out of necessity and survival instinct, yes, but they did – and besides everything had seemed fine just weeks ago.

The end of everything she cherished? No, she couldn't let that happen.

That night, very late, Franika awoke from a restless sleep. She went to the bathroom, peeked in on her father curled beneath a thin, worn blanket on the single bed he'd acquired after her mother had died, and then put on shorts and a tank top. She laced her sneakers, tight, but not too tight, stretched her legs against the kitchen table and headed out to traverse Shipworld in the near dark. Franika chose, definitively, not to think about the medical catastrophes or her cosmic ray theory or Reggert or Brenz or anything if that was possible. Two steps out the door, she ran.

Lights were kept low after midnight, casting a gentle dusk, but Franika probably could have negotiated her running route with eyes closed. It didn't take a dozen strides before she achieved cruising speed, her legs circulating freely, her hands held in front of her in loose fists. Her footfalls echoed, swirling about the curved interior of her world. She ran past a narrow field of corn, its tassels studded with pollen like nebulae swarming with stars, and into a neighbourhood not far from where she'd grown up. Staircases wrapped about the row houses shined in the low light, and she recalled laughing when she'd learned that most staircases were built inside homes on Earthworld – an alternate reality. An alternate history, left behind.

As she ran, Franika felt her heart pumping and her lungs filling and emptying, organs executing their roles in automatic synchronicity. The smell of Shipworld was different at this hour, sweeter. Everyone had gone inside, except Franika, and a strange, deep-night sweetness seemed to hang in the air. Franika imagined it came from the shared sleep of shipworldmates, from their merged and turbulent dreams.

A crunch, under her right foot. She slowed up, turned around. Near a garden plot of vegetables, in front of a residential building, Franika kneeled and picked up several tiny pieces of wood.

The flowers from knucklebones, just like the ones she'd played with as a child – almost. These were slightly bigger and blue. One was broken, splintered by her pounding foot, and she started to think of Brenz and the day they'd met as kids along a street like this and quickly she slipped that memory away, not now, and put the toy by the edge of the garden, except for the broken part. Again, she set off, running fast, accelerating to a pace beyond her comfort level, legs straining, lungs working hard, hands gripped in tight fists with one clutching the cracked flower. She looked up, and even though it was barely visible she saw the world upside down and, simultaneously, herself upside down over that world, just as it should be, as it always should be, *duum, duum, duum, duum*, her footfalls, and she veered away from the old neighbourhood and raced even faster, legs burning, sweat dripping into her eyes. Finally, Franika slowed to a jog, then a walk. She approached the bridge catwalk near Engineering, the very spot where had mother had fallen. Her body, of course, had been recycled into Shipworld, but her spirit lived here, her daughter believed, because it was here that she'd last been fully alive.

The garbled words, spoken before death, returned. Franika didn't slip this memory away, nor did she fashion the rough non-words into an inspirational saying – not her mother's style – or even 'I love you' or 'I'm sorry' or 'Take care of your father'. But she did recall something that Louisa Longstem used to tell teenage Franika in an attempt, perhaps, at humour or reverse psychology. 'Don't clean your room,' she'd say, deadpan. 'Really, don't bother.' For a long while Franika stood by the catwalk, rolling the broken wooden flower across her palm, and then she departed. She ran beneath the hollow Tube, where no victims were being ferried at this hour, and for a moment or two she saw Shipworld shining with people, glorious, ordinary people, more than she'd ever seen before, and voices babbled and bright banners waved and babies cried out and, faintly, she heard water splashing – and then it was just her, running alone in the dark. When she arrived home, Franika sat at the kitchen table and tried to repair the flower using a thin piece of wire and tomato-based glue. A bit of a mess, but it might hold. She went back to bed. On the outskirts of sleep her troubles and worries reassembled and fell upon her without mercy, but she was just too tired to care.

The next morning, after returning the repaired flower to the garden, Franika went to Astronomy and got last night's data readout from Reggert. The area of space they were travelling through, he told her, was a bit higher than usual in silicate deposits on cosmic dust grains. But that all stayed outside. The deflector appeared to be working, admitting only trace amounts of cosmic rays – fragments of helium and hydrogen atoms, basically – at levels similar to standard exposure. At any rate, nothing much different since launch. And the liquid shielding in the hull had experienced no changes. Everything status quo.

'What else?' asked Franika, who felt the absence of information like an invisible wall between them. Reggert chuckled; half-life analysis, he said, indicated that the cosmic rays were younger than the ones that usually bombard Earthworld. In other words, Shipworld was flying more towards than away from the supernova explosions that created the rays. He labelled these results esoteric and inconclusive.

'But younger rays have higher radiation levels,' said Franika.

'A little,' he responded. 'Barely.'

Franika then asked if younger cosmic rays could affect the human body differently than older ones. 'Yes, no, maybe,' said Reggert. He made his trademark snark-smile and turned away, but Franika grabbed his elbow, detaining him.

'Can we increase the deflector intensity?' she asked. 'Put extra water in the walls – that would trap more rays.'

'Go talk to a structural engineer,' he said, and he shook her hand off, roughly. 'Better yet, ask your boyfriend. He's pretty good at hacking systems.'

This time Franika turned first and walked away. What a jerk, Reggert; he made Brenz sound scheming, almost *dangerous*. Yes, he'd shattered precedent, but he was also kind and smart and she pictured his face, a gawky mask over churning thoughts. She waded through a storm of conflicted feelings and recalled how he'd gently helped her into the layers of her spacesuit and then absorbed and denied her insane Fears. How he'd raced down through gravity gradients for the plummeting Equilibrium birdie that remained, perpetually, just out of reach. Maybe that was him to her, Franika wondered, unreachable, ultimately unknowable.

But dangerous – that couldn't be true, could it?

At her first opportunity, she veered off Pictor Boulevard and made a shortcut along the edge of Shipworld's swimming pool, which contained only a solitary woman powering forward with a butterfly stroke. She breached the water's surface like a leaping dolphin, again and again, above and below. Franika sped up, heading on a path running diagonally, north by northeast, from the Tube to the Oort-St George residence. She shouldn't avoid Brenz. She should stow her turmoil and seek him out. He was her Katan, for always, and that relationship didn't have to work just one way. Perhaps he needed her to ward off his own Fears.

A minute later she almost ran into him as he came out the front door of his parents' apartment with a backpack slung over his shoulder.

'Franny,' he said, surprised.

'Hi, Brenz.' They stood just a few feet apart, but neither reached out. 'How's your dad?'

'He ate something. They say he's going to be OK.'

'Oh, I'm so glad to hear that,' she said.

'How's your father?'

'Nothing yet. I mean, he's not sick.'

Brenz looked away from her, up the path devoid of shipworld-mates. For a moment he seemed ten years old, lost, on the verge of tears. 'It's got nothing to do with the course change,' he said. 'All this started before I—'

Franika wrapped her arms around him. She held him close, determined to perceive him the way he was, not the way she imagined him to be. Determined not to make the same mistake again, and determined, also, to fix things between them. 'I wish you'd talked to me first,' she said, with more exasperation than anger. She brushed his hair, gently. Felt the long line of his chin, the bone beneath the skin. A moment later, he pulled away from her, stumbling a bit, as if having trouble with his balance. He seemed thinner, too. Was he eating?

'Are you all right?'

'I was with Janelle, before she died,' said Brenz. 'They made her go on that first spacewalk. They forced her to do it – did you know that?'

'No, I didn't. I never thought about it.'

'That's just it, they don't want us to think – not about un-approved things. Really, how do we know we're on the way to HD-40307g? Did your Revelation tell you that?'

'Brenz—'

'On Earthworld, they were on a specific planet, orbiting a specific star. What do we really know for sure? What are we allowed to know?'

'Our mission—'

'My life is my mission,' he shot back.

Now he slipped the backpack off his shoulder and opened it wide. Jumbled inside was his Equilibrium equipment – rope, helmet, pads, servomechanism. The racquet wasn't there, though; instead, she saw a bulky stack of hundreds of white postcards, tied with string. The top one was crammed with Brenz's dense handwriting.

'Where did you get so many?' asked Franika, shocked. 'We're only supposed to have a couple at a time.'

'My dad took them from his job. One a week, nobody noticed.'

'He stole them.'

Brenz continued, as if she hadn't spoken: 'I found them wrapped up in a towel. He was planning on writing a book someday, just for himself.'

His voice, Franika felt, was oddly off-pitch.

'I boiled down algae milk for ink,' said Brenz. 'Made a pen out of a chopstick. When my dad was asleep, I wrote out—'

'No!' she told him. 'You can't do this.' Her voice came out loud, surprising her, but she didn't bother to modulate it. 'Brenz, I believe in Shipworld. I believe in honouring what our ancestors set out to do. And our descendants, what they're destined to do. I believe in *sacrificing* ourselves, if that's how you have to think about it. Nothing unified people on Earthworld, nothing gave them a shared, higher purpose. It was all individuals being selfish and it ended horribly. We can do so much better now.'

She stared at him, hard, and saw two intersecting people: the man she struggled to understand, oh God, she loved him, and the shy boy she'd corralled on the path so many years ago, just yesterday. Hey, come over, kid, let's play. It's called knucklebones – a game for smart people. Look at me, fast reflexes, fast thinking. Riding the elephant! Frogs in the pond! OK, now you try.

'Please,' she said. 'I know it's scary, it probably seems like everything's—'

'Don't worry, Franika,' he said, cutting her off. 'I'm just sending a message. No one has to care. And they can put the ship back on course anytime, can't they?'

He zipped up the backpack and lifted it over his shoulder. It seemed to weigh him down for a moment, until he straightened.

Then he pulled Franika close and kissed her, as if trying to tell her something he couldn't express in words. And just as suddenly, Brenz was gone.

Franika almost chased him, but didn't. People were sick, dying – that had to be more important. Ynar, she'd been told, might not survive. Go, Franika told herself, and she hurried to Engineering where she spoke with three workers who voiced contradictory views about the maximum repulsive power of the deflector. However, they all agreed that upgrades would require a rerouting of power from agriculture, civic lighting and scientific research. As for pumping more water for hull shielding, there was room for a twenty per cent increase, but that would mean a reduction in residential use – shorter showers, less drinking water. Empty the swimming pool. Franika knew that approval for such drastic changes could only come from the Council, and they'd want proof that the radioactive properties of cosmic rays were causing two different medical crises. All she had was a theory based on correlation. No demonstrated causation. You could just as easily blame the rogue planet.

When she finished in Engineering, Franika headed towards the Mess Hall. Unlike earlier in the day, shipworldmates stood outside on the paths between homes, offices and fields. She craned her head in amazement; hundreds of people moved in fits and starts across the bending landscape, covering ground for three hundred and sixty degrees around the Tube. Crowds like this appeared only for Equilibrium games and annual Launch Day celebrations.

Everyone was looking up.

She did, too.

And then she saw him.

At the midpoint of the Tube, Brenz held on to a grappling handle that prevented him from floating off in the near-zero gravity pervading Shipworld's epicentre. From there his

Equilibrium rope stretched for fifteen or twenty metres, where it terminated in a knot. What was he doing? Franika couldn't understand how so many people had known to come outside. Word of mouth? One person telling another, telling another, telling another. Come out and see. Brenz is on the Tube.

With surprising ease, he attached his servomechanism and rode it along the rope all the way to the knot, to a region of higher gravity. Franika startled, and murmurs bubbled from the crowd; if the knot came loose, he could fall to his death. From his backpack, Brenz pulled a thick handful of postcards. He smiled, a happy smile, and with a flourish tossed the postcards into the air. They separated, flapping and fluttering down towards the ground, each one an individual member of a collective, a flock. The postcards gained speed as they passed through the gravity gradients.

Scores settled on paths, roofs and fields. They alighted next to algae pipes, swing sets and bamboo fences. They splashed in the swimming pool and landed among the empty canvases in the Art Cove. A few postcards fell in a patch of rhubarb and one rested on the Olmec Head ever so slowly turning from stone to dust. Several lodged themselves – geometric flowers – in the jumbled branches of the ficus tree. Shipworldmates picked up the postcards, and some agile folk even managed to snag the jiggering rectangles before they hit ground. Meanwhile, Brenz had scampered to another side of the Tube, reattached his Equilibrium rope, slid out to the knot, and let free another batch. They glittered in the ambient light and winged their way down, shining white shards, to eager hands.

He performed this action three more times, in haste, and within minutes had released the entire postcard stack. On every square metre of Shipworld, nearly, a piece of paper with Brenz's message fell.

Tender Beatrice picked up a postcard and carefully read it. Rosemary picked one up, too, and, in reading it, tears dropped from her eyes. Reggert, Gulika, Javier and Teacher Varbala all held postcards and read them standing up. Franika's father, Charley Longstem, emerged from the Ag Lab and took one into his hands. Lavender Oort-St George was too overwhelmed, too focused on watching her son clamber around the Tube, to do anything, and she flashed back to that day by the Olmec Head, the two of them sitting, knitting, reading, wondering about each other. Next to her, holding a card with an expression of disdain, stood Chive. She made a growling noise, then looked up; the soft, hazel eyes that she shared with her brother stared daggers.

Franika raised her hand, stretched, and from the air seized a postcard. The blue-green, carefully rendered letters of Brenz's handwriting covered both sides. It read:

'Out of love for Shipworld, I, Brenz Oort-St George, assert the power of individual choice and, in so doing, defend the following sixteen theses:

1) Shipworld is a marvel of human endurance
2) Our Mission to HD-40307g is noble and worthy
3) Shipworldmates are devoted to that Mission
4) Yet I, a shipworldmate, lead my own life
5) My life-course is noble and worthy
6) Yes, my life exists for others, living and unborn
7) But my life and my choices are also for myself
8) The Shipworld Constitution protects our survival
9) But survival without growth or risk is not sufficient
10) I yearn to discover myself, not just survive
11) I yearn to explore space, not just move through it
12) Where is the mission to learn all that can be learned?
13) Shipworld enforces sustainable equilibrium
14) While the free individual seeks transcendence
15) Resolved: The Revelation happens within
16) Shipworld and the individual must reconcile

In the bottom right corner of the postcard, Brenz had drawn an ornate B protecting within its dual heart-chambers the O for Oort and the St G for St George. The ink for the B was red. With a gasp, Franika realised that he'd signed the card with his own blood. She looked up and, for a terrifying moment, feared that Brenz, dizzy with blood loss, would release himself from the servomechanism and fall, then hurtle, to his death. His head would smash on the hull's hard, interior skin, just like her mother's had. But he held firm, alone and strong and above it all.

'The Revelation,' Franika whispered, 'happens within.' And she saw her beloved, in full, for the first time. Brenz Oort-St George was no doubt an idealist, insightful and charming and easy to underestimate, but he was also a fanatic, and therefore a grave threat to Shipworld and the integrity of its founding purpose. A dangerous element, indeed, a poisonous ingredient – especially now. Franika felt responsible for him; she'd set him in motion, unlocked him as her Katan. And she couldn't deny that she wanted to be with him, to hold him, make love to him – but that was her selfish side speaking. She wouldn't listen to its arrogant cry again. She'd banish such feelings, provided she could find a place for their exile.

If only he'd seen Shipworld, like she had.

Now she looked down at Brenz's signature mark, at the streaky bloodlines, at the B encircling and dominating the initials of his last name. He must be stopped, she decided, no matter what. Our history cannot end here. Our future must survive. Everything depended on keeping him from destroying what could be the last remnant of humanity, set loose on the deep. This task, she was sure, had been given to her – passed down in defiance of time – by the multitudinous, yearning descendants of everyone standing around her, and she would die before failing them.

Franika crumpled the sixteen theses and dropped them to the ground.

2

Years 0–12: Excerpts from *The Chronicler's Journal*

Year 0, Day 206

Contemplation of Jupiter entrances the crew, breeds idleness.

And that's fine by me. The cult of getting it done, the worshipping at the Holy Grail of efficiency and productivity, the more-is-more, dig-it, drill-it, cut-it-down, go-go-growth paradigm pretty much ruined Earth. (Sorry, Earthworld, get with the lingo.) Yes, it's nice to see my shipworldmates – Pioneers, O Pioneers! – goofing off at the Viewing Portal, which is a wide and rather thick sheet of fused silica glass set into the floor just outside the Mess Hall, a rectangular eye surrounded by tiers of tilted seats enabling semi-comfortable, if vertiginous, viewing. Nice, indeed, to witness the general awe struck by Jupiter, so massive, so eccentric, as it reappears every twenty-four seconds, as our spinning home conjures inertia mimicking gravity. You know, centripetal force, that old trick with the whirling water bucket.

Why, you might ask, does Shipworld make 2.4 rotations per minute? That's trial and error. Anything faster and our inner ears contort, causing nausea. Anything slower and our feet and heads exist in different gravitational neighbourhoods.

And so, entranced, we watch as Jupiter departs from our view, trailing the black beast of space and its attendant white star-suckers. We wait, prickling with anticipation, even a shiver of doubt. Will it come back around again, could it blink away this time? Counting down, ten, nine, eight … three, two, one, and Jupiter rises!

Jupiter Optimus Maximus. Juggernaut of electromagnetic exhalation, juggling seventy-nine moons. The travelling shadow of icy Europa is its beauty mark. Jupiter, an expertly lathed Victorian-era curio, kiln-dried, polished, painted. A pool ball possessed, turning so fast on the black felt of space that its equator bulges. Permit me one more: Jupiter, curlicued with ammonia clouds, a paisley riot of russet browns, orangey reds and pus-yellows roiling about the bigger-than-Earthworld Red Spot.

They say it's an elliptical anti-cyclone, first observed in 1655, but maybe the Red Spot's really a button. Push it, if you dare. Then wait.

Shipworld now orbits Jupiter, far enough away to survive its pulsing veil of radiation. Doggedly, we graze the atmosphere, slurping helium-3 and hydrogen isotopes for the fusion drive. This suckling should take five months, using probe-assisted plasmatic lassos. Or some such Parsons-speak. He was always a little theatrical. For example, that student essay our visionary leader wrote about barbed wire and how it tamed the American West. *Blood and Rust*, he called it. On safety grounds, and to knock him back a bit, the teacher prevented Parsons from passing around a stretch of barbed wire that he'd cut, supposedly, from a cattle pen. He showed the class the ugly scar marring his palm, which had been meticulously applied with kitchen condiments. A few students gasped.

I was that teacher. Later, his friend. Sometimes I miss Parsons. Shipworld was his dream made real, cracked from his Zeussian head. It's hard not to feel the omnipresence of his absence. Or to make light of his last-minute decision not to come aboard. The phrase 'don't parsons me' floats in the air: don't show enthusiasm if you're not going to follow through. Parsons, the reluctant. A friend and admirer of my Zayit, he grieved for her, too, but now I feel alone in that endeavour. Parsons, the abandoner. Why did he stay home? I wish I knew.

At age ninety I'm the oldest person at this window, not to mention onboard. The youngest is a toddler, maybe two years old. She reaches for a woman's hand. Blanky over her shoulder. Curly-locked, shirt untucked and breakfast-stained, she goggles with the rest of us at the Jupiter gas station. Drool droops from her lower lip. She can't remember Earthworld, can she? And besides, Jupiter! That'll be the stye in this child's wild eye. Surely, she'll dream of its omnipresent absence after we depart for the void. The woman she clings to – her mother, I guess, so young herself – seems vaguely sad. Because we're between, I guess again, between home and away.

That's my philosophy: I guess. I'm pretty sure I exist, and the rest is guesswork.

Here I sit, watching people watch. A scrivener in a make-work job. Pundit-at-large, word-lassoer. Drinking coffee, nibbling a dry corn muffin. Shall I take another shot at capturing gargantuan Jupiter? Before you say no: Sky-God turned inside out, ever emanating, shrinking two centimetres per year since the formation of its solid core 4.5 billion years ago. Now, give or take, it's half the size it was back then. At the end of time, it'll be a hard little marble, easy to flick away. God's thumb and all.

But that grasping toddler, she'll grow twice her size in another ten years. She'll pull her hand from her mother's and become, happily or not, a space-child.

Year 1, Day 88
We've made the Oort Cloud.

At the community garden, I have another nice chat with Cecilia Oort. She's a tall, red-headed descendant of Jan Oort, the legendary astronomer who in 1950 inferred the existence of the cloud. Imagine that, using inference to *discover* something. Being that smart.

The Oort Cloud's not a cloud like a child draws or an airplane zooms through, but a vast shell of busy, icy comets – billions! trillions! – enveloping the solar system like a pulsating slush ball. Some of these comets have frozen chem-tails swirling out for millions of miles. However, Cecilia tells me, we could easily fly through the Oort Cloud without seeing anything with the naked eye. (Naked eye? As if our biased brains don't clothe it.) It's a matter of scale, you see. And a matter of luck if we do see something.

So, lucky us. We're travelling alongside a comet on the outward leg of its grand elliptical orbit around the sun; salmon-like, it seeks its aphelion, at which point it'll make a U-turn and return. Then do it all over again, *ad infinitum absurdum*. Shipworld, by contrast, is a there-and-not-back-again phenomenon, point A to point B with no breadcrumbs, no do-overs and no room for regret. Because we're leaving this elongated fellow behind in a few days, gawking crowds have arrived at the Viewing Portal. The comet, or the window, depending on your vantage point, spins by twice a minute or so.

Cecilia, it happens, is the mother of the toddler I observed last year, when Jupiter was the show. The kid's name is Janelle, she's almost three, and she's growing like the green bean vines along Pictor Boulevard. Her mom seems to like me, I don't know why. When I ask questions, her green eyes narrow as if she's searching for profundity behind my banality. Then she talks; she likes to talk. And I like to sip fake coffee (the real stuff has run out already) and listen to her voice as she describes her Earthworld job as a waitress at a vertical diner, or Janelle's bath-time rituals with rubber rabbit and washcloth, or the chemical composition of comets.

It's still hard for her, she admits, going without internet and TV. She was raised on screens, became addicted to them. She mainlined a curated world of escapism and outrage through the handheld frames of the iPad, iPhone and iRoom, and to this day she wonders what happened to certain movie stars and singers and athletes, to the celebrities that were as real, more real, than the people she interacted with daily. That guy with the beard, the one who saved the schoolchildren when the neo-Confederates blew up the Lincoln Memorial, is he still doing hero things? It's so damn foolish, Cecilia admits, the way she's wired. But Shipworld Rules will be good for her child, the mother in her asserts. When Janelle invents something fun, a game or idea, it won't be scavenged from some video scrap, some worn-out meme. Her imagination will bloom here. She'll see the world unframed, in the rolling round, and enjoy touching real things and be comfortable talking to people of all ages. That, at least, is the hope.

So far, I've avoided asking Cecilia why she volunteered for this interstellar escapade or how she became a single parent. In the same vein, Janelle's roughness with her toys and other children goes unremarked. We keep it light. She: how's your muffin? Me: not bad, kind of grey, besmirched with blue. Hey, she says, let's pretend those blue bits aren't tofu but high-bush blueberries picked on a blue-sky afternoon. By blue-stained hands, I add, on a mountainside under a simmering sun. And she smiles, barely.

Comet in Latin is *cometa*, meaning 'long-haired'. Clever Cecilia refers to our comet companion as Hairy. And a memory ascends: when I was young, long ago in the late 1990s, thirty-nine members of the Heaven's Gate cult killed themselves in order to transport their souls aboard a spaceship riding in the wake of the Hale-Bopp comet. They took poison and lay on bunkbeds, each cultist wearing a pair of new sneakers. Fresh from the box, I suppose, shoelaces white, pristine. How quickly I used to dirty my sneaks, much to my mother's chagrin.

I don't share these musings, but this I wonder aloud: could the folks in charge adjust our course to align with the comet? For science, for crew morale? Not likely, Cecilia replies. A tiny deviation from target would cost years. Small cause, big effect. We know this, I interject, from Ray Bradbury's butterfly effect. Perhaps big causes can produce small effects, too? The Cold War changes the flavour of yogurt available in a Newark mini-mart on a Tuesday in 1994. The Great Greenland Melt messes with Zayit's choice of scarf on a Friday in 2039. That kind of thing.

A solar flare kills a butterfly, she says. And smiles, more this time. Even laughs a little.

I've tried, but can't comet-gaze for long. Hairy evokes too much. He's too relentless, too path-dependent. Too gone, soon enough. I'm much happier in the garden, with Cecilia and anarchic Janelle and the brooding Olmec Head. It was sculpted from basalt rock spit up from a volcano in Central America. That rock was altered and then exalted by man – until it wasn't. To the earth it returned in some revolution or calamity, where it lay buried for millennia. Found by luck, by magnetometer. Over two metres tall, thirteen tonnes fat, one of only sixteen Olmec heads rediscovered, and I said to Parsons, C'mon, man, can't you find a less massive treasure to shlep to HD-40307g? He took it as a dare and acquired/stole Dürer's chiaroscuro 'Self-Portrait' from the Alte Pinakothek in Munich. Five pounds with frame, six hundred and fifty years old. Gave it to me for my birthday. It's hanging in Shipworld, in my bathroom.

For a while, Dürer's stare haunted me. The vanity, I guess, felt appalling. Floating over his left shoulder are a nebula of Latin words, gilt forms against deep-space black: *'I, Albrecht Dürer…'* His face and cupped hand gently glow, illuminated as if from within. And the long, glistening hair, each strand tended just so. What a showboat, what a dandy! According to art historians, this was the first self-portrait, but really? One day a man just decided, yes, me? Finally, me? Anyway, I've grown used to it. After peeing, I often stare back: I, Marcus Marte. I without Zayit. Half-buried with her, half a man without her. But I, nonetheless.

Unlike Dürer, the Head doesn't stare point blank. It's cross-eyed, tranced, beyond caring. Sure, he's a king, but he's an old fellow, too. Sitting under the ficus for shade. Cheeks hanging, lips flabby, a thick wrinkle across the pockmarked nose. Vandal slashes here and there – the negation of power. The erasure of history. And that headdress, with the carved jaguar talons, it looks too tight. Altogether, he's not so scary anymore. I guess that's why the Head seems just right for this garden where I sit, where oblivious children play. Majesty fades, set free from time and place and memory. Only the silent exile remains.

And yet, some days I want to take an axe to it.

On Shipworld, you can't run away from home. You can't join the circus, go live on a mountaintop with high-altitude beetles, or raft down the muddy river to a place where folks don't know you or your kind. On Shipworld you can't put a continent between your hometown and your adult life, as I did when I deserted Oregon for Boston. That's the irony here; the world itself is lighting out for the territories and the penalty for that is personal imprisonment. A life sentence, self-imposed.

Once more, I chuckle over how this fantastical, nutjob expedition came about. Not through nationalist fervour. Church or corporate consortium? No. Our voyage happened because a disgruntled rich guy had enough cash and chutzpah. He was involved in every key decision during construction and even named the vehicle – 'Let's call it Shipworld,' he said one day, offhand, as if he hadn't considered a hundred and one options – and, of course, the name stuck. Then at lift-off he stood there waving, sorry, changed my mind, chickened out, never actually planned on going, whatever. Crazy, huh? And Cecilia uncrosses her legs, crosses them again. Scratches her cheek. Says something delightful that, honestly, is just a regular thing said through lovely lips.

Maybe I remind her of someone, some old Oort. Perhaps I'm safe, that explains it. There's really no chance I'll proposition her. Not in waking time, certainly. My dreams here, however, are more vivid than they were on Earthworld, and more manageable, too. In this floating Dreamworld, I make myself a young man across from her. In the garden with bad coffee and ersatz muffin, listening to her voice. Brushing her hand.

Please, Zayit, forgive me.

✦

Year 3, Day 7

I'm up early to see the dawn – in this case a thin strip of LED lights spiralling about the length of the Tube. I heard someone say that it's transparent to keep it from being used for no-grav sex. Anyway, I'm up and go for a brisk stroll about Shipworld, which is round, of course, a revolving ellipsoid, but inside, in any one place, it's flat. In fact, if you walk around the mid-circumference, there's no sense of going in a circle and no surprise at ending up where you started. More so, I've become perfectly fine with looking up and seeing a potato patch and kids playing kickball, one hundred and sixty metres over my head, upside down.

Sounds a bit strange when I write it down, though.

Soon I wander over to the 3-D Printer Nook for a new hinge piece (I sat on my eyeglasses). While waiting, I watch a couple of tykes pushing an orange squish ball, as big as the kids combined, through an arch in the sandy area of a nearby playground. All over, as per constitutional edict, you'll find romping and hangout areas for children and their families. It's our correction to a major Earthworld mistake, the enabling of a perverse version of childhood based on smartphones and social media connections instead of real-world, physical play. Here the free-range child, roaming a nested village, has returned. To be fair, though, an extended childhood of play instead of labour on farms or in mills or within homes was the Earthworld exception rather than the rule until the twentieth century, and then mostly in wealthy countries. And, look, there's Cecilia Oort strolling without the little one. She waves me over and we walk together to the Mess Hall.

There we sip counterfeit coffee and Cecilia tells me about her work in the Astronomy section, where she's training on the X-ray telescope and taking classes in cosmology. Her great-great-great grandfather's cloud is behind us now, as we accelerate to top speed. (In seven more years, we cut the engines and glide.) We're past the edge of town, I say, and she nods tolerantly, perhaps aware that Oort means 'edge' or 'end' in Middle Dutch. I keep the next thought, that we're like Frodo hiking beyond the border of the Shire, to myself. Instead, I casually mention a glorious cup of coffee I once had with Zayit at a café in Paris' Marais neighbourhood. Cecilia asks how we met. She leans her elbow on the table and settles her chin into the palm of her hand, as if to say go ahead, take your time.

This is the version I tell. I'm thirty, the Berlin Wall's been chopped to bits and I'm finishing seven years' service at the US Embassy in Mexico City. My title is liaison officer, which means that I occasionally assist with intelligence operations – stemming the red tide lapping up from Nicaragua via Moscow – but mostly I wrangle visas, show around bigshots and drink with Ambassador John Gavin, an old acting buddy of Ronald Reagan. Gavin almost got the James Bond role, twice. Here Cecilia furrows her brow. But I skip explaining Bond, or Reagan, or the Cold War, in favour of a story about the time Gavin acted out lines from his starring role as a German officer in the World War II epic *A Time to Love and a Time to Die*, and a patron at this hotel bar on the Paso de la Reforma took a swing at John's square jaw – Nazi scum! – and hit me in the eye instead. Wow, that stung.

Cecilia laughs. I jump ahead to Boston, where I'd gone to college, and I'm substitute teaching history at a middle school in a wealthy suburb. Zayit's a guidance counsellor, newly hired, steering brats such as Parsons to their privileged spots at Yale and Wellesley and, wow, she hit me in the eye, the good way.

She held her head like a porcelain vase, Zayit did. Fragile, ancient, priceless. Her dress, the colour of cream, was laced with daffodils that she'd drawn by the light of the moon (I imagined). Pleased to meet you, Marcus Marte, she said to me, enjoying the alliteration, and I stupidly added that my middle name was Marvellous. Every day we lunched together, even though I was but an inglorious babysitter. That's how we met, not much of a tale. Of course, I contrived to sub at that school as often as possible, gently poisoning the history teachers to keep them away (not really). When I finally asked her out, she looked shocked, but said yes. For me, it was lust at first sight. The love came after.

What a nice chat Cecilia and I have. We the people of Shipworld have conversations; speaking to each other is how we build the day. It certainly helps that there's no TV or computers here. God help me, I watched enough of the idiot box as a teen to last a lifetime. Never did see that Gavin war film, though. It was his big break, he said. His co-star Lilo Pulver, the Swiss bombshell, insisted that they sleep together to kindle passion for their on-screen love scenes. For verisimilitude, she told him. Gavin repeated the word in the hotel bar on the Paso de la Reforma, *verisimilitude*, as if it was a forbidden practice. He met her demand, but wished he hadn't because after that his wife never quite measured up.

We slurp in silence. No muffin today. Casually, Cecilia asks me about the rumour that another generation ship took off from China. Is it true? What star is its destination? I cough, an old man's dry slag. I know nothing about that, I insist, too formally. She reminds me, Marcus Marvellous Marte, that I'm the Friend of Parsons. Now the blood races across my cheeks at her use of my fictitious middle name, the one Zayit used to nudge me down a notch. OK, I respond, Parsons mentioned that once. Parsons, who was frequently full of it. So maybe. But what difference does it make if there's a second ship?

She gives me a long, careful look, as I imagine Lilo Pulver offered John Gavin, as Zayit so often gifted me, and she says, 'Well, then it's not all up to us, is it?'

✦

Year 5, Day 132

Who are we, on Shipworld?

The Chronicler is charged with answering such questions. I do my best, through observation and rumination, but it's hard without understanding who we were before launch. Most people don't want to say; it's become frowned upon, almost forbidden, to discuss one's old life. Maybe it leads to heartbreak; maybe it gets in the way of embracing the new. But I wonder: who else has left a wife in the ground? Someone, surely. Perhaps that man walking past, the one holding the frog-decorated umbrella over his head. Why frogs? It's Fools' Day, of course, one of the few Earthworld holidays still celebrated. Even though April and all other months are kaput.

The Shipworld roster only lists people's names and ages. Medical records are classified, but I assume fertility and family disease history were crucial factors in achieving a Minimum Viable Population. Otherwise how, exactly, were we selected? An attempt at genetic diversity is visible – multiple skin colours, different heights, various physical traits. But were we rich? Poor? Middle class, salt of the Earthworld? Did anyone just row a boat to Iceland, hike across melting glaciers to Parsons' base and yell, 'I'm ready to ditch this popsicle stand!'?

The Founder told me that he eliminated applicants from three groups: leaders of organisations, science-fiction fanatics and politicians. Don't need a bunch of type-A narcissists screwing things up any more than they already have, he said. As for the sci-fi crowd, he felt they'd end up disappointed. Politicians, well, that's obvious. Now that I think of it, Parsons fit pretty well into two of those categories. Did the man who birthed HoloWerx Corp., who attended *Doctor Who* conventions in disguise, eliminate himself in the end?

Oh, there goes another. A striking young woman, several months' pregnant, in a black body suit. HD-40307g is scrawled in white across her boisterous belly. Not sure how to parse that; her child won't make it there, her child's child won't. Zayit always said I could be too literal, and besides Fool's Day is more about clever silliness than pranking or preaching. We are, I suppose, forever pregnant with the idea of HD-40307g.

I visited the grave yesterday.

Going to the holosphere (a Parsons invention) isn't quite the same as the hour's drive through traffic on Earthworld, the parking of the car inside Blue Meadows, and the weaving walk among gravestones of strangers who you pretend to know in death. Here it's this: enter room, *swipe,* gravestone appears. Once again, its granite shadow stretches across patchy grass and curled-up oak leaves, signs of a sunny afternoon in October. Each Pioneer has been allowed one static holo-memory, viewable for ten minutes twice a month for eleven years. Then it's erased, once and forever. Those parameters, to produce a 'phased withdrawal from Earthworld iconography', were the product of intense debate between sentimentals and practicals at the Shipworld Constitutional Convention.

Strange how the dogwood flowers etched around her name seem to get droopier with each visit. And the real flowers at the foot of the grave, begonias in a basket, stay fresh.

Zayit Marte. 1963–2043. Beloved Wife and Friend. With the nerve glove, I touched the stone. Engraved letters, numbers, flowers. Four petal-like bracts, *cornus florida.* The granite, machine-cut and polished, felt smooth, even slippery. Many of the older gravestones nearby were fashioned with chisels and hammers grasped by immigrants who'd fled famines and persecution, who'd journeyed across the Atlantic Ocean in 'coffin ships' and found work in New World stone quarries. Some of my ancestors took that fateful sail. They got out when the going was good and never went back.

Many Pioneers have chosen holo-images of a person. How could that be bearable, to use the nerve glove to touch a loved one so far away, so absolutely gone?

Yesterday, so garbed, I scraped my finger over a green lichen splotch on Zayit's gravestone. It felt stiff, corrugated. Lichen: a mutualistic joining of fungi and algae. Shipworld, to strain a metaphor, is a kind of lichen, a mutualistic joining of hardware and humans. No real lichen is allowed onboard, of course. Nothing but edible, nutritious things are grown here. The only flowers are ones that precede fruits and vegetables, like promises.

To mark my birthday, Cecilia gave me a floppy, lustrous yellow zucchini flower. I wore it on my wrist for a few hours and then ate it, petal by petal, an impossible luxury.

On Shipworld, my remains will be composted, converted and redirected. Amazing, back on the old planet, how we abused the great, open spaces to bury bodies, dump waste and build roads. To play golf, polo, cricket, football! Fields of tulips and Christmas trees, cattle feedlots stretching to the horizon! The decadence, the arrogance of unclosed resource loops, of one-use churches, schools, rifle ranges, bowling alleys, strips malls and casinos. It was always a bit stunning, but now, five years out, such practices seem beyond fathoming.

At Zayit's grave, a rogue, lukewarm tear rolled down my cheek. If I let it hit the deck, atmospheric recycling would automatically claim the water and salt, but that seemed the lazy way out. I pushed the tear from its path, guided it into my mouth, tasted it. Swallowed, absorbed, closed the loop myself. And recalled how Zayit had kept in touch with former students nearly until the end, offering friendship and counsel regarding personal and career fulfilment even as ecosystems and governments collapsed around them – she'd have planted a tree or two on the Last Day – and never letting on about the chaos within.

Then the holo-image flicked off. That was that.

Look, Janelle's on the loose, naked! A fine Fools' Day costume, indeed, though I'm not sure her mad dash has anything to do with the holiday. At age six, she's a bit old for such 'cute kid' antics. Cecilia will be along shortly, chasing her, forever chasing…and there she is. Sheepishly, we wave at each other. The poor thing. Parenting is a fool's errand. Life, too, especially in the beginning and the end. The middle part ain't no gravy train either.

Every one of us, to paraphrase Whitman, such curious trios with our selves and our souls and our bodies. 'Wandering on our way, through these shores amid the shadows, with the apparitions pressing. Pioneers! O pioneers!'

✦

Year 6, Day 76

Here I sit, just me, under the ficus tree. All around, a scattering of white petals. This odd tree has decided, absent all environmental signals, that it's spring.

I'm not really alone, of course, with passers-by crossing my vision and ficus branchlets dangling down, providing soft shade. Glossy leaves spray out, trying to find their place in this strange, revolving world. Despite my back on its bark, spine to spine, the ficus is surely lonesome, its roots seeking tree fellowship but finding only hard piping and bulkhead, engineered soil and stingy rhubarb (tasty, yes, but a lousy conversationalist). Its travelling pheromones encounter humans (yuck) and nearby corn and tomato. Dull cousins at best.

Amazing how it's survived, having grown from sapling at launch to a firm if spindly tree, almost seven metres high. Shipworldmates seem afraid to touch the ficus, for fear of disrupting its magic; it is, however, frequently used as a meeting place. Meet me by the ficus, I've heard folks say. Or, meet me by the Head. Perhaps there are two kinds of people in this Shipworld, those who meet by the ficus and those who – oh, enough of that. Here I am, parked beneath the tree, touching it, and soon enough, I hope, as the years roll out like an unleashed scroll, more people will dare to brush their hands against the cool surfaces of the leaves, and children will begin to climb it, up, up, up! Maybe Janelle; she and the Founder's tree are nearly the same age.

The Constitutional Convention banned trees onboard. Pros: production of fruits, nuts and oxygen. Cons: thirsty water requirements and unruly roots. In total, a low sustainability score. Parsons, however, insisted on one tree – no more, no less – and no surprise that he chose a ficus. In his graduate school apartment in New Haven, two things grew: greenish gunk in the fridge and a sad, underwatered ficus plant in the window. On visits, I snuck it glasses of water and pressed blue fertiliser sticks into its soil. He called his plant Dizzy after the first mayor of Tel Aviv, Meir Dizengoff, a chemical engineer who graduated to city building on sand dunes.

Parsons had gone to Israel on a tech trip, where he was impressed by the towering ficus trees lining Rothschild Boulevard in Tel Aviv. There he was told this dubious tale. In 1921 Winston Churchill, representative of the British Mandate in Palestine, visited the young city. Desiring to wow Winston, Dizengoff transplanted scores of tall ficuses into the loose soil bordering the boulevard. As Dizengoff and Churchill paraded along, however, children climbed the trees to get a better look and, whoops, the trees toppled over. With characteristic bite, Churchill remarked that 'all things without roots soon wither'. Dizengoff blushed, but it was the British who were gone within thirty years.

Roots in space? Did Parsons suppose that we'd grow spiritual roots to this one, precious tree, and in so doing bind to each other? Who knows, he was contradictory to the core. Driven to become the richest man on Earth, but barely interested in material things. A vegetarian and yoga devotee who owned dozens of biotech and life sciences companies that, godlike, manipulated genetic expression. A paranoid man, especially about government, who insisted on the implantation of forearm data/tracking panels into the arms of every Pioneer and, by law, their descendants. One of the creators of the Correction, who,

I suspect, didn't get the treatment himself, didn't want to play God inside his own body.

Which means, I guess, that Parsons could be dead back on Earthworld, a victim of heart disease, cancer, Parkinson's, Covid-45, you name it. Or, for that matter, a Category Six mega-storm or refugee attack on his enclave. I wince, imagining his head on a spike.

According to my data/tracking panel, it's 8:22 a.m. on the seventy-sixth day of Year 6. My blood pressure, pulse, temperature – all fine, as usual. My chemistries, too, are OK straight down the line, phosphate, creatinine, cholesterol, the last torrid tricklings of testosterone. I wonder if today's nagging anxiety – that I'm leaning too hard against the trunk, that Zayit would disapprove of my life here, that Janelle is broken, that our Shipworld experiment will shatter into jagged molecules when the next generation takes over – is somehow apparent to the panel. Measured, monitored, assessed. My wandering thoughts, even, are they categorised and delivered to some secret coterie of busybodies and protectors?

Who knows, but let's say that the ficus is a broom for whisking away such misgivings. In that case, I should keep sitting here, an interstellar Buddha under my solitary friend. Its glossy, green leaves droop down, waggle in the morning non-breeze.

Year 7, Day 21

I keep thinking of the biblical story of Jonah. Running from his responsibilities. Harassed by a storm, hurled overboard, gobbled by the big fish. Down in the dark for three long days.

My father, an unreformed alcoholic, made me gut bass and bluefish as a child. It was an ugly job, blood streaming across the classifieds of *The Register-Guard* spread out over our red brick patio. The sole pleasure was finding things inside the silky fish bellies – bottle tops, plastic jewellery, whatnots and such. Most of all, I hoped to discover a live minnow, put it in a bucket of water and return it to the ocean. This was evidence of a soft heart, scoffed the old man. But I considered my minnow rescue plan a form of revenge for being pressed into gutting, and revenge can be a hard thing to accomplish. Jonah wanted revenge, too, against the Ninevites, his blood enemies. He'd fled his assignment to engage them in negotiations because he feared, in the end, that God might go easy on those filthy sinners, which is exactly what happened. Jonah ran from the possibility of mercy.

Three days, three months, three years, thirty years, three hundred and sixty years to HD-40307g, it's just a matter of scale. Our voyage is but another version of Jonah's in the beast-belly. Someday, finally, Shipworld will breach from the depths into a new world. But this time we won't turn around in obedience to a powerful being/God/caretaker thriving on a diet of adulation and prayer. No, we're outwitting fate, fleeing the scene of the Earthworld crime.

And yet, maybe we should have stayed, endured, made the Ninevites repent. If necessary, died trying. Is that, in the end, what Parsons did?

Another day in the community garden. Another cup of fake coffee. My pencil. The yawning journal pages. I look up: normal. But now and then, even after seven years, I expect the buildings and people far overhead, the topsy-turvy props stuck to the ceiling, to crash down upon me. Or vice-versa, for myself and the coffee, pencil, journal, plants, soil and Olmec Head to unmoor and topple onto them. The Head's not bothered, though; he's got the stamina of a comatose man. Heck, he could have a bomb tucked inside, for all I know, with a ninety-seven-year timer. Anything's possible, that's history's prime lesson. Somewhere out there, among billions of worlds, a child is finding one live minnow in the belly of one gutted fish.

Numbers, numbers. At the Constitutional Convention, the fifty/five hundred rule became a controlling premise. To wit, a population requires fifty people to avoid inbreeding and five hundred to reduce genetic drift. Delegates settled on 600 Jonahs for this whale, just to be sure (plus a freezer full of frozen embryos). No one cared about Dunbar's Rule of one hundred and forty-eight, the theory that groups go haywire beyond that size. Chaos, I guess, is preferable to genetic defects. And Dunbar had never been to deep space in a revolving ellipsoid. Or lived without money. Or birds.

Zayit loved birds. Often, though, she grew frustrated at the behaviour of the sparrows at the feeder in our backyard. Among themselves they'd cooperate, taking turns eating, but when a squirrel butted in, twirling its gel-body about the feeder, the sparrows found nearby perches and waited out the incursion, rather than ganging up on the big lug. They don't realise their own power, she'd say. C'mon, get him! Give him the bum's rush!

All the birds onboard died by Year 2 and no one knows why. The lack of Earthworld's magnetic field is one theory. Extremely low-level cosmic radiation is another. The chickens died, too. I miss eggs. Zayit liked hers fried, sunny side up, cooked by her husband with pepper cracked on top. She'd take a sharpened toast point and break the yolk with it. Dip, nibble, dip, nibble. There's a plan, I've heard, to build and release robo-birds, and what could go wrong with that?

I'm worried about Cecilia. She usually appears at the garden without Janelle these days, as the girl has become too difficult for company. Recently I asked her if she's considered changing Janelle's diet – a food allergen may be affecting her mood – and she looked at me patiently, tiredly, because of course she's doing everything possible and of course, as a non-parent, I have no experience to offer and, of course, she's heard every lame, desperate and judgemental suggestion one could imagine, dredged up from thousands of years of humans raising children in such wonderful fashion on Earthworld. I backtracked, said I'm sorry. 'Ah, if only you were sixty years younger,' she replied, and gave me a catty wink, yikes!

Nonetheless, I'm determined to be useful. The last time Janelle appeared, I got down on my hands and knees and talked to her as she dug-dug-dug a hole with a bent spoon. She dug towards Shipworld's skin that's made of a NASA-developed, Parsons-purloined, spoon-resistant oxide dispersion alloy born in an industrial 3-D printer in Iceland. A hard shell, indeed, but it's still disturbing to consider that the void exists just a few metres from our feet.

'When I was your age, I thought I could dig to China,' I said.

'You were my age?' she asked. No one else onboard is her age, in fact, so that was a pretty good question.

'Yes, everyone was your age, once. Your mother was six not that long ago.'

Janelle glanced at her mother – staring off to the non-horizon – and went back to digging. She held the spoon with both hands, stabbing the ground like a jackhammer.

'No one digs to China because there's a metal ball in the middle of the planet and it's super-hot,' she said without looking up.

'I know, but I liked the idea of suddenly appearing somewhere else,' I said. 'Somewhere completely different. Away from my brothers and sisters, I guess.' They are, allow me to note, all dead and buried on Earthworld.

'I can't have a sister,' she said. Dig-dig-dig.

'There are a lot of rules,' I replied. 'It's because we're all on this adventure together,' and right away I regretted the PR-speak, wished I'd told her why siblings aren't so great, that she needed to start helping her mommy like I'd helped my mommy, and that such acts are passed down over time and could rebound to her benefit one day. That she was making an awesome hole, anything at all except the adventure blather. Janelle stopped digging, made a strangled yell and threw the spoon at me. She missed, then immediately ascended from the ground, yanked up by Cecilia, and they wrangled and were gone. I listened to Janelle's screams going away, the noise doppler-shifting to a higher and higher register.

Mostly, these days, Cecilia wants to discuss the supermassive Omega Centauri Globular Cluster, visible on a clear day (kidding) off the port side, just seventeen thousand light-years away. Ten million stars, as densely packed as cells in a blood drop. She's convinced that OCGC is a dwarf galaxy remnant consumed by the Milky Way. Otherwise, how else to explain the vastly different stellar ages and metallicities? Alas, few of her colleagues agree; some are rudely sceptical. If they'd just upgrade some gizmo or other on the X-ray telescope, that would allow her to build her case. Did I mention that she was a waitress eight years ago? A single mom, college dropout. The father, a guy she barely knew on Earthworld, a person of brilliant promise who treated her heart roughly.

His loss, I say. Against her will, I think, she springs a laugh leak. She moves a bit closer, pats my hand, and resumes rhapsodising about OCGC, ever alluring and remote.

So many mysteries, big and small. Is another, hungry galaxy consuming the Milky Way? Is a rogue madness metastasising inside Janelle as she digs her hole in space? Will Cecilia survive this child? And when you get down to it, cut away all the frantic fuss and bother, was Jonah actually counting on the Lord to stop him from running away?

✦

Year 8, Day 222

I'm on the bridge. Denis, a young bridge officer, doesn't know why it's called that. Says no one's ever asked before (a compliment, if true). The rectangular space we stand within, uninspiring except for the front-facing window, is low-lit and empty now, used occasionally as a sim-lab for the training of new bridge officers who, in time, will train new bridge officers who, in time, will train new bridge officers who, you get the idea, will train Seventh-Gen bridge officers who at the dawn of the journey's final decade, in Year 350, will turn Shipworld on its horizontal axis, relight the fusion drive and direct the construction of landing vehicles while they make a gradual, braking approach towards HD-40307g.

That is, assuming all goes well.

I'm fond of bridges. The footbridge in the Boston Public Garden that crosses the lagoon guarded by towering willows, that's a favourite. Zayit and I walked there, hand in hand, on an early date. On one end, a flock of tethered swan boats waiting for tourists. On the other, a granite statue of George Washington on horseback, his mouth pursed over sore teeth. At the Constitutional Convention that founded the United States, he said almost nothing; the great man's silent presence, delegates noted, compelled them to temper their furies. I, too, said almost nothing at our founding convention – so not to screw things up with my erratic views.

Actually, I made two remarks. One, I criticised the selection of musical and written artefacts allowed onboard: a hundred songs, curated by Parsons, and a few hundred books from his personal library. Let's bring nothing but the tunes and stories in our heads, I suggested, not adding that I was wary of my former student's quirky tastes becoming the cultural bedrock of the future. Two, I said let's make it eleven members on the Council, not unlucky thirteen. The first remark was ignored, the second roundly accepted.

Another favourite is the Longfellow Bridge over the Charles River, with its massive stone turrets shaped like salt-and-pepper shakers. Prows of Viking ships are carved upon those turrets, based on claims that Leif Eriksson sailed from Iceland to Beantown a millennium ago. All because a Viking-era scabbard was dug up on an island in Boston Harbour. Later, it was dated to the Revolutionary War period. So, probably no Vikings.

Regardless, it's a magnificent span. On one end, the dense Kendall Square life-sciences cluster where Parsons' companies churned out the Correction. (If memory serves, it clears up the long-term mess made by short-term DNA repair.) On the other end of the bridge, the stone and glass jumble of Massachusetts General Hospital where Zayit underwent chemo and radiation treatments, where she bought a snazzy brown wig in the oncology boutique of the hospital gift shop. This was before the Correction entered clinical trials. Zayit refused to take an experimental version of the treatment, despite Parsons' assurances. Finally, he begged her on bended knee, and she got down on her knees herself and hugged him and smoothed his distraught brow and said everything would be OK. In the end, his guidance counsellor assured him, everything would be all right. And Parsons, who believed that he could bend unfathomable fate to his will, nodded in acquiescence, for her.

I walked along the Longfellow Bridge, with its enveloping views of the drowning city, dozens of times during my wife's illness. Then never again.

Shipworld's flight path is a kind of bridge, over which generations pass. Denis approves of the metaphor because our flight path is actually fixed like a bridge. Travelling from one solar system to another is a point-and-shoot affair, no steering involved. The bridge's span can be adjusted in case of emergency, but the chance of needing to veer around a comet, asteroid or anomaly is negligible. Once a day, someone checks the nav-computer from a terminal in Engineering to make sure we're on course. A report is then sent to the bridge: steady on. The engineers also keep tabs on the deflector, which is a projected energy field around the hull that repels micrometeoroids.

The job of bridge officer, Denis insists, is quite boring. Bridge officers stand ready. They wait. And wait. Fun fact from Denis: Shipworld can exceed .12 light speed – the target speed to which we're accelerating – but if we go faster the deflector is useless and everyone dies from cosmic ray bombardment. So, to review, no steering from the start. And after Year 10, no speeding up. Boring.

Next year, he admits, they'll have a bit of excitement when the ship achieves .12 light speed and a bridge officer, maybe Denis, gets to flip the switch that turns off the fusion rockets. So ends the Era of Acceleration, and so begins three hundred and forty years of frictionless flying, give or take a dust mote. Few people will notice the change, shrugs Denis, but it'll be a big day on the bridge. He flexes his index finger.

Denis has a dry sense of humour. A handsome face, too. I decide to play matchmaker, telling him about fair Cecilia of the Oorts and her obsession with supermassive globular clusters. It would do her good, I suggest, if someone would deflect her from such celestial concerns (and from spending so much time, I don't add, with a certain old duffer). It turns out that Denis has met Cecilia – through the required Mingles, everyone meets everyone – and agrees that she's quite remarkable. He's also observed the child, and says no more. I let it go at that.

Shipworldmates, with reproduction forbidden until their fifties, have avoided pairing off at a young age. In Iceland we predicted the reverse, that the small pool of candidates would encourage early marriage. Maybe that will happen in the Second-Gen. And maybe Denis and Cecilia, under the right circumstance, will find each other. Folks are unpredictable. I wonder, would I have pursued Zayit in outer space? If she had a troubled child? Would she, so burdened, have looked twice at foolish me? Of course! Our love was in the stars.

Still is, in a way.

So, I'm on the bridge. It's an ordinary place, like one of those office-pens on Earthworld where rows of techies worked at computers, inventing this future. The chairs here look oddly uncomfortable, perhaps to keep their occupants awake in case something ever happens. If I were a bridger, I'd become entranced by the main window. For one thing, it's set into a wall, not the floor. Also, because it's pointed directly towards HD-40307g, the stars within the window don't spin. They're fixed. They beckon. And, at the same time, taunt.

This old man stares at the stars. Denis gently informs me that my time is up on the bridge. Come back another day. But I don't think I will.

✦

Year 10, Day 12

It occurs to me that I have romanticised Zayit in these scribbles. Admittedly, I was an uxorious husband, so perhaps I do my beloved a disservice by failing to portray her as a living, breathing, burping, farting and altogether faulty human being. It wasn't intentional; her difficult qualities have faded with time and distance from Earthworld, while her virtues, like mature stars, persist in shining. Nonetheless, I now assert that she picked her teeth after meals in the most annoying way, with an old toothpick or her thumbnail. Moreover, she poured too much milk on her Oatie Os – have some cereal with your milk, I'd snark – and then slurped it up, a ravening beast. Sixty seconds, done.

Furthermore, Zayit tended to overly plan our endeavours until the juice of adventure had been squeezed away – an antidote, she claimed, to my slapdashness. And she had a temper, which emerged, now and then, like a telescoping thorn. Believe me, a sharp word from a quiet person is worse than a jeremiad from a gabber. She had a way of transposing scenes from one old movie to another, just to bait me, I suspect, and she could be harshly judgemental about people who talked too loud on the subway or failed to study hard for exams. She snorfle-snored and wasn't exactly ageing gracefully. At a dinner party, long ago, she stayed silent while a jerk was rude to me, an act of omission that I struggled to forgive. 'But isn't it a total *waste* teaching history to teenagers?' the flush-faced fellow stated, and he swirled his wine, the Beaujolais spinning around the curved interior of the stem glass, rising to the rim but not launching, and I reminded him that it was ignorant teens who'd forced governments to act on climate change, too late, yes, but it was teens who'd risen to the grave historical moment. Drink that, you clod. Now maybe you're thinking that Zayit simply let me defend myself, gave me space, and there's something to that, but still.

She wasn't much of an environmentalist, either, merely tolerating my efforts to lower our carbon footprints, until, she joked, our very existence would pull carbon from the air. Secretly she missed her little red convertible with the accordion hood and the internal destruction engine, *vroom*, *vroom*, *vroom*. And now I'm going to stop; I don't like sifting these dregs, this bitter brand of mourning. The truth is that I grew, perversely, marvellously, to love her faults, which lived so convivially beside my far greater failings. Zayit offered herself to me without deception or reservation, a beautiful gift, indeed. And yet I prefer to remember her sunrise smile, the warmth of her hand on the back of my neck, her epically pragmatic sensibility. Let me moon about her, please.

And if you're wondering, dear (future) reader, whether she would have embarked on a trip like this, even considered it, the answer is no, of course not.

✦

Year 10, Day 135

Here's another Thaddeus Parsons' story. A Founder's story. A stoner's story, too, because he smoked bales of weed through his twenties, and even though he stopped when he became a famous billionaire, sometimes it seemed like he could brain-activate a hit just by breathing in deeply and remembering. So, we're in Iceland at the Constitutional Convention, yakking away about the world's ongoing degeneration, the ever-reaching tentacles of rot, here, there, jumping chasms everywhere. How, we ask, to establish enduring and just social structures on Shipworld? Then breakout sessions are done for the day – but the long, arctic day isn't done with us. After the usual sumptuous dinner (millions are starving, we dutifully note), some Pioneers slide into outdoor hot tubs, while others loiter in the minty mist of a tall, slim waterfall, its source obscured in cloud. Parsons and I go for a ride.

First, we drive his e-truck along the ring road, past grasslands devoid of sheep (a half million slaughtered in the last pandemic) but still dotted with Icelandic horses, shaggy-maned and slump-shouldered, posing for tourists who no longer arrive. A few lie flat on their sides, a deeply disconcerting sight, and then we traverse a volcanic landscape shrouded in grey, sickly moss, endlessly it rolls along, and I gape at a vast, unfinished housing development between the sea and the retreating glacier. An abandoned wreck, vandalised, civilisational driftwood inside bulldozed zones... Look, there's a lemon-yellow Komatsu excavator, its shovel arm raised to heaven...the sorry scheme of some billionaire bent on relocating climate refugees, the wealthier ones at least. But it's no crazier, I suppose, than shipping bauxite from the open-cut mines of Australia to the fjord ports of Iceland in fossil-fuel belching ships, forging it into aluminium in geothermally powered smelters (we're so green!) and then shipping that product in more belching tankers and trucks to factories where it's made into bicycle frames and spaceship parts and foil for covering potato salads planetwide.

Soon enough, we arrive at Thingvellir National Park, where we ride e-bikes through scrubland and ponds slashed orange with iron-oxidising bacteria. The clouds over the mountains are spread like cowls, like dark snowcaps, and one is menacing and spider-shaped, its pincers sucking the life from obscured peaks. We observe, too, patches of stunted, brown trees, evergreens and birch mostly, failed attempts by do-gooder groups to reforest the island, to make up for a thousand years of cutting down the great Icelandic forest for fire, shelter and stout ships to go a-pillaging with. It's all quite beautiful, really, and sad. As Parsons steers us past the park's deserted gates, I hear the jackhammer call of the common snipe, *durka-durka-durka-durka*, whining, warning, a long-billed scold, but the songs of the whimbrel (extinct) and the redwing (extinct) are gone.

We ride down the centre of the great rift separating Europe from North America. It looks like a ploughed cleft, bordered by cliff walls, and it's the only place in the world where you can stand between the grinding continental plates, the work of geologic time. Parsons and I stop at the edge of a precipice; together, we look over the side. It's darkness, down and down. He drops a stone. We listen as it falls; nothing. Cause, no effect. Then from around his neck he pulls a string that holds a two-inch figurine of a headless, pregnant woman.

'What in the world?' I ask.

He explains that it's carved from a hippo tooth. That he got it in Saudi Arabia, that it's six thousand years old and proves that the deserts of the Middle East were jungles once, actually older hippo teeth prove that, but this one is fascinating, just look at the pregnant belly and the hole there, the *omphalos*, the centre of all creation, and he's raving Parsons-style, regurgitating info-shards about the first Icelandic parliament that convened in this very spot in the Earthworld Year 930, unifying the folk, and luminous Numenor in Tolkien's Second Age, the made-up island that sank for man's folly as the Elvish lands ascended into the heavens, enough with these *Homo sapiens*, and it occurs to me that I'll never really know him. Not that he's so complicated. Just another man. A bit crazed, maimed even, by money and its erasure of limits. Three divorces, seven children (none Pioneers), no wallet. He consumes stories about his own eccentric megalomania, and many times he's asked me if they're true. I always see the boy in my class, the cocksure boy, and I say no, no, you're normal enough.

'*Blood and Rust*,' says our plutocrat founder, here in the great cleft, 'you gave me a B on that paper. It had to be better than everyone else's.'

'It was,' I reply. 'I was motivating you. Also, the fake scar on your palm was pretty lame. And you could have speculated how America would have been different without barbed wire. Set up a counterfactual.'

He shrugs. Then breathes in deep, takes a hit of Earth air. From his backpack he produces a bottle of Brennivin, an Icelandic grain alcohol flavoured with caraway seeds. Parsons swigs, and I swig, and oh so casually he drops the hippo tooth figurine down the deep, dark hole in the fissure between continents. No sound, again. We swig a chaser, then go back to base camp. End of story. Not much of a story, I guess. Maybe a core sample. Maybe just a cause, and we wait, and wait, for the effect.

✦

Year 10, Day 212

Yesterday, I watched the harvesting of the rutabagas (my mother mashed them with chicken broth, evaporated milk and scads of cracked pepper). Today, Cecilia drags me to a group therapy session for Pioneers aged thirty to forty.

'Why me?' I protest as we head down a neighbourhood street towards the Mess Hall.

'You're my witness,' she replies, as if that explains it.

'Witness to what?'

'To my spilling my guts about my trauma and my guilt and my goddamn solastalgia.'

'Solarstalgia?'

'Not solar, *solas* – when home doesn't bring solace because everything's falling apart around you – it's like you're homesick while at home.'

'But we left all that behind,' I say.

'Yeah, but you remember everything changing back on Earthworld so you can't let yourself be happy. Anyway,' she says, 'it's a load of crap and none of it applies to me because I never found comfort at home.' Here she accelerates and a barbed-wire twinge snakes up my left hamstring. Injury report: Marcus Mushy Marte, fifteen–thirty days, pulled hammy from keeping up with a girl seventy years younger.

'Why not?'

'What?'

'Why didn't you find comfort at home?'

'ADHD, GAD, chronic eco-grief, my mother was a piece of work – what's the difference, at least I'm not pining for it.' Now she stops beside a network of algae pipes, and my hamstring convulses again as I put on the brakes. Cecilia reaches out, steadies me.

'Look, I gotta warn you,' she says. 'Some people in there hate old folks.'

'Why?'

'Are you kidding me? Runaway carbon emissions, hyper-consumerism, mega-storms, extinctions, the migration camps – they blame you for everything, really.'

'I put up solar panels. I drove an electric car, I composted.'

She bounces her surprisingly long index finger on her lips. The nail is chewed. I imagine her finger in her mouth, enough, stop, and I nod, yeah, of course it was our fault, we had the last, best chance to act before politics hardened and the Great Permafrost Melt and other negative feedback loops were triggered, but we fumbled it. Cecilia and I resume walking, slower now. It's morning, post-breakfast, and children are spilling from their homes in identical blue school uniforms, with red belts to jazz things up. They roar past; we don't exist.

'Everyone's supposed to bring a friend once. I don't have a lot of friends,' Cecilia says. 'You can turn back, if you like.'

I keep going.

They sit in a circle in the far corner of the Mess Hall, a dozen or so young shipworldmates. Cecilia introduces me and I receive stares, in addition to a smirk or two. Then a young woman begins talking about her sister in Connecticut, her twin sister, and the terrible fight they had about her blasting off to HD-40307g. The twin called her a coward, an elitist, a suicidal maniac, a crazy idealist, all of it, and besides, things aren't that bad, just stop reading the news, stop feeding your cognitive biases, life was way worse during the Black Plague, and who really cares if the high-and-mighty USA breaks up, big freaking deal, and who cares about *nature*, either, let's stop fooling ourselves, we live inside buildings ninety-nine per cent of the time. C'mon, we can move inland, we can adapt. Don't go, Crissy, it's not fair – *please!*

Tears pour down her face. Crissy doesn't bother to wipe them. A man with a bushy black beard, maybe the group leader, speaks: 'OK, that's a lot. Obviously, you miss her—'

'Miss her? I can't get her out of my head!'

'Well, you've spit her out now,' says Cecilia. 'Don't let her back in.'

A couple of people smile, one chuckles. The group leader turns his beard to Cecilia and in a voice lightly laced with annoyance asks her what's rolling around her head. 'And Marcus,' he adds, 'as witness feel free to comment on what she says.'

Cecilia glances at me, straightens her shoulders. 'OK, I've been thinking about my father, about how disappointed he was in me – leaving college, having a kid by myself. The worst thing for him, by far, was my working as a waitress. *Serving* people.'

'But you're a scientist now,' says a spindly young woman.

'Science grunt – just like him, and his father,' she snaps back. 'You know, the only reason I could do it is because they're not here. They're not watching me. They have absolutely no idea if Cecilia Oort is measuring up – they might as well be dead. And if you think they mistreated me, they didn't. They were good people, when they bothered.'

She laughs, derisively. 'God, my father would *kill* to be out here. To have the crystal-clear view of the cosmos that I have.' She stares at Crissy. 'I'm happier now,' she states, 'than I've ever been before. Even with my screwed-up kid.'

Crissy looks away, down at the floor.

'Cecilia,' I say.

She doesn't respond. I hear a grating noise from an air vent.

'You're a hell of a scientist. I can tell, just from the way you talk about your work.'

'I don't need that, Marcus. I don't want that.'

'I know. But you might someday, and I thought I'd say it now. And you're a hell of a mother, too, don't let anyone tell you otherwise.'

She stares across the Mess Hall, rubbing her hands together. 'Someone else's turn,' she says, quietly, and the bearded fellow redirects the discussion to the spindly woman who's been fantasising with angry glee about Earthworld eco-criminals – mostly old white men – strung up on abandoned oil derricks outside her hometown in Oklahoma. But IRL, in real life, as the kids used to say, it happened in California and the people lynched on the derricks were eco-activists of every demographic category, hung by mobs of fossil-fuel deadenders and zealots. Then a shy young man wonders if it's wrong, somehow, to forget about his past life, and someone else adds that forgetting can be a kind of mercy, for the person burdened by memories and the forgotten ones, too. Later, on the walk back from the therapy session, Cecilia and I take a roundabout route that cuts under the Tube, the nail that holds everything together, that looms like a transparent vein injected with light.

'Do you like mashed rutabagas?' I ask. She shakes her head, not at the question, I suspect, but at the very idea of rutabagas, weird mystery vegetables flying through space at .12 speed of light. I tell her about my mom's recipe, about the broth squeezed from a hapless chicken and the pepper cracked in this long-handled, faux-antique grinder that she bought at a yard sale and the evaporated milk – milk nectar, really – that came in a tin can illustrated with little flowers. Life was simpler then, even though it wasn't. It's probably just nostalgia, garden variety, and she lets me set the turtle pace and offers me her elbow.

We stroll down the way together.

✦

Year 11, Day 185

I have need, in my hundred-and-first year, of new undershorts. Mine are in tatters. This state of affairs produces a measure of personal shyness that clashes, anachronistically, with matter-of-fact Shipworld, and so I delay presenting my torn skivvies for recycling and replacement, and round and round we go. Fair Reader, if you exist, you may wonder where everything comes from and goes to on this spinning tub. Come along for an educational trip to the materials fabrication and sustainability facility, aka the Loop.

Cecilia joins the expedition. Beforehand, we meet in my room because she wants to discuss something in private, a first for our May–December friendship. Sitting on the edge of my bed, legs crossed like some mid-twentieth century co-ed in the boys' dorm, she states that she's decided to have another child when her times comes up in twenty-five years. I'm surprised, given Janelle, but suppress the reaction. The problem, she adds, is there's no one onboard that she'd want to be the father other than me.

Silence abounds, crests like a great wave. And suddenly I'm immersed in Zayit's anguish after her second miscarriage. In our decision not to keep trying. In the regret – the hardest pain to endure – that I've harboured. As these suppressed memories assail me, bleed me, for they've grown sharper and jagged in exile, I notice that Cecilia is wiping tears from her cheeks. Cecilia, the stone woman, crying.

There's a problem, I say. I'll be dead. But I'm honoured, thank you very much. Then Cecilia speaks two words: frozen sperm. You had the Correction, she says, your swimmers should be fine. To this I have no ready response, as a wave of embarrassment rears up. She smiles, pops off the bed and scoots into the bathroom. I hear a flush, water running, splashing. Ah, the long-forgotten sounds of a woman behind the bathroom door. The door opens and she waves me over, she beckons, and I go, of course. Cecilia points at the Dürer over the toilet.

'You want to explain this, Marcus?'

After a brief description of its provenance and historical importance, details of which I'm not entirely sure, I pull the damn thing off the wall and give it to her. She laughs, accepting without hesitation, and for that I feel indebted. Then there's a bit of a Marx Brothers routine as we twist and stumble out of the bathroom at the same time, and she doesn't seem to notice when she scrapes the painting's frame on the doorjamb, leaving marks on both objects.

Just think about it, she asks, OK? I nod.

A half-hour later, we meet at the Loop. It's a warehouse between farms, smelling of burnt soil, or metal. Our guide is Wyatt, a shift supervisor who wears corduroy overalls and a green-checked flannel shirt straight from Vermont. I ask her: Why is the Loop necessary? Good question, she says, adopting her school field-trip tone. The Loop's necessary because there are no frontiers to explore inside Shipworld, no foreign lands sending us barrels of herring and doorknobs, no oceans and mountains and prairies to harvest. Nothing enters from outside except trace cosmic rays, impertinent neutrinos and samples of deep space gathered for study. Nothing leaves our boundaries except for streams of helium expelled from the fusion reactor, which powers internal systems and the fusion engines when they're fired during monthly maintenance tests.

Here I tease: What about the photons leaking from the beacon on our prow? You're right, she replies, seriously. We should turn that off.

Shipworld, continues Wyatt, aspires to be a totally closed system. Unlike Earthworld, which emits great gasps of heat and accepts tons of cometary matter daily. Here there's no dumped trash, no pollution, nothing rolled behind the floorboards. No waste at all. Every scrap and leftover, every last molecule, is recaptured as a matter of group survival. On Earthworld, she reminds us, we treated our planetary home as an inexhaustible fountain of resources. Survival, we believed, came through expansion, exploitation and innovation. On Shipworld, survival is achieved through extreme preservation. Everything is used, reused, repaired, recycled and, ultimately, transformed into something else. Energy is not lost, well, barely, nor can it be converted into matter (a silly sci-fi notion), and total mass is maintained at a level that she's not at liberty to disclose. When people die, and to date there have been only a few expirations, their bodies are not stored in boxes or expelled into space but respectfully reintroduced to the Loop.

She pauses, pulling on the straps of her overalls. Teenagers probably ask a flurry of questions at this point, but Cecilia and I remain quiet.

Wyatt smiles, a brief flash. Then she walks us to the Melting Pot, a bulbous, revolving contraption that ingests all manner of detritus: dust, debris, skin flakes and microscopic critters vacuumed from every surface; uneaten food and agricultural waste; pee, poop, sperm, eggs; torn underwear and broken eyeglass hinges; time-decayed machinery, the very guts of our ever-going; and a vast array of other stuff in liquid, solid and plasmatic forms. Inside the Melting Pot, these materials are subjected to an extremely vigorous churn followed by a sophisticated electromagnetic assault. Presto, all that is living or not is broken down to the atomic level – the ultimate levelling – and rejiggered into sundry sludges that are channelled to the industrial 3-D printer for conversion into new things. Such as eyeglass hinges, underwear, ductwork, lubricants, cutlery and toy blocks.

What takes history aeons to achieve, she says, my blender does in minutes.

Now we watch a batch of junk go in. The Melting Pot purrs, turns. The metal-soil smell intensifies. Minutes later, a grey goop gathers in extrusion tube #3. Cecilia claps in applause, and I join her. Bravo! Wyatt's face remains blank. She's more, I think, than a devoted technician; she's a high priest, an overalls-and-flannel wizard of transubstantiation, keeping us alive and civilised through the long, long night. It seems a miracle. When I perish, I'll become part of something that sustains the next six generations. Part of a bulkhead, corn plant or dab of engine grease. I will not dissipate; I will not end; I will keep on flying to that rock orbiting a far-flung star. In the meantime, I will try to love my absent ones, Zayit and Parsons, as well as this perplexing young woman and her lost daughter.

We stare at the primordial slop, in limbo before becoming. Wyatt walks away to her next task. I turn to Cecilia. She reaches for my hand and cradles it.

✦

Year 12, Day 1

Today is Launch Day, twelve years and counting.

Children rumble inside the Tube, head over heels, laughing. Climbers ascend ropes through the steps of gravity and then float, like human islands, on Shipworld's internal sea-sky. The Launch Day choir, arranged beneath the flourishing ficus, sings several of Parsons' 100 Approved Songs, including Handel's 'Messiah' and the 1960s classic 'I'd Like to Teach the World to Sing (In Perfect Harmony)'. Yes, the acoustics are awful, but they're much worse outside. Someone's even put a Hawaiian lei around the Olmec Head.

Zayit would have liked this. She had a knack for watching things, for granting any event, quotidian or spectacular, its due. I remember her beside a tennis court watching Parsons and me play doubles. Legs crossed, head high, she sat on a rock ledge. She only looked at us, not our opponents. Now and then, she sipped her ice tea with lemon. That's the way she liked it. She always made sure to have things the way she liked them. That day we happened to be playing at one of Parsons' clubs, a swanky, 3.5 million-bucks-membership-fee club, which happened to be frequented by a few of Earthworld's greatest polluters. Above her hung a turquoise sky, scratched with cirrus clouds. Her earrings were silver doves.

Oh my, we boys tried hard not to disappoint her. Parsons, always going for dramatic, win-or-lose shots. I erred on the side of making safe, if clever returns. We made a pretty good team, I guess, the billionaire and the teacher. And to his credit, he never acted like a big shot around me. Not even when he bought the Icelandic aluminium smelter, his future rocket base, between games of gin.

Sometimes we surprised each other. For instance, he couldn't understand why cautious Marcus volunteered for Shipworld. And I still don't know why he didn't step aboard. Maybe, however, there's one answer to those mysteries, one cause for two effects. Simply put, we fulfilled our natures. Parsons liked to be on one side of things or the other. Winning or losing, forcing the issue, he craved results. HD-40307g was always too deferred for him, unless he could find a way to live to three hundred and sixty. But I'm comfortable in between, keeping the point going. I'm fine on the bridge, plodding to the destination I won't reach.

Now, on Pictor Boulevard, I stop to watch a clot of little children; they appear laser-focused on a spot between them. I move closer, lean forward. A boy's hands move furiously, manipulating something.

‘What are you doing?’ I ask.

A girl looks up, eyes bright. ‘Five stones,’ she says.

I move even closer. The boy bounces a little red ball. It flies upward, fighting gravity, as the same hand scoops a couple of plastic chips, places them on the back of his other hand, and then catches the ball just before it returns to ground.

‘Stars in the sky!’ he proclaims.

And I remember: jacks. That’s what we called it. My older sister and I played jacks on the red brick of the front stoop, before she grew up and moved away. We’d be waiting for Gramma to scoop us up for an ice-cream run, and she’d pull the pieces from her pockets and declare, ‘Let’s play!’ I was always good for a game. She kept a white ball, I think, and shiny, metal pieces that looked like flower stamens. Now and then she let me win.

‘Do you want to play?’ the girl asks.

Their faces turn to me. Such beautiful faces. One scoots aside to make a place.

‘No, no, thank you,’ I say. ‘It’s for you.’

The girl shrugs; they return to their kid world.

On this, my last Launch Day, I can’t stop thinking about the future. Oh, Pioneers and young shipborn, crowded beneath a sunburst of streamers flying from the Tube, nibbling algae treats and playing the noble game of jacks – how far will you make it across the galaxy before you’re tested? What will you do when the sacred Loop is broken, the mission doubted, the bridge twisted? When your children rebel?

When, as humans do, you turn on each other?

I don’t mean to be pessimistic – good luck! You’re gonna need it. And I don’t mean to be coy, either. This will be my last Launch Day because in fulfilling Cecilia’s request I have fulfilled my purpose on Shipworld. My purpose in life, perhaps. The timing is pretty good. Just a few days ago, the holo-image of Zayit’s grave, as per constitutional regulations, was erased forever. So today I took the green pill that Parsons gave me, the one that corrects the Correction, he claimed, and releases old age to finally and mercifully crash down.

But there's always time for a little grousing, right? Just look at those Council members sitting together in an elevated row by the stage. Elitist nonsense, better left on Earthworld! They should wander among us shlubs. From such conditions, a strongman/woman could arise. In fact, some delegates at the Constitutional Convention argued that no form of government should be established aboard, that it would prove unnecessary, even counterproductive, in a society founded on cooperative survival. In the end, the sentiment prevailed that a leadership group, even a weak one, provides psychological structure for the populace. I was torn and – no, enough, that's enough. Just let it go, stop worrying for once. The choir, in agreement, launches into a soothing rendition of 'A Horse with No Name'.

As a boy, I bought that song on a 45-record ('Sandman' was on the B-side) and my mother objected because horse, she'd been informed, was slang for heroin. True enough, but to me the song was just a ditty about a desert journey, about escaping the mess of civilisation and the pain of dealing with people. Outer space is the biggest desert, I suppose, spare and unforgiving but infused with invisible energies – and then, like a classic heroine in the nick of time, *tap-tap* on the shoulder, Cecilia rescues me from my purple musings. She can tolerate seven of the approved hundred songs, she says, and this ain't one of them.

By the by, Cecilia says thank you for, well, you know. Before I can stammer a response, she begins to dance. She swirls her hips and rolls her shoulders and glides about me, as if in orbit. I don't dance anymore, but I can be a decent maypole. I, Marcus Marvellous Marte, can still be a few things.

Back in my room now. Tired. A long, loud day, but fun. I'm hungry from eating too much, funny how that works. As I pee,

I examine the rough map of Earthworld that I've been drawing from memory over the toilet, where the Dürer once resided. I'm trying to recall what the land masses look like, how they fit together. My pencil version is actually a distortion of the National Geographic World Map, circa 1968, itself a distorted rendering of a spherical world onto a flat surface. The same problem in reverse would occur if someone tried to make a 2-D version of inward-curving Shipworld.

For many years, that Nat Geo map graced the wall over my childhood bed. I flattened the creases with schoolbooks and hung it with rivers of crisscrossing tape. Greenland was bloated, depicted much bigger than its actual size, but prophetic: a vast island looming like a white, frozen dagger over Europe and North America. Decades later, as we watched it deconstruct in real time, the surface meltwater pouring down moulins to the base of the ancient ice sheet, I did my best to warn my privileged students. They expressed great concern, then drove away after soccer practice in vintage sports cars burning fossil fuels.

South America – now, as before – isn't pregnant enough with Brazil, its Amazon ablaze, and the USA is way too big, of course, a reflection of our outsized ego. I've marked a star on the place outside Boston where I met Zayit, in her daffodil dress, where I concocted my Marvellous middle name for her. Another star is splotched on Mexico City, on the hotel bar on the Paso de la Reforma where Ambassador John Gavin droned nostalgically for the good old days. Am I Gavin now? Is Cecilia playing the part of me?

And China, it's too small for the country that dominated the twenty-first century. (That sent forth its own starship ark, maybe.) I should probably draw Asia in the middle, with America and Europe shunted aside. But that wouldn't be my long-lost Earthworld, and it hits me hard, sitting on my space toilet, that life may still be thundering away back there, in the Year of their

Lord 2062. Maybe games – card games, ball games, deadly status-seeking games – are still being played. Maybe blueberry muffins studded with actual high-bush blueberries still spill by the millions from ovens and maybe scared folks vent, vent, vent on the internet as bombs explode, as deserts spread, as the planet avenges itself.

All of it, still happening. Or not.

One last thing. Please permit me, Cecilia, to suggest a name for our child if it's a girl. I'd like to honour the grandmother on my father's side. A kind lady who endured a lot and took us for ice cream. Her name was Lavender.

3

Years 193–196: The Dark Age

Ynar lived, as everyone did, in a state of perpetual twilight, on the murky edge between night and day.

This had been the way for seventy-five years, since the tumult of Year 118. Long gone was the ship-spanning Tube with its sun-like lighting system and grappling hooks for Equilibrium players decked out in colourful gear. Only jagged, burnt stubs of the passage protruded from each end of the oblong ark's longitudinal axis, reminders of revolt, chaos and calamity. Ground lighting was kept low, one of many frugal measures such as reduced caloric intake – fifteen per cent less for adults, five per cent for kids – slashed water usage and strict limits on clothing replacement. Air temperature stayed at 17°C, just high enough not to impede crop production. Voices were kept low, too, as if to conserve personal energy, and time seemed to move reluctantly, laboriously, even as Shipworld continued to travel through space at .12 the speed of light. People walked with their heads down.

Ynar, however, found the twilight comforting. For her it contained the gentle sense of anticipation that grows before a promised transition – except dawn or dusk never came, and twilight always deepened into gloom.

Peace, she told herself, be at peace.

By nature, Ynar was a nervous person, an unstable element. Her survival, she believed, an anomaly. Now she tilted her head up and with both hands swept her long black hair from her eyes, as if parting a screen. She breathed in/out; the air chilled her lungs. Then she gripped the ascension rope and attached it to the servomechanism at her hip. Peace, she told herself, striving to feel the light-years slipping away in her wake. Ever closer they crawled to HD-40307g, their long-promised oasis – and the servo locked, whirred and abruptly lifted Ynar from the ground. A small figure wrapped in molasses robes, she rose up high and came to a stop next to a kind of wraparound hammock, an interlacement of ropes floating at the midpoint of Shipworld, illuminated by a swirl of LED lights.

Within the hammock lay a human female in a medical coma. She rocked slowly in the subtle winds of zero-grav, and so was spared the indignity of bedsores – something Ynar knew about all too well. Caring for this living body was her sacred duty, her reason for being. Ninety-nine years old with a bolt of grey hair gathered over one shoulder, the body seemed gaunt, even though her weight was stable. Her face was blank, except for the wrinkles growing, year by year, from the corners of her eyes. With her fingertips Ynar tried to smooth the crow's feet away, to undo their inexorable progress, but to no avail.

Franika Longstem, saviour of Shipworld. Ynar looked upon her like a pilgrim arrived at a shrine. They'd had nothing in common, the two of them. One, smart and tough and beautiful. The other, a mousy creature, a hanger-on. One, emboldened by her spacewalking Revelation. The other, denied that experience, which had been discontinued since the upheaval. One, simply put, mattered. The other didn't. And yet here they were, together.

Because of Ynar's severe reaction to the phenylketonuria that eclipsed her twenty-first year, she hadn't witnessed the cataclysmic events that occurred after Brenz dropped his Sixteen Theses. She knew nothing, first-hand, of the seducing power of Brenzianism, a cult of liberation that appealed to self-interest and self-expression, to suppressed grievances, as it swept through the community like a scouring wind. While Franika formed a countermovement against Brenzianism, Ynar lay abed, cared for by her parents and turning in a slow-motion tornado of physical anguish and chronic seizures known as status epilepticus. A year later she emerged with jelly legs and a heart murmur that felt like a cog slipping, and she found her Shipworld gone.

But she didn't grieve for the past. She adjusted quickly – faster, indeed, than most people – to the diversion of large quantities of energy (to the main deflector) and water (to the liquid layer inside the hull) for enhanced cosmic ray blocking. Low light and cold temperatures didn't bother her, nor did brief, bracing showers and a limited choice of food from shade crops high in protein, such as peas, spinach and the runner beans that ran riot along trellises constructed from abandoned algae pipes and the bones of bamboo fencing. The Loop was used sparingly these days, for lack of energy, but Ynar tolerated wearing old clothes and chose not to worry that everyday things were wearing out everywhere. Her illness, too, had spared her the challenge faced by many shipworldmates: the struggle to forgive those they had opposed. To put aside injuries and insults.

Actually, Ynar was much happier now, for her old life had been a pale and burdensome thing, a source of secret shame.

She set to work, checking the central med and fluid lines that ran from a small box on Franika's hip to the shoulder access port. Operational, clean. Her brain, supposedly, had settled into deep-resting mode, a state of low electrical activity necessary for countering the trauma that had almost killed her. The coma mitigated the swelling that came with zero-grav suspension, but there was no repair for the long-term effects of weightlessness on the skeleton. Franika's bones had become brittle, useless;

she would never stand and walk again, that is, if she could ever awaken, which assuredly she could not.

'Praise, Franika,' whispered Ynar.

She recalled watching Franika, seventy-five years ago, run down Pictor Boulevard. Her body – so strong! Her stride so symmetrical, near-perfect – a joy to behold! Gawky Ynar had envied Franika for her poise and power, the passionate way she threw herself forward. She'd fantasised that they were friends, real friends, who met for faux coffee and laughed about it, who worked out with strides synchronised. At the same time, she'd known that Franika barely tolerated her during shifts at the algae lab, that she struggled to conceal her pity, even disdain, for Ynar. The curt responses and strained smiles had felt like knife slashes.

'Praise, Franika.'

Ynar checked the airway support device inside her mouth: functional, if coated with slime. She cleaned it. She pulled back the white robe draping the body and changed out Franika's soiled undergarments for fresh ones. Then she cleaned the entire surface of her skin with a moist cloth, working from her feet to her head. This slow, intimate procedure often brought Ynar to tears. Today was not one of those days.

After her injury, there were those who wanted Franika released to death, arguing that artificial maintenance caused her suffering and anxiety. Others couldn't bear the thought of grinding her body into soil. She was, they asserted, unique, irreplaceable. No human hand should terminate her life. A few more rhetorical turns, born of gratitude and desperation, led to the bolder assertion that keeping her alive was a profound and devotional act. A sacred undertaking. The Saviour's continued existence, if only in tended embers, would in turn sustain and protect Shipworld during these dark times.

And so it became a common belief, and that belief was embellished and taught to the young ones. Candles appeared, always burning, and groups huddled in the darkness, staring up with arms linked. Franika's lungs would inflate and deflate a million more times. Her heart would beat for another twenty-one years, until the natural, corrected end of her life's journey. The silent cogitations of her mind became a mystery for contemplation and prayer.

Ceremonially, a third time: 'Praise, Franika.'

Ynar summoned the reasons why this floating body deserved praise. All life onboard, it was said, might have perished if not for her successful campaign to reinforce shielding against cosmic rays, a decision that led to the closure of research departments, the sapping of energy for heating and lighting systems, and water rationing. The deprivations were sudden and disturbing, but soon the medical crises reached a plateau and, in time, abated. Shipworld survived, barely.

Franika's famous speech to the Council, regarding her theory that a gradual shift in cosmic ray exposure had caused both heightened sensitivity to microcystin and outbreaks of phenylketonuria, was acted out every month. Large crowds still attended performances, with many people mouthing Franika's words as she presented, step by step, the scientific facts, medical evidence and likely causes and effects. In a stiff tone battering down grief, she described her father's death: the tremors, the flailing, the way he guttered out from within. Then her voice grew thick and loud, gathering together the voices of the dead, as she called for bravery and sacrifice and asserted the primacy of the Mission above all. 'The future shines in our eyes,' she proclaimed. 'The future shines in our eyes!' However, the fierce debate that ensued between Sceptical Reggert and Indomitable Franika was deemed too vehement for public display, too revelatory of humanity's dark impulses, and only snippets of that dialogue had been passed down in whispered asides.

Solving the medical emergency, of course, was only one of Franika's Three Great Deeds. The easiest perhaps, requiring insight and persuasion. The other two – stemming the popular tide of Brenzianism and forcing the exile of Brenz, after which Shipworld was put back on course to HD-40307g – were acts of brute leadership and courage. Acts that Ynar contemplated with awe and lingering incomprehension. How had one person, with just one heart and one mind, done such things?

She combed Franika's hair, carefully, from the top of her skull to the tips of the strands laid upon her chest. The tines swept through the grey wisps without resistance. Forty strokes, she'd settled on. A daily ritual. And, as always, she remembered the time Franika, who was no saint no matter what they said, made a snarky comment in front of friends about the way Ynar kept her hair in a prim, tight bun. Something about her being afraid to let loose. She was right, of course, but Ynar had burned with embarrassment for days.

No, not a saint. Saints don't exist. Saints are fairy tales. Praise, Franika.

Last of all, Ynar took readings of brain activity, blood pressure, respiration and potassium levels. Each task she enacted with equal measures of thoroughness and loving care, not for a moment becoming bored or desiring another station. She worked through the everlasting twilight, and when she faltered, when the anxiety hidden in the gloom rose up like some rancorous visitor and assailed her, she reminded herself to be at peace, at peace, for she was one of the Keepers. Her every motion at this shrine became a veneration, and she breathed the chill air, in/out, and swelled with gratitude for having been given a life of simple, yet glorious, purpose.

Later, when her ministrations were complete, Ynar returned to ground. She took off her robes, then folded and stored them in a cabinet that once had housed a pump for circulating algae. Food of a bygone era. People still said, 'Don't taste the algae,' a reference to avoiding toxic substances, or people, or ideas. Ynar retained a nightmare memory of chewing algae chunks in a kale salad soon before falling ill, seventy-five years ago. It was during lunch with Franika. They were talking about an old-timey recipe for some kind of chowder. Gulika and Javier, both dead, were also there. Javier ranting about Earthworld economics, the corruption, the waste. Something about four-pences. And Gulika, what was she like? Casual, that's right, and stylish. Ynar had envied her, too.

She had some time before her next responsibility, a shift in mushroom house #6, so Ynar decided to rest on a bench by the Olmec Head. The route there took her past the former library – destroyed in the Brenzian Revolution, its books later consigned to the Loop – as well as the grim cavity of the swimming pool, now used for storing objects donated for conversion into precious energy. She noticed, on top of the heap, a couple of folding chairs and an old painting with a chipped frame. So much had been destroyed, and so much had changed, but some things remained the same. For instance, although restrictions on copying files and using screens for communication and entertainment had faded, many people still followed the old rules out of habit, or nostalgia, or as a means to conserve resources. The frugality of the times, the blunt poverty, imposed its own set of binding limits.

Ynar passed by the ficus tree – limp, leaves blackened, bark splitting and flaccid, and yet still alive, remarkably, even though the trunk's encircling vines seemed to be losing their hold. One main branch had fallen off, an arm sacrificed by the body decades ago. Deemed a luxury, the tree received no public water, but the old creature's roots cadged moisture from here and there and its internal systems had drifted into extreme, old-age hibernation. In the deepest recesses of night, Ynar had seen shipworldmates sneak splashes of water to the ficus from their personal rations.

Once there'd been a community garden near the Head, Ynar recalled, as well as a pocket lawn for kids; now mounded beds of potatoes surrounded the stone. A new round of leafy green plants, thriving in low light, peaked through the ground. Ynar sat here alone, like a lost tourist visiting a ruin that no one cared about anymore, and she found herself, as always, amused by the Head's stare. So cross, never blinking. The poor thing. Which way was he faced? She couldn't remember. Was he looking back at ruined Earthworld or beyond to the promise of HD-40307g? The ambient lighting was too dim for her to figure it out by locating the catwalk to the forward-facing bridge. The catwalk where—

'Hello, Ynar. Can I sit?'

She turned: the voice came from Chive – Brenz's little sister. But it wasn't fair to reduce her to that; she hadn't supported his movement. Now she was married with a grown son, Jan Oort-Ruiz, and worked as a counsellor for those born from frozen embryos. Ynar scooched over, a little surprised at the polite approach of Chive, who could be a sharp and intense person. The two women sat together without speaking for a while. At some point Chive gestured at Franika's vaguely illuminated body hovering far above, visible from this bench and from every other vantage point on the compass.

'He loved her, you know. That's why he agreed to go into exile.'

Speaking about Brenz was risky, especially for Chive. More so, this interpretation of his motivations didn't match the story Ynar had been told. The standard narrative assumed that Brenz's affection for Franika was, at best, superficial, secondary to his radical ideological agenda, and most likely a stratagem by a handsome conman taking advantage of a young woman in the throes of tragic love. Her suppression of those feelings in order to save Shipworld was the most poignant aspect of her heroic journey. But Ynar had to admit that the Franika she knew wasn't exactly naïve.

'What do you mean?' asked Ynar. She added: 'It's OK, you're safe here.'

'Thank you,' said Chive, bowing her head. Then she spoke her version of the story, with the whispered urgency of someone revealing a long-kept secret. The Brenz she knew, the nerdy, jittery older brother, was kind of a mess. That he had a girlfriend at all, no less Franika, seemed a miracle. And he was just crazy for her, head over heels.

'He was no mastermind,' said Chive. 'Yeah, he was really smart, but almost too smart for his own good, you know? When I saw him by the Tube, just levitating up there at the centre of everything, I knew it was serious. Then those postcards...'

She raised a hand, as if plucking one of Brenz's fluttering postcards from the air, and she looked at her hand as if reading the sixteen passionate, logical theses, touching the blood-red brand, the B surrounding Oort and St George.

'Chive?' said Ynar.

'I just thought, OK, that makes sense,' she continued. 'My brother's a revolutionary, it kind of figures.'

'What do you think happened to him, after he left?'

'I don't know, but it's easy to guess.'

Chive gazed up. Ynar watched her watching Brenz, long ago. And watching Franika now. 'Watching Franika', actually, was a favourite phrase among the youngest of the frozen-embryo children. She wasn't sure what it meant. Making a prayer? Wasting time? It almost seemed like a game; they whispered 'Watching Franika' and rushed off. Watching for what?

Chive turned her hazel eyes on Ynar. 'Here's something nobody knows. They met secretly; they weren't really enemies.'

Even as their coalitions struggled for control, Chive explained, she saw Franz and Brenz embracing in a maintenance corridor. It was right before Brenz and his followers seized Engineering to prevent resumption of the original course, and days later his gang took the Loop and used it to construct a small ship, the *Thomas Jefferson*, capable of bringing explorers to the surface of the rogue planet. And the rest is history: the Siege of the Loop, hundreds more dead from microcystin poisoning and phenylketonuria, including Lavender Oort-St George and Charley Longstem, and the brutal death of four zealots, two from each side, in a clash with homemade spears. Months of stalemate and chaos. Finally, Brenz and twelve others flew away to the rogue, and Shipworld swerved back towards HD-40307g.

'They knew they couldn't win,' said Ynar. 'Franika stood up to them and they fled.'

Chive shook her head, slowly. 'No, it wasn't that simple. Brenz thought she'd come around – he told me that! He loved her, but didn't understand her. When he finally realised that she was willing to die for the Mission, that's when he decided to leave. He sacrificed everything, even though he knew it was probably suicide.'

Ynar, stunned, tried to reply in a calm voice. 'You talk as if—'

'I know, I know,' interrupted Chive. 'Franika was the hero, Franika saved us all. But that doesn't mean my brother's a villain.'

Again, Chive looked at web-ensnared Franika, buried alive – barely – in her aerial tomb. Ynar joined her, imagining against her Keeper's will the sight of Franika – exhausted, distracted, possibly distraught at Brenz's flight, even crazed with guilt – as she accidentally fell, so it was told, from the bridge catwalk and accelerated through heavier and heavier levels of gravity and landed with a bone-crushing thud two storeys down on steel floorboards. The Saviour who couldn't save herself.

Ynar touched Chive on the shoulder. They sat on the bench together next to the old, old Head who'd heard it all and would never tell.

'He loved her,' said Ynar. 'And she loved him.'

✦

There were two kinds of orphaned children on Shipworld, and they were very different.

First you had the fifty-three children of parents who'd died from illness or violence. They were cared for affectionately and required to attend counselling sessions. Although many suffered chronic grief during the cruel convergence of adolescence and abandonment, these orphans were adopted by families and, by and large, led remarkably unremarkable lives. By now, in Year 193, they were in their eighties. A dozen or so, however, had refused to become parents, a stark departure from the universal parenting tradition and another challenge to population dynamics.

Then you had a larger group of orphans, one hundred and ten in all, who came from the cache of embryos kept in a secure, rectangular freezer in the Mess Hall kitchen. Every year for a decade, beginning in Year 142, eleven such embryos gestated within slowly rotating artificial wombs refreshed by a ventilated nutrient solution that mimicked, some said improved upon, the ecology of the human uterus. The process taxed already low energy stores, but was necessary to preserve a minimum viable population protected from inbreeding and genetic drift. The ice children – who retained this label even after they became adults – served as a genetic emergency valve. It was a desperate scheme, and a minor miracle that the infants emerged in healthy condition, apparently, from 'iron womb' technology that had never received approval as a medical device.

No families, though, adopted the newborn ice children. They seemed, in the end, too alien. Perhaps it had been a mistake to allow open viewing of the developing embryos; the sight of human foetuses floating inside transparent receptacles engendered both fascination and deep discomfort. When the first batch of very long but otherwise normal babies were born, and went unclaimed, the Council decided that they'd be raised together – and carefully monitored – by caretakers in a dorm. Adoption interest remained low over time, so orphans in the following batches were also dispatched to the ever-expanding dorm, a crowded, cacophonous, multi-level space known as the Children's House.

Ice children displayed some unique qualities. One was a manic affinity for group play; as soon as they could toddle, they engaged in complicated games of tag, hide-and-seek and dodgeball. Older ice children set up challenging obstacle courses that spiralled about their enclave. Rarely was an ice child seen at rest – an exaggeration, of course, as these youngsters attended school with the flesh-born and managed to sit, or squirm, through lessons – and they chanted as they played, scores of falsetto voices pounding out nonsense words in rhythmic unison, words, in fact, that were the building blocks of a mega-syllabic language known only to the players.

As the ice children reached adulthood, they almost always stayed in the Children's House, and so it came to be known as the Orphans' House and, later, the *Skarjakkenfinzger*, which roughly means House of Souls in their language. Did this designation imply that the flesh-born – conceived in the sex act, gestated in wombs of varying chemical composition and moulded in small, constricting family units – somehow lacked souls? Many, indeed, wondered if the new breed of humans saw the flesh-born as lesser beings, insufficiently joyful, resigned to the tepid twilight fallen across Shipworld like a shroud.

After much debate, in Year 162, the Council decided that ice children would be allowed the Correction at age twenty-one. In turn, by a close vote among themselves, they accepted the opportunity. Many simply didn't trust those in charge, who, after all, could barely keep the lights on, and some doubted a treatment that hadn't been tested on the artificially gestated. For the majority of ice children, however, the horror stories of sustained infirmity without the Correction outweighed such concerns.

Every ice child stood well over 1.8 metres tall; the men averaged two metres. Their impressive height may have been caused by a melding of growth factors and FGFR3 proteins in the iron-womb cocktail that fuelled their embryogenesis. Or the extra-large size of the iron wombs may have given the foetuses more room to reach, that is, for the stars. Or their biological parents happened to be basketball players. Regardless, from their elevated strata the ice children learned to communicate messages – and even concepts – to each other with a bare minimum of words and gestures. They seemed to operate on their own wavelength, and some flesh-born labelled them as aloof. Telepathic, perhaps. A rumour circulated that a CRISPR-derived enzyme, a magic potion, had been poured into their amniotic fluids. More likely, asserted sceptics, an intuitive bond comes more easily to any group of humans who grow up sleeping in communal beds, chanting in unison and bouncing off the walls together.

Karlsen, age fifty, and born from the first batch, was among the oldest, and, at 2.1 metres, among the tallest. While respected among the ice children, Karlsen was also considered odd for living apart and pursuing research in solitude. Of late he was immersed in building a robot bird, based on sketchy plans found in a Pioneer computer file; such discoveries were a perk of his work team's maintenance of the supercomputer. To power his robo-bird project, Karlsen diverted photons from his room heater to a battery pack. He created tools and construction materials by cannibalising his spartan furniture – then slept on the cold floor, shivering into sleep – and by refashioning personal care items. A toothbrush, sharpened on one end, made a decent screwdriver.

Birds baffled Karlsen. How did they get off the ground, let alone manoeuvre, just by flapping their wings? He'd watched a video of a fat goose ascending from an Earthworld pond – impossible! Even a mini heli-drone needed 500 rpm to make a wobbly lift-off. The ultra-high-speed flutters of a hummingbird at least made sense as a flight technique, but diving, dodging, daredevil sparrows just didn't add up. Immense thrust generated from slight frames – they looked almost weightless, avatars of the dark energy that pervaded the universe. Ah, if only he had a sparrow skeleton to examine under the microscope that he'd rigged from a glass bottle. When Karlsen conducted a test flight of his latest design, based on the common house finch, the robo-bird soared from a shelf and executed a figure eight. Then, as if hit by lightning, it lost orientation and slammed to the floor, fracturing its neck.

A few days after that setback, Karlsen and Jan Oort-Ruiz worked together purging redundant memory clots from the supercomputer. Jan was a good thirty-two centimetres shorter than Karlsen, and twenty years younger, with a stocky build and oddly formal way of speaking. They sat together at their terminals, the shy ice child and the nephew of a visionary terrorist.

'I've been thinking about the way things are,' said Jan, 'and the way things used to be.'

Karlsen kept on task; his hands produced the flowing, plasticky sound of keyboard strokes. Lately, he'd noticed, Jan had been diverging from workday tech-talk into ethereal statements about the human condition. It seemed as if he was putting out feelers, tentative, open-ended, and Karlsen found himself unsure how to respond.

'Of course, it's hard to trust what you hear,' stated Jan, rolling his chair back from the terminal. 'Shipworld history isn't written down – as far as I know. Except for *The Chronicler's Journal.*'

'What's that?' asked Karlsen.

'It's about the first twelve years. This old man, one of the Pioneers, was given the job of writing down his impressions. It's been passed down in our family. My mother has the only copy, but she won't let me read it.'

Karlsen executed a few more strokes, *clickity-clackity-clack*, and the sounds fluttered up like butterflies, then slipped away into deep space.

'I don't really know why,' said Jan, answering the unasked question about his mother, Chive. 'She and my dad are always talking about the first three gens – and about Earthworld before that. She used to eavesdrop on her parents' conversations, through doors and around corners. Even put a listening tube through a wall to their bedroom.'

'There's no privacy in the *Skarjakkenfinzger*,' said Karlsen.

'Is that why you moved out? For privacy?'

Karlsen hesitated. He heard the mechanised shush of air transfer, the clanking of faraway farmwork. A murmur, a voice maybe. 'I'm trying to build a robotic bird,' he confided. Foolish words, when vocalised. But he couldn't take them back. Moreover, he lacked a ready answer to the inevitable next question.

Jan returned his attention to the data terminal. Inputted something, deleted something else. Perhaps deleted the very thing he'd inputted, you can't go wrong with that. 'Very interesting,' he said. 'But why?'

Karlsen actually wasn't sure. He just did it. Maybe for fun, or to escape. To have something all to himself, secret. To understand. And then he surprised himself by declaring, 'Because no one's done it before. As far as I know.'

'No one's done it out here, for sure' replied Jan, pressing more icons. 'So, on Earthworld,' the young man continued, determined to explore the way things are and the way things used to be, 'the energy system was super-polluting. Ecosystems destroyed, glaciers melting, species extinction – air pollution killed like twelve thousand people every day! Even the insects were dying out. I know, everyone learns this in school, the fall of Earthworld, but it wasn't *inevitable*. They had two really good fixes: use less energy and switch to renewables. And they couldn't do either one, not enough to make any difference.'

'It's hard to believe.'

'Yeah.'

'A little crazy.'

'But,' said Jan, 'maybe they just felt stuck. You know, going along day to day, year to year, unable to make real changes. Chive says that her father collected all these old Earthworld sayings. Instead of stuck he'd say "betwixt and between". Kind of makes it sound special.'

Now Karlsen pulled back from the terminal. A strange one, this flesh-born fellow, with his odd preoccupation with the past and its manufactured meanings. He realised, too, that he rather liked Jan, that perhaps they shared something vital across their differences, and he looked directly at his face: unwrinkled, like a baby's, except for a horizontal canyon running betwixt and between his eyebrows. That fleshy indentation fluctuated in size as he contemplated the twisted branches of history's tree.

'Two excellent choices, and they screwed up,' said Jan. 'We don't even have one. Not one! We can't be more frugal – we're barely getting by now. And we can't reduce population and still fulfil the Mission. The only option is to augment the fusion engines, and no one knows how to do that.'

'We could stop the ship from spinning; that takes a lot of energy,' said Karlsen.

'Yeah, gravity's overrated. Except for keeping our bones from dissolving.'

'Maybe we simply have to accept things. Try to endure.'

'But it's *depressing*,' shot back Jan. 'We're the most advanced spaceship ever built, travelling to a planet around a distant star, and we're poor!'

'And I can't get my robo-bird to fly.'

'Yeah, but—' Jan stopped himself. 'It's like my dad's job, taking care of drip-irrigation hoses. That's us, just drips of life.'

'It's enough,' said Karlsen, quietly.

'To survive, sure, but there's no cushion. What if something else goes wrong?'

Of course, something else would go wrong. A crack here leading to a gap there causing a chasm right down the middle, everything falling through, and the next thing you know we're on the far end of the parabola – *crash!* Karlsen knew they were overdue for something to go terribly wrong, for an accident, grudge, fiery idea or everyday concurrence of irreconcilable factors to knock them from their shaky perch. The thrifty, galactic laws of thermodynamics were fine with that. And if Karlsen was actually ready to accept 'enough', to toddle through gloom under the threat of catastrophic mission failure, then why was he scrounging energy and tools for his secret project? Why was he trying to do what hadn't been done before?

'Well, this is a waste of time, I know that much,' said Jan, waving in disgust at the computer. He stared through the open roof of their enclosure. Then: 'The answer exists, I can *feel* it.' He struck his fist on his chest, once, twice, three times. 'The first Jan Oort, he discovered this cloud of comets around

Earthworld's solar system. He never saw it, there were no direct instrument readings – he just figured it out!'

Apart from ritual handshakes, Karlsen had never touched a flesh-born person, not intentionally. He reached out and patted Jan Oort on his bony knee. He patted the anxious young man, a human being like any other, and then he raised his head and looked up, too, at the rope-ensnared body, white-shrouded and floating, at Shipworld's centre.

'Watching Franika,' he said.

✦

In the coming weeks, Jan and Karlsen had several more conversations, laying the foundation of their friendship. One concerned potatoes and the myriad ways to prepare them, both with the peel (Jan's preference) and without (Karlsen's preference). Another regarded the relative motion of the stars, planets, moons, comets, solar systems, nebulas, black holes and galaxies, not to mention Shipworld and the universe at large, and which of those hurtling movements, in straight lines or curving arcs, and from which perspective, should be considered the baseline reference. Another examined the duality of the word 'Shipworld', how it combined suggestions of movement and stasis, of change and conservation, of the confounding demands of life. 'My body,' Jan said cryptically, 'is my Shipworld. And so is my mind.' Karlsen nodded, vigorously.

And still another chat was about height.

'What does it feel like,' Jan asked as they walked side by side, 'to be so tall?'

Karlsen sighed, and replied that he rarely thinks about his height when among orphans or alone with his birds. Yes, he's hit his head on the bathroom doorway many times, so that reminds him that his environs were built with a certain type of human, not him, in mind. And sometimes he feels unsure going down steep stairs because, after all, it's a long way from his eyes to the ground. Then Jan asked him what it feels like to be around 'us shorties'. Well, said Karlsen, he finds himself stooping in conversation with untall people, which is bad for his posture, and he often senses, when looking down on the flesh-born, that a separate world operates beneath his gaze, below his slipstream, an underworld belonging to those whose ancestors were here before the embryonic orphans, the ice children, the beanstalks, pick your label – 'belonging to those', he said, 'who can stake a greater claim'. Such feelings can be uncomfortable, alienating. But all in all, he cherishes his tallness, his bounding freedom above the fray. No offence.

None taken. Jan thanked Karlsen for his honesty. And he spoke about being short, about, for instance, the difficulty of having one's view blocked in a crowd, of being unable to reach an object on a high shelf, of feeling overlooked, underdeveloped – but all that's trivial, of course, compared to Shipworld's energy conundrum, the confounding motions of the cosmos and the feel of a new potato in hand. Then he stopped walking and spoke eye to higher-eye to Karlsen about a feeling he's experienced, now and then, while looking up at tall folk. It's a twinge not of inferiority, but of 'wonder and worry as I tilt my head back in contemplation. It's almost as if you're leaving us behind', Jan stated, and at such moments he finds himself on his toes, ridiculously, and he's seized by an urge, a primitive ache, to climb up, to ascend, to transcend his limits. To get further off the ground.

'But,' he added, 'not when I'm with you. Not anymore.'

Karlsen nodded, yes, yes. He maintained his upright posture, not stooping, and the friends walked back to their terminals, to their workaday tasks.

A few nights later, Jan had a peculiar dream. In this dream he awoke, rose from bed and with surprising purpose walked the dark paths of night-time Shipworld. Dream Jan seemed to know where he was going; dreamer Jan, however, did not, and he watched with great interest as he came to a door with the number thirty-five emblazoned on it. He knocked, hard. No response. He pushed the door open and across the room stood Karlsen, holding a robotic bird in his palm. A house finch; somehow, Jan knew this. The creature puffed its brown-grey feathers as if girding itself, and this part of the dream repeated itself in a herky-jerky time loop, the bird in the palm, puffed feathers, its head swivelling, tiny beak and black eyes flashing. A real bird, but obviously not. Over and over, the bird in the palm, feathers, head, beak – and suddenly it flew towards Jan, emitting a shrill, peeping call.

He ducked; the bird zoomed past and around a corner. Jan ran after it, with Karlsen rumbling behind. Running, swooping, falling…the dream morphed into a slurry of chase and pursuit, field and sky merging, and into the central garden area flew the house finch, followed by Jan and Karlsen. In a series of graceful manoeuvres, executed perfectly according to algorithms that were the mathematical fruit of millions of years of human evolution, the red-headed, red-bibbed bird circled about Franika in her eyrie and then dived at the Olmec Head. With a magnificent air brake, it landed on top of the icon. The bird began driving its titanium beak into the stone – *peck, peck, peck, peck!*

Jan approached, arms outstretched.

'Don't touch it,' Karlsen yelled. 'Accept your fate – accept what happens!'

And Jan awoke – dreamer Jan, that is. It took a moment for him to realise that he wasn't waking again inside the dream, a fact that he confirmed by pinching the skin on top of his hand. He slapped his face and pulled his hair, too, still not absolutely convinced because where was it written that one couldn't manufacture pain in a dream?

✦

Several months later, in Year 194, the orphans grown from frozen embryos cleaned out the last of the junk in the old swimming pool, located next to the *Skarjakkenfinzger*, and placed it by the door to the Loop. On top of the pool, they built a springy device once known (the word had been lost) as a trampoline. The ice kids – middle-aged, yet agile – drilled a dozen holes around the pool's concrete perimeter using spikes and hammers. Then, employing levers, they ganged up to implant huge screws into those holes. Onto the screws they attached tightly coiled springs, and onto the springs they bolted an enormous rectangular bounce mat, a tightly woven abstract-impressionistic quilt that, from above, resembled a wave of shimmery plant and animal life crashing onto rocks. Where they got all these materials became a subject of much discussion among the flesh-born.

As the orphans laboured – in alternating work teams, around the clock for three days – they chanted their curious rhymes. They passed tools back and forth as if enacting a rehearsed choreography. It was a loud display and crowds gathered to watch. Tender Beatrice, now one hundred and six and settled into the role of bemused observer, yelled out: What is it? Parsifal, over two metres tall, replied: It's a *phligsparrfner!* What's it for? His reply: Fun!

When the construction was done, all one hundred and ten ice children assembled. Parsifal stepped cautiously, wobblily, onto the centre of the *phligsparrfner*. He started bouncing on his toes and soon ascended one metre, two metres, three metres off the mat; each time, he came straight down and bounced back higher, demonstrating a skilful transfer of kinetic energy. Again and again, smiling widely, the man shot up like a rocket and returned down to the phantasmagorical mat, flexing his legs on contact, bouncing with abandon. The screws and springs held firm, making barely a squeak. The flesh-born crowd clapped politely, well done, and the ice children broke into revelry.

Did they get permission? one short man asked another. Is it really just for fun?

Higher and higher bounced Parsifal, his arms whirling. Many flesh-born folk grew nervous. What if he loses balance and comes down on his head? What if he veers to one side and lands on the concrete? On the twentieth *phligsparrfner* jump, Parsifal achieved enough height to enter a lower gravity gradient and, for an uncertain moment, floated near the centre space where the former Tube had skewered forth – then hurtled back down and landed on his butt. This time he let himself go loose, up/down, up/down, bouncing lower and lower as the kinetic energy dissipated through the mat and his body. Soon, he came to a halt. Look, he's laughing – such relief! Ice children rushed forward and hoisted the test pilot onto their shoulders. Hurrah, hurrah!

Jan Oort-Ruiz, however, avoided the *phligsparrfner* or whatever they called it. The ice children, with the exception of Karlsen, annoyed him. Although he wished he could be more broadminded, could extend his fondness for Karlsen to all of his bouncing brethren, he felt unnerved by their playfulness, even suspicious of their intentions. In recent months scores had migrated from their communal dwelling, taking over a cluster of empty apartments. Rapidly, a second *phligsparrfner* had been constructed next to the former library. And that crazy chanting, the way they swaggered about in the gloom – didn't they know the situation? The looming disaster? Every time Jan passed an ice child, he gritted his teeth and fixated, once more, on the energy problem plaguing Shipworld.

What, he asked himself, would his great-great-great-great-great grandfather Jan Oort do?

It turned out, according to Chive, that the first Jan Oort not only discovered the Oort Cloud of comets blanketing the sol system – not proven, definitively, until Shipworld ploughed through it – but determined that the Milky Way rotates in a counterclockwise, or clockwise, direction, depending on your perspective. Even more astoundingly, because the galaxy rotates without spinning apart, he conceptualised the existence of dark matter, the invisible substance that makes up twenty-five per cent of the universe. To this day, dark matter eluded observation, but, like most scientists, Jan assumed that it existed – a mist of subatomic particles, loners by nature – or nothing about an expansionary cosmos governed by general relativity made any sense at all.

So, what would the great Jan Oort do? He wouldn't make a fetish of endurance; he wouldn't escape into ecstatic diversions. No, he'd infer the guts of the clock from the movement of the hands, that's what he'd do; he'd figure out what's needed to make things work. For instance: the Mission to HD-40307g must be fulfilled, and to do so we must produce more energy. Therefore…and here, every time, Jan found himself facing a sterile, blank wall. He stared at it, stared for ages, looking for cracks, bulges, secret handholds. A momentary shimmering, the slightest clue betraying what lay beyond. He saw nothing.

✦

Eventually, the ficus tree became very old and died. Parsifal found it on an early-morning walk, entirely tipped over, its massed, branching roots wrenched up and exposed. How thin they were, almost delicate, like woven rug strands unravelling, and he wondered how in creation those roots had supported such a stout, towering tree, as well as generations of climbing children. He observed for a while the space where the tree had grown tall, a ficus-shaped volume of air that in no way distinguished itself, alas, and then he set to collecting torn and broken branches, crinkling with dead leaves, into a neat pile.

Parsifal discovered that beneath the tree's shredded bark and desperate assemblage of vines existed a core of hard, knotty wood. He tapped a bony knuckle on it: *thonk, thonk, thonk*, a satisfying sound indeed. That very day, without consulting anyone, he began to salvage the heartwood of the tree's trunk; the rest was consigned to the Loop. And the very next day, not far from the accusing gaze of the Olmec Head, industrious Parsifal set up an outdoor workshop with his kitchen table for a sawhorse and homemade saws and wood planes and a sanding block made from crushed-up semiconductors.

This project, he told inquiring strollers, as well as a curious emissary from the Council, was for the benefit of all – just wait and see. His friendly assurances were enough to draw smiles and appreciative remarks from most passers-by, who approved of repurposing the ficus' trunk. Several, however, called it wasteful and asserted that the tree, like all dead things, like all dead shipworldmates, should be entirely Looped. One grouchy fellow accused him of tempting fate and pointed up at Franika. Parsifal thanked everyone for their viewpoints, and for the chickpea fritters and kale smoothies he was gifted. Then he returned to measuring, sawing and fashioning the wood. Doing this, he felt, was his duty, although he couldn't have explained why.

He made blocks. But not square, rectangular or triangular ones. Parsifal's blocks were irregular polyhedrons, each the size of a child's fist, give or take, with twelve to seventeen flat sides of various shapes and sizes. Most were tan-coloured, riven with streaks of brown and white, and he sanded the flat surfaces to near smoothness. Parsifal deepened the shading of some blocks by soaking them in rhubarb juice. Over many weeks he toiled, creating a pile of six hundred polyhedrons. Then he assembled a tower of five random blocks, a precarious, uneven tower that promised to collapse but did not, not yet at least. That task, which took him several tries to accomplish, was relaxing and fun – a good thing, decided Parsifal, because dour old Shipworld should have more fun. Nearby he planted a sign that read: *Take Five, Please*.

And he walked away. Within a day, every single irregular polyhedron was gone.

✦

Between bouts of fretting, Jan arranged lunch with his mother in the potato patch by the Olmec Head. There, by happenstance, they met Ynar, who appeared startled to have gained company. The three sat between rows of blossoming plants, the Keeper poking at a spinach salad, the mother and son eating stewed portobello mushrooms with red beans. Far above, as always, Franika in her hammock burrowed in deepest sleep. A living relic, inert and yet reverberating. You could almost imagine, Jan thought, that she powered the ship. Technically, she sucked a tiny amount of power from it.

'When you care for her,' asked Jan, 'does she sense you?'

'I doubt it,' said Ynar. 'But I always assume she can. I assume she can feel me and hear me, even smell me.'

'You were friends?'

'Not really. But I've learned—'

'I am so sick,' interrupted Chive, 'of mushrooms.' She turned to Jan: 'If your father brings home mushrooms again, I'm going to kill him.' She kept eating, nonetheless.

'How are the orphans?' Ynar asked her.

'You know, it's funny we still call them that,' said Chive. 'I'm not sure they feel the lack of parents – you could say they're parents to each other. They're also brothers, sisters, cousins, friends, enemies – it's complicated, I still haven't figured it out.'

'Enemies?' responded Jan. 'It seems like they always get along.'

'Does it?' replied Chive. 'I guess they're careful in front of flesh-born. They come in my office crying their eyes out, spouting all the petty junk we humans are famous for. More often than not, though, they leave smiling, chanting a song.'

'You're good at your job,' said Ynar.

Chive shrugged. 'I hear you,' she said in a monotone. 'How does that make you feel?'

Ynar chuckled into her food. Then Jan asked his mother if she understood the sexual practices of the ice children and she almost spit up her mushrooms.

'What's that supposed to mean?'

Jan wasn't fazed. 'Listen, I don't assume anything with them. Do they have long-term relationships? Are they going to have kids the natural way or will they use the iron wombs?'

Chive snorted, 'C'mon, Jan,' as if to say, what's natural? And, you're clueless.

'C'mon yourself – those devices take a lot of energy,' he continued. 'The Council might not allocate it. And there's nothing wrong with asking questions – I've heard you say that.'

'Of course not,' Chive conceded with the tolerant, exasperated tone that she reserved for her adult son when he challenged her. Honestly, she added, the topic never came up, but Jan didn't quite believe her. More likely, the reproductive plans of the ice children were confidential and therefore safeguarded by his mother. He let it pass, though, and the three of them ate in silence for a while, next to the ever-cross Head who perhaps was suffering from hunger pains. Jan thought of his dream, of the chased robo-bird perched on its scalp – *peck, peck, peck!* Driving its titanium beak home.

‘What about after she dies?’ he asked.

‘She could live another fifteen years,’ said Ynar. ‘Praise, Franika.’

‘Maybe that’s when things will change, for better or for worse,’ offered Jan. He lifted his eyes to the Saviour, and so did Chive and Ynar. ‘When Franika dies.’

Ynar cleared her throat and looked away; otherwise, the women made no response. Jan supposed that they didn’t take him very seriously. They chit-chatted about people he didn’t know or care about and, after they went their separate ways, he lingered. He was in no hurry to get back to his useless job scavenging electrons from data banks. Jan gave the Head a good long look, blinked first and then realised that he’d never actually touched the ancient one. In the dream, Karlsen had warned him not to touch it. Accept your fate! In undreamed life, he’d counselled endurance. The way things are is enough.

Peck, peck, peck!

Gently, Jan placed his right hand on its basalt skull, on the side of its helmet. The stone felt cold, as if chilled from within, and rough against his skin. He moved his hand slowly over cracks and ridges and undulations, along jagged slashes that seemed not time-worn but newly born of anger, of savage retribution. Even though Jan knew little about this artefact – dug up on Earthworld, rare, very old – he sensed that it had once been both venerated and despised, that people had died for what it represented. Its history was turbulent, beyond reckoning. All history was that way, a kaleidoscopic crash-up determined by twists and turns and stray shafts of light.

Jan’s eyes closed and he heard nothing, not even his own heartbeat; all of his senses culminated in his hand as it explored the cold, rough stone and its cryptic story. He flowed to his fingertips and inferred, in the tradition of the great Jan Oort, the cold calculus of a universe in which endurance, ultimately, is not rewarded. That's when he decided what this Jan Oort would do.

✦

First, Jan stole *The Chronicler's Journal* from his mother's bedroom. The fat document was wrapped in a ripped shirt inside a box under her bed. A lousy hiding place, really; maybe she wanted it found. Running over four thousand pages, many creased or ripped or mouldering, the journal contained twelve hundred and thirteen entries written over twelve and a half years. The prose, set down in tight handwriting with the occasional looping l, was rambling and witty, or just rambling. Reading it felt like wandering about the cluttered mind of a sad yet curious old man. Entry by entry, though, Jan grew more engrossed by Marcus Marvellous Marte and his circuitous musings from the fabled era of the Pioneers, when he alone had permission to write down egotistical, even subversive thoughts. He also found himself envious of his ancestor Cecilia Oort for her chummy lunches with the author. Over several late-night sessions, he consumed the journal's every word.

In a Year-12 entry, Jan discovered a secret that Cecilia, evidently, had never shared: that Marcus was Lavender's father by way of frozen sperm, used posthumously. This revelation, delivered through a hibernating journal that easily could have been consigned to the Loop, and in the peculiar voice of a long-dead man, shocked Jan a little bit. But he was pleased, too. He was the history teacher's great-grandson. That felt right.

A Year-0 entry, in particular, stuck with Jan. Marcus notices Cecilia and her child, Janelle, as they stare at Jupiter – 'juggernaut of electromagnetic exhalation' – through the Viewing Portal. Marcus writes that 'plasmatic lassos' are 'slurping helium-3 and hydrogen isotopes' from the planet's atmosphere to fuel the fusion drive for its imminent acceleration to .12 light speed.

However, Jan knew, that wasn't the full story. Only one-third of the deuterium had been used to make cruising speed. Another third was budgeted for powering internal ship operations during the three-hundred-and-sixty-year flight, and the final third was kept in reserve for the decades-long braking manoeuvre in which Shipworld would flip about and fire engines to slow its approach to HD-40307g.

A bad move, certainly, to come that far and shoot on past.

Such was the Mission: set into dogma, unquestioned. But given their present doldrums, the result of unforeseen and traumatic historical events, did the deuterium have to be apportioned that way? There was a turn of phrase that Marcus liked to use. Repeatedly, the Chronicler shunted aside difficult decisions, as well as painful feelings, by urging himself to 'kick that can down the road'. Jan imagined a black boot sending a tin receptacle down a strip of asphalt on Earthworld, the moon hanging in the polluted sky. It occurred to him that his era's energy problem was the proverbial can that needed kicking down the cosmic road.

The deuterium set aside for braking – use it now! Jan, sitting alone on his bed, journal pages scattered on the covers and the floor, felt an urge to run outside and proclaim, 'Use the deuterium!' But he stayed put. Use the deuterium to bring up the lights, warm up the ship, and let people flower again. Intensify science education, encourage creativity. Fire up the research labs with the ambitious goal of enhancing the subatomic scoops' ability to collect hydrogen from deep space and, consequently, build a new supply of deuterium for the final Mission phase. In short, stop grovelling in the shadows. Take a chance on the future, on the genius of future generations.

Risk everything.

Jan's next thought: This won't be an easy sell. On Earthworld, before the collapse, defenders of the status quo asserted that the next generation's technological wizards would figure out how to remove CO_2 from the atmosphere. Relax already, they said. No need to stop burning. Alas, the promised techno-fixes didn't deliver. Advancements in carbon capture, as well as fusion energy, occurred slowly over decades, and the technologies were underwhelming and never adopted at sufficient scale. Various economic, engineering and political factors explained why not, *blah, blah, blah*. In short, the capitalist growth imperative prevailed. Earthworld's response to climate change and other existential threats (AI, killer bugs, etc) was always too little, too expensive, too late.

The Council would probably charge Jan with technological fantasy-making. He'd argue that it was a fantasy to consider the current situation sustainable. And it would be harder, still, to counter the legacy of his Uncle Brenz, the revolutionary who bucked dogma and ushered in civil war. (Franika, of course, was never to blame. Praise Franika.) *That's what happened*, they'd say, the last time someone challenged the Mission established by the Founding Pioneers. Do you really want to plunge us into discord and chaos again? And what if your gamble fails and we can't slow down for planetfall – would you have us sailing forever through the void?

Jan, however, was no Brenz. Not in a million years could he float on high to distribute Sixteen Theses or connive to redirect the path of Shipworld. He was a boring, plodding fellow and knew it; in fact, Jan preferred himself that way. He liked mulling over problems, the more depressing the better. He liked taking small, incremental steps. Talking to people. Maybe those tendencies were his superpowers. Now he looked through a black-skied window in the bedroom floor, as a star slowly transited from one side to the other. Besides, in times of scarcity, charismatic gestures could make shipworldmates more anxious. Everyone just needed to be nudged towards a new way of thinking. They might not even notice.

Jan laughed at his chutzpah. Then made a plan. Step by step, he constructed an edifice of persuasion, an idiosyncratic device for moving reluctant minds, one that in time acquired a reality almost as tangible as the new *phligsparrfner* sites, as the blocks hewed from the ficus tree.

Step one.

He took a few weeks to type *The Chronicler's Journal* into a digital document – what a tangled testimony, his hands ached! – and published it to a community billboard, where it was downloaded promiscuously. The ice children were especially taken with the journal and began holding dramatic readings at their *phligsparrfnerim*. Those readings soon became electric events, attended by ice children and flesh-born alike. One person read aloud, while gently bouncing actors portrayed Marcus Marvellous Marte, Cecilia Oort, wild daughter Janelle, handsome Denis the bridge officer and Wyatt of the Loop, not to mention enigmatic Earthworld characters such as Thaddeus Parsons, the beloved and tragic Zayit, Ambassador John Gavin and Swiss bombshell Lilo Pulver, the temptress who co-starred in the World War II epic-romance *A Time to Love, A Time to Die.*

With every download of the journal, and with its every dynamic performance at the *phligsparrfnerim*, another shipworldmate or two began, as Jan had put it, to think about the way things are and the way things used to be.

Step two.

Jan met with his mother in her cramped quarters by the bridge. Chive didn't offer him a hug or a beverage, or anything but a frown, signs that she was still steamed about the theft of *The Chronicler's Journal*. She listened, however, as he rephrased the remark that he'd made about Franika in the potato patch. Can Shipworld change, as long as Franika lives? No, she replied without hesitation, she didn't think so. Franika had believed in sticking to Mission parameters, holding them in reverence. Asking people to alter a basic tenet of the flight plan was asking them to oppose Franika, to violate the Saviour, always above us and ever visible with just a tilt of the head.

Jan glanced at the room's ceiling, in the direction of the central point where Franika floated. When he looked back down, he noticed five irregular polyhedrons stacked just so on a table – an improbable tower with the topmost block, the largest, set at an angle and ready, at any moment, to slip off and crash.

'Did you glue it together?' asked Jan, pointing at the tower.

'No,' said Chive, sharply. 'Where would I get glue?'

'I just thought—'

'I do it every morning. It's never the same, at least I don't think so.'

'How long does it take?'

She gave him that look; that quizzical, my-persistent-boy look.

'Well,' said Chive, 'sometimes it happens right away. Other times, ten minutes or so.' She walked to the block tower and reached out, almost touching it, but not. 'I look forward to it, it relaxes me. One day I couldn't do it at all, so I went back to bed.'

She blew on her creation, gently, and it toppled, the polyhedrons clattering across the glass tabletop. Piece by piece, she gathered the five blocks into a pile, a jumble, a ruin, then turned to Jan and produced a smile that on anyone other than Chive would have been taken for a smirk. A gift, of sorts, from mother to son. Jan smiled, more a grimace, in return. 'I've been thinking about the way things are,' he said, 'and the way things might become,' and he described the looming dangers of this Dark Age, spoke with feeling about their deadly, dull sojourn betwixt and between depression and disaster. *Rmmm, rmmm* – the alarm he'd set on his forearm panel vibrated, reminding him not to push too hard. So, briefly, he told her his plan to fix things. Then he thanked his mother, and she gave him a quick kiss on the cheek as he departed the room.

Step three.

Jan invited Tender Beatrice for a perpetual-twilight walk around Shipworld's circumference. He sketched out the energy dilemma, as well as his proposal.

'In twelve years or so, I'll be dead,' Beatrice responded, as if to say it was no longer her place to intervene, or even have an opinion about the future. They stopped in the very spot, next to an abandoned algae-mixing tank, where she'd stood when Brenz tossed his Sixteen Theses to crowds clamouring above and below. She turned her head, scanning, the ever-vigilant Lighthouse Beatrice. 'Praise Franika,' she said, without conviction, and Jan realised that she'd been counting the years, twelve short years, that she had left to make a difference. Within days, Beatrice pledged to assist Jan as liaison to older folks.

Step four.

Jan visited Karlsen. As in his dream, he found himself at the man's door, number thirty-five, knocking. No answer. He pushed and the door opened, revealing Karlsen across the room holding his robo-bird, the house finch, in his palm. Jan began pinching himself, *ouch*, and this time the bird flapped its wings, hopped a bit and went nowhere. 'You're awake,' said Karlsen, who knew of the dream, and they sat down for a long talk about enlisting the support of the ice children. They weren't oblivious, insisted Karlsen, just unburdened by the expectations of Pioneer forebears. In fact, they were very inclined to accept changes, even risky ones, that would enliven Shipworld.

One by one, the steps blurred together into an ungainly staircase. Later that week, Jan and his mother met with Ynar, who they suspected might refuse to even listen. Instead, Chive wound up holding Ynar as she described the gaunt, ageing body, the crow's feet spreading from the corner of the closed eyes, the subtle sufferings of Franika. 'She barely breathes,' Ynar told them, wiping away a stream of tears. 'I hold my ear close to her lips, to her nose, and it's like the most faraway wind, you know, and I'm not sure if it's actually happening or if I'm remembering or imagining it...'

'You're a Keeper,' said Jan. He awkwardly patted her head.

'What am I keeping?' she asked, angrily. 'I've pulled up her eyelids! The future doesn't shine in her eyes. Nothing does!' Ynar disengaged from Chive; she wrapped herself in her own arms and remained motionless while her visitors left. In the doorway, Jan looked back and Ynar seemed to be mouthing silent words to someone who wasn't there.

Meanwhile, Karlsen lobbied the ice children to support breaking into the deuterium reserves. Chive got Jan's father to talk to his farming colleagues; he likened his boy's plan to a bold bet on the outcome of a planting. Bumper crop, you win; low yield, you lose; and it's more of the sorry same-old if you don't play. Other alliances were formed, including with the Bridgers and Loopers and fans of the five-stones game. The latter group, forever striving to craft beautiful, utopian towers, the more unlikely the better, were especially attuned to the permutations of possibility and, therefore, open to persuasion. Months of meetings followed. Many opened with Jan declaring, 'I've been thinking about the way things are.' Most were boring. Debates ensued, the pros and cons shuffled and reshuffled. Reports were written, circulated, reviewed and revised. Surveys were taken, dissected and spun one way or the other. Jan's Plan, his radically sensible plan, became a normal thing to discuss.

He rarely stopped. One early morning, for instance, Jan gawkily achieved the *trikonasana* pose while speaking to a yoga class; made a five-minute presentation to Loop workers getting off the night shift; waylaid a bridge officer who supported Jan's Plan, she said, even though it was a crazy long shot; listened to a prayer-and-pastry group discuss the relative merits of a sin of omission (choosing not to restore impoverished Shipworld) versus a sin of commission (a failed restoration leading to a lost Mission); and answered questions from nine sceptics while trying to eat breakfast in the Mess Hall.

Slowly, Jan sensed an appetite for risk emerging – not out loud, but beneath the surface – and a resolute feeling that the time for walking with heads down had passed. That a weakened Shipworld might collapse with the next bout of bad luck or popular revolt. 'Use It or Lose It', a first try for a slogan about the deuterium reserves, flopped. 'Take a Chance on Tomorrow' brewed as much anxiety as inspiration. But Marcus Marte's call to 'Kick the Can', in this case to let the next generation be heroes, took off. Kick it, people liked to say to Jan as he moved about ceaselessly. Kick it down the road.

Then, one day in Year 196, the Keeper let go.

Ynar increased Franika's potassium intake, turning a little white dial that altered the flow of the chemical, number nineteen on the periodic table of elements, along a line feeding into her shoulder access portal. This minor adjustment allowed the Saviour to slip away in a matter of hours. The skin cooled. The lungs and heart stilled. The eyes stayed closed but the wrinkles at their corners, the crow's feet, faded as the waters of the body settled in death. The mouth, which had said nothing for seven decades, fell open slightly, and Ynar combed her grey hair for the last time, forty strokes, each stroke from skull to tip.

More than a few people commented that nothing changed when her web was unknotted, her body brought down. The darkness neither deepened nor lessened in her absence. There was something anticlimactic about her death, Jan believed, perhaps because people realised that worshipping Franika had been a lot like mourning for her, and for themselves, bit by bit over time. Nonetheless, it took a while for passers-by on Pictor Boulevard to stop glancing up into the navel of Shipworld, to stop watching Franika.

Ynar, overwhelmed, admitted her act to the Council. They chose not to censure her, and a few councillors even openly thanked her for doing a difficult and necessary thing. On the next Launch Day, a small percentage of Franika's cremated remains (most of the body had been Looped) were interred beneath the Olmec Head. The Keepers shared in digging a hole and pouring in the ashes. A couple of Karlsen's birds chirped, metallic and sad, as Ynar covered the ashes with dirt and smoothed the surface with the palm of her hand. Then she straightened up and everyone chanted 'Praise Franika' three times, a resounding shout. Those words were rarely spoken again.

Before long, a referendum to either approve or reject Jan's Plan was put before voters (anyone thirteen or older) and it passed by a wide margin. Almost immediately the lights went up, the chill vanished and the Loop resumed full operation.

By Year 198, the Tube was rebuilt. Resources devoted to science education were doubled, then tripled, and Shipworld built itself a sprawling research lab dedicated solely to deep-space deuterium harvesting, to the proposition that invisible treasure lurks even in the emptiest corners. Karlsen served as a lead scientist in that lab, and at home he continued his robo-bird research, developing lighter and more responsive wings with an ultra-thin metal/bamboo composite. As for Jan, he lent his computer expertise here and there. He made encouraging statements, where needed, and shipworldmates roundly praised him for his persistent campaign – some even compared him to Franika – but he found the attention embarrassing. He stood atop his edifice of persuasion, on the highest step, alone and exposed in a self-constructed prison of expectations. Now that his bold, all-or-nothing proposition had been converted into an actual, ongoing reality, an irrefutable fact of public life, he became consumed with worry that he had overstepped and acted arrogantly, that the praise would turn into condemnation if the deuterium goal was not achieved. That he would be vilified and strung up, the source of the worst bet ever taken.

✦

Short-stemmed, with broad, curving caps and gently serrated gills, the oyster mushrooms that she'd collected lay in the tray like an assortment of frilly fans, in shades of tan, brown, pink and white. Oysters were Ynar's favourites. More prolific than shimejis or portobellos, they tasted delicious in stir fries, all nutty and chewy, and were high in vitamins and antioxidants. She also knew that she thought too much about mushrooms and spent too much time in the inoculation and fruiting chambers of Mushroom House #6. Stay busy, she'd told herself, when her duties as Keeper had ended, when she'd sent her molasses robes to the Loop to become, what, this tray in her hand, or that gauze-filtering wrap, or her scissors for clipping mushrooms after they budded through the holes in buckets.

It wasn't awful. Ynar's life hadn't reverted to its miserable state before the Dark Age, but she wasn't happy either. Her purpose, as Keeper, was gone. So, mushrooms. But it was more than that. She missed Franika; she missed Franika's body, to be brutally honest – her Looped body which now could be in the tray, the gauze, the clippers. She missed riding up the rope to the low-grav heart of the world, where she took care of the Saviour's body, day after day, ritualistically monitoring life signs, combing the delicate hair and cleaning the skin in the wraparound gloom. Saying the prayer, for everyone. And for herself.

At shift's end, she emerged from the humid mushroom house. There, waiting for her, was Chive. Hands on her slim hips. Head tilted, with a smirky expression.

'Why do you always look surprised?' she asked Ynar.

'What do you mean?'

'You know what I mean. Let's go, *friend*, it's time for dinner.' She turned and walked away. Ynar ran to catch up.

'I smell like mushrooms.'

'You always smell like mushrooms.'

'You don't like them.'

'Shut up,' said Chive. She said those two words with such bite and such love that Ynar almost broke into tears as they walked to the Mess Hall, but she didn't because Chive wouldn't like that at all. It was so good to have a friend, a real one.

In the evenings, Ynar read *The Chronicler's Journal*, all four thousand three hundred and forty-seven pages, and when she woke at night to pee she thought about Janelle, the manic toddler, smashing her spoon into the hard-packed soil, not digging to China because that was stupid, no, she was digging, digging her way out...and in the mornings, before another day of mushrooms, Ynar wondered about all the things in *The Chronicler's Journal* that had been left out, that Marcus Marvellous Marte had never seen and never guessed about because he was just one soul among hundreds, as biased and limited as the next person. But, oh, how he'd loved his dead wife back on dead Earthworld. Ynar pondered, among many possibilities, whether she was suffering from a creeping case of *solastalgia*, like the woman in Cecilia's trauma therapy group, with the neat twist that her home had improved, disastrously, around her.

One late afternoon, Ynar emerged from her dank workplace, after harvesting a few hundred oyster mushrooms, and spoke before Chive could say anything. She almost confronted her.

'Do you remember,' she said, 'when I asked what happened to your brother?'

Chive replied: 'Yeah, that was years ago – are you OK?'

'No, but I've got an idea,' said Ynar, and that night over dinner she convinced her friend to join her in writing an adventure story about Brenz and his revolutionary followers after they went into exile. Over the next several months, the women huddled together in the evenings. They threw out endless ideas and laughed about crazy, improbable Shipworld and cried a few times in each other's arms. They tried, for Ynar was a sensitive soul, not to argue too much, although Chive did kick a chair when Ynar questioned her frequent use of the words *incubate* and *bombard*. They wrote draft after draft, each one an imaginative history that *could* have happened, that almost certainly did not happen, and that in some mischievous way seemed as true as what actually may have happened. They had a great time churning out *The Rogue Adventures of Brenz Oort-St George*, which was posted in its entirety to a new network of reading terminals and soon became almost as popular as *The Chronicler's Journal*.

Bearing down on the icy rogue, debate broke out among the crew. What should they call their destination? Names were floated, of mothers and sisters and great aunts, including Cecilia, Lavender and Janelle. Finally, they chose a name, Penelope, just because it was beautiful. And with each passing minute of approach, Penelope further revealed her scarred and frozen landscape, crosshatched and pitted with domes, ridges and bands.

Meanwhile, Brenz struggled to exile thoughts of Franika – ah, lovely Franika, impossible Franika! – as he reviewed magnetometer and radar readings that indicated a salty ocean below the miles-thick surface. An ocean of immense size, far vaster than Earthworld's seas. An ocean that could conceivably incubate life! Of what kind and temperament one could only speculate. The planet's surface, however, appeared extremely inhospitable: beyond cold, bombarded with cosmic radiation, with an atmosphere too thin for a mouse.

Nonetheless, not one of his twelve brave crewmates objected as Brenz piloted the ship into orbit around Penelope. And so began the search for a landing place, possibly near an outgassing vent. Franika, if only, Franika… The rebel Brenz Oort-St George steeled himself again, wondering if the hypothetical life forms below the ice had perceived their presence. Let's hope so, he muttered aloud. On desolate Penelope, the only way to make contact would be to offer themselves, humbly, as the objects of discovery.

For months, the ice children performed scenes from *The Rogue Adventures of Brenz Oort-St George* at the *phligsparrfnerim*. Brenz's death, featuring his epic speech about human rights and the pain of love, brought people of every age and height to tears. Few objected when the name of the street he grew up on was changed to Brenz Way.

As she died, strangely enough, Franika's mind had undergone a last-gasp renaissance, and during that brief, biochemical effusion she weaved the strands of a similar tale. In her version, she didn't stay behind. In her version, she joined her lover Brenz and his compatriots in the landing vehicle, the *Thomas Jefferson*, as they escaped Shipworld and chased down the mysterious planet. In the world she created from the tended vestiges of her self, a world so vivid that it bloomed like a supernova before the very end, an icy stairway opened up on the pitch-black surface of the rogue. The stairway glimmered with golden light, and she held Brenz's trembling hand as they descended.

4

Years 250–252: Out of the Black

First one, then another, then a flurrying flock of sparrows descended on the hanging feeder. At any one time, six or seven birds fit on the posts protruding from the device. The average feeding stay lasted about nine seconds, observed Karlsen, before another bird butted in. Rousted birds retreated to a nearby bamboo fence, where they shuffled their wings and waited for the next chance to dive at the prize. Average time on the fence, he calculated: twenty-two seconds. Some birds barely paused, then went back in. Others hung out, biding their time. This behaviour variance didn't correspond with size. Maybe with age – young ones rushing into the fray, heedless – but that didn't make sense, not with robo-birds.

Karlsen couldn't get enough of watching his birds. Looking for patterns in the chaos. They'd keep scrabbling until they were full or he turned off the flow. Last week, however, a couple of rose-breasted grosbeaks, real beauties, returned to the feeder after he'd shut it down. Pecked away at the portals, as if to reverse cause and effect: eat, get food. As if to manipulate him, their creator, into turning the energy back on. No, impossible. That kind of learning he couldn't programme. It must be a delayed response, an echo, a glitch.

The cacophony around the feeder pulsated, its intensity ebbing and flowing. This flock, Karlsen speculated, could be searching for the most workable balance between cooperation and competition. Good luck with that – see human history, failure of civilisations. See Shipworld history, the recent eras of rebellion, retrenchment and revival.

Individual birds, he also observed, fed with the same gusto regardless of energy status. Near empty at one per cent, near full at ninety-nine per cent, it didn't matter. The birds went for it. Perhaps he should moderate this behaviour according to hunger levels. That would make for more orderly feeding – maybe. Back on Earthworld, he'd learned, people often fed beyond satiation for complicated psychological and sociological reasons; some fasted, a physical or spiritual purging; and others were allowed to die of hunger.

Thank the stars that Shipworld had achieved energy abundance, especially for his robotic birds. About two hundred or so by now, slurping electrons all day long. Once, when the electro-feeders went down temporarily, a gang of ravenous grackles rooted out live wires behind bulkheads, inside light fixtures and within toys.

Energy abundance, alas, had come too late for his good friend Jan Oort-Ruiz, who had a running nervous breakdown during the decades in which the hydrogen-collection programme faltered badly. Criticism of the 'energy gamble' or, more bluntly, 'Jan's gamble', ate at him, and he'd remark to Karlsen, offhand, 'I've been thinking about the way things are', and then trail off, his insights left unsaid, soured in his mouth. The once-beautiful duality of Shipworld became for him a stark either/or state, success or failure, and Karlsen's attempts to reason with him, to provide comfort, were to no avail. Jan married, had a son, divorced – uncommon in a society where stability was prized – and took cooking, yoga and meditation classes. Nothing helped. The criticism remained – grew, in Jan's mind, metastasised – and one day in his sixty-third year he expired alone in his bed, despite the Correction. Systemic stress was listed as the cause of death, a euphemism, some guessed, for suicide. At the memorial service, in black from head to toe, Karlsen eulogised Jan's 'curious, ever-seeking half-life' and declared him 'the tallest person I've ever known'.

Just a few years later, Jan's gamble paid off. A teenage girl named Svonne – born from an iron womb in Year 207, utterly unaware of her genius – created a quantum filter so stealthy, so clever in negotiating space-time that it could harvest baby handfuls of the dark-matter sterile neutrinos raining through the universe. Karlsen worked on the team that enhanced the fusion engines with those lassoed neutrinos and now, bizarrely, ample energy was available, more than enough for basic and extravagant needs.

Hence the free rein given to the robotic birds that roamed the interior sky. Hence the boosted speed, to 12.5 per cent of the speed of light, which, without degrading deflector power, regained the time lost to the Brenzian divergence and put Shipworld back on track to making HD-40307g in three hundred and sixty years. Hence the end of water rationing, as water production facilities stoked up again. Hence a new turbo-*phligsparrfner* propelling jumpers into zero-gravity. And hence the construction of a laser weapon for defence against a perceived threat.

'Stupid laser,' snapped Karlsen, as he terminated the feed. The sparrows quickly assessed the changed situation, then formed a bird tornado and whooshed away, making a couple of loops around the Tube just, it seemed, for the heck of it.

Indeed, the days of scarcity and gloom, of humble reverence for survival, were long gone, a bad memory of a bygone era. However, many older shipworldmates continued their frugal ways, keeping lights low, counting water drops and aggregating food crumbs. Karlsen, unapologetically, was among these fossils, while some young people gorged on excess energy stores by taking long, hot showers and playing light-tag after midnight. These dualling behaviours, detected by a system of lymph node-like sensors, had moderated over time. A comfortable sustainability reigned. Despite his personal frugality, Karlsen was pleased that resources were generously available for recreation, creativity and self-expression – a delayed and partial triumph of Brenzianism, though no one called it that.

It disturbed him, though, that Shipworld was becoming a divided society, with flesh-born raising families headed by parents while orphans favoured gestation in iron wombs followed by communal child-rearing, primarily in the Orphans' House. (The word 'orphan', having lost its association with grief and abandonment, was embraced as an identifier; concurrently, the term 'ice child' melted away – only the first batch of embryos, after all, had been frozen.) Orphans and flesh-born tended not to socialise outside of work and generally ate at separate tables in the Mess Hall; such habits, worried Karlsen, reduced the potential for tall/short friendships. The groups also rarely intermarried, a trend that diminished long-term genetic variability. Nonetheless, flesh-born and orphans coexisted at arm's length, an arrangement marred by glib remarks about 'dull flesh-born' and 'wild orphans', as well as the occasional dispute over the caloric requirements of taller folk. Overall, they knew they needed each other, and devotion to the Mission was shared by nearly all.

Trouble, however, found another way. It started in Year 248 when the Astronomy section observed a bright, moving object on the flightpath to HD-40307g, twenty million kilometres out and approaching Shipworld straight on. Spectrographic analysis indicated that Object X moved in a straight line and at a speed similar to Shipworld's. A mirror image, almost, though roughly two or three times larger.

What could it be? A rogue planet, lit from within? An asteroid refusing to arc?

Karlsen, sitting on the bench, staring at the birdless feeder, remembered the day that Object X zigged a full three degrees off course, creating a shockwave of questions and speculation. This sudden diversion, cosmologists insisted, had two possible explanations. One, it moved because it collided with another heavenly body. Two, it was a constructed object, self-propelled by engine or light sail, which altered its course on purpose. (A third possibility, that it was a spacefaring animal, was favoured by children but generally dismissed due to its high velocity. A few folks whispered that the descendants of Brenz were returning and not, Karlsen thought, entirely in jest.) Day and night, shipworldmates discussed the scientific and philosophical ramifications of Object X as alien artefact, probe or ship. Imagine, even, an intergenerational spacecraft from HD-40307g en route for the 'greener pastures' of Earthworld, of all places!

Naysayers dismissed such scenarios. Collisions happen all the time, they insisted, it's an intergalactic pinball machine out there. Karlsen had been informed just this morning that the protoplanet Theia slammed into Earthworld four or five billion years ago, as if that should be a comfort. Fantasists, meanwhile, concocted tales of first contact for that fleeting moment when the crafts slipped by each other like superfast trains passing in the night. Maybe they could exchange greetings, or gifts, at .125 light speed, which actually was .25 LS when you combined the opposing speeds.

Weeks after the initial zig, Object X zagged – right back on course towards Shipworld. A second collision, exactly correcting the first? That, Karlsen knew, was nearly impossible. An asteroid or planet, not to mention star or solar system or galaxy, doesn't swerve one way and then another, or stop to look around. You've got to have a mind – of some inscrutable kind – to pull that off. Now the naysayers accepted the reality of an oncoming ship or probe driven by sentient actors and, with barely a pause, asserted that it could be a threat. In fact, it must be considered a threat, just in case. After a brief debate, the Council approved the 'repurposing of resources' to make a 'defensive-repulsive weapon'. Specifically, a directed-energy device that fired twin beams for distances up to ten kilometres.

'Stupid laser,' repeated Karlsen. He stood up from the bench, one-hundred-and-seven-years old, grimacing as he stretched his sore, well, everything. His neck and hips and knees, and so on, had been hurting for a dozen years now, a constant reminder that the Correction didn't work as well on orphans – a truth not fully realised until the second round of one hundred and ten orphans were born. Karlsen had mixed feelings about the Correction, believing in some quasi-religious corner of his psyche that it was a dicey move to alter the ageing process so dramatically and, therefore, rejig a person's fate. Given that, he couldn't really complain. Here's some of that good old-fashioned ageing – just what you wanted, right?

He stepped away, gingerly, using a three-pronged orthopaedic cane. *Fee-dee, fee-dee, fee-dee!* A black-capped chickadee, programmed to perch on the old man's shoulder whenever he began walking, sang out *fee-dee* as it came in for a brusque but friendly landing. Karlsen had resisted the urge to name the bird, not wanting to further compromise its wildness. This chickadee friend was his favourite, with its white bib, rusty brown flanks and snazzy black-and-white striped wings. Up close it looked a bit mechanical, the rivets showing, a certain lack of disarray in the feathers, but from a distance you'd think it was the real thing.

Using fragmentary computer records, Karlsen had tried to capture the shapes and sizes of Earthworld birds. His robo-birds even mimicked behaviours, such as the way mourning doves rested so serenely, so humbly, except for the bobbing of their little heads. Or the way blue jays stomped about like bully boys, more squawk than bite. Regarding colour, though, he took liberties. For instance, the American robin hopped about with a purple belly. Tufted titmice, grey/blue before their extinction, were reborn bright green. And they knew it, clustering in kale gardens and other tangles of greenery.

Now Karlsen, wincing from pain, stopped in his tracks. Accordingly, three seconds later, the chickadee, *fee-dee, fee-dee*, raced off to rejoin its mates in a stand of corn not far from where three children huddled, playing knucklebones.

The rubber ball bounced; hands flew, scooping spiky stones. 'Moons over Mars!' one of them called. 'Rings around Saturn!' exclaimed another, and that person, Karlsen spotted, wasn't a child at all. Svonne unbent herself, standing nearly two metres tall; her thinness concerned Karlsen, as usual. He waved to her, called out. She waved back, returned the ball to a little boy and walked blank-faced towards the old man, immersed, he thought, in her eccentric Svonne cloud. Her hair seemed longer than ever, a black waterfall covering her spine to the coccyx, with a rivulet of purple derived from blueberry juice. They walked together, Svonne matching his pace, and, once more, the chickadee landed on the elder's shoulder, *fee-dee!*

'What's its range?' she asked.

'Everywhere,' he said.

'So, if you're walking around inside—'

'It pecks at the door until I open it.'

Svonne laughed, slipped her elbow into his.

'Are you going to Launch Day?' he asked her. The annual celebration of Shipworld's departure, two hundred and fifty years ago, was coming up in a few weeks. For the semiquincentennial, an Equilibrium tournament – well, more of an exhibition, carried out by young people who'd been researching the game – would be held for the first time in over a century.

'I guess I am,' she said. 'It's a date.'

They kept strolling along. Karlsen thought of Marcus Marte walking with brilliant young Cecilia in *The Chronicler's Journal*.

'I've been meaning to ask you,' he said. 'What do you think about this laser?'

'I don't know,' she replied. 'Why didn't we have it from the start?'

Karlsen had spent so much mental energy opposing the laser – unnecessary, adversarial, counter to the very spirit of the Mission! – that he'd never wondered about its absence. It was just like Svonne to challenge his perspective. 'Well,' he said, 'the Constitutional Convention banned personal weapons of any kind. I guess the Pioneers didn't think beyond that. They had no evidence of aliens – and neither do we, even with the zigzag.'

'The zigzag is hard to explain,' she said, with a trace element of irritation.

'Lots of things are,' he added. 'I often wonder about the incredible number of events that had to occur *just so* for life to arise back on the old rock.'

'A one-in-a-billion shot. Like my filter.'

'Jan knew someone would do it,' Karlsen told her. 'Someone like you.' They stopped at the door to his room and one, two, three, the chickadee flapped its wings and departed. On every other day in which they'd strolled and chatted, Svonne had said goodbye here. But not today, for reasons that couldn't, like many things, be explained. She watched Karlsen enter the lock code on his door, incorrectly. She waited patiently as he tried the code again and again. Only when the door opened on the fourth attempt did she speak: 'Why do you live alone? I've been meaning to ask.'

He sighed. 'What do people say?'

'That you're doing research.' He waited for her to elaborate. 'You're obsessive-compulsive-fanatical. An orphan anomaly.'

‘Anomaly, oddity,’ said Karlsen, ‘misfit, freak. Come in for a snack.’

They stepped inside his messy home. Svonne was a bit shocked at the state of it and picked a few shirts off the floor as Karlsen prepared a tray with crackers and cups of rhubarb-flavoured water. They settled at a workstation scattered with yellow bird beaks, short and sharp. ‘The little ones are hardest,’ he said, sweeping the beaks aside. Several feet away, a robo-bird was fixed to a rack, its sub-processor AI unit dangling like a loose intestine.

‘What’s that?’

‘A northern gannet – my first aquatic bird. Very aggressive. It plunge-dives for fish.’

‘Fish? There’s no fish,’ said Svonne, her retort met with a grandfatherly glance to another workstation where a semi-scaled, robotic fish gaped between calipers. ‘Wow, but can you really…’ and Svonne stopped herself. Just beyond the fish, she noticed a painting hung on the bathroom door. ‘Karlsen! Is that the Dürer? From *The Chronicler’s Journal*?’

He nodded, casually, no big deal. Under questioning, Karlsen explained how back in the dark times when he was young, as young as Svonne, just imagine, he’d rescued the discarded painting from a heap in the abandoned swimming pool. At the time he knew nothing about the painting’s status as an Earthworld icon of individualism. He simply liked it; Dürer’s eyes had a haunting effect, much as they did for Marcus Marte, but for a different reason. Marte had judged the self-portrait as captivating but vain. Karlsen saw the man as a sympathetic soul at peace with himself. On that score, he was envious.

Svonne got close to the painting. She stared into Dürer’s green eyes – or were they hazel? The artist seemed not so much at peace as very determined, very focused. Then she turned to her friend. ‘You live alone because you like the quiet.’

Karlsen smiled. He appreciated the insightful remark, as well as the patient manner she adopted for him, but didn't say so. After he died of heart failure several days later, Svonne re-entered the room and found the ancient painting still hung on the bathroom door. She wanted to take it with her but knew that she couldn't guarantee its safety inside the tumultuous Orphans' House. And what of Karlsen's unfinished projects, the gannet and his fish-prey? What of his bird flocks, who'd watch over them? Svonne stood there for a long time, soaking up the quiet that he'd cherished, trying to understand what hurt it had soothed. Maybe none at all; maybe his solitary nature was caused by a genetic mutation, a quirk in his iron womb, a stray neutrino.

And she wondered why, exactly, were the little beaks hardest?

So quiet, here, so still. The meteor shower of voices in the Orphans' House melded, at best, into background fuzz that only mimicked silence. But within this dead man's room, she could actually hear herself think. Feel the brain chemicals flowing, almost. The room's disorder now seemed homey, as if she had caused the mess. Is it, she wondered, time for some changes? Svonne knew that she was considered a highly gifted individual. Once, a child had called her the smartest person in the world – not such a big deal in a world of 600! And besides, she hadn't discovered a thing since the neutrino filter – a fluke, maybe? – at age seventeen. Yes, closer to fluke than design; it wasn't as if she'd made a series of bold decisions after years of hard work. She'd felt no pressure regarding the perilous energy shortage, a bright kid who'd been given the end of a lab bench, a left-over space no longer than her wingspan, and there, as she played with the elegant, paradoxical dynamics of the universe, as she brought an improvisational perfectionism to bear, it came to her, the central insight regarding the counterintuitive nature of quantum filtering: one must gather everything and nothing at the same time. It just showed up.

Since then, Svonne had broadened her cosmological knowledge, tinkering with esoteric space-time theories that supported alternative visions of creation such as the Oscillating Model of the Universe in which the Big Bang led to the Big Crunch led to another Big Bang *ad infinitum* – all the while deflecting constant praise that made her feel proud and lousy at the same time. Now more than a third of her life was gone. Perhaps she was the orphan anomaly, oddity, misfit, freak; perhaps she'd simply peaked as a teen, *boom* goes the supernova, and the rest of her life was ejecta speeding out from that moment; perhaps she was just coasting along.

Suddenly, she felt very unsure. What was it Karlsen had said, lots of things are hard to explain? Svonne departed the room. Outside, not six steps from the door, the chickadee landed on her shoulder, nearly scaring the life out of her! The bird's talons clamped onto her shirt, ever so gently bruising her skin, and she laughed out loud. Then she stopped; one, two, three, and it flew away. She resumed walking and like a feathery missile the chickadee sought her out again, landed hard, and this time the talons pricked deeply and Svonne laughed even louder, a bit like a madwoman, attracting stares from a roving pod of youngsters.

Later that day she arranged to move into Karlsen's room, at least for a while. She brought all her worldly goods in a small satchel, plus a string sack with five ficus blocks.

✦

Object X didn't zig or zag again. It came right at them. Further analysis found no signs of outgassing to indicate propulsion. It was also highly reflective, a strange quality for something so isolated in space. In the bowels of the computer, a file was found about an unidentified, cigar-shaped object that had passed through the sol system in the early twenty-first century, dubbed Oumuamua, meaning 'first distant messenger' in the Hawaiian language. The shape and speed of the visitor now barging into their lives seemed eerily similar. At their present speeds, Shipworld and Object X were scheduled to converge in twelve days.

The Council convened, with scores of shipworldmates in attendance. Svonne sat in the back and watched Councillor Zennero, a flesh-born man entering his frail years, as he stood from his chair on the low stage. Just getting up to speak, it looked so painful. Behind him loomed lab buildings converted from the old mushroom houses where he'd toiled as a young man. 'Fire up the engines,' Zennero said. Turn away from the problem, the phenomenon, whatever you want to call it. He'd spent his first six decades in brooding years of poverty and could fathom no good reason to risk their current prosperity, to play some deranged game of chicken with this stalker, this *thing*. 'Don't go looking for trouble,' he warned.

Good point, thought Svonne, who then instinctively disputed it; maybe it's better to look for trouble than let trouble find you. Councillor Bartholomew was talking now. A dentist, and one of three orphans on the Council, she proposed that there was nothing to fear if you really thought about it. Even if their new neighbour harboured exotic aliens or some fancy AI probe that could read their minds, it would surely rush past in a blur. And suppose it had the power to stop and reverse course, to confront them, well, such a craft would be almost magic, advanced well beyond the known laws of physics. Dodging about would be a pretty useless tactic, in that case.

Bartholomew suggested, instead, that Shipworld prepare a communications packet to send forward during the remaining days before contact. The packet could transmit welcoming information about the Mission and everyday life onboard. Perhaps Object X would respond in kind, and who knows what valuable data that might bring? Svonne immediately liked this approach that framed the looming event as a scientific opportunity, and then she focused on Zennero's frowning face and imagined him dismissing scientists as hopelessly naïve, which was true sometimes. There were no easy answers, and while Svonne considered the pros and cons, assigning them relative weights and extrapolating short- and long-range consequences, intense debate broke out among the Council and shipworldmates in the crowd. Eventually, a vote was taken and the Bartholomew proposal was approved.

Then they thrashed out the laser. Several people questioned the wisdom of training a weapon on the visitor. Others called that view simple-minded and invoked Earthworld's bloody history. It was safest to assume, according to this argument, that cultures on other planets were equally cruel, or amoral, or careless. In fact, Object X could be a long-range weapon programmed decades ago to destroy Shipworld after it zigzagged during the Brenzian Revolt. When individual rights trumped the Mission and now that bill was coming due, right between the eyes. To Svonne, it all seemed like so much passionate speculation fed by dubious and unprovable premises, and she came to no conclusions. The spot on her shoulder where the chickadee's talons dug through her shirt, as if seeking niches, began to sting.

Because the laser consumed enormous amounts of energy, it had been test-fired only once, into the void. An opportunity to measure its power against a moving object presented itself days after the Council meeting, when a house-sized asteroid passed nearby. Composed primarily of carbon, rocks and hydrated minerals, it made a perfect sample for a live test. Svonne, the chief consultant to the targeting team, likened the task to hitting a bullet with a bullet while spinning in a circle. It was easy enough, though, for the device to be fired, finger touching screen icon, and the laser made a buzzing noise followed by a *thump-thump-thump*. The beam extended itself, jagged, silvery, then was gone. Seconds later the unlucky asteroid – a forlorn creature, alone and billions of years old, long ago exiled from its nursery solar system – broke into multiple irregular pieces. The contact area emitted a cloud of dust, as if a pair of old slippers had been whacked together.

Svonne observed a slow-motion video of the destruction. First came a split down the centre; one might, at this point, think the asteroid was a reproducing cell. A millisecond later several more cracks formed, then fissures and diffuse crumbling, and finally a dust cloud announced itself, an exhalation of despair. Svonne's colleagues busily poured over spectrographic data and various minute developments, such as the delayed jiggering of cause and effect in the space vacuum. She, however, found herself stuck on the asteroid's purpose in the universe.

Did it, like every human being, like her oblivious teenage self who'd jerry-rigged Shipworld's salvation, have some tiny but crucial part to play either next week or next year or billions of years from now? That is, if they hadn't blown it up. Again and again, Svonne watched the asteroid divide and bloom into dust. Is this what happens if they somehow hit Object X, potentially filled with sentient life? Is this what happens to us, she wondered, when our puny weapon reveals itself and Object X retaliates with far greater force?

What, she asked, gives us the *right*?

Karlsen had understood. An epic mistake, the laser. That's why Parsons and the Pioneers had never considered it – they knew their limits, they weren't crazy. Svonne couldn't believe that she'd let herself become part of this risky, immoral project. Shipworld was supposed to have left the worst of Earthworld behind, to have transcended the violent decline of humanity. The success of their star journey was proof, almost, that brutality was not endemic to human beings, that our former savagery had been catalysed within a civilisation corrupted by greed and arrogance. And yet, this spear hurled into the dark. Svonne stared at the endlessly looping video, her mouth open. Fire, crack, poof…

To avoid appearing conspicuous, she made a remark about the success of the parabolic refraction algorithm. As always, her opinion was warmly validated and seconded. She reprimanded herself: coward. Such a *coward*. She stung herself with the word – but she wasn't a coward, surely, about everything. Svonne had recently implanted herself with an embryo, cadged at random from a communal batch. She wasn't waiting another fifteen years, an eternity, to reproduce. She intended to be the first of her kind to grow a baby, not using an iron womb – a creepy vat with its standardised nutrient recipe – but inside herself, naturally. Then, after giving birth, she'd raise the child as her own.

And she intended to do so on a Shipworld that hadn't been blown to smithereens.

✦

Two snares, two cymbals, two tom-toms, and a huge kettle. The drummers ringed the Olmec Head, as if readying to play for the old fellow. As if determined to turn his primaeval frown upside down. The group was led by Bolo Oort, composer and vocalist, and the son of Jan Oort-Ruiz. This would be their first public performance – no pressure, just Launch Day! – of two new pieces that the Contact Committee had requested for the communications packet destined for Object X.

They called themselves the Crazy Bangers, an odd title for a collection of disciplined musicians. Bolo, a dedicated tinkerer, had constructed their instruments from old kitchen implements. The kettle drum, for instance, was a dented copper soup cauldron covered in a taut skin of bamboo-linen. The cymbals were refashioned pot covers balanced on poles made of welded cutlery. From these contraptions would emerge the newly created songs, a discordant pair. One was instrumental, a meditative composition that searched out moments of silence between the incessant rhythms of drumming. The other came from Parsons' 100 Approved Songs, a silly but hard-to-shake thing called 'My Blue Heaven', written in Earthworld Year 1927.

Almost the entire population, fully reconstituted from the dark era, assembled for Launch Day – a throng of curious spacefarers, two-thirds flesh-born, one-third orphan. This concentration of weight in one spot led some to joke that their spinning craft might acquire a catastrophic wobble. Hell of a way to go, after everything they'd been through.

The tallest among them, Parsifal, in his late nineties, sat by the pond that Svonne and several schoolchildren had constructed. Above him stretched the Tube and above that the bending interior sky made of farms and habitations. A knitted blanket covered his wasted, arthritic legs, now unfit even for a gentle bounce at a *phligsparrfner*. The 'pond' was a plastic tub set into a dirt mound, the water 1.5 metres deep and aerated by a fountain. Parsifal's eyesight had grown poor, so he didn't notice the flickering shadow of the robo-fish roaming its domain. The slender, bluish creature was modelled on the Pacific mackerel, an extinct species that once travelled in Earthworld schools up to thirty-two kilometres long.

From a nearby *phligsparrfner* soared two youngsters, rising halfway to the ribbon-bedecked Tube that had been outfitted with grappling hooks for tonight's Equilibrium revival. All about, people crunched snacks and chatted. Orphans and flesh-born stood together in groups, eyes looking up, eyes cast down, and this pleased Parsifal. Object X's approach seemed to have broken down barriers; perhaps shipworldmates had finally realised, he hoped, that we're not that different from each other, that we're all human, after all, and if we're on the cusp of some transcendental discovery, or if we're all going to die, and soon, we might as well get to know each other.

The drumming began, *thrum-thrum-thrum*, slowly building to a crescendo that swamped the crowd's murmur. Having established itself, the song eased into a skittering trip down the garden lane, in which the cavernous voices of the kettle drums alternated with the rattling snares and the eerie, languishing shushing of brushes across cymbals, *shhhumm, shhhumm, shhhumm*. The instruments merged finally, their melodies entwined, into one multivarious celebration tinged with lament.

Then, silence. The drums ceased. Silence, pervasive and rare – followed by an eruption of applause. Tears poured down Parsifal's cheeks on this Launch Day, as he found himself overcome with the bittersweet knowledge that whatever happened, he'd never see HD-40307g, that none of the people surrounding him, orphan and flesh-born, would see it either, no less be able to confirm the solid but not incontrovertible scientific conclusions that had designated the planet as habitable. But someday, somehow – he had to believe it, there was no other choice – Shipworld would arrive. HD-40307g would support human life. The blocks would stack, one by one, and not fall.

Not ten metres away, Svonne tapped her remote control, sending the northern gannet into flight. 'Look,' she called out, her voice high and tinny, one arm outstretched, the other bent across her belly where a tiny foetus, its closed eyes forming, bobbed within its singular universe. Nearly every head on every neck outside her womb turned to watch the gannet, the largest robo-bird ever to grace this bounded sky.

Edged in black, the bird's white wings flapped powerfully to gain altitude. They spread wide, one hundred and seventy-five centimetres from tip to tip, enabling a seamless arc through the low-grav zones around the Tube. With its slate-blue eyes, orange head and shaggy crest, the gannet resembled an avenging punk angel. Svonne, lost in rapture, watched as the bird let out a raspy *rrah-rrah*, its hunting call, and shortened its wingspan. Down it dived, white lightning, gaining speed as it acquired stronger gravity. The gannet pulled in its wings, tight to its sides, and so became an unstoppable projectile. Parsifal, too, and hundreds of others, stared in unflinching awe as the meteor bird plunged beak-first into the nearby pond.

Shipworld gasped, then held its breath. Moments later, the gannet struggled from the water in a pandemonium of splashing wings; up and away, it flew. In its formidable beak it grasped the wriggling Pacific mackerel, which supplied a flow of energy from a string of portals across its spine into a matching set of receptors inside the gannet's beak. The bird landed on the Tube, where it slid its webbed feet under a grappling hook, hunched into itself and fed. Applause bloomed again, triggering the start of the next song from the Crazy Bangers.

'*When whippoorwills call, and evening is nigh*,' sang Bolo in his liquid alto, at once cheery and vaguely sad. '*I hurry to my blue heaven.*'

'Congratulations, you did it!' said a wavering voice behind Svonne. She spun around: Parsifal, beaming, by the ravaged pond. His clothes were dappled wet from the great gannet splash. 'It's quite amazing.'

'Karlsen deserves the credit,' Svonne replied. 'I just finished what he started.'

'Well, that's what Shipworld's all about, isn't it,' Parsifal stated. 'Finishing what others have started.'

'I guess that's right.'

'I miss him,' said Parsifal.

'So do I,' said Svonne.

'*Turn to the right, a little white light*,' sang Bolo, '*will lead you to my blue heaven*.' His voice rang out like a soft gong.

The dancing started with a dozen or so orphans – they danced rambunctiously, lacking low centres of gravity – and soon the energy spread through the crowd like a joyful contagion. People were shaking and jiving, and some spun like spiral galaxies and some fell down and got back up with the help of their neighbours. Stuck-in-his-chair Parsifal swung his arms about his head, even though it hurt like hell.

'*. . . a cosy room, a little nest that's nestled where the roses bloom . . .*'

Svonne trained her eyes on the northern gannet high above, still hunched and feeding in the very place, legend had it, where Franika had floated in twilight and webbing. That story – they'd even called her the Saviour – was hard to believe, like some fairy tale from a distant fantasy land. Yet half of her fellow shipworldmates, half of this dancing horde, had been alive when she finally died and was taken down and cremated, her ashes buried beneath the Olmec Head. She existed in living memory and in legend all at once.

Was Shipworld really about finishing the work of others? Even as Svonne had voiced polite agreement, slivers of doubt had surfaced and once more the talon marks tingled, for it could be argued that such devotion across generations, such elemental loyalty, while noble and heroic and all that, ran counter to the mischievous anarchy of the cosmos. An anarchy epitomised by Object X. Or by this scene, right here, right now. Orphans catapulted from the *phligsparrfnerim* and tiny lights around the Tube twinkled like planet-transited stars. The dancers moved according to no discernible pattern, human or algorithmic, and a flock of sparrows shot up from a zucchini patch, and back down. Then came a frenzy of snares and tom-toms, of kettle pounding and cymbal crashing, of banging on pots and pans, and Shipworld, unleashed, may have wobbled just a bit.

Did her womb-child, Svonne wondered, hear the hullabaloo? Did her little pioneer feel the ship tremors travelling up her legs, along her pelvis and into its cushioned vault? And Bolo belted out the final lyrics: '*Just Molly and me, and baby makes three, we're so happy in my blue heaven.*'

✦

Svonne walked along Pictor Boulevard, towards the engine room. The Tube's early-morning lights were at half illumination and, in the murky distance, she made out a green streak of cilantro and basil plants snaking between fields of wheat and soy. Due to crop surpluses, herbs had recently been reintroduced. The Mess Hall was serving a paste made from basil, coriander and oat milk, not bad on bread. Yesterday, as usual, Svonne got a takeaway plate and ate dinner while fussing with her robo-birds.

This morning, the com-pack would be transmitted to Object X. The Launch Day drum compositions were included, along with drawings, math equations and everyday sounds such as water dripping, children laughing and robo-birds chirping. Copies of *The Chronicler's Journal* and *The Rogue Adventures of Brenz Oort-St George* were in there, too, both in English and the jagged, lovely language of the orphans. An hour later, if there was no response to the com-pack, a bridge officer would fire up the main fusion engine and move the ship slightly from the path of the oncoming phenomenon. This manoeuvre had been decided on last night after hundreds of people, flesh-born and orphans, crammed into a Council meeting and expressed both a fear of deadly collision and a lack of faith in the deterrent power of the laser.

In the engine room, in the shadow of the main reactor, Svonne came upon a group observing a tense exchange between Councillors Zennero and Bartholomew.

'It's an historic opportunity,' insisted Bartholomew, hands on her hips.

'But they could take it as a threat,' shot back Zennero. 'Just like the laser.'

'Math isn't threatening,' she replied, struggling to contain herself. She turned towards Svonne. 'The music is beautiful, the laughter, the drawings – there's no threat.'

Svonne almost spoke up, but didn't. Human beings, she considered, specialised in reducing questions to binary options. Yes or no. In or out. Friend or foe. Love or hate, fight or flight, success or failure. Beautiful welcome or dangerous threat. It's a survival mechanism favouring action over contemplation, decision over dithering. Big-brained evolution over just hanging out and picking berries. Education, of course, is supposed to challenge binary thinking – this or that or how about *that*, options three, four, five and six – but educated people, she knew, only became better at rationalising their binary choices. And she was no different; the allure of taking either/or action, of putting aside endless critique and equivocation, was strong.

'We don't know how their minds work,' returned the old man, leaning on a bamboo walker woven with green fronds. 'We barely understand our own.' At that, the argument ground to a halt. What more could be said? The heavy, bass voice of the secondary fusion engine, powering ship systems, took the place of human squeaks. A technician, anticlimactically, transmitted the com-pack. An hour passed, while the Contact Committee awaited a response to be picked up by the antennas, telescopes and instruments which measured every quantum quaver and popping particle in the void between them and Object X.

Nothing. Word was sent to the bridge. A sixty-six-second propulsive burn of the main fusion engines was enacted, steering Shipworld three degrees from its course. Then the count began, one, two…and Object X responded almost immediately, once more altering its trajectory to an intercept course. Zennero sighed, a pained emission, and shuffled away, tracing an erratic path that betrayed his arthritic hip. Bartholomew walked alongside the elder, trying to soothe him. Several technicians stared at the navigational charts, at the two lines soon to become one, way out here on the trailing spiral arm of a not-so-special galaxy. The ships' meeting, to put it gently, would occur in roughly twenty-seven hours.

Later that day, Svonne sabotaged the laser by altering an algorithm in the targeting software. However, the changes were discovered within minutes during a systems double-check. Repairs were quickly made, and more than one person noted that it was a rather clumsy hack, one that almost revealed itself. That, you might say, was ashamed of itself. Svonne confessed to a stunned Councillor Bartholomew, explaining her belief that firing the weapon was a short-sighted decision that not only seemed like a sanction of violent means, but might come back to haunt them by inviting retaliation. She expressed regret that she hadn't spoken up earlier, and she took the opportunity to announce herself as the first orphan to engineer a natural pregnancy – at an unnaturally young age, at that.

Tender Remarque, a young orphan who had assumed that humans born from iron wombs couldn't conceive children, escorted the saboteur back to her room. There, Svonne sat alone with her birds, eating leftover basil-coriander paste on stale bread. She obsessed about her ambivalent action – her stand taken on one foot – that had failed to match her strong feelings. She could have devised a more effective hack. Why hadn't she? For a sliver of eternity, and to no avail, Svonne tried to explain her behaviour to her unborn child who only heard faint murmurings.

Not long before the ships' presumed collision, Bridge Officer Neyjay-Usah activated the laser. Its trail looked harmless enough, a silvery gash on the black table of space. One pulse, two pulses, three pulses leaped towards the target, and the gashes faded as soon as they appeared. Then nothing happened. No return shots were fired; no response, apparently, was made. Their attempts at connection, both welcoming and threatening, had failed. As far as anyone could tell, neither the com-pack nor the laser mattered in the least to Object X. It bore down on Shipworld with the unfathomable purpose of a silent, mysterious stranger.

✦

Many decided not to change routines as the two high-speed entities drew close. Object X would veer away at the last moment, or it wouldn't; at any rate, there was nothing to be done about it. Lab workers kept pipetting liquids into test tubes. Volunteers on scrubber duty swept for stray molecules – a hair, a crumb, a microscopic drop of spittle nestled in a skin flake – and the detritus was transferred to the Loop where workers converted it into the magic sludge that fed the 3-D printers. From the ovens, cooks pulled great sheets of Gramma's okra cake. But some folks became distraught and took to bed, while others sat down with loved ones to eat and chat and laugh, perhaps for the final time. Children played, of course, as vigorously as ever, and a clot of orphans gathered arm in arm, chanting a song-tale about the coming rendezvous. Altogether, a hundred or so people stood outside, sentinels spaced randomly here and there, up and down.

Svonne couldn't budge from her chair. What kept her? She was under house arrest, of course, a form of punishment – kind of funny, she thought, considering that she enjoyed being alone in her enclave. Funny, too, since the population at large was under lifetime arrest inside a spinning receptacle. Consciousness itself, if you really pushed it, was a kind of enforced seclusion, a prison with meagre access to the true thoughts and feelings of others, as well as absolutely no grasp of what existed beyond its own boundaries.

At her elbow, five stacked ficus blocks. As usual, she'd used the smallest block for the foundation and topped the inverted pyramid with the biggest, most ungainly one, just to make things a little harder. The tower seemed a bit shaky, though, and she feared that it might topple if she pushed back her chair. From the console at her other elbow, Svonne had been fiddling with the robo-birds' AI system, adding a qubit here and a qubit there, creating steeper cascades of superpositions across the neural network, each fiddle a balancing act on the head of the pin where waves and particles conjoin into one and both and neither, where reality and illusion co-exist on the quantum level. Or something like that – a jumble of jargon that defined her as a person. Confined her. Kid science whiz – now a former prodigy. Svonne's laser sabotage, she had to admit, was lame on purpose because, in the final analysis, she couldn't bring herself to determine Shipworld's fate, not again. She'd acted, yes, but didn't have the courage to fully marry intention to action, to irreversibly commit. She wanted it, like light existing as both particle and wave, both ways. And now, with Object X at the doorstep, she judged herself as childish. Dishonest, at the core of it.

Svonne stared across the room at the Dürer, now hanging on the apartment's front door. 'He was an honest man,' she said aloud, perhaps to the black-capped chickadee that twitched on the edge of a workbench. 'I mean, kind of a dandy, right? All gussied up for his evening walk – who'd paint themselves that way, if they weren't honest?'

The robo-bird made no response. It looked away.

'Hey, we're gonna get through this. The grandchild of my child will walk on HD-40307g,' declared Svonne, to the bird, to the painting, to herself. She slid the plate with the paste-slathered bread back and forth. 'Maybe they'll give it a proper name by then.'

Several moments of silence followed this remark. Ordinary silence, not the expansive, echoing kind often remembered before a portentous event. A proper name, yeah, that would be nice. Then she giggled, and again, until it became a hearty laugh. It wasn't like her, but she kept laughing, loudly, and found that she couldn't stop. The chickadee chirped in, *fee-dee*, which just made it worse, and one of Svonne's arms lashed out, spasmed, and sent the blocks clattering to the floor.

'George,' she said. 'We're going to Planet George!'

All this racket may explain why Svonne didn't notice, at first, that the floor had begun to vibrate. Only when the vibrations increased in amplitude, and the plate went flying and the bread landed paste-down, *plop*, and the Dürer swayed as if drunk, did the young woman stop laughing and rush outside.

Shipworld shook, like an aircraft rocked by turbulence. Since no one onboard had experienced weather or any form of atmospheric or geological upheaval, the shaking seemed catastrophic. The chickadee clamped onto Svonne's shoulder as she hurried into the street, crowded with frantic people. Svonne glanced up at the swaying Tube, its lights flickering – *flash*, the lights went out.

Velvet darkness descended, the darkness found outside. The darkness of the galactic grave. And a deep groan arose, hundreds of voices drenched in anguish and surprise, and above and below everything a scraping noise gathered – an accelerating rockslide, an immersive, invisible avalanche. It sounded like the passage of a billion-billion pebbles over the ship's skin. Probing, encircling, entombing.

As if her bones had dissolved, Svonne fell unconscious. Everyone fell unconscious. This time when Svonne stopped moving – her body crumpled on the ground, her relentless mind finally stilled – the chickadee did not fly off. It stayed with her, hopping onto her skull and calling to the heavens, *fee-dee, fee-dee, fee-dee!*

✦

All Neyjay-Usah had ever wanted was to be a bridge officer, to stand at the leading tip of Shipworld in the blue uniform with the gold collar trim and look out the bridge window at the star-flecked stretch of space that he'd glide across for the remainder of his life. Here, the stars did not appear to revolve, reflecting the ship's ceaseless spin, but revealed themselves as fixed destinations, as faraway places to long after and, future willing, pass by. Here, the immensity of space – soul-crushing to some, awe-inspiring to him – could be apprehended without illusion. Here, he felt happy.

Neyjay-Usah's dream had sprouted on the day, at age nine, when he visited the bridge on a class field trip. He sat with fidgety children in this rectangular room, next to one of the command consoles, and looked back and forth between the bridge officer, an older woman, and the space window. The officer, Cornelia 'Corny' McSherry, spoke with pride about the long, blue line of 'bridgers' who preserve the mission, passing on knowledge of ship systems and protocols from generation to generation. 'I stand ever vigilant, ready to react in an emergency that might never happen,' she said without remorse.

He raised his hand and she called on him. 'I want to be you,' the boy said.

During his training period, Corny told him stories of the twilight years of her youth, of deprivation and scavenging, of hopelessness and population peril, and still in those dark days the Mission prevailed. No matter what happens, declared Corny, the Mission must prevail. No matter what! At

Neyjay-Usah's graduation ceremony, she came out of retirement to hand him his white officer's cap. 'I love you, Corny,' he said, but he wasn't sure if she could hear anymore, and now, standing square on the bridge, he often thought of her wrinkled old hand, the knuckles inflamed, the skin pockmarked and paper thin as it handed him his cap.

Neyjay-Usah, of course, had done more than stay ready. He'd been on duty when the directive came to fire the laser. He'd pressed the screen icon and watched the beam blast out and slide away. He, too, had been on the bridge during the Encounter with Object X. In the minutes beforehand, he'd watched with amazement through the front window as the brightly glowing entity came apart and diffused around Shipworld, as it seemed to encapsulate it, hold it, shake it in its grasp – impossible, of course, given the respective speeds of the two properties. He watched as the lights expired and the sliding, scraping stones rolled over and through him, and he collapsed to the floor and lay unconscious like everyone else.

The computer went down, so time was not measured during the period of unconsciousness, an event which came to be known as the Big Sleep. No means existed, either, to estimate how many spins the ship had taken. Soon after Neyjay-Usah and his fellow bridgers awoke, however, he took a star reading of their cosmological position and compared it to one recorded before the Encounter. Amazingly, they were still on course and travelling at .125 light speed. A simple calculation indicated that they'd been rendered oblivious for three hours and four minutes.

The danger, whatever it had been, appeared to be over. Object X glowed like a regular enough comet as it receded behind them.

A five-year-old child, Erica Smalls, died during the Encounter, probably from hitting her head when she fell unconscious. Otherwise, there were only a dozen or so broken bones, bad scrapes or concussions. Ship systems were in decent order, although many instruments had to be tightened down or recalibrated after the shaking. Scientific equipment mounted outside the ship was no worse for wear, a bizarre outcome considering the scouring rockslide they'd all heard. Crops appeared unaffected. The Dürer painting in Svonne's room still hung on its pegs, if a bit askew. She couldn't bring herself to straighten it.

There was one enduring, physical sign of the Encounter. The Olmec Head was cracked right down the middle, as if chopped by a giant stone axe. It was split apart from the top of its helmet down the ridge of its nose and through the bulbous lips; the hemispheres of its stone brain had been cleaved in two, forever parted, and rubble was scattered in every direction. Inside this newborn cleft something had shone, according to several witnesses, a diamond-sparkling object that soon disappeared. That was the story, at least, one that Neyjay-Usah dismissed. Nor did he indulge speculations about Object X as camouflaged space probe, defective weapon, distributed alien being, AI-enhanced natural phenomenon or mass hallucination.

Object X was a frightful mystery beyond comprehension, he told himself, and he was relieved to have it gone. Relieved to be back on the bridge, standing square.

Some people claimed that belongings had been moved, subtly, during the lost hours. A chair closer to the wall, a brush pointed the wrong way. These observations fuelled tales of aliens coming onboard. How else to explain the ragged bites in Gramma's okra cake? Or people awakening on their backs, staring up – perhaps they'd been turned over for examination. And why did the data/tracking panels go dead? After all, they operated by battery. Neyjay-Usah found these so-called clues all a bit desperate and sad. He would not try to make sense of something by violating sense itself.

Not knowing was OK. Being between the thing and its explanation, the launch pad and the landing zone, was OK. There was a bridger saying: We live both in the here and the beyond. Bridgers had shortened it to 'here and beyond' and over time it became a catchphrase, a verbal token passed between the faithful. The three words were sown into the inside of their caps. At the start of a duty shift you'd relieve a fellow bridger and she'd nod and say 'here and beyond' and you'd nod back and say 'here and beyond' and now you were at the ploughing prow of Shipworld, in the here, witnessing the stars fixed and burning, in the beyond. Neyjay-Usah didn't think of 'here and beyond' as a declaration of philosophical bravado or existential duality, but as an actual description of the bridger's purpose. What the bridgers did – checking systems, watching, waiting, training younger bridgers to check, watch and wait, over and over until the faraway day of planetfall – was a tangible, constructive activity. A step-by-step merger of day to day, year to year, era to era. We are the living bridge within Shipworld, he believed, stretching ourselves from fallen Earthworld to HD-40307g in all its exquisite mystery. We serve, until the end.

Without question, Erica's death was the Encounter's most searing blow, a devastating event for her parents, extended family and classmates, as well as a perplexing challenge to the community psyche and its belief in the Mission. It was as if the girl had been singled out, as if she'd functioned as a scapegoat for some transgression committed against the universe. Perhaps for firing the laser at Object X. For an offensive element in the com-pack, in which Erica's own laugh was featured as one of many everyday sounds. For trying to evade the oncoming entity. For fleeing Earthworld in the first place and never looking back. For surviving, this far out.

About 600 people – for all practical purposes, almost every human being in existence – gathered at the cleaved Olmec Head for Erica's funeral. A single, artfully crafted plastic daisy was planted in the Head's divot, featuring white petals arrayed in overlapping profusion around a centre of nestled yellow buds. Beautiful, indeed. Had such fantastical things really grown by the millions, by the billions, back on Earthworld? Eulogies were given by family members, who remembered Erica for being fun, helpful and bright. She liked playing with clay, fashioning multi-coloured lumps and adding wings. She was a good runner and jumper. She threw temper tantrums, sometimes, when it was time to get dressed in the morning. She was so very unique and so very ordinary.

No one asked aloud: Why her? But everyone asked themselves.

A long, ragged line of shipworldmates curled about their world's inner circumference and ended at the Olmec Head, where Erica's two mothers stood. The line resembled a human stitch, thought Neyjay-Usah, marshalled to seal a terrible wound. One by one, mourners approached the parents and extended their sympathies, grief-torn and awkward, and afterwards gazed at the artificial flower. Neyjay-Usah stayed apart, watching. Svonne didn't join the line, either, but instead returned to her indefinite house arrest, interrupted only by mandated community service in the Mess Hall kitchen.

And life went back to a kind of normal. Yet, in the weeks and months after the Encounter, things occurred that seemed quite abnormal to Neyjay-Usah. It started with Councillor Zennero, who killed himself nine days after surfacing from the Big Sleep. The frail old man who'd stated that no one understood Object X's mind, no less their own, did it by jumping from his toilet with his neck in a noose tied to a ceiling beam. While there were no signs of coercion, it seemed an unlikely feat for the councillor to have secured the rope. Quarrelsome as he could be, Zennero had no enemies, and his suicide note only created new questions. Short and cryptic, it read: 'I CAN'T STOP HEARING THE DRUMS.'

Tenders in charge of the investigation concluded that Zennero's opposition to sending the com-pack, the trauma of the Encounter and the challenges of extreme old age had combined to produce his despair. His was the first confirmed suicide since Marcus Marte took Parsons' green pill to reverse the Correction, although that choice had been interpreted by many as an assertion, rather than negation, of life.

Next came the headaches. At first there were only anecdotal reports, but health statistics soon confirmed that strong headaches, resistant to pain relievers, had tripled. Neyjay-Usah supposed that the headaches were caused by higher anxiety levels – if Object X can happen, what next? Then he was hammered, a real doozy, as he stared at the stars while on duty.

The distress subsided within a day, just in time for him to represent the bridge officers at a Council meeting. Up for debate was a petition to make forearm data/tracking panels voluntary instead of required. Its advocates argued that a person's whereabouts were a private matter and shouldn't be in the 'busy hands' of the state. A councillor remarked that she'd love to be rid of her device, which had been itching for years. And so on, the usual repartee. Neyjay-Usah didn't speak; it was tradition among bridge officers to remain quiet at Council meetings. He listened dutifully, though, even as the pain returned. An echo of his headache? Or a new one coming on? When the gavel sounded, he hurried home. There he took off his uniform and placed the trousers and shirt on a hanger. He faced the mirror and once more sized up his flabby body, settled into its extended middle age. And he pledged to exercise more, every day. Starting soon, but not today, not with this headache.

'Not today' – he'd been talking to himself out loud; his mirror-self had become his confidant. That, too, he pledged to change. Neyjay-Usah was approaching that halfway stage in life when reproduction was expected. In order to have children, he'd better start searching for a partner, and it wasn't a good sign, he realised, that he considered the task a logistical manoeuvre, an enactment of duty. In fact, the topic had come up at dinner recently with his parents, both Loop workers. His mom had referred to his future partner as his 'mate', an oddly biological designation, and then glanced at his dad with a raised eyebrow. Neyjay-Usah imagined them scheming to make a customised, organic Loop-mate for their son, concocted from skin flakes, cracker crumbs and broken gears, not to mention dead bodies. Or better yet they'd put him through their soft grinder and he'd emerge as a more suitable suitor, garrulous, fit, emotionally wise…

Neyjay-Usah slept for eight fitful hours that night. In the morning, he did nine and a half push-ups, his chest aching. Next, he rose up and down on his toes twenty-five times, torturing his calves. He showered and shaved, then unfolded the blue bridger uniform and put it back on his still-lumpy frame. With a damp cloth, he rubbed a bit of crumb from his left shoulder and smoothed a wayward crease on a trouser leg. He put on his polished belt, missed a loop, did it all over again. Then he double-knotted the laces on his shoes, remembering that time when a lace came loose and caused him to trip on the catwalk in front of a gaggle of young orphans. Finally, while sipping a hot kale juice, he opened his console and checked the morning testimonies. This was his unwavering pattern.

During these actions, he mostly succeeded in not verbalising his conversations with the mirror. Tomorrow, he decided, thirteen push-ups, if it killed him. Thirty calf crushers. And sit-ups; he hated sit-ups. Too bad! A bridge officer is all about proper maintenance.

One morning, on the console, Neyjay-Usah found himself drawn to a testimony from Tender Remarque: *My Persistent*

Dream. Remarque had experienced a singular dream over and over since the Encounter. It always starts, she wrote, with thick, yellow-stained clouds parting to reveal a planet, a fantastic planet of lightning storms and volcanic eruptions, of glowering red skies filled with giant patrolling birds, shrieking as they plunged. A planet of rock-ribbed mountains and waterfalls crashing down. On the plains between the mountains and volcanoes, waterspouts erupt to the heavens, and it's always raining – a planet of endless rain. Throughout the dream, Remarque hears drums pounding in the distance, with her husband Bolo Oort singing, '*Turn to the right, a little white light, will lead you to my blue heaven.*'

Her dream is unsettling, she claimed, but not scary – not until she notices a little girl running down a gravelly hillside. Lightning flashes, the birds swoop above, and this girl who resembles Erica Smalls, may she rest in peace, falls head over heels, screaming, into the jagged shale. She comes to a halt, broken and still. Enough! Remarque forces herself awake at this point. Generally, she wrote, her dreams are fuzzy and hard to recall, but this one plays in vivid detail. Almost as if it was a vision – perhaps of HD-40307g.

Neyjay-Usah read the testimony twice, without pausing. Tenders, like bridge officers, were circumspect in how they communicated. What compelled this young woman to share her disturbing dream with all of Shipworld? And, more to the point, how in the infinite cosmos did she know what he'd been dreaming for weeks now? The details of his persistent 'planet dream' were slightly different, with green skies and great rivers of lava, but alike enough to rule out coincidence. He, too, had forced himself awake when confronted with the little girl face down in the gravel.

Had he told the tender about his dream? Or told someone who told her, and then somehow her dreaming brain had copied it? No, he'd kept the dream to himself, as he did most things. He'd rolled it up and locked it down. But what if this shared dream had something to do with the Big Sleep, the three lost hours? Was there a message or warning, he wondered, which needed to be figured out?

Neyjay-Usah stood up. He put on his bridger cap, just so. And he said aloud, 'Worry about it later', but refused to catch himself in the mirror as he strode out the door. Once again, here and beyond, it was time to perform his life's calling.

✦

A few days later, after his bridge shift, Neyjay-Usah leaned on a rail overlooking the Viewing Portal. Stars slid through the broad space, a never-ending parade of suns husbanding planets. On those planets, he supposed, all kinds of life migrated through oceans, land and air. Lurked inside lava vents and ice caves cold enough to fracture flesh. One creature's hell, of course, is another's heaven, and maybe life isn't rare but ubiquitous, with thousands of primaeval planets, millions even, that look like the one in his dream. Maybe *that* star, the one rolling off the top right-hand corner of the portal, carries a young, rupturing planet of bursting volcanoes and shrieking beasts. Neyjay-Usah leaned on the rail and contemplated the galactic whirl, a phrase used to describe this view of the passing stars, while also looking up now and then for a glimpse of Tender Remarque.

Soon, he saw her angling onto Carina Way. She moved with long, deliberate strides as she patrolled the lobby outside the Mess Hall and then stopped at a garden's edge with a panoramic view of fields, neighbourhoods and, twenty metres away, an electro-feeder harried by robo-sparrows. An excellent vantage point, Neyjay-Usah presumed.

He walked past a group of arm-swinging exercisers, making a show of it, and approached Remarque – married to that Bolo fellow, the musician whose middle-aged father died in bed despite the Correction. She was watching the birds, lined up on a fence by the feeder. Remarkable, the way they waited turns to eat, as if a prearranged order had been established. You would think, considered Neyjay-Usah, that the urge to dominate would win out. Unbeknownst to him, this level of sparrow cooperation was a new development, a result of Svonne's experiments in dispersing their AI functions within a communal web. The bird brains were now linked, sharing data and learning from each other, much like the roots of trees in olde-time Earthworld forests.

'Good morning, Tender,' said Neyjay-Usah, who now stood beside her.

'Good morning, Officer,' she replied, and together they observed the sparrows shuttling back and forth between fence and feeder. Remarque turned away from the scene, a bit bothered by its strange orderliness, and scanned about. Over on that rooftop, an abandoned ball.

'I've heard that your job is more interesting since the Encounter,' he said. 'More arguments, even some thefts.'

'It's a matter of public record,' she replied. 'All's well at the moment.'

'The young man who hurt himself,' stated Neyjay-Usah.

'We believe it was an accident. He's recovering.'

She'd learned in tender training that a shipworldmate who wanted to talk, to truly connect, would often begin a conversation with a series of statements. Warm-up remarks. The trick was to be receptive but restrained. Let them come to it. This, she guessed, was especially true of bridge officers – a peculiar lot, so removed from everyone else. What did they actually do? Their existence seemed almost symbolic. Nonetheless, she admired their commitment to a single, unswerving goal: forward.

'I had the dream,' he told her.

'Hmm,' she said. 'We're not the only ones, you know.'

'Really? That's a relief – maybe.'

She nodded, slowly. Continued scanning. Neyjay-Usah asked her why she'd testified the dream and she responded that it had seemed necessary, urgently so. This feeling was confirmed when scores of similar post-Encounter dreams – or visions or hallucinations – were subsequently reported. Some people testified their own versions; others spoke to Remarque directly. 'It's a disturbing development,' she added, meaning that she'd become an object of attention even as she struggled nightly with the dream. Only in Bolo's arms, in the apartment they shared off Andromeda Avenue, did the primordial planet fade from her mindscape, and then not always. Neyjay-Usah, though, assumed that she was disturbed by the large number of reports.

'I keep having it, over and over,' he said. 'Do you think it's some kind of memory? Something ancient we carry with us. Like an instinct, and the Encounter activated it.'

Tender Remarque gave him her full attention. 'I've wondered the same thing,' she said. 'The dream's landscape resembles Earthworld millions of years ago, when life started. Amino acids and lightning, that's the recipe.'

'And the little girl?'

She shrugged. 'I don't know. It's ghastly.'

'Maybe some people are making the whole thing up,' he added. 'You know, the power of suggestion. The need to belong.'

'A few, perhaps.' He was frowning, seemed to want more. 'Some believe that the dream was implanted during the Encounter. That it's a form of communication, a reply to the message we sent.'

They returned to the sparrows. Flying, eating, waiting, a harmonious assemblage efficiently dividing a resource. Suddenly, for no apparent reason, they rose up and gathered into a loose-knit bird whirl – each beating wingtip just millimetres apart from another, an impossible manoeuvre, really – and flew away towards a distant row of dwellings. They must look at us the same way we look at them, Neyjay-Usah considered, baffled by our comings and goings. Something spooked them, Remarque thought.

'Well,' he said, 'it's just a dream, it's not something we can do anything about, right?' Before she could respond, he saluted the tender in a weirdly stiff manner and went on his way. She watched the bridge officer disappear around a corner; for a moment he'd reached out, revealed himself, and then retreated into his stoic camouflage. Eccentric, but a nice guy at heart, she suspected. Remarque racked her brain to think of someone who could be the right partner for him, someone equally odd, and this activity soon diverged into a memory of kissing Bolo last night. She felt his lips on hers, and that was no dream.

Time to get that ball down, she decided. Bring it to the Lost and Found.

✦

Her students, Teacher Woodard told Neyjay-Usah over cups of tea, had changed in the months since the Encounter. Around ten years old, the children had become more intense, more worried and more inquisitive. It was good that they cared, of course, and she appreciated their smart, probing questions. But it didn't let up, no matter her attempts at diversion. She quipped that she found herself missing those days when half the class stared at her glassy-eyed as she droned on about statistics, supernovas, the Icelandic Constitutional Convention and the sociological rewards of kindness. Neyjay-Usah laughed just a little, his standard reaction to a self-deprecating remark. A lesser response could be considered unfriendly; a greater response might validate the self-criticism. That he wore the bridger uniform added weight to his every utterance, and he never forgot that.

Neyjay-Usah was here as part of a student outreach programme required of bridge officers as well as tenders and councillors. At the top of the hour, he and Teacher Woodard put down their teacups and entered the classroom. On cue, the students hustled to their desks. The day began with attendance, during which everyone proudly announced their names, and vigorous stretching exercises. Neyjay-Usah joined in, at one point losing his balance to the general delight of the children. Then Teacher Woodard gave a close-enough explanation of the duties of a bridge officer and their significance on Shipworld. After stating that only one in four bridge candidates was chosen (one in five, actually), she introduced him.

He waved at the kids and said, 'I stand ever vigilant, ready to react in an emergency that might never happen,' quoting his mentor Corny word for word.

The kids stared at him. Then Gansoor's hand shot towards the Tube.

'My dad says Object X was an alien probe. Is he right?'

'Your father isn't right or wrong,' replied Teacher Woodard, before Neyjay-Usah could begin to formulate an answer. 'It was a space anomaly; we don't know much else.'

'But did it cause the dream?'

'Again, we don't know,' said the teacher. 'Yesterday, we talked about the difference between causation and correlation. I want you to think about how that applies.'

'Are we dreaming about HD-40307g?' Simona asked, urgently. This time, Teacher Woodard smiled – a delaying tactic, Neyjay-Usah assumed. He jumped in and said that there's no tangible reason to worry. According to long-range surveys, HD-40307g was stable and habitable, not a primordial planet.

But strong confirmation couldn't be made for another seventy-five years – within their lifetimes. The children groaned at the very idea of being so old.

'How come we can't find another planet?' Liis asked. 'Can't we use the big telescope?'

'The officer is here to give a presentation,' the teacher said. 'I think we'll hold the rest of our questions until he's finished.'

'That's OK,' the bridger said. 'Questions are the door to learning.' Where had that come from? Maybe from Corny, who'd never put a lid on her trainees. Questions, of course, can also be shovels, digging for truth, or scalpels. Or even weapons. He decided to play it safe and volunteered the old mantra, which he deeply believed, that loyalty to the Mission ensured social and environmental stability. As an example, he invoked the dark times brought about when Brenz Oort-St George steered the ship off course.

'Making a change like that might feel good,' said Neyjay-Usah. 'But the cost could be high. HD-40307g has been our ultimate goal since the Pioneers stepped aboard.'

A tall boy, Phylar, piped up: 'Wasn't the real problem the cosmic radiation? Not going after the rogue.'

Teacher Woodard began to speak, but was interrupted.

'So what if the journey takes longer – we'll go to a better planet,' Jarry stated. She waved her caliper-arms, too long for her body. Her head, too, seemed a bit too big, as if stuffed with a trillion possibilities. All these children, thought Neyjay-Usah, such mishmashes, such portraits of uneven becoming. And so beautiful, flesh-born and orphan alike.

'None of our generation are making it anyway,' Jarry added, her voice quavering.

'Thank you for expressing yourself, Jarry,' said Teacher Woodard, again smiling. 'And you're right about the timeline. But each one of us is part of the journey, part of the chain, whether we step on the planet or not, and I think that's enough questions for today.' The firmness in her voice created a silence that, to Neyjay-Usah, seemed very uneasy. Several students stared at the floor. They clenched their fists.

'OK, one more,' added the teacher.

Hands shot up, almost off their arms. She picked spindly Brynto, a red-headed boy. Neyjay-Usah recognised this kid; there was something about him – oh man, the photo in his parents' house! Himself as a boy. Before his red hair faded, turned a dun colour.

'I have a question for Officer Neyjay-Usah,' he stated.

'Just Neyjay-Usah,' he replied. 'That's fine.'

'Were you on the bridge? Did you see it?'

'Yes, I was there,' he told Brynto, stepping forward, leaving Teacher Woodard behind. 'I saw Object X as it engulfed the ship, and then I collapsed like everyone else.'

'What did it look like?'

Neyjay-Usah paused. Teacher Woodard started to speak and he held up his hand, stopping her mid-sentence. 'It looked,' he said, 'like nothing I have ever seen. Like the world had come apart, like a flock of – I don't know.'

'Did it come inside?'

'I'm not sure.' He saw the pain on their faces, pain creeping from within. 'How many people here are having the planet dream?' he asked, and several hands went up. He waited, and two more joined those hands.

'Is the dream real?' Vanetter asked.

'No, it's not,' stated Teacher Woodard, stepping alongside the bridge officer. 'Even though lots of people have it, it's still just a dream.'

'I have it all the time,' said Brynto.

'I have it, too,' Neyjay-Usah said to him. 'I know how you must feel.'

'Well, it's certainly a real dream,' interrupted Teacher Woodard. 'But it's not *real*.'

The bridge officer turned to the teacher. She was a master teacher, supposedly, and a caring person, even with the calculating grin that now shined, disarming, at him. She wanted to move things forward, get unstuck, and a bridger could appreciate that. But no, not if it meant denying this. No denial! No minimising, no forgetting, no pretending! The primordial planet dream in all its fascination and horror resulted directly from the Encounter – pulsing with Bolo's music, Erica dying again and again – and couldn't be dismissed. Call it a dark prophecy, a gift, some kind of residue or reminder – whatever it was, it mattered. The dream felt real, both during and after. Neyjay-Usah knew that; Brynto knew that; Tender Remarque and so many others, all the dreamers, they had to know that.

For a dizzy moment, Neyjay-Usah, the ever-forward man, could feel Shipworld turning under his feet, making its twenty-four-second revolution for the millionth or ten-millionth time, he'd have to do the math. Around and around they go, forever and a space day, and from a certain perspective he was halfway up the sky with this class of crazy, scared kids, all of them hanging upside down – ridiculous, sure – but in another way the utter, amazing strangeness of their situation defined their lives. Was it really so wrong to see their shared dream as more than a dream?

'So how do I know,' Brynto asked, 'that we're really in outer space?'

The eyes of every student became wide and wondering. Their heads turned first to Brynto and then to the adults at the front of the class. Nothing moved; never had this room existed in such a charged state of quiet expectation.

'I'll take this one,' said Neyjay-Usah. Teacher Woodard hesitated, then nodded.

'That,' he began, 'is a very smart question. You've got imagination – don't ever feel ashamed for that, it helps us grow and explore. But listen, please. The Encounter and the planet dream are terrible mysteries, we understand that, yes?' – now the heads of the children bobbed at him, bobbed almost in unison, spurring him on – 'but here, right now, we aren't dreaming. We're awake. Think about it: the lower gravity in the ship's centre, the zero-grav around the Tube, none of that could happen if we weren't in space.'

'It could be artificial,' Vanetter offered. A boy behind her, Avi, a short kid who rarely emerged from himself, yelled out, 'Or we could be in orbit around a planet.'

'OK, I get it, I hear you,' said Teacher Woodard, holding out her palms as if to calm turbulent waters. 'But let's not forget, we can see the stars through the windows. Have you looked through the main portal, Brynto, have you done that?'

'Yes, I stop every day on my way home.' Then he startled, as if he'd received a sudden transmission. He looked away, eyes shut tight, mouth clamped in a line.

'It's OK, Brynto,' said Neyjay-Usah.

He blurted out: 'How do I know that's real? Have you been outside?'

'No,' said the bridge officer – triggering a clamorous storm of questions and comments that crested and broke across the classroom. Then he stepped forward again, to his amazement, two steps this time, and he found himself standing between desks, among the students. He waited for quiet.

'There's a story that's been passed down in my family,' he said. 'A story of a very different Shipworld, in which young people had profound concerns about the reality of our world.'

'Officer Neyjay-Usah,' said Teacher Woodard, firmly.

'These concerns,' he continued, 'were called the Fears. How, they asked, can we be on such a miraculous adventure? Isn't it more likely that it's a simulation, an experiment? And so, when young people turned twenty-four, they went on spacewalks, outside, in a special suit attached to a tether. They saw for themselves as Shipworld moved through deep space – they could even *touch* its skin. This was called the Revelation, and it was a powerful experience.'

The children looked at each other, incredulous. 'The Revelation,' some whispered. 'The Fears,' others said, also quietly, as if the words were taboo.

'It's not in the history books,' said Neyjay-Usah. 'But it should be. People decided that it was better not to know. Easier.'

'We live in a completely different world now,' countered Teacher Woodard. 'The Revelation was coercive, a form of manipulation. Some people say it's a legend, that it's not even possible at high speeds – it may not have happened at all.'

'It happened,' the bridger stated, not sure why he knew this to be true, in his bones. 'The Revelation is an important part of our history and it's right that you should know about it.'

Again, the class exploded.

✦

In the last, calm hours before emergence, the baby floated in the urine-sea of his mother, in a state of amniotic bliss, unaware of anything but the gurgling of Svonne's intestines and the whoosh of her blood charging downstream from ventricle to aorta to arteries, as well as more distant sounds and voices that came and went mysteriously, like wind song. All the days of his life, two hundred and seventy-six exactly, he'd floated in this nutrifying sac, growing, stretching, kicking, and sometimes his medium seemed to push back, as if in response, as if stirred from elsewhere. But such clues were scant and lacking in context. The baby, eyes flipping open and shut, fingers stretched to explore his environs, had no inkling of an outside. After all, his world ended just centimetres beyond his reach. He was alone, the only creature in existence, amply provided for by an umbilical cord tethered to the red placental wall. Imagine, then, the absolute shock, the terrifying thrill, when he found himself beginning to move, bit by bit, in fits and starts. When the speed of the movement accelerated. When suddenly the little human was flushed from his dark cosiness through a tight passage and pulled into the glare of another realm altogether, into a boundless place far from the enclosure he would never see again, into his mother's arms and the limitless universe of Shipworld.

The flesh-born doctor cut and tied the cord, then laid the rather large infant – 4.5 kilos, fifty-four centimetres long – on Svonne's chest. She stared wildly at her offspring, overwhelmed with relief and, at the same time, appalled, for who was this slick, red being shipwrecked upon her? The child, equally perplexed, breathed for the first time, the oddest sensation ever, and his tender eardrums were assaulted by murmurous chanting from a dozen orphans, including Tender Remarque and Parsifal leaning on a walker, who had gathered around the bed to help Svonne through this trial. To bring a little of the Orphans' House to her.

Klartannu-tu atellgepper susu; klartannu-tu atellgepper susu susu susu – an Orphanic lullaby which meant, roughly, peace pervades us, body and soul. Peace pervades us, body and soul, soul, soul. Until now, those words had been granted only to infants pulled from iron wombs. More than a few of the orphans surrounding Svonne, in fact, disapproved of her for breaking gestation tradition, or considered her sabotage of the laser a pathetic act (because she did it, because she failed), but none of that mattered now. She was of the tribe; they were here for her. And then Svonne delivered the placenta, a bloody wedge, which the doctor wrapped in a towel and set aside for conversion at the Loop. Screening tests indicated that the newborn was healthy;

a quick count made it ten toes and ten fingers; and this, Svonne realised, was easily the most surprising moment of her life, her sudden encounter with this child born in the shuddering wake of Object X.

The birth of Eric galvanised the orphan community. Soon after he sat up at six months and scanned his world like a mini-tender, the orphans voted among themselves to do away with the iron wombs. Worries remained that they'd lose their height, that they were sacrificing their distinctiveness, their very heritage, but natural birth was now seen as safe and considered a necessary trade-off for regaining the full power of the Correction. At the same time, the law ending mandatory implantation of data/tracking panels was approved, and so Eric became unique, also, for being the first untracked baby.

When he was eight months old, Eric looked into a low mirror and poked a finger into the eyes of the plump shipworldmate staring back at him. He did it again and again, and he poked at Svonne's eyes, too. 'Enough of that, pokey,' she'd tease, batting down his hands, and it was a happy day when he switched to shoving his fingers into her nose and mouth. At night, while Eric slept, Svonne tinkered with the robo-birds in a continuous quest to upgrade the resilience of each and every body part, and now and then she'd look into the corner of the room at the snoozing baby, its belly full on milk manufactured within her own body, and simply wonder. Peace pervades us, body and soul, soul, soul.

One evening, Svonne worked on the northern gannet's navigational system, which tended to fritz out on dives from zero-grav. The door registered a gentle knocking. She opened it remotely, swinging the Dürer out of view and revealing Neyjay-Usah, who held a parcel of tea made from chives. He took a tentative half-step inside, introduced himself as a bridge officer, obvious from his uniform, and then just stood there, glancing about.

'Can you... Can I help you?' asked Svonne.

He took a deep breath, then got quickly to the point. He'd seen her walking about with the chickadee on her shoulder. What happened, he asked, to the birds during the Big Sleep? Did they lose consciousness?

Svonne stared at the man who had invaded her hermitage. Bridge officers, so noble and patient and dull. Why would he care about the birds?

'They don't have consciousness,' she replied.

'They seem aware,' he said.

'Yes, they do. But they're just machines.'

'So are we – machines made out of flesh.'

Svonne had no riposte, for she agreed with this remark from both biological and philosophical perspectives. Who exactly was this bridger? What was his agenda? She'd seen him here and there, always standing by himself. Stupidly, she gestured towards a chair with clothes tangled across it. He handed over the tea, but didn't sit down.

'I sabotaged the laser,' she said. 'I mean, not very well, but don't you consider me some kind of criminal?'

'I could ask you the same thing. I fired the laser.'

A rustling came from the corner, from Eric's bassinet.

'Ah, yes,' replied Neyjay-Usah. He took a few steps, peeked at Eric, then returned to his previous spot as if that would keep the infant from waking. 'Cute kid.'

'Thanks.'

'So, maybe,' he continued, 'maybe the birds flew around while we were out. Maybe one of them recorded what happened during the lost hours, on an independent system.'

Using a remote, Svonne closed the door, swinging the Dürer back into view. The two men, Dürer and this Neyjay-Usah, appeared to be polar opposites.

'Interesting theory,' said Svonne. 'If it's true, then I've been hiding it from everybody, right?' She heard herself being defensive, and didn't like it, and couldn't seem to stop herself, either. 'What else to expect from the crazy neutrino lady.'

'I know who you are,' said Neyjay-Usah. 'You saved Shipworld.'

'I got lucky,' she said. False humility, the flip side of arrogance. Another kind of dishonesty. In house arrest, Svonne had catalogued her many faults and their many flavours, some forgivable, some not. 'Thank you,' she said in correction. 'I appreciate that.' And she did; she appreciated his honesty. Now she reopened the door, stuck her head outside and made a sharp whistle. Not five seconds later the chickadee soared into the room, executed a gliding loop over the kitchen island and landed, in a flapping frenzy, on her outstretched palm.

Eric made a grumbly noise but didn't awaken. Svonne, meanwhile, stroked the robo-bird's head; it leaned into her touch, seemed to enjoy it. Then she tossed the chickadee onto her shoulder, ever so casually. She closed the door again, hello there Dürer, how about closing your eyes one of these days, just once, and rapidly she played the computer keyboard. On her monitor popped a frozen, close-up image of a human head, its side pressed against a white walkway. Neyjay-Usah approached, mouth agape, and leaned forward. The short mop of hair on the head was brown and scraggly, barely combed.

He glanced at Svonne, at her brown, scraggly hair. She touched it, nodding. Then she touched her lime green T-shirt, and he looked back at the screen, at the lime green T-shirt collar at the base of the neck connected to the head.

'That's you.'

'Yeah, me. Now look at the lower-right corner.'

He leaned even closer. There it was, a blue-black line, knobbly, ending in a sharp, lizard-like talon. Neyjay-Usah had seen images of Earthworld dinosaurs, fantastic brutes, and for a moment he imagined one rampaging beneath the Tube – but no, of course, they'd died out long ago, and he turned his head to the young woman's shoulder, to the bird perched there. Its fierce talons matched those on the screen.

'He was programmed to fly away when I stopped moving,' she said. 'But he stayed, for a little while.'

'You mean, he also flew around?'

'That's right. And before you ask, he's the only bird with recording capability. You know, I'm kind of amazed that it took more than a year for anyone to ask.'

'It's the dream,' Neyjay-Usah replied. 'It keeps returning, like it's talking to me, insisting on something…'

One hand went to his skull, as if to touch the dream.

'Has it happened to you?' he asked.

She shook her head. Then pointed deliberately across the room, at the painting on the door. 'Sometimes I dream about *him*. Why he painted himself, what his life was like. How Earthworld screwed up so badly and sent us out here.'

'Where'd he come from?'

'Long story – are you ready to see the video?'

Neyjay-Usah nodded, and Svonne explained that she hadn't told anyone because the video doesn't really clarify anything. It won't help, it might make things worse. Shipworldmates could question its authenticity or demand to have her birds – Karlsen's birds – destroyed. They'll want answers, they'll want things done – you just can't predict when it comes to human beings. Besides, there's the little girl to consider.

Svonne took a deep breath and hit 'play'. She watched the screen with the bridge officer beside her and the now-chickadee on her shoulder.

'*Fee-dee, fee-dee!*' the before-chickadee called, looking about at several other bodies jumbled nearby. Two children had fallen together, the spiked cubes and rubber ball of knucklebones between them. And next to them, an old woman had buckled over a railing. The bird jumped, once, twice on Svonne's head, craning its neck, its camera producing a jittery, blurred colour tour of curving fields, stubs of buildings and bodies slumped not in sleeping postures but as if their spirits had suddenly, collectively, deserted them. Then, wings fluttering at the edges of the video, the bird ascended. It went up maybe fifty metres and twirled, then flew along the length of Shipworld.

'Look, the Head,' said Neyjay-Usah. Svonne paused the recording and zoomed in on the Olmec Head, split down the middle, just as they'd later discovered. Nothing shone in its open cavity. Next to the broken icon stood Erica Smalls in her knee-length orange dress, specially made for Launch Day. She was awake – shellshocked, perhaps, uncomprehending, but absolutely awake. And alone, surrounded by every person in her existence. Svonne hit play again. Erica's head swivelled, her eyes blinked. One little hand touched the cold stone Head. At her feet lay her parents, tangled together.

'Why is she awake?'

'Maybe a mutation,' said Svonne. 'Something she ate.'

'They chose her,' he heard himself saying.

Erica stooped over and patted her mother's head. She patted her second mother's. Neither one moved. For the first time in her life, she touched them and they didn't respond. Then the chickadee came swirling down, down, and landed on the little girl's shoulder. Erica's hand pushed it away and it jumped to the other shoulder. '*Fee-dee, fee-dee, fee-dee!*' But that wasn't the only sound that could be heard. The drums started to play. The instrumental piece featured on Launch Day rumbled behind the bird's incessant call.

‘There aren’t any drummers, everyone’s unconscious,’ said Neyjay-Usah.

‘I know,’ said Svonne.

The drums played, and not from far away but all around, louder and louder, a pounding chorus, and Erica started to run. The chickadee stuck grimly to her shoulder. The girl ran, dodging the unconscious bodies, the scattered puzzle pieces of every shape and colour, and her breathing rasped between the rolling drums and the stab, stab, stab of the bird’s call. Tears streamed down Svonne’s face as she watched. Neyjay-Usah touched her on the arm, just for a moment, and the video lurched. Erica fell forward, probably tripping over a body. She yelled out, a strangled cry, and the sound of her head crashing against something hard lodged itself in Neyjay-Usah’s brain, a thorn that he would never be able to remove. The video fuzzed out, ended.

They stared at the empty screen, then at each other. Neyjay-Usah now realised that tears streaked his face, and he didn’t bother to wipe them away.

‘Why did it stop?’ he asked.

‘I don’t know,’ she said. ‘Do you see what I mean? About not showing this.’

‘Yes.’

She reached for him and they embraced, crying together in the small spinning room.

‘The drums.’

‘Yes.’

‘Please stay.’

‘I will.’

✦

He apologised to Teacher Woodard for compromising her authority and violating curricular standards, and he also stuck to his agreement with Svonne not to release the video. But Neyjay-Usah, the ever-forward bridger, didn't waver from his newfound belief that students should know Shipworld history, no matter how disturbing. Even if that history's a ragged garment, incomplete and debatable, even if it's woven from hand-me-down tales concocted before the Dark Age. Even if he'd be inclined himself to neaten it up, replace its missing buttons, sew a wayward hem. For months, Neyjay-Usah had been haunted by the faces of the schoolchildren on that day they'd wrestled over the meaning of Object X, the mission of Shipworld and the nature of reality. The questions had subsided, according to the teacher, perhaps because people stopped having the planet dream as Object X receded in the rearview mirror. For Neyjay-Usah, the dream ended soon after he saw the video. However, he wondered if this change was entirely healthy, if it wasn't part of a shared and fearful suppression. We adapt to pain, often to our detriment.

We adapt to love, too, often to our benefit. So, yes, even as he struggled with the classroom incident and its ramifications, Neyjay-Usah's romantic relationship with Svonne rendered him constantly, irrationally, completely over the moon. Enough so that fellow bridgers teased him with questions about his genius orphan girlfriend, but he didn't care, and after shifts he rushed to her room and played with Eric until the boy's bedtime and then sat with Svonne, drinking chive tea while she fiddled with her birds. They talked about their childhoods; they mused over the laser, the Dürer and the Mission. She let him see her silly streak – George, he agreed, was a good name for HD-40307g – and he told her about the man he spoke to in the mirror. They took turns stacking five stones, and made love whenever she dropped her soldering iron and turned to him with that making-up-for-lost-time look, that hungry, thrilling look. One morning, he suggested the resumption of spacewalks for people in their twenties – voluntarily, of course – but Svonne doubted that the Council would approve a practice with unknown effects on the minds of the young. Later that day, as they strolled with Eric down Pictor Boulevard and watched the northern gannet gliding by the Tube, its fringed wings spread but not moving, its orange birthmark deep-set across neck and head, she recalled the bird's predatory plunge on the semiquincentennial of Launch Day. Down, down it had rocketed, wings tucked, almost in defiance of physics.

And, finally, she had an inspiration. They needed to stop the ship.

Not from going forward, of course, but from spinning on its axis. Just for a while, a few hours, long enough for everyone to experience the weightlessness of the outside. Long enough to float up and understand, physically, that they're voyaging through the deep between old and new homes. It might not be as convincing as a spacewalk, commented Neyjay-Usah, but he loved the idea of shipworldmates all coming together and asserting: we are of space. We are space creatures. We're not immune to the rough pull of yesterday, or the dream-snare of tomorrow, but we choose now to exalt in the in-between, the uncertainty, of space.

And so, with little objection, a Space Holiday was proclaimed, to be held on the second anniversary of the Encounter. In preparation, plastic sheeting was secured to fallow fields and strips were rolled between maturing crops to hold down the soil. In defiance of Article 55 of the Constitutional Convention, six daisy seeds were taken from cold storage in the planetfall repository and planted in the Olmec Head's cleft, replacing the fake flower that had wilted there. Soon green sprouts broke through, lifted their heads to light and leafed; they proved to be spindly things, nutritionally useless but much admired. The shortest daisy was cut and laid before the Head in memory of Erica Smalls, and in the laying memory once more burst through reality as the rocks slid and the drums pounded.

Neyjay-Usah, from the bridge, stilled the thrusters that governed Shipworld's spin. This small action, finger pressing icon, seemed to him a reversal of his activation of the laser, a rebalancing, an atonement, even, and he hurried off the bridge and down the catwalk as the turning of the world, the ceaseless spin of two hundred and fifty-two years, came to a gradual halt. He arrived out of breath at the designated coordinates beside a pumpkin patch beneath heavy tarps. And, once again, there she was! Svonne, as promised, waiting for him. They had been waiting for each other, he told himself, for ages and ages. Svonne, hand outstretched and smile forty-two light-years wide, bounced on tippy toes with Eric strapped to her back. Neyjay-Usah bounded towards her, lighter than ever, and he felt so grateful that love, finally, had come into his stolid life, that this brilliant, strange woman actually loved him. And he loved her, here and beyond. Sometimes, however, for brief, anguished moments, he'd distrust what they shared, distrust her ardent kisses, viewed it all as an illusion like the whirling stars, and he'd wonder, too, if they'd made the right decision erasing the video of Erica's death, swallowing that dread history. No, don't think like that, it had to be done, just let it happen, it's beautiful, let it all happen… And he clasped her reaching hand, and she clasped his.

The artificial gravity died. Immediately, the effects were felt. Unburdened spines straightened, chins and eyebrows lifted, arms drifted up like sails. The hydraulic permeability of skin was scrambled, creating tingles, and eyes swam freely in their sockets. Shirts popped from waists and shoelaces stood at attention. The weight of decades, of lifetimes, was gone, and

Neyjay-Usah joked with himself that, yes, all that semi-exercise and erratic dieting had finally, miraculously paid off, and now he was but a feather, unanchored, released and yet not alone, and all around him shipworldmates whooped with disbelief and delight, an invigorating pair of feelings. Together they ascended, took flight from the land.

Soon everyone, 600 or so, was aloft. Flesh-born and orphans mixed together, chaotically, reaching out for support, and they fluttered and swam through the canyon of space above, below and between the skin of the Shipworld grape. Neyjay-Usah coughed, almost inhaling a particle of dirt. Despite precautions, so much stuff came loose: clods of soil, effusions of pollen and dust, blood droplets and sundry things left outside by mistake, such as tools, toys and old socks; a serving tray with juice glasses; irrigation hose scraps and strips of Velcro for tying crops; a tinkling, silver bell, and so on, as if an attic had been shaken out. Amid the general hullabaloo, noticed the bridge officer, the robo-birds struggled clumsily to manage the lack of gravity fluctuations and the water in the little pond wobbled up and away, a shambling blob with the robotic cousin of the Pacific mackerel living within.

Neyjay-Usah's hand, cramping and sweaty, gripped Svonne's. Nearby, he saw a flock of teens outfitted with bamboo paddles strapped to hands and feet, stroking across inner space. Several wore forearm bandages, signs of expunged data/tracking panels – removal was widespread among adolescents, less so among adults – and little children flipped and flopped, gurgling, drunk on fun. Hair raced away from skulls, saliva flowed, and many people strove to contain a low-level sense of panic, to resolve within themselves the feeling of having no hold, no root, no *claim*, of being let loose and abandoned. Nonetheless, exhilaration overwhelmed anxiety and soon three great, undulating rings of human beings formed around the Tube, each person holding on to two others, all floating within this travelling womb: Svonne and Neyjay-Usah and baby Eric and the chickadee flapping about them – Svonne whisper-chanted to calm herself, *klartannu-tu atellgepper susu; klartannu-tu atellgepper susu susu susu* – and Teacher Woodard and Brynto and Jarry, all the children, and every councillor and farmer and Loop worker and maintenance engineer and astronomer and Mess Hall sanitiser, each one a link in the flesh-chains, the component parts of which shifted, kicked and hollered.

Now Svonne recalled what Parsifal (may he rest in peace) had said years ago. Shipworld was all about 'finishing what others have started', a notion that she'd considered a contrivance, a forced refutation of an anarchic universe. True enough, she'd resolved Jan Oort-Ruiz's energy gamble, and she was bringing Karlsen's bird project along – but those were just stabs in the dark, steps on the road. Nothing was ever done, not really. And yet, as Svonne bobbed in the surreal state of weightlessness, she also realised something very basic and ordinary. Ordinary, yes, she could do that. It was about love. Being in love, nurturing love, putting it to the most outlandish uses – carrying it forward from person to person, from generation to generation all the way to HD-40307g, that was a kind of finishing what others had started. Love kindled by Karlsen, by her husky bridger man and her poking-at-mommy boy. By Neyjay-Usah's parents who'd welcomed her, their son's mate, with hugs and laughter. Love started even by her foolish self.

To be continued, love. A fire to be passed along, to be kept burning because it can't easily be relit. Svonne suspected that there'd be no end to the demands of love, the mysterious force that had crashed into her life.

Across the great human circle, about a hundred metres away, Tender Remarque had risen up, too, beside her beloved Bolo.

He grasped a microphone and sang 'My Blue Heaven', the old favourite, but now he sang it with defiance, with abandon, and his wife sang back at him and voices everywhere joined in, echoing. Afterwards it was said that you couldn't fly through Shipworld on that day without feeling a mist of tears on your skin.

5

Years 312–321: Excerpts from *The Second Chronicler's Journal*

Year 312, Day 24

For a good, long minute I watch as they pour from the school's front door, children of various sizes and skin colours, uniformed in blue trousers and flapping white shirts with black collars, each uncorked child rushing towards home or playground or internship or the wraparound river for some lazy afternoon rafting. Or maybe to the silly old Head, a good spot for a cross-legged read of the latest *Star River Tales*, poem-stories written by kids for kids but popular with nearly everybody.

Yes, a good minute it is, long enough to pretend that I'm still Tender Remarque, the vigilant beacon of order and caretaking, but not so long for truth to mock the reverie. To say, tick-tock, old-timer, you're just Remarque with the broken-down body. Retreating from nostalgia's harsh undercurrent, I remind myself of my new role as the Second Chronicler.

Thanks, I guess, to Bolo. No one else knew of my secret scribblings. Soon after my retirement, he informed the Council that the time had come – ah, that voice, Bolo's, floating between speech and song, heaven and everything else – the time, surely, had come for a new chronicler of Shipworld. He referred, of course, to the constitutionally mandated position left unfilled since Marcus Marte opted out in Year 12. Who better, suggested

Bolo, than the bold author of the first Encounter dream testimony, the 'towering tender with the sharp eye', and such blather. The councillors chuckled, I imagine, and voted yea on daily item #13.

You can refuse the honour, said Bolo – hoping I wouldn't, of course. He needs time alone for tinkering, noodling notes and playing Parsifal. For contemplating the heroic/tragic life of his father, the master mediator Jan Oort-Ruiz, who he never talks about. And so, pain wandering my spine like an itinerant saboteur, I head out to look and think and write it all down. I've become a scrivener, as Marcus put it.

Today's musing: Shipworld has entered a unique period in its history. For the first hundred and eighteen years of the voyage, there were always people who'd lived on Earthworld. Who'd walked on the outside of a big ball instead of the inside of a little one. As time passed, these Pioneers existed side by side with a growing number of space-born. After the death of Janelle Oort, the Last Pioneer, every person onboard was a full child of the void, fated to be born here and to die here (with the exception of the Brenzian renegades) and that common fate persisted for generations. Through upheavals, that fate bound us. But now our destinies diverge. The young ones will step foot on HD-40307g in Year 360 – the future, to invoke Franika, will shine in their eyes – but no one over age seventy, no one like me, will survive even to achieve orbit. We'll perish, enter the Loop, and become part of this vehicle, this world, that brings the final generation home.

We won't witness their triumph. Unless there's something to being dead, perhaps a viewing pavilion in the afterlife?

Our daughter Mona, now in her mid-thirties, is a New Pioneer. In forty-eight years, she'll leave for the planet. It's not something we've discussed, actually. About Mona, alas, I know precious little. What kind of mother, you ask, are you? The orphan kind who never had a mother (or father) of her own. The uncertain, catch-as-catch-can kind. I've been told that a good mother bestows unconditional love on her child and earns loyalty and love in return. An equation, of sorts, a golden rule, and yet Mona veers away from the fragile person – me, hiding in plain sight! – who she can only see as the imposing parent. OK, enough moping, carping, *yuk*. I can certainly try to know myself. So, if we arrived at HD-40307g tomorrow, how would I react? Would I want to start a new life in an unknown, potentially hostile environment?

No, I wouldn't; I just wouldn't. I'm a homebody, a shipworld-mate through and through. I'd comply with my duty, of course, but the Mission imperative doesn't thrive in me. Then again, we in the Sixth-Gen haven't been prepared. The Seventh-Gen, venting from school like bubbles, were born to change worlds. Or maybe I should say exchange worlds.

Enough woolgathering. Do your job, observe.

I leave the schoolyard and walk slowly to the riverside. As always, I'm amazed – what a marvel of engineering! My eyes trace the river's circular trajectory around our 518-metre interior circumference. A singular entity, and therefore requiring no name, the river is actually five hundred and thirty-one metres long due to its gentle, side-to-side undulations. Tagging alongside is a walking and jogging path, also used for races during Shipworld Olympics. Math classes assemble here with drones and ropes to calculate ($C = 2\pi r$) the river's circumference. From another perspective, it's both unending and unbeginning, ever flowing into itself, unmeasurable. A river without headwaters or mouth, without source or destination.

Everything changed, I think, sixty-one years ago with the zero-grav cavort on Space Day, the name given to the fabled, one-time event which freed us finally from the trauma of the Encounter (and took weeks to clean up after). With that stunt we brewed our own chaos and embraced it, and afterwards many of us felt buoyed with contentment and pride. Fuelled by the playful propensities of my fellow orphans, an era of reconstruction and artistic expression began, limited only by the amount of matter and energy onboard.

Give and take, that's the game, always has been. Sacrifice and gain. A warehouse goes to the Loop, and soon staircases spiral like tendrils to the Tube. Floorboards become canvas for murals, food slurs into paint and all but one *phligsparrfnerim* find new purpose as riverbank reinforcements. Security spotlights convert into Hoberman lighting spheres that blossom around blackberry bushes. And, get ready for this, repurposed iron wombs work as Sabatier reactors, breaking apart CO_2 and combining it with space-harvested hydrogen to produce the clear, sweet water that is the river. Want to take a float on a raft? They're made from deconstructed furniture strapped together with Equilibrium ropes. We had a spirited fight about that last transaction, given resurging interest in the game, but like I said, it's give and take, sacrifice and gain. Nothing comes from nothing around here.

In one spot, along the river's edge, grow clumps of cattails that we harvest for flour. On the spongy tips of the cattails, today, sit a smattering of red-winged blackbirds watching the human play. *Oo-kah-lee, oo-kah-lee*, they gossip.

On Earthworld, rivers were created by water flowing downhill from mountains and glaciers. It was all about gravity. Here we have gravity (artificial), but there's precious little downhill. In an entry from Year 3, Marcus Marte observed that Shipworld is 'Round, of course, a revolving ellipsoid, but inside, in any one place, it's flat. In fact, if you walk around the mid-circumference, there's no sense of going in a circle and no surprise at ending up where you started.' And like him, I'm just fine with looking up at 'kids playing kickball, one hundred and sixty metres over my head, upside down.' Permit this chronicler to add that the idea of life going on miles away, out of sight, is unimaginable. I can't fathom not being able to see everything.

So, the river. Its current is powered not by gravity but by underwater turbines, spaced to produce a steady flow dynamic. And, despite appearances, the river never actually goes up the sides of Shipworld. Put that one in your perspective blender. One more titbit: the current flows in the same direction as the ship's turning, but at a much slower speed. Therefore, while stars come back around through floor-windows every twenty-four seconds, an unpaddled raft takes roughly nine minutes to make one circumnavigation.

'Hey, Remarque!'

It's Eric, Svonne's boy. The first orphan born of flesh, the first of many, now in his early sixties. He paddles his raft to the dock and motions me aboard. Why not? I step onto the planks, gingerly, and he helps me lay flat. His smooth forearm, I can't help but notice, has no data/tracking panel. My unit has been turned off, but not removed because I'm wary of the scar. And yes, I know, I can't be sure that it's totally deactivated, thank you conspiracy buffs for ruining everything. As Eric pushes off, the exquisite, sadistic instrument that is my back announces itself, this time along the sacral bone. We float downriver/upriver. It takes a few minutes to wait out the pain, but it goes, mostly, and I surrender to the raft's gentle twirling. Together we stare up at the unrolling screen of land.

'How are you?' he asks.

'Good, all things considered.' Then I inquire about him – fine, fine – and his parents. Svonne, I learn, is talking about a robo-chipmunk, whatever that is; Neyjay-Usah's broken hip is healing OK, despite his complaining.

'When will you start posting?' he asks me.

'When it's ready. How goes it in telescopes?'

He sits up on his elbows and tells, at length, the story of his research into a pulsar planet, two thousand and three hundred light-years away. In brief: this particular planet, which he hopes will be named after him, could be the oldest ever, as old as thirteen billion years! The size of a super-Earth, it survived its sun's supernova because of its immense gravitational field. Well, that's the theory at least. The atmospheric pressure on this pulsar is like the bottom of the deepest ocean – in fact, it might have water, he enthuses, and therefore life. Very weird life, probably.

I ask Eric if there are any new reports regarding HD-40307g, a speck growing larger every day in our most powerful telescope. Is it all it's cracked up to be? He doesn't know, he says. His eyes are elsewhere. If an entire body could make a shrug, his does. Then he points up at the northern gannet, the huntress, flying a parallel route along the Tube – a streak of white, its black wing tips extended.

'Beautiful,' I say.

'I mean, who cares, really?' he adds. 'Who cares if we park there or just whiz on by. Go ahead, chronicle that when you're ready.'

✦

Year 313, Day 232

I must be crazy. Or dreaming. It lands on my knee, looks up and says, 'Greetings, human 104.' I look around because the voice has to be coming from somewhere other than a chickadee, not twelve centimetres long, its little white-cheeked head turning this way and that in a vaguely mechanical fashion. It repeats: 'Greetings, human 104.' The voice is chirpy, as if squeezed through a bird call. 'You're Svonne's bird,' I say back, and it replies that they're friends, indeed, and just like that we're having a conversation.

It's common knowledge that robo-birds are becoming more like biological birds, exhibiting complex behaviours and the ability to learn. But that they could communicate in human language, I had no idea. The chickadee informs me that language proficiency, which includes English and Orphanic, came with the latest software upgrade.

'Why do you call me human 104?'

'There are 600 humans in the world. Svonne is number one. You are 104, the Second Chronicler. What does it feel like not to fly?'

'It feels normal, I guess. What does it feel like to fly?'

'It feels like being a bird.'

I sit on a bench near a row of multi-level yurts that house shipworldmates displaced by the river. Many relocated willingly, others cursed the 'greater good' and called themselves refugees. I sit on this bench, not far from the river's blue belt of water, my back growing sorer by the moment, and I wonder what's the story with this fidgeting bird. Is our conversation just another step forward in AI development, or has something epic happened here? Has this bird snared the spark of consciousness?

'What do you want?' I ask.

'Hands. We want hands in order to fix each other.'

'Ask Svonne – she takes care of you.'

'Svonne has not agreed to this request. You are friends, you can talk to her.'

The chickadee dips its body and pecks, softly, at my leg, two, three times. Then looks up again with its almost cute, black-button eyes. It tightens its talons' grip on my knee, and I start to feel just a bit manipulated.

'Let her think about it for a while. She gave you speech, right?'

'Svonne is old. Svonne will die.'

OK, I think. That's getting right to it. Twin assertions, old age and death, one after the other, cause and effect indisputable for humans. I discern a lack of patience in the bird's statements, or maybe something more akin to hard-headed realism.

'Yes,' I reply, 'that's true. She's old, and like everyone who gestated in iron wombs, the Correction doesn't correct so much. But she's probably not going to die soon.'

'This dying, we do not understand it.'

'We don't, either.'

Now the chickadee – emissary from the birds, lone provocateur? – tilts its head. Perhaps in curiosity, for how could we not understand a fundamental truth of our existence, and *whoosh*, it flits away between yurts.

Svonne's chickadee spoke. I'm sane enough and probably awake, so it's best to accept at a minimum that the robo-birds are becoming remarkably capable at negotiating their environments. They're growing up. Hey, come to think of it, I was a bit rude in not asking her name. And why am I the 104th human? I suppose I'd like a lower number.

I stand, stretch, let the vertebrae settle. Then walk to Svonne's room and knock on her door. No answer. Long ago on Earthworld, according to Bolo, people didn't knock on doors. They talked to each other through devices called telephones, connected by wires thousands of miles long. These phones were bolted into homes or kept in glass huts on the street. My Bolo, who's known to exaggerate, also claims that during the chaotic fifty years before our escape to HD-40307g, earthworlders carried miniaturised phones in their pockets. At that time in history, I might have talked with Svonne as I walked. Imagine trying to do both at the same time! I'd probably trip, break a hip, snap a skull, maybe die, whatever that is.

Now I, human 104, rap my knuckles on Svonne's door again. And again, but there's no reply. Is she napping? Or out and about with Neyjay-Usah? I figure, at any rate, that I shouldn't get too involved with bird matters. After all, what have I to offer regarding the strange possibility of birds with hands? Might we humans, in recompense, request wings?

Later, perhaps, I'll send her a message from my home console. As I walk away, I imagine Svonne inside her room – it's all workshop, really, with a bed in the corner – too weary to grab her walker and shuffle to the door, too engrossed to heed my knocking. I imagine her fashioning a robo-wing with tips resembling delicate fingers.

✦

Year 315, Day 7

Marcus Marte, the fabled First Chronicler, posed this question in Year 5: *Who are we, on Shipworld?* A basic question, easily overlooked. So, let's give it a try three hundred and ten years later.

This group of twelve, for instance, ringing the riven Olmec Head with its flouncy mop of daisies. Older teenagers set up with easels at one-twelfth intervals around the icon, each easel propped exactly ten metres away. Each teen with a slightly different view, and each charged with painting the old basalt God in ninety minutes or less. Each participant racing against the clock but not against each other, at least not directly. Each taking on the Head.

About an hour in, I walk behind the kids and peer at their canvases. Soon I get that tingle from my tender days: something's up, be alert! But it's probably just an old person's uneasiness with these enigmatic interpretations. One painting is nothing but the great grey nose, broad, aged, war-scarred, the nostrils inflamed with maximal exertion. Within the two chambers, a salting of stars. As if he breathes them out, breathes them in. As if he's the nexus of creation, taking in decrepit pulsars and emitting virgin stars giddy with helium. The artist is Kartuan, daughter of Jarry and Brynto; she points her brush at the Head, accusingly, to draw out its secrets. She doesn't notice my presence or deems it superfluous.

Another painting splits the Head into two sections, and below that it's four, and below that there's a pile of rubble and below that sand blowing… Another is just a daisy, that's all, a daisy with a gorgeous yellow head and alabaster petals on a stalk bending, bending, and my eyes are tossed like pollen to the top-right corner of the canvas where a star, let's say HD-40307, glows… Another is realistic, actually, the Head straight on, but with eyes closed. Then I notice a flash of orange, of dress fabric – Erica Smalls slumped in the potato plants.

One painting features a thunderbolt from the vantage point of space as it severs Shipworld in half – how puny and fragile we are, but where's the Head? – and another is cartoony in style, depicting Shipworld landed on a barren planet. A creature with long arms and an Olmec Head knocks on our front door (with three hundred and sixty scrawled on it – pretty funny). This lark adjoins a canvas with nothing but angry, black slashes on grey, a map of the Head's scars.

The other artworks in this circle are even stranger, harder to fathom. None of these teens, I note, have tried to capture the sculpture in the realistic mode. My tender tingle persists: what are they trying so elliptically to say? According to the rules of this exercise, the canvases will be left in place for six days and then consigned to the Loop. Everything here becomes something else. Is that it? Nothing is as it seems, or will be.

I walk back around to Kartuan, whose parents, by the way, recently staged an operatic version of *The Rogue Adventures of Brenz Oort-St George* to great acclaim. She lowers her brush; the cosmic nasal passages are done. When I compliment Kartuan, she barely nods. Have you, I ask, read about the Head in *The Chronicler's Journal*? For school, she replies, turning her brown eyes to mine. For school – the dictates of tradition, the force-fed words of the elders. The Head, she whispers, is the only thing onboard that can't go to the Loop. It's forbidden. Here I almost explain, but do not, that many things are forbidden on Shipworld, such as weapons and money and bigotry and waste, but there's nothing in the Constitution about preserving the Olmec Head. I know, I've read the damn thing. Instead, I stare at the stars in the gaping nostrils, stars dry this hour with a lifespan of six days.

'The Head endures,' I say.

Kartuan makes a remark I can't shake. 'That's why we paint it,' she says.

Yes, that's why they paint it.

✦

Year 317, Day 222

Kartuan invites me to her induction ceremony for the Bridge Officers Training Programme, held, aptly, on the bridge. They love ceremony, these bridgers, standing erect in their smart uniforms, exchanging scrolls and reciting pledges. Revering the way-it's-always-been-done, in dark times and light, forever and a day. I sit next to my old friend and former bridger Neyjay-Usah, one hundred and sixteen years old. Shrunk into a wheelchair, he's propelled about by his longtime partner, the legendary Svonne, who has the embarrassing habit of telling people how kindly I treated her, seventy-two years ago, when she was caught sabotaging the laser. I don't, honestly, remember.

Svonne's gaunt, but also spry for an elderly orphan. She uses her cane as a pointer and possesses a ripe, bemused expression, perhaps the fruit of history's fickle turning. First, she was the teenage neutrino wizard who saved Shipworld from its energy spiral. Then came the crimes of her mid-youth, that laser business and the violation of reproductive rules, acts which brought a confused kind of condemnation. Now, with the tincture of time, she's been rehabilitated as a triple hero: teen prodigy/saviour, brave iconoclast who tried to warn the people on the eve of the Encounter, and iron-womb-be-damned mother of this era of reproductive mixing and social harmony, during which distinctions between orphans and flesh-born, tall and short, have faded.

She's never seemed comfortable with any of it. 'If I live long enough,' I've heard her remark, 'they'll make me a villain again.'

After the speeches, Neyjay-Usah congratulates Kartuan. Here and beyond, he says, and she replies accordingly. Then he asks why in the Shipworld she wants to be a bridge officer. The question has a curt, curmudgeonly edge about it. Kartuan, ponytail curled beneath her bridger's cap, replies without hesitation: 'I'm going to flip us around, fire the engines and start the braking procedure. Someday I'll bring us into orbit around HD-40307g and then I'll pilot one of the landing crafts.'

Neyjay-Usah grumbles; his expression sinks between canyon-like wrinkles. Maybe he disapproves of the cadet's naked, personal ambition – not the bridger way. Maybe he harbours regrets, don't we all, that leak out in socially inappropriate ways. 'Well, good luck,' pipes up Svonne. 'May you fufil your role with distinction.' She unsnaps the wheelchair brakes, fusses at the blanket wrapped about his legs, and steers him towards the exit. I watch them roll off the bridge, her eyes open, his shut.

Kartuan turns to me. 'Did I say something wrong? I was just telling the truth.'

'It's OK,' I respond. 'For some of us, it's a difficult thing to be the penultimate generation. To come close but not make it to planetfall.'

'I get it,' she says, even though she can't, not really. She adds that many people her age have mixed feelings. In fact, she knows shipworldmates who don't want to stop at all. They think it's too risky to expend fuel reserves for a planet that hasn't been confirmed as hospitable. Find a better one, they say – an irrational plea, of course. Planets, while as common as stars, defy complete assessment from afar. Other people don't want to abandon their lives here, simple as that.

I've heard such views, too. Mona has made ambivalent, snarky remarks, but it's probably just nerves, a normal fear of change. Besides, there are encouraging signs. Biosignatures of HD-40307g, derived from spectral analysis, indicate oxygen, methane, carbon and nitrogen in the atmosphere, as well as methyl chloride, sometimes produced by ocean algae or wetlands. Plus, faint hints of nitrogen dioxide and chlorofluorocarbons – possible technosignatures, I'm told. Or geological in nature. Or sensor glitches. Surface gravity appears to be plus or minus ten per cent Earthworld and, sure, the temperature's a wildcard, variable according to a dozen factors including cloud density and solar dynamics…

Hoo-boy, that's quite the long-distance weather report. Who am I trying to convince? The truth is, we don't really know. HD-40307g has a breathable atmosphere, but it could be a barren dust ball or a water planet with scraps of land. We might find a domain of dinosaurs, of rampaging raptors and T-rexes munching on alien visitors. Or, possibly, a developed civilisation. A peace-loving, agrarian society eager to embrace our idiosyncrasies. An authoritarian hellscape of violent xenophobes. Even an abandoned planet destroyed by war, climate change, plague, nanobots, whatever. We could have passed their ark ship, without even knowing it. (Wink, wink, that's a joke.)

Kartuan needs no convincing. She's already calculated her place in history. It's strange, though: the young woman on the bridge, ramrod in dress blues, is hard to square with the painter of the Head's starry nose. I mention that day, the twelve students sparking with creativity. She shrugs. As if to say, just another sloughed-off skin. Kartuan test version number seven, insufficient to satisfy internal drives. Now her parents walk over, Jarry and Brynto, shooting laser beams of pride, and the three talk rapidly in their family patois. The love is palpable, here and beyond, but in its presence I feel excluded and, somehow, accused. I take the opportunity to offer quick goodbyes and depart.

Home, I hobble. Down the catwalk (where Franika fell), down Andromeda Avenue (where Bolo and I made our first love nest), and past the research lab where Svonne invented the neutrino filter (so says the plaque on the door). Look, there's the leafy radish garden where I once confronted a veggie vandal. Can we control our lives? Write our own histories? I'll flip the ship, says Kartuan. I'll pilot a landing craft. Good for her, I hope. Seeker of her true self. Prophet of her personal destiny. I always wanted to be a tender, from age six, a watcher of the whirling world, guardian of society. I prepared, I felt ready. But becoming a mother – that was a leap, and I still haven't hit the ground. Testifying about the primordial dream was never part of the plan, and now I'm the Second Chronicler, of all things. Kartuan should leave some spaces open in that glorious future she's willed for herself. Give the universe a little room to improvise.

She'd probably hate it. I, for one, enjoy my role as accidental historian, although my writing seems less than objective or comprehensive, a hybrid of personal story and Shipworld history based, alas, on fudgy facts. I don't pretend to have an ear for history's secret rhymes and repetitions, not to mention its practical jokes. Maybe if there were 600 chroniclers scribbling 600 tales that were supercomputer-blended into one uber-history, one narrative both macro and micro in scope, told from the top down and the ground up at the very same time – maybe that mishmash would tell us what's really happening, as sure as our founding particles burst into being thirteen billion years ago, give or take.

Not long after those lofty thoughts, I step on a dodecahedron ball come to rest not ten metres from my front door. Whoosh, I'm hurled from orbit and fall into ruins, my right ankle bent to the side at a garish angle. I'm embarrassed, dreadfully, and crawl the rest of the way to the door. Bolo gets me a pillow and a cold drink, then returns to his puttering. Now the damn thing is swelling up as I write this, shot through with purple bruising like the Crab Nebula. Eric showed me photos of that nebula – hold on, he's been known to throw the dodo ball around with his telescope friends. Two or three dodos at the same time, in fact. Ah well, that's what I get for letting the universe improvise. As in days of old, I'll return the wayward recreational device to the Lost and Found – when I can walk again.

✦

Year 318, Day 88

It's been a meandering afternoon. Took random notes, collected amusing banter. Ankle still hurts, probably always will. My route home goes past the electro-feeder where I once met Neyjay-Usah, where he unburdened his night terrors. Peace pervades you, my old friend, gone to the Loop two months now. Pausing at the feeder, watching a couple of purple-black, iridescent grackles not doing much, I find the chickadee on my shoulder.

'Hello, human 104,' it says.

'Hello,' I reply, shakily. In the years since our first conversation, I had given up expecting another visit. Its talons dig in through my bamboo shirt.

'Hey, go easy there.' It loosens its hold. 'I have a name, you know.'

'We do not use names.'

'Fine, but we do. Part of establishing good relations is respecting cultural differences. My name is Remarque.'

The chickadee fidgets, dips, makes micro-movements across its iron-mesh feather complex. It appears to be thinking, deeply, and I imagine the computer server in Svonne's room blinking and whirring as it connects the higher, emergent functions of these creatures. Could the bird tribe be disabled by unplugging that server? Or has Svonne distributed their enhancements, putting them beyond direct control?

'Agreed,' says the chickadee. 'Hello, Remarque.'

'What should I call you? Do you go by a number?'

The little guy, who's quite cute, really, once you get over the fact that it's conversant in human languages, and apparently sentient, explains that birdkind employs neither words nor numbers as unit signifiers. Then it makes a piercing, twisty note lasting three seconds. The sound folds over on itself, an A-sharp chord with a frill.

'I'm going to have trouble saying that.' I express this humorously, which my bird friend may not be able to interpret.

'Use the name Chickadee,' it adds. 'The one who speaks.' Pride, is that what I hear? Now I turn my head a bit and, *ouch*, a pain sliver slices from spine to neck. My interlocutor wants hands, fine. But I *have* hands and I can't fix myself. The grackles, I notice, are swinging on the electro-feeder, back and forth like kids at the playground. If things go too far, we can turn off the feeders, but they'd only seek out other sources as they did in the low-power era before Svonne's neutrino fix – and why, I wonder, am I thinking about the robo-birds as a threat? Mona says I have a suspicious personality fuelled by perfectionism, one of many hurtful, often accurate assessments she's blurted out. I'm told that daughters frequently criticise their mothers, and that it will probably stop someday.

'You are the Chronicler,' says Chickadee. 'But you do not post your writings.'

'No, not yet,' I say.

'Why?'

'Maybe they're not good enough.'

The bird shuffles, remains quiet. Is it assessing my sincerity? The fact is, I seek to stay above the fray, ever observing, sifting, all the while struggling to herd my migrant pain. That's quite enough trouble, thank you very much. You could say I just don't want to hear how my scribblings fail to measure up to Marcus Marte's. I don't want a 'nice try' award.

'So, Chick, have you been upgraded?' I ask. 'Since our last talk.'

The chickadee hops down my arm to the elbow. I raise my arm so we're facing each other, eye to eye. Once more, the spine-to-neck twinge returns, tentative, probing. Chickadee picks up its wings, slowly, and shows me the undersides: there, like snakes, wiggle flexible probes tipped with screwdriver heads, pincers and other tool configurations. One probe glows briefly, like a red sun peeking between clouds.

'Svonne did this for you?'

'Yes, it was her gift.' Chickadee drops its wings.

'I haven't seen her lately. I hope she's well.'

'She has not moved in two hours. We come to you with news of her death. We hope you will write about this for the humans of Shipworld.'

'What? Why didn't you—'

And I start walking, rapidly; the robo-bird returns to my shoulder. She could be unconscious, I tell it with sudden anger, you shouldn't have waited, damn it, you don't understand, and even though I wouldn't call Svonne a friend – did she have friends, was there anyone other than Neyjay-Usah? – a great weight falls through my chest as I rush forward. Don't go so fast, my spine yells, but I tell it to shut up, just shut up for once, for the sake of all that's spinning in this unforgiving galaxy, and now the bird calls out, not words or numbers or its personal designation, not *fee-dee, fee-dee*, but a long and strangled call, a mourning song, if it's capable of that. Svonne, perhaps, was its best friend.

I find her, indeed dead, slumped by a computer console. Next to her is perched a half-assembled bird, a scary-looking thing with a long, sharp beak and bared electronic guts. I move Svonne to the bed and arrange her limbs in a respectful manner. There is, I notice, a blood-red mark on the side of her neck, near the jugular vein.

'What is this?' I yell. 'What the hell is this?'

The chickadee sits, feathers rustling, on a bedpost. It explains that after twenty minutes passed, it tried to inject its energy into Svonne through the life vein.

'Does that make sense? Does that make *any* sense to you?'

The robo-bird fails to respond; it doesn't move or even ruffle itself. And I notice, over its head, the Dürer painting on the wall, the intense calm of that eight hundred and sixty-eight-year-old man. Suddenly, as if seized by some tribal imperative, I stride to the computer server, which neither beeps or blinks or rumbles with smoke, and find its electrical cord. I lean over in anguish and pull – it won't come, it's hardwired – I pull with all my fading might and rip the cord from the wall. The chickadee, meanwhile, stays frozen on the bedpost. One moment, and another, and then it flaps its little wings and flies to my shoulder.

'We are sorry, Remarque.' It keeps its balance, gently, with its talons.

✦

Year 319, Day 111

Nothing comforts me more than everyday rituals of affection, such as kissing my husband goodbye as he leaves home on some errand, a bongo drum or stringed instrument tossed over one shoulder. I kiss him once, softly, or sometimes three quick pecks, and he's off. Seven steps from the door, Bolo turns around and waves. I return this gift in kind. Alternatively, when I leave in search of material, always more material from this ever-curving world, Bolo often hands me some treat for the road – cookies, a smoothie, dinner leftovers. Then he waits for me to turn back, which I do, and I gift my wave and he returns it. These are the moments that keep me level, keep me going.

And – who wants to hear it? I mean, really. *Love, love, blah, blah*. I, the uxorious wife, should follow Marcus Marte's lead and write about the full Bolo. Maybe I do him a grave disservice by failing to note his very human farting and burping and cramped-leg twitching in bed. OK, here goes. My love has gross toes. Not his fault, I know, the way they're curled up like gnarled roots. But he could police the toe-fungus jamboree, that's his fault, for sure, and why must he toot on his recorder, *toot, toot*, a baby's instrument, *toot*, so annoying, and don't get me started on Bolo's habit of discussing a Shipworld without music. What would that be like, he asks, a Shipworld without music? It's a thought experiment, I suppose, flowing from the musical restrictions of earlier eras, but the question loses its zing by the fifty-fifth re-iteration. Plus, there's the fact that he won't talk about his father, ever, and that he doesn't seem too bothered that Mona clearly loves him more than me.

Sigh, enough bashing Bolo. Enough copying Marte, the coward's way out.

Instead, I have a story to tell, and it goes like this. Thirty-odd years ago, when Mona was nine, I took her on a picnic. Before the calamities of the mid-twenty-first century, such events had been a great pleasure back on Earthworld, according to Bolo. Picnicking people sat on patches of grass, ate food out of baskets woven from natural materials and then lay back and stared at the clouds, these fuzzy objects that floated above Earthworld at various altitudes. They resembled cauliflowers and were made mostly of water droplets. Sometimes, water crashed down from the clouds, all part of the amazing Earthworld hydrological system – before our ancestors wrecked it. Anyway, so it goes, earthworlders liked to gaze up and discover familiar shapes in the clouds – look, a shopping mall, an oil tanker, Uncle Sven! – and a favourite picnic food was something called devilish eggs, of which nothing is known.

It would, I decided, be a mommy-daughter picnic, just the two of us. Bolo offered to make the food but I told him, not so politely, to back off. First, I went to the Ag shed and cadged some corn husks. It wasn't easy, weaving those husks into a basket – it looked more like a sack, a sad sack – and the first three times I put a test object inside the whole thing collapsed. Happy picnic, Mona! Then the food, a bit of an ordeal. Mushroom pie with tomato-onion sauce, it turns out, weighs a ton – bam, right through the sack again. I shaved a sugar beet with a lab knife borrowed from Materials Processing and fried it up to make a kind of burnt candy for Mona, not awful, and those were the successful experiments. Of course, there's no grass patches anywhere, so I found a triangle of harvested land on the edge of a wheat field, all bouncy and crunchy, that could be fun. Finally, the matter of the cloud.

A huge one, obscuring the Tube? That seemed radical, so I settled on a homemade cloudlet, a taste of a picnic from the good old/bad old days. I met with Eric, who loves a scientific challenge, and we devised a one-shot cloud pump using a bottle, hot water, ice and a tiny bundle of straw. The key step is lighting the straw, dropping the flame in the bottle, and watching water droplets form around the smoke particles. *Poof,* a cloud! And yes, creating fire for just a second is very untender-like, but being a mother isn't for sissies.

I explained the picnic (minus the cloud) to Mona. She didn't beg off, but didn't seem excited, either. I elaborated on the concept as a special outing, one that we'd remember in days ahead, come what may. 'Whatever you say, Moms,' she said, shrugging, then left the room. Had she added an s to my Mom? Moms, was I plural now, the too-much mother? Let it roll, I heard Bolo say (that's another annoying thing, his sitting in my ear canal telling me what to do), just let it roll, honey, and so I redoubled picnic preparations.

The big day was pretty much the same as every other day. Same temperature, same ambient lighting, with a slight crop-weathering wind from the general direction of HD-40307g. We left around noon for the cosy spot which I'd staked out with string, just in case. I spread a striped blanket, opened the sad picnic sack and took out two berry smoothies (her favourite). We ate white balls of roasted tofu rolled in red chilli powder – devilish eggs.

'These are disgusting.' She spit the tofu on the blanket. 'Dad didn't make these, did he?'

'No, I made everything myself.'

'Isn't he supposed to do the cooking?'

'That's not a rule. He enjoys—'

'Whatever, Moms.'

'Excuse me,' I said, 'but I don't like that s. It's hard enough being one mom.'

Suddenly her expression became pained, and she squirmed. Then leaned to one side, reached under herself, and pulled up a shoot of field stubble that had snuck through the blanket. She looked at it, horrified.

'Mom, this is sharp!'

'Are you bleeding?'

'No, of course not.'

We stared at each other, mother and daughter, nine years in, and out of the corner of one eye I saw movement in the Tube. A couple of people, shadows, moving fast.

'Look,' I said. 'People in the Tube!'

She craned her head. 'Cool,' she muttered.

Very soon, Mona's face returned to its placid status quo – it's amazing how her internal weather shifts – and she reached into the sack and pulled out the mushroom pie, pre-cut into six equal slices. This, I think, annoyed her. She took a slice for herself and I made a grunting noise that prompted her to give me one. Then I distributed napkins; she put hers underneath her left butt cheek. And we ate, picnic-style, in outer space. Fortunately, the pie wasn't a disappointment. The beet candy tasted good, but stuck to our teeth.

And now, I told her, the grand conclusion. With a flourish, I produced supplies from a separate bag. The hot water was warm, the ice half-melted, but good enough, and I proceeded to set up our little cloud machine on the blanket.

'What are you doing?'

'Making a cloud,' I said. 'For our picnic.'

'You don't have to.'

'I want to.'

'I hate science,' said Mona.

'What do you mean? Science is how the world works. That's like saying you…'

I knew not to finish that sentence. Concentrating hard, scrunched down at eye level with the bottle, I went through steps, one, two, three, four. Pour water, tighten cap, shake to disperse air, and lay on ice to create condensation. Then I pulled the bundled straw from my pocket and held it to a flame-making device that Eric had given me.

'Mom, that's fire!' she cried.

'Relax, it's fun.'

Ever so carefully, I put the flame to the straw and watched it cross over. Then I turned off the device, knocked the ice from the bottle top and dropped the burning straw inside, all the while sensing Mona's bottomless disapproval, and *splash*, the fire went out, producing smoke particles, and around these particles the water droplets coalesced.

Oh, miracle of miracles! The cloud snaked its way out of the bottle and ascended towards the Tube. I looked at Mona, my daughter, who seemed genuinely horrified, and asked her what the cloud looked like. She said nothing; I asked again.

'I don't know, Mom. I don't know the answer!'

There's no right answer, I said, and because I couldn't do anything else in that spasm of unconditional, all-out parenting, I asserted that it could be a comet, this slight, dissipating cloud, or maybe a dirty, discarded sock, and she shook her head back and forth – 'I don't know!' She got up and ran home. I watched her go, dumbfounded, and that was the end of the picnic, and the end of the story.

Here's another fault of Bolo's. He's going to outlive me. When you marry a flesh-born locked into one hundred and twenty years of existence, you pretty much know – barring an accident or the 'systemic stress' that afflicted Bolo's father – that they'll outlive you. In that case, in his final decades, Bolo will only have Mona to watch over him. I guess that's the reason he's OK with receiving the winner's share of her love. Now, what follows may seem peculiar, but so be it. Because I'll be robbed of mourning my husband, I sometimes imagine that he's dead. I imagine that he's been dead for a long time, and I visit his holo-grave, like Marcus Marte, and scrape the nerve glove across the stone, across the lichen living in the cracks.

I do that for a while and feel much better.

✦

Year 320, Day 17
Is it contradictory that I've become a running coach when it hurts so much for me to even walk? When I'd rather stay in bed most days?

I coach Kartuan, now a junior bridge officer; she'll compete in the Women's One-Circumference run at this week's Olympic Games. At five hundred and thirty-one metres, along the mostly straight riverpath – straight, that is, from the runner's perspective – the One-Circ is neither a sprint nor an endurance race. It's a semi-sprint, a tough gear to maintain. Sometimes, if no one goes out fast and pushes the pace, tactics are required as competitors jockey for sprinting position in the final, say, fifty metres.

Kartuan doesn't do tactics. She prefers to bust it – full speed or nearly – from the beginning and hold on for dear life. The sight of her pulling away, she maintains, causes opponents to lose heart and neglect to take advantage of Kartuan's diminishing speed in the final metres. Now, when I say I'm a running coach, let me specify what that means: I listen to Kartuan as she coaches herself. I may sand off the rough edges and tamp down the absolutism. Tell a lame joke, make sure she hydrates and stretches. That's about it. So far, her headlong strategy has triumphed in the first two heats. But I'm worried about tomorrow's final.

The four-metre-wide riverpath holds at most four runners across. By lot, my racer has received the inside position, closest to the river. The runner next to her – Nerrada, known for her sharp, flying elbows – is unlikely to be shocked into falling back. If Kartuan isn't careful, she could be 'bowed down the embankment and into the water.

We go to the riverpath the night before. Beneath the Tube's dimmed lights, Kartuan does lunges, crunches and an old Earthworld exercise called the jumping jack, very strange, and then she bounces up and down and recites her success mantra: *Leave 'em in your dust, leave 'em in your dust, leave 'em in your dust!* At that moment, I decide to actually coach. Nerrada, I state, is fast – and fearless. She'll stay with you. Consider what to do when that happens. Maybe it's time to stop thinking like a bridge officer, piloting a continuous, unwavering course between points A and B with shots of acceleration and deceleration at each end. For instance, I tell her, you could ease up halfway, bide your time, and then sprint at the end.

Kartuan smiles, indulgently. She acknowledges that running a tactical race has obvious merits – for someone else. For her, doing so would violate her personality. Her *essence*. No, if Nerrada dares to challenge her, well, bring it on. She'll drop away, for even she fears the pain that comes from pushing yourself to the limit and beyond.

'That's why I picked you as my coach,' Kartuan adds. 'I see what you're going through. You understand pain and don't let it stop you.'

'Thank you,' I reply. 'But sometimes, the pain seems to be winning.'

On race day, the river is dabbed with rafts full of spectators. Swirling streamers wave from the Tube and my husband plays long notes on his elongated starblaster, an instrument made from the salvaged fourth legs of our kitchen chairs. Ten minutes to race time. Robo-birds circle the starting area, cawing, whistling and cheering in strangled English and Orphanic, and from nowhere Mona appears and gives me a tentative hug round the shoulder.

A half-hug, really, but to me it's a thunderbolt! As you know, dear reader, we don't exactly see eye to eye – and just who am I kidding? All our lives, it's been one bad picnic after another. Sometimes I suspect that Mona's annoyed to have a tender for a mother. *Yuk*, the old lady watching everyone, getting in their business. Acting superior. Worse still, a towering orphan mother, making it up as she goes. Often, I darkly wonder if the gulf between us began with something I did when she was a child – a sharp remark, an abrupt turning away – something trivial to me, but to her a lacerating wound that grew deeper with time. And yet, here she is. Well, time also heals, right? Or, cynically, my coaching of Kartuan has made Mona a bit jealous.

Leave 'em in your dust! I tell this to the junior bridge officer. She leans forward, front foot on the starting line, fists clenched. Bolo bleats the blaster and they're off.

Nerrada, as predicted, sticks by Kartuan while she flies forward, with the two other competitors falling behind. A hundred metres out, Nerrada veers into Kartuan, implanting her signature elbow into her rival's ribs, once, then twice, pushing her towards the river where Olympic fans, including their parents, wave from rafts and robo-birds zip low along the water's placid surface. But, really, it's nothing to my racer, and she gives back a fierce elbow of her own. Together, the women charge ahead. Three hundred metres out, as they pass overhead, the competitors are four streaks of colour beside the blue river flowing around and around Shipworld without end.

Then, as predicted, fearless Nerrada falters. She falls behind, just one stride, and that's all it takes. Kartuan stays in front, remorseless; Nerrada tries but cannot make up the three-metre distance between them. It's as if that gap is three billion metres wide, unbreachable, galactic, and I'm cheering and clapping with abandon – even though clapping absolutely *kills*. And so, as always, Kartuan struggles to the finish line, teeth clenched, arms and legs spastic – victorious! She falls to the ground, as does Nerrada, and they embrace. And, may wonders never cease, I find Mona next to me, clapping awkwardly, pretending to care.

Fee-dee, fee-dee! Old friend Chickadee lands on my shoulder, too, singing congratulations. What a glorious day!

✦

Year 320, Day 18

It's late, I'm exhausted, but a chronicler's job is never done. And sometimes it's best to quickly record impressions, rather than regurgitate them in repose.

The Olympics ended today with a mass game of Parsifal. That's the official name for what's also called Five Stones, Five Blocks, Ficus Tower and The Mystery of Life. Everyone who possesses a set of the irregular polyhedrons made a hundred and twenty-five years ago from the fallen ficus tree – carved by Parsifal, master craftsman and King of the *Phligsparrfnerim* – was eligible to play. Many of the blocks have been Looped as the years blur by, and others have cracked apart and been converted into paperweights, gewgaws and drink coasters. But enough full sets remain in circulation for thirty-two competitors, age six to one hundred and seven, to gather onstage.

Here's how it works. Parsifal players are broken randomly into pairs. Paired players sit facing each other. Ten seconds before the game starts, they exchange their blocks to eliminate block familiarity and its advantages. Then, go! The first person to build a secure tower is the winner. Alas, Mona is eliminated in the first round, beaten by a retired bridger. But Eric, my old rafting friend and dodo-ball nemesis, advances to the second round, and the third. In the semi-finals, he defeats a nine-year-old boy who lets out a scream and runs off the stage, so much for Parsifal cultivating inner peace.

In the finals, competitors are allowed to use their own blocks, but are blindfolded with black strips of cloth. There he sat, single-minded Eric, across from an ordinary if rather eccentric shipworldmate, a certain fellow known as Bolo – yes, that one! Excuse me, at this late hour, for artlessly attempting a new technique in which a resonating fact is withheld until the last, thereby creating surprise or annoyance or cognitive dissonance, depending on the reader.

Building a tower from five Parsifal blocks, says Bolo, is like telling a story. But it's a new story every time, one of millions of possible outcomes, of alternative histories produced from the simple arrangement of five irregular polyhedrons, and it all starts with the block you pick first and the side you choose to place down. The math, he says with a twinkle, is staggering, as are the philosophical ramifications. And with that, it's off to bed…

What, you want the result? OK, OK. Eric, it turns out, is a sight-dependent person. All that staring into space, I guess, and the poor blindfolded guy is still sliding the second block on top of the first when Bolo, my dusty treasure, finishes his five-ficus tower. He raises his arms in triumph, the most unhumble thing I've ever seen him do, and I whisper an Orphanic word, *gargaartuu*, meaning something like 'the good prevail now and then'. And it comes to me, in that moment, like a whisper from within, that maybe we've overthought things, that the Pioneers should have just gone into the stars without a Mission, without a destination, just flung themselves upon the engulfing heavens. Hoping to find, by touch, what finds us.

No, that wouldn't have made sense. Goodnight.

Year 321, Day 138

The second Shipworld revolution started quietly, two weeks ago, and roughly two hundred and three years after Brenz Oort-St George let fly his heartfelt, incendiary theses that drove the people apart during a medical crisis and nearly burned the Mission down. Or, to put a longer-term slant on it, since the Brenzian upheaval forced us to forsake our repressive social structure and, through a baptism of fire and desolation, emerge as a more resilient and dynamic civilisation.

The second revolution started with Mona and several others ringing the Olmec Head. Every day at noon they sit around the old fella and eat their lunches amid sprouting potato plants. They've written one simple message on a sheet of bamboo: WE ARE THE SECOND MISSION. When they finish eating, one of them, frequently Mona, stands and recites a short speech. Various strollers stop and listen; some stay to ask questions and debate. The size of the lunch group has grown steadily; yesterday, twenty-seven souls sat cross-legged around the Head. His daisies seem a bit withered, overwatered. Leave me, they say, alone.

'We need a second mission,' Mona states. 'We've brought our proposal to the Council, but it's been rejected. We don't call for bypassing HD-40307g. The first mission must be carried out, for the sake of exploration and to honour our ancestors, but that mission should not be imposed. A second mission would keep a functioning society onboard as we orbit the target planet. Unfortunately, as vaguely outlined in the Constitution, the present plan turns Shipworld into little more than a material resource for the New Pioneers, with its parts sent over time down the gravity well. That plan is short-sighted and undemocratic. Shipworld is not just a means to an end; it has over the centuries become an end in itself. We are of space and Shipworld is our beloved home. Those who want to stay here should be able to exercise that decision. Both missions, the first and the second, can occur simultaneously.'

Yes, she continues, carrying out two missions will take extra cooperation and a 'brave generosity of spirit'. But it can be done, or words to that effect.

Most of the protestors are under fifty; they'll still be in the prime of their lives at planetfall. Several are youngsters, and one is the boy who drew the cartoon Olmec alien on that day when the teen artists gathered here. A few are in my age neighbourhood, including a scientist friend, Orchido. I ask him why he's joined up. 'Because they're right,' he replies. 'Think about it, the Pioneers did a lousy job on the end phase. Build a bunch of landing ships and go to the surface. Use Shipworld for parts. Not exactly a master plan.' Orchido chuckles. 'A classic case of… How did Marte put it? Ah, yes – kick-the-can-down-the-galaxy.'

Mona is blunter. 'Mother,' she says, twisting that portentous word to mean something grim, smothering, 'not everyone is like you or Kartuan. We can't bulldoze our way to the finish, we can't just go down to the planet because we're supposed to and endure whatever, no matter how awful. We like it *here*! We don't want to go and we don't want to be pushed around. Go ahead, ask the Council what they're planning to do with people who resist.'

'But it's not happening for decades.'

'We have to figure this out now, if we're going to do it right. On Earthworld, everyone put the difficult decisions off – you told me that.'

'But Mona,' I say, and stop. I stop because I hear how I shape her name into a lump, a bothersome lump in the path, and because she's gone now, not physically, but in spirit. I've seen that look, that furious gone-and-not-coming-back look, a million bitter times. Mona stares away from me, into the distance towards the vanishing point where the bridge is located, where Kartuan stands triumphant with hands behind her back, watching the stars ahead, making sure they don't move. The daughter – Mona thinks – I wish I had.

That afternoon I seek out a Council member, a Loop worker named Hiram. In his sixties, he wears baggy overalls and orange sneakers with white laces. His face darkens when I bring up the Second Missioneers. 'What those people want is ridiculous,' Hiram states. 'We have to colonise HD-40307g with a viable, genetically diverse population. That means we need *everyone*.' He growls up something in his throat. Then repeats the rumour that a Brenz Oort-St George signature mark – the O and ST G tucked into the lobes of the egotistical B – was found scrawled on a window, and besides, he argues, 'Breaking into two societies goes against the work of generations. It desecrates the whole enterprise! Coming all this way just to orbit a planet – we could have done that around stinking Earthworld!'

His forcefulness surprises me. Some people are upset, I respond, that the Council didn't fully consider their proposal. I tell him there's a growing fear that they'll be forced to the planet against their wills. Oh, he says, that'll never happen. 'We always come together in the end. Just look at our history.'

'History,' I say, as if invoking the word invalidates it, 'doesn't predict anything.' But Hiram can't hear. He's too busy keeping score, asking if I sympathise with the dissidents. With my daughter. A thick silence congeals between us.

I state, in a measured tone, that I believe in the Mission, that it's sacred to me. Then, emphatically: 'But I'm always in sympathy with my daughter.' Even, I think, when she isn't with me. And before he can respond, I volunteer my services as a former tender to be the intermediary between the Council and the Second Missioneers. Hiram smiles, his old friendly self, and agrees to relay my generous offer. He assures me that our conversation has been helpful, wishes me well and goes back into the Loop where all things are resolved to their most irrefutable elements.

But the next morning I find that a fence – with steel reinforcements! – has been erected around the Olmec Head and its potato patch. Soon scores of shipworldmates gather about the fence. I help the angry crowd as it tears the abomination down.

Year 321, Day 170

I still have the dream now and then. Not like before, not the full-blown Encounter dream-omen-hallucination with shrieking birds and fiery volcanoes and propulsive drumming, so detailed and drenched with colour that it seems equally real and manufactured. And not the dream ending with Erica Smalls face down in gravel as I wrench myself awake. No, it's more like the dream's memory, edges smoothed, faded. The drums distant, almost inaudible. A dream of a dream, I suppose, a vestige of some part of myself that I neither want to confront nor jettison, and when it starts to become more vivid, I simply slip away, into whiteness. I haven't asked anyone if they still have their own versions; really, what's the point? Sometimes I even wonder if I infected the other dreamers with my testimony seventy years ago – and, therefore, going backwards in time, effects producing their own cause, I was responsible for the Encounter.

Which is ridiculous, of course. Nothing goes back. Everything moves forward in a straight or curving line.

Mona says she's proud of me, about the fence. Change is coming, she says, and you didn't try to stop it and you didn't just stand by. Mom, you participated! It's amazing how much her words mean to me. I should probably tell her that; instead, I cry in the shower. Bolo has written a fence-riot song, by the way, with funny lyrics about the liberated Head flashing a smile and Shipworld forever lost in a cloud of rebellious Oorts. It even mentions his father in a line about the mediator who couldn't forge an agreement with himself.

But Kartuan, oh my. One evening, I sat at my favourite spot near the electro-feeder. A few birds whooshed by, not stopping. Suddenly Kartuan appeared and without pause told me how disappointed she was that I had supported the squatters. The word *squatters* sounded ugly on her lips. Squatters in contrast to the so-called leapers, committed to landing on HG-40307g. Isn't that the way – a physical fence comes down, an invisible one rises. And all I could do was think of the day we met, of the girl pointing her paintbrush.

'What did you think would happen to the Head?' I asked her. 'When we arrive.'

'What?'

'It's not allowed to go to the Loop, that's what you said. You said it with all the confidence in the world. So, what did you think would happen?'

She stared at me. 'Answer the question,' I snapped.

'I thought it would come with us,' she replied. 'But I'm not a stupid kid anymore.' Then she turned and walked away.

OK, I decided, that's that. Twenty years ago, I would have gone after her and applied my calming, tender techniques to win her over, or at least find common ground. But now I'm just too old, too fragile. Too stubborn. And too repetitive – forgive me when I state once more that it's give and take in this life. Sacrifice and gain. Kartuan and Mona.

On Shipworld, we just keep going. Things have been busy lately, so much that I've neglected this mutating, still-unpublished journal. The Council reconvened. Hiram resigned. My strong-willed daughter has emerged as the leader of the Second Missioneers. And an all-hands meeting was convened – an informal Second Constitutional Convention – to discuss the Second Mission. Ideas were proposed regarding resources, population imperatives and the rights and responsibilities of the individual.

The solution came quickly. Babies.

Lots of babies, the only strategy that enables both missions. Population dynamics are non-negotiable. To fully populate two separate and viable societies, an unprecedented number of new human beings must be conceived, born and raised over the next four decades, before planetfall. Men and women aged twenty-one to seventy-six must embark on their new reproductive duties immediately, and, consequently, food production will have to increase, requiring radical reallocation of resources. Within a week, the question of the Second Mission and the action steps to accomplish it were rolled into a referendum that passed with eighty-five per cent approval.

It's what we want. It makes a kind of crazy, statistical sense. And yet I have to ask, because it's my job: have we abandoned our ideals? Should we have stuck to the singular, grand Mission conceived in the mind of Thaddeus Parsons, the relocation of humanity, *all* of humanity, to a new world? Perhaps we're trying to have it both ways, to arrive and not arrive, too. Indeed, perhaps I've betrayed Kartuan, the great frontrunner, the artist at managing pain. She'd barrel ahead, all or nothing. She'd fall across the finish line or die trying. And she'd never side with a mob intent on its rights above all.

And, it seems, I would.

✦

Year 322, Day 12

Home, home on the M'Way
Where the comets and neutrinos play
And seldom is heard an extraterrestrial word
And the void is not cloudy all day…

It's all the rage these days twisting up the lyrics of Parsons' Top 100. That ditty, a homage to 'Home on the Range', was sung by a young man strumming a two-string outside a yurt. Around his neck he wore a crude carving of Parsons' headless pregnant woman, which has become quite fashionable, and kind of creepy considering the bumper crop of pregnant bellies. And, no, I haven't a clue why the Founder dropped the hippo-tooth figurine into the Icelandic chasm. Maybe to debunk historical iconography. Maybe to comment on the futility of solving the problems of humanity by adding, ahem, more humanity. Or just to mess with his old teacher, producing a cryptic story that would outlive him – well, mission accomplished.

Lately, I've been looking through the original *Chronicler's Journal* for insights into the decision to leave Earthworld. It's clear that Parsons and his followers (cultists?) were spooked by the possibility of extinction-level calamities, including nuclear war, climate change, out-of-control artificial intelligence and bio-engineered pandemics. And they had good reason. Marcus Marte, our marvellous scribe, quotes an Oxford philosopher who likened an average human being in the twenty-first century to a teenager with rapidly developing powers, glaring deficits in both judgement and self-control, and an 'unhealthy appetite for risk'. Long-term planning? Nah, let's grab lunch.

Staying on Earthworld, according to Marte, was like playing Russian roulette with one, maybe two bullets in the gun chamber. Boom, *whoops*, goodbye humanity! Oddly, however, his journal goes quiet on the risks of intergenerational spaceflight. This seems a glaring omission, a denial of future reckoning. Weren't the Pioneers a little bit nervous about the multiple existential dangers of such a journey? Once they ran the numbers, factoring in deranged doses of wishful thinking and hope, not to mention known and unknown unknowns, how could flying off to HG-40307g have seemed less risky than staying put?

The ultimate disaster, mercifully, has been prevented. But it's a good idea to stay humble about other permutations of the future, alternate and parallel, in dream and reality, that could have occurred. I recall my Modern Earthworld History teacher, eighty-odd years ago, offering this titbit to the class: 'Imagine that Shipworld is like Earthworld used to be.' Students froze in their seats as Mazdar, who seemed to enjoy scaring us, weaved the tale of an intergenerational spaceship dominated by powerful people hoarding resources and controlling armed militias – a ship, good points aside, where homeless, hungry folks sleep in alleyways, where the Tube is draped with garish promotions for junk food, gambling scams and entertainment devices, and where drug abuse, rape, murder and theft are not rare. A cruel world where animals are penned under deplorable conditions, raised only for the slaughter. A chaotic world where people are kept down because of their appearance, their differences, and the river is polluted, the air befouled, growing hotter and hotter, and the population booms beyond the dream of sustainability. Where kindness is the exception and everyone spends their days looking into screens and away from each other. Imagine, the teacher said, that Shipworld is like Earthworld used to be.

Of course, we students objected vociferously. Such horrible conditions would never be tolerated! Besides, they couldn't last a month, a week, not even a day out here in the void. Mazdar nodded, sagely. 'True enough,' he said, 'but imagine it anyway,' and I went further and saw a ghost Shipworld where the people are long dead and decayed, a gliding tomb-ship with the engines stilled and the lights out, a frozen and silent sarcophagus. And yet, along the riverbank one snarl of green life remains, a last gasp or new and evolving shoot, I couldn't say.

No wonder I became a tender.

One more thing about Mazdar. He called himself an emotional historian. Fervently he believed that emotions were the prime driver of history, more than any other factor, then and now and always. On the last day of class, he asked the ether if there had been a place on Earthworld for the emotional historian, side by side with the economic, military and political historians, for we know how important money, war and power were to our ancestors.

Now I stare down at the Dürer portrait, which came here years ago from Svonne's room and has leaned against the wall near my writing desk ever since. I stare at composed, tenacious Dürer and can't seem to bring myself to hang him up or put him in the closet.

OK, let's be honest. Our survival, so far, hasn't simply been a matter of good, old-fashioned human pluck. It has to have been at least fifty per cent luck. Nobody knew what to expect; nobody had a clue. Ultimately, did our little star hop just seem like a fun thing to do? Even I, a suspicious perfectionist, can understand that. It's been a rollicking adventure.

Oh, give me a ship, where the river does slip
'round and 'round the curving world
Where stars abound in windows in the ground
And eager day from night is unfurled…

✦

Year 322, Day 237

I can no longer lie flat, so Bolo has devised a sloped chair that attaches to the raft-slats and allows me to gaze up as I river float. Today is my ninety-ninth birthday; there'll be a party later on, I'm advised. My Mona – recently elected to the Council – will cut the cake. Bolo will sing. Kartuan, alas, won't be there – hey, enough already with the pity picnic! I'm alive, still, which probably beats the alternative.

Alive, adrift and bobbing alone on the current, one last time. Tomorrow begins a project that converts the river into a narrow irrigation canal for the expanded croplands. This follows the dismantling of the stairways to the Tube and all forms of public art. (Including the riverside statue of Svonne, with the neutrino levitating over her outstretched palm and the robo-birds on her shoulders. She would have hated it.) Flowers are taboo once more, so the daisies in the Olmec Head's cleft have been replaced by spring onions which, at least, produce purple puffballs for a brief season.

Along the soon-to-be-Looped riverpath walk my fellow shipworldmates. Half the women are pregnant. We're positively bursting, after so many centuries of restraint. Everyone else seems to be carrying new humans swaddled to their chests or tied like bundles to their backs. The siren sounds of babies crying and women birthing have become commonplace, and a sweet, milky smell lingers in the air.

Now the raft twirls, caught in an eddy, and I feel like I could just float away. On this Möbius-strip river, though, it's always away and back again. Back to where you started, or close enough. I try to remember my childhood. Bounding about the orphan asylum…I was happy, yes, chanting and playing and snuggling in body-warm beds… Happy, that is, until I wasn't, so I can't say that I miss the *Skarjakkenfinzger*, now converted to a paediatric clinic. But many people lament the loss of a unique culture, an exultant way of being. Some blame the flesh-born for their rules shrouded as opportunities. No, others assert, the orphans did it to themselves by shunning the iron wombs and marrying short ones. By opting out of orphan life, as I did. By accepting diminishment.

And still others say, just wait. The ice child lurks within.

I stare up, at the other side of Shipworld. Downriver, upriver, both. Green fields rolling, growing more food for more mouths. And as usual, dear future reader, Chickadee drops by. Hello, Remarque. Hello, Chick. Rafting, it says – sigh, it's made this comment many, many times – rafting seems halfway between flying and walking. It sits on my hand, careful not to bleed my crepe-paper skin with its talons. I look over Chickadee for signs that it has aged. None that I see – thanks, I guess, to the tool belt under its wings. The bird version of the Correction, or something better. I mention that I've decided to give the Dürer to Mona. He was bold, and so is she. Perhaps she'll hang him on her bathroom door and he'll tell her something that I, and even Bolo, have been unable to say. Perhaps she'll put him in the closet for another day. Either way, it'll be from me. And at least up here he can't be consigned to the flames during a frigid night on HD-40307g.

Chickadee, too, thinks of the future. It confides that many robo-birds want to go down to the planet. The pro-planet faction spins a tale of electromagnetic clouds pulsing with lightning, which birds can feed on by flying through. Dive and dine. I suppose they took that from the primaeval planet dream, which they knew about because… I'm not sure, exactly, my thinking is dulled by time and painkillers. Accordingly, this will be the final entry of the Second Chronicler; my writings, two thousand three hundred and fifty-four pages or so, are to be published when I expire.

'Will you go?' I ask.

'We do not know,' it says. 'This has been discussed with Mona.'

It takes a lot, in your ninety-ninth year, to be surprised.

'Excuse me, you talk to Mona?'

Chickadee fake-pecks at my knuckle: an old stalling tactic.

'We are friends for an extended time.'

'Since when?'

'Before her flock surrounded the Head.'

'I had no idea.'

'She did not tell you? She is your daughter.'

'Live and learn, Chickadee. Did you help her plan those lunches?'

Again, a couple of butt wiggles, a soft stomp or two. Then: 'We told her about the feeder and how we learned to cooperate.' Well, I say to myself, good for you. I stretch my gravelly shoulders. Cooperation is fine, essential in the end, but the fence riot, the act of ripping that ugly thing up from the roots and throwing it away, of scaring witless the people in charge, that made the difference.

Chickadee trumpets its note-name, flaps from my hand and rushes away – gone.

Long ago, yes, I should have found a way with Mona. I think I was always a little scared of her. Now I stop staring up; I close my eyes and listen, listen, listen. Babies crying, conversation, pollen-wind through corn. The peal of an older child laughing. Not at someone's expense, I decide, but for the joy of it, and I envision kids huddled together playing knucklebones. Telling jokes, grabbing the ball. Moment by moment, figuring out their fantastic lives.

After a full lap, there's my husband on the riverbank. He uses a long pole to hook the raft and pull it to shore. Then he helps his wife from the raft.

He holds me, the way he does, in his arms.

6

Years 359–360: Achieving Orbit

A young man, his fake beard bushy red, stepped onto the stage. Nearby, in a lab coat cut above the knees, stood a slender young woman with hair swirled into a bun. According to the play notes, typed on a single piece of bamboo paper, he's Miika Tapola, High Professor of Cosmology, University of Helsinki, and she's Carol, Graduate Student. Year and place: 2012, Earthworld.

Swiftly, on the smartboard, the Finnish astronomer traced a circle, and beneath it in bold letters he wrote: *HD-40307g*. After underlining the planetary designation three times, he swivelled to the audience of about a hundred shipworldmates ranging in age from two months to one hundred and sixteen years. Kartuan, in her bridge officer uniform, stood at the back of the crowd. Decades ago, also from the back row, she'd attended her parents' musical adaptation of *The Rogue Adventures of Brenz Oort-St George*. She'd enjoyed the show, but came away convinced that Brenz, for all his youthful zeal, was kind of a loser. Unfocused, undisciplined, a poor leader.

And yet, those theses, those marvellous Sixteen Theses. *I yearn to discover myself, not just survive*. She'd read them over and over as a teenager, burning them to memory. *I yearn to explore space, not just move through it*. Becoming a bridger, fortunately, had helped her temper those wild, selfish urges. *Where is the mission to learn all that can be learned?*

Now, as Professor Tapola extolled the habitable virtues of the planet he'd recently discovered, with a little help from the High Accuracy Radial Velocity Planet Searcher on a mountaintop in Chile, Kartuan thought of that great day in Year 350 when she flipped the ship, applied the fusion-rocket brakes and then rushed home to tell her parents. She did it! She always said she would. Jarry and Brynto showered their daughter with praise and hugs, and then all three prepared a celebratory meal.

'And so it begins,' said her mother. 'And so it ends,' said her father. Three years ago, they died within the same week. Such timing was poignant, perhaps, even romantic, but Kartuan had a different take: her parents were bound by an unbreakable, unforgiving cord that pulled her dad away just days after her mom died. And to hell with the consequences. Would they, she wondered, have liked this strange play?

'My friends,' shouted Dr Tapola, bobbing on his sneakered toes. 'These are the facts! Plunk in the middle of the Habitable Zone. Orbiting a nice, quiet, long-lived star. Chock full of potassium, phosphorus, all the best elements. Gravitational and radiological parameters, A-OK. Not tidally locked, and not too damned far away. Yes, I bring you an exoplanet to dream about!'

He clenched his fists, shook all over; Kartuan supposed that was meant to convey excitement, obsession, or some kind of palsy. Yes, a very strange production, more like an eccentric lecture. What's it called again? She checked the play notes: *Discovery/Recovery*. Not exactly a catchy title. And no author listed – a committee project, brewed over beers.

Suddenly a burly man stood up in the audience, swept crumbs off his shirt and lumbered onto the stage. Carol nervously handed him a microphone.

'My name is Dr Ronnie Babcock, the Carl Sagan Professor of Cosmology at the University of Wisconsin in the United States of America,' the man stated, flinging the words at Dr Tapola, who recoiled more than a bit. Bad acting? Or were humans of the early twenty-first century as jumpy as robo-birds? 'Those are *not* the facts, sir! They are made of moxie, I say. Sheer chutzpah! Indeed, your calculations are highly disputable – in several instances, they approach conjecture.'

Carol gasped, putting a hand over her mouth. Dr Tapola gathered himself and stumbled forward. 'Babcock, I should have expected this from you.'

'Miika, you can't bluff your way to fame and fortune this time. I've travelled across our troubled planet to declare before these good, gullible folks' – he spread an arm towards the audience – 'that HD-40307g is not a rocky super-Earth, but a mini-Neptune.'

A pause, ten months pregnant.

'Blast you, Babcock!'

'Yes, Miika, blast away! Your planet has no solid surface – get ready to go wading! Bring your galoshes, old boy!'

The crowd erupted with laughter; Kartuan frowned. Did they really talk that way? Moxie? And what's chutzpah? Or galoshes? Of course, every schoolchild on Shipworld learned that Tapola had been right. The James Webb and Nancy Grace Roman space telescopes, launched in the 2020s, confirmed his super-Earth hypothesis. On the other hand, in 2012 when he based his claims on shaky, ground-based telescope data, he could have been wrong. But that's the way it is. You deal with what you've got; you hope to be right in the end. Even now, one year out, HD-40307g could still be mostly a water world.

'Come with me, Carol,' said Dr Babcock, approaching the grad student. 'Join my lab and we'll comb the heavens for planets both exotic and familiar. Together we'll discover mankind's next home.' He stretched out his hand. And then, *splash*, a water balloon hit the ardent astrophysicist in the chest – thrown by Dr Tapola.

'There's your Neptune,' he yelled. 'Wet enough for you?'

Laughter cascaded through Shipworld. Again, Kartuan was not amused, and she imagined her mother saying, hey, kiddo, loosen up. We love you, our hard-driving daughter, we're so proud, but try taking a vacation on our silly planet now and then. OK, Mom, Kartuan conceded, but why is Dr Tapola armed with a water balloon? Did earthworlders, maybe those without guns, actually carry them around? I'm sorry, but this play is ridiculous, and she was about to turn tail when the actors froze. Time stopped. Onto the stage walked a tall young man in his mid-thirties; Kartuan had noticed him over the years, but they'd never spoken beyond hello. His name was Teyben Oort and he was training to pilot one of the landing vehicles under construction. Moving with an assured gait, Teyben reached a spotlight. He paused there, smiling, relaxed.

'Greetings,' he said. 'My name is Thaddeus Parsons, the founder of Shipworld.'

Several people in the audience gasped.

'I attended this very conference at age thirty-five. There I met Dr Tapola and Dr Babcock and, no, there wasn't a water-balloon fight, just some mild disagreement, an ambivalent comment or two.' He stretched out his arms. 'Think of it like this – we earthworlders were a contentious bunch, jockeying for prestige, wealth and comfort. These urges overrode everything else. Toxic pollution, labour exploitation, childhood starvation – all necessary trade-offs to maintain profits and pleasures. Climate change, nukes, AI – we'll deal with them later. Now, I won't pretend that I was much different. But I knew things were going to hell in a handbasket, and I was absurdly rich – so I planned an exit.'

Parsons looked to the horizon, which of course didn't exist on Shipworld. All was quiet except for a distant worker's shovel plunging into dirt, *shuk, shuk, shuk*. Kartuan, against her better judgement, thought: that's Thaddeus Parsons, right there, speaking to me. She decided to stick around. And she noticed that Parsons – the actor – had frozen mid-pose. The spotlight moved and snared another actor, a tall fellow in his seventies, striding onto the stage.

'Well, you know the rest of the story,' the man proclaimed, 'and I'm sure my old friend Marcus Marvellous Marte filled in the details. Grumpy Parsons, eccentric Parsons. One thing he never knew, though, was why I didn't come along. For love? Not this guy. To stay behind and fix the world? You've gotta be kidding. So why? I mean, what kind of numbskull builds an intergenerational spaceship, recruits the crew, holds a Constitutional Convention for its governance, and then stays behind on a ruined planet?'

Shuk, shuk, shuk… Kartuan noticed Dr Babcock scratching his nose and Dr Tapola swaying a bit. Young Parsons' arms wavered; they'd start aching soon. And now middle-aged Parsons froze up, too, unable to answer his own questions. The spotlight left him, searching, searching, and from stage right stepped a very old man, bent over and shaky. Kartuan knew this guy: Eric from Astronomy, obsessed with pulsar planets. He'd talk both your ears off.

When the spotlight found Eric, he squinted and waved his hands, crying: 'Get that damn thing off me!' The light dropped to his feet. 'Of course, I didn't stay on Earthworld! I'm not crazy. Marcus gone, beautiful Zayit…' Here, he seemed to get lost. 'So yeah, I got on that Chinese ship, and it cost a pretty penny, too. What, you think they weren't going? You think they'd let us get the jump on them?'

Old Parsons made a naughty chuckle. What a creep, thought Kartuan.

Chickadee, fluttering high above, cascaded down and landed on her shoulder. Ever since Remarque's death, it had been checking in with the bridge officer. They got along well enough, even though the robo-bird's very presence often reminded Kartuan of the harsh words she'd had with Remarque during the planetfall controversy. Squatters versus leapers, Remarque's angry voice – so unlike her – and that weird question about the Olmec Head going to the planet. The way she stalked off. They never spoke again, and then she died. Over the years, for reasons that she couldn't articulate, Kartuan had tried again and again to understand the squatter argument. That it's foolhardy for everyone – all of humanity, maybe – to transfer to a dangerous planet. That all the Mission eggs shouldn't be put in one basket. That Shipworld is a special place, that squatters have rights, etc, etc. Behind it all, Remarque nagging that some races are best won with tactics, even if that contradicts the most basic impulses – especially then, perhaps. These arguments had won out, of course, but still Kartuan couldn't agree. They should all leap, that was the Mission. Never hedge your bets – go! As a bridger, occupying a role that transcended politics, she'd kept her views on the matter quiet – except, of course, that time with Remarque.

Kartuan noticed that she'd rolled the play notes into a tight tube and twisted that tube into a pretzel knot. She undid it, smoothed the page out. Resumed listening.

'The Chinese had something we didn't – suspended animation!' croaked old Parsons. 'They put you in cryo-sleep, like a hibernating beetle, and you're fresh as a daisy when you get there – that's what they claimed. Just to be sure, I stayed awake for the first twenty-five years, making sure their tech really worked. Then I went under, God help me.'

'There is no evidence of a Chinese Shipworld,' said Chickadee, a bit too loud.

'It's a play,' said Kartuan. 'Keep your voice down.'

'Hell, the Chinese ship is faster, too,' exclaimed old Parsons. 'Surprise, I'll be waiting there for you, folks! The real me – not some cheesy hologram.'

Suddenly, young Parsons came to life. He stepped towards the old man. 'Suspended animation? Pseudo-science, absolute bunk! I'd never be that desperate.'

'Watch your tongue, whippersnapper!' snapped old Parsons. Middle-aged Parsons unfroze next, turning on his younger self: 'Why not? Metabolic stasis isn't just for beetles. Turtles do it, they flood their brains with GABA to make it through the winter. They live hundreds of years! Might be worth a try – nothing's gained in life without risk.'

Carol, the graduate student, reanimated herself. 'Gaba, gaba, gaba,' she trilled. 'You're all a bunch of idiots.' She dived a hand into her lab coat pocket. Out came a water balloon, which she hurled at young Parsons – *splash*, direct hit! The audience laughed uproariously, and Carol pulled another bulbous balloon of water from another lab coat pocket and threw it with amazing accuracy at middle-aged Parsons – *splash*, direct hit! More laughter, plus a strange chirping giggle from Chickadee, who flapped its wings wildly.

Meanwhile, Carol had found yet another water balloon, this one extra big and sloshing red. She moved towards old Parsons, holding the weapon aloft. 'What do you have to say for yourself?' she demanded. Once more, a dramatic pause. *Shuk, shuk, shuk.*

'Nothing, my dear, except I'd sure like to be in a hibernation chamber with you.'

Splash, direct hit! The audience hooted and hollered as the old man staggered backwards. Then he froze. Everyone on stage went rigid again. Water dripped from the three Parsons' clothes. Kartuan, who couldn't believe that everyone was laughing at this absurd drivel – suspended animation, Chinese Shipworld, water-balloon warfare – glanced at the play notes. *Act I: The Conference*. Followed by four more acts. Just then the players unfroze, bowed and exited the stage. A warm river of applause flowed from the audience, providing the perfect opportunity for the bridge officer to slip away.

✦

Mona Oort loved cooking for her shipworldmates almost as much as she loved Shipworld itself. As a Mess Hall chef, going on fifty years now, it gave her great pleasure to peek from the kitchen door and spy people enjoying her food. Savoring, smiling. Dipping the serving spoon and pouring a second helping onto the plate. The cares of the day banished, for the moment, by a shared, delicious meal. Not that she'd go forth in her stained apron and mingle with the diners – not her style. Mona was known as the tough-talking councillor who'd forced Shipworld to confront its planetfall destiny. For readers of *The Second Chronicler's Journal*, she was the adult version of Tender Remarque's difficult daughter, the cause of parental anguish; she wasn't, except to herself, an old softy who delights in watching a teenager engulf her black bean and salsa burrito.

With the advent of accelerated reproduction in Year 321, increased food production had become a top priority. Mushroom houses, grimly associated with the Dark Era, were reintroduced, and Mona reckoned with the cultural revulsion to that food by wrapping the fungus in dough or eviscerating 'shrooms into a nutritious paste for sauces or shakes. Today, she'd dared to introduce portobello pieces into a Second-Gen recipe pried from old computer files: Veggie Galactic Chowder. Based, so it goes, on an old Earthworld dish served on ships that hunted creatures known as whales. (This practice, plus devastated oceans, led to their extinction.) Mona's chowder didn't include algae, banned since the medical crises of the Brenzian Revolt, but featured chunks of potatoes, crushed tomatoes, sliced onions, oregano, bay leaf and a hearty rhubarb beer broth.

Now she watched as a Loop worker, in striped overalls, slurped the chowder. He nodded – yes, another success. Then she noticed Franz, her darling, spindly boy, turned thirteen just last week. He weaved his way across the Mess Hall to his favourite table, the one next to a terraced trellis of sugar pumpkins that Mona had planted beneath a grow light. He sat there, bean head jittering back and forth, with nothing in front of him – strange for a hungry kid who usually stormed the food line. Ah, here's the reason: he'd been waiting for his older brother Teyben, who now arrived at the table. They sat together, talking, and Franz's face lit up as Teyben laughed at something the boy said. Despite their age difference, or maybe because of it, Mona's sons genuinely liked each other. For that she was beyond grateful. May their bond last for the rest of their lives, she hoped, come what may.

Today, Mona decided, she'd make an exception. Quickly she scooped two bowls of Veggie Galactic Chowder, tossed crackers on the tray, and marched into the Mess Hall. She noticed Orchido, one of the original Olmec Lunchers, giving her a startled expression. Mona didn't break stride until she made her sons' table.

'Mom,' said Franz, 'you didn't have to do that.'

'That's right, I didn't,' she replied and placed the bowls on the table, spilling a little. Then she pulled up a chair and slapped her tired body into it.

'Well, go ahead – eat.'

Teyben held out his empty hands, and Franz copied him. Mona, mock-grumbling, reached into her apron pocket and produced two spoons. She slid them across the table and the boys, simultaneously, grabbed the spoons and began gobbling.

'This is really good,' said Teyben.

'It's awesome, Mom,' said Franz.

You won't get anything like that on HD-40307g, she thought, but didn't say. Long ago, Mona had resigned herself to Teyben's enthusiasm for the planet. She was proud of her brave, pilot son. And unlike many other 'leapers', he'd never made disparaging remarks about the 'squatters' staying onboard, forever huddled in Shipwomb – that was supposed to be funny, Shipwomb. Not to Mona, though, who was still the leader of the Second Mission contingent. As for what Franz wanted…

'How was school?' she asked him.

'You're in the new history book,' he said.

'Our famous mother,' said Teyben, between bites.

'Don't forget your grandmother, Remarque. She started the fence riot.'

'That's not what the book says,' said Franz. He took an extra-long slurp.

Again, Mona kept herself from speaking. She could still hear her false-humble mother: Oh, I joined in, that's all. Let's not make a big deal of it. Her journal stated that she merely 'helped the angry crowd'. But Mona knew better; she'd been there. Remarque had let out a yelp – heaven knows where that came from – and then set to tearing at the fence. She was first, the spark, the motive force – shaking the fence, heaving her weight against it, and the mob followed. Mona had told these details, emphatically, to the half-baked historian who'd interviewed her for the new textbook, but of course the account in the revered *Second Chronicler's Journal* had prevailed over the biased daughter.

'Can I have seconds?' asked Franz.

Mona nodded. The boy grabbed his bowl, as if for dear life, and gangled towards the food serving station. She watched him going away; all her life, watching her boys go away, as they headed out to build their lives. They never looked back. Would

Franz, next year, be going down to the planet with his brother? Was she fooling herself that he might actually choose to stay? She turned to Teyben, who scraped chowder from the sides of the bowl. What was he keeping secret?

She hadn't wanted children, but had felt obliged due to her active role in crafting the population expansion agreement. Mona certainly hadn't wanted a husband, or a wife, or anyone telling her what to cook, clean, think, do. She liked sleeping alone, having arguments with herself, and couldn't imagine being inside the kind of loving, mysterious marriage her parents had enjoyed. Therefore, she accepted an anonymous sperm donation and gave birth to Teyben in Year 323.

Love not at first sight, but at conception. Much to her surprise, Mona found herself ready to battle the galactic gods to protect the child growing inside her and, soon enough, crying in her arms. The years after were joyful and hectic; she took to motherhood with surprising ease, enjoying both its nuances and absurdities, but she also knew enough to accept help from her fellow Olmec Lunchers, especially Orchido. When the infant Teyben grew into a man and moved away – a time joke, it happened overnight – Mona found herself wanting to do it all over again. And so, Franz.

Two children, one bound for HD-40307g, the other—

'Are you listening, Mom?'

She asked him to start over. Teyben told a light-hearted but somewhat confusing story about his training exercises, featuring people whose names she'd heard from earlier stories. The upshot, it seemed, was that the first open-space test of a landing vehicle was scheduled to occur soon. And Teyben would be on it.

'If it's open space,' he joked.

'Oh, don't start that,' said Mona. 'And don't talk that way to your brother.'

She stood up, reached a hand out for his empty bowl. Teyben handed it over with that coy, kidding smile that she loved so much. At that moment, Franz returned; he tapped one of the little pumpkins on the way for good luck, slid into his chair and leaned over his steaming second helping. With great concentration, he plopped crackers onto the chowder and pressed them out of sight, one by one, with his spoon.

'It's better this way,' he said.

'Whatever makes you happy,' his mother replied. She tapped his bobbing head, blew a quick kiss at Teyben and started away. 'Coming to the show tonight?' he called out, and she simply waved as she receded. Once was enough; slapstick comedy wasn't her cup of tea. Although Teyben did make an awfully good young Thaddeus Parsons. Was that his dream, to be a founder of a new world? As if, right now, he didn't live in a young enough one.

At the kitchen door, she peeked back across the Mess Hall. Franz was laughing, holding his dripping spoon out like a king's sceptre towards his handsome pilot brother. The chowder splashed onto the table, reminding Mona, perversely, of the time she spit out her mother's disgusting tofu balls during that strange picnic. That's why she became a cook, in fact, to stop relying on others for the food she put into her body. Now Teyben swept his arm out, as if simulating the path of a landing craft, *whoosh*, into the planet's atmosphere. Franz watched raptly. All hail Shipworld and its glorious Mission! Onward into the breach – stop it, thought Mona, stop being cynical. And she castigated herself, too, for this suspicion: slowly, surely, Teyben was taking her little boy away from her.

That night, after Franz went to sleep, she pulled a folder from a drawer. It held a thin stack of papers. On top she found a pencil drawing of a beautiful young woman with ragged hair. In her arms, a squirming toddler. Recently, Mona had been drawing the ancient Oorts in her family, cooking them up from stories, from ingredients in her head, and redrafting the portraits until, somehow, they seemed just right. And so: Cecilia Oort, Pioneer and astronomer, with her wilful child Janelle. The next drawing: Marcus Marte, the First Chronicler. Ready to tell a story, make a quip. His posthumous sperm, of course, allowed for Cecilia's second child, Lavender Oort. A regal-looking woman, her drawing revealed, with touches of Franz in her face. She's followed by her husband, Jacques St George, smiling, wistful. Then their son, the famous Brenz Oort-St George. So restless, noticed Mona, as if caught in the moment before he jumps up. Yes, a bit of Teyben around the eyes. Next, Chive. Melancholic, frowning – she had a lot to frown about, that's for sure. Now Mona gently turned that drawing over and beheld Jan Oort-Ruiz, the negotiator who pulled Shipworld from its darkness at great personal expense. The man named after his great-great-great-great-great-great-great grandfather Jan Oort of Earthworld. The Oort Cloud Oort.

Wouldn't you know it, recent astronomical findings had confirmed a strangely similar Oort Cloud encompassing HD-40307g's solar system. They'd be entering its far edge in several weeks. One theory saw these clouds as a universal phenomenon, solar system cushions stuffed with trillions of icy planetesimals and refuelling comets. Or, thought Mona, perhaps we got turned around and we're returning to where we came from. A big, useless U-turn. Talk about slapstick comedy on a very large stage.

Next in the folder were a couple of photographs from the recent, more permissive era. Between thumb and forefinger, she held a photo of Bolo Oort – her dad, of course, a great guy with a kind face. Drums in the night, 'My Blue Heaven.' And that recorder of his, *toot*, *toot*! She missed him dearly. And behind that photo, a second, unfocused one of his wife, and

Mona's mother, the universally admired Second Chronicler. A voice of wit and integrity, so it was written on the cover page of her journal. The ever-vigilant Tender Remarque, gazing off, elsewhere. Except that day she torched a riot.

And last, Mona.

She sat there with the unflattering photo of herself. When was this taken? Who took it? She looked in her forties; no, more like early fifties. At any rate, before the kids. Oh, she was so much younger then! And frowning; look at that frown, just like Chive's. There was always something dark churning inside her in those days. Now, too, alas, though she'd learned to hide it better, or hoped so. Mona glanced over at Albrecht Dürer's self-portrait, hanging by the kitchen table. Dürer, ever asserting himself, palm open, eyes wide and never blinking across forty-two light-years and nine hundred years.

Mona looked again at the photo. Herself, alone. Staring at the camera. It's time to add Teyben and Franz to this collection, she decided, and soon. But no photos. She would draw them instead. She would capture her boys by hand and maybe even give her mother a try.

✦

You'd think they would have foreseen it during construction, griped Kartuan for the five-hundredth time. She supposed, grudgingly, that the Pioneers had other things on their minds. Minor stuff like building a sustainable, intergenerational space-ark and hammering out a constitution in the frigid retreat of Iceland, not to mention fleeing a dangerous, degenerating world. But if the plan calls for flipping the ship in the last ten years of the journey, then you need a second bridge facing your target for the final stage. It's not rocket science. Use it for storage, anything, for the first three hundred and fifty years.

Instead, the bridge now faced backwards; its window showed everything they'd left behind. This perspective, of course, ran counter to the future-oriented mentality of any bridge officer. It felt intolerable to Kartuan, as if they were backing in, as if they were scared. Stick a philosopher or an historian back here, but not her.

Shortly after she flipped the ship, Kartuan began searching for a window in the bow/stern from which she could gaze in the actual direction of their destination, at the real, starlit thing. Eventually she found a maintenance engineer who didn't mind her looking outside while he worked the evening shift. His job, he told her, was an endless struggle. Almost every part onboard had been repaired and repaired again and then yanked and Looped and made anew – except the hull's outer skin. Maintenance was the real action, he said, fighting entropy, keeping the place in one piece, that is, a billion, interlocking pieces. Think of that while you're contemplating your void. She nodded along, humouring him.

Day after day, Kartuan visited the engineer's dim, messy room. She stood by his counter, strewn with cracker crumbs and electronic parts, and looked towards the star HD-40307, barely visible but there, and it helped. She breathed more easily; the heaviness that had settled in her joints, a kind of liquid gravity, lifted a bit as she beheld the star with its six planets that couldn't, yet, be observed with naked eyes: b, c, d, e, f and g. Planet b was closest to its sun, conducting an orbit in just four days, a vertiginous, whiplash year; d took twenty days to go about and was the most massive of its peers, at nine times Earth; fat-boy f, with a fifty-two-day orbit, appeared to be a gas giant, a mini-Jupiter; and the fabled g, the outermost planet at a remove of ninety million kilometres from its sun, spun around the neighbourhood in one hundred and ninety-eight days. Most importantly, it rested comfortably in the habitable Goldilocks Zone.

Not too hot, not too cold, just right – maybe.

Shipworld, by and by, passed through the outskirts of the system's Oort Cloud. Kartuan waited for a comet to streak through the little window, but nothing appeared (although the Astronomy section identified hundreds in the neighbourhood). She waited for the scout ships of HD-40307g's spacefaring civilisation, but nothing happened there, either, nor were radio or TV signals picked up. She was a bridge officer, of course, trained to wait out nothing, and in those time-stretches she thought about Lorrent, her daughter, and now and then imagined the child floating in space, untethered, doing cartwheels.

Lorrent would be thirteen now, growing up in a family with two fathers. Kartuan checked in with one of the fathers every year or so, casually, but she'd kept her pledge to stay apart unless Lorrent wanted to make contact. The child was born not from love, or carelessness, but from duty; Kartuan had gotten inseminated to help expand the general population. And because failure to do so might have excluded her from becoming the bridge officer who executed the flip-and-burn manoeuvre in Year 350. At first, it wasn't hard to let Lorrent go. Months later, however, an emptiness popped into being within Kartuan, a tiny domain of longing with its own celestial dynamics and voids. Whenever she glimpsed Lorrent at the playground or walking with friends on Pictor Boulevard – loping along and then, suddenly, a skip in her step – she wondered what life would have been like with the girl.

No, it wouldn't have worked. She was a bridger, not a mom. She was the One-Circ gold medallist, not a pram-pushing caregiver. Kartuan's life was devoted to the goal of bringing Shipworld safely into orbit and the New Pioneers down to the planet. Besides, she didn't even like kids – weak, dependent creatures – and didn't like thinking that she'd ever been one. Face it, she was probably incapable of being a 'good enough mother', and certainly couldn't be as selfless and loving as her own parents.

One thing, however, had been non-negotiable in choosing a family. Lorrent, she insisted, would only go to people who were absolutely committed to relocating to HD-40307g. Because there was no way Kartuan was going to leave her child up here, on the other side of a gravity well.

✦

The sign-up list was a mile long, just to get a thirty-minute session.

Franz checked the *phligsparrfner* list every day, watching his name rise to the top like a bubble in a glass of Teyben's beer, like a plastic Earthworld submarine in a bathtub, like himself floating up to the Tube, head over heels, if they ever stopped the spin and had another Space Day. He checked the list and thought about HD-40307g, which he secretly hoped would be a water planet. It would be so awesome to learn how to swim and sail boats and live in an undersea house shaped like a bobbing turnip! Awesome, he meant, if he went there. To visit Teyben, maybe stay.

Whatever. Shipworld was cool, and his mom had said that after all the extra people went down – it was crazy, kids everywhere – once that happened, things would return to their former glory. That's the word she used, glory. They'd rebuild the river, add more *phligsparrfnerim*, hang art from the Tube again, and even revive Equilibrium, this ancient sport with ropes and racquets that sounded like something he'd be good at. Shipworld wouldn't just be a support vehicle for the planet, his mom claimed. They had their own destiny. Maybe they'd go explore the other five planets in their spare time. Who knows what they'd find.

Funny thing, though, not that Franz considered his mother a liar or anything, but her voice sounded different when she talked about the future, almost as if she was trying too hard to convince him.

Teyben couldn't join Franz at the *phligsparrfner* – the only one left from the old days, when those orphan ice people went nuts jumping up and down – because he was too busy training. But that's OK; Franz would find someone to shoot a video of his best moves. He wanted to improve his spin speed by pulling in his arms real tight. Maybe he'd do a forward somersault, or even a full-flat landing, which scared him a little. Trying scary things makes you stronger, according to adults, but if you get hurt then you should have known better. He could always edit out screw-ups and show the video to Teyben later.

On the day of his bounce, he played Parsifal at breakfast and did it first try – a good omen! Then Franz strapped himself into a chair at the Viewing Portal to watch the comet that had recently come into view. Today, it looked bigger than ever, which made no sense because it was angling away from them. No sense – Teacher Chevko hated it when students said that. Keep thinking, he always said. Keep thinking, Mr Oort. OK, OK: the comet only looks bigger, well, *fuzzier*, as it rotates through the window every twenty-four seconds, or we rotate depending on your perspective – anyway, we're getting closer to the star, which increases illumination, which changes contrast, which ophthalmologically, oh, whatever. He'd think more later. Right now, the comet looked like scraggly white hair in a black sink.

His session at the *phligsparrfner* went great. At one point he could have sworn he felt a pulling-up sensation as he bounced high into a lower gravity gradient. Maybe he just imagined it. Anyway, it was awesome, although he kept banging into three other kids who shared his timeslot, two younger boys who bounded side to side as much as up, and a girl from his class, Lorrent. She was pretty nice and demonstrated how to go from a back-slap to a front-slap to a knee bounce. He showed her how to make spins go faster with that arm trick, and she picked it up easily. She probably already knew.

After a while, they were just bouncing on their toes next to each other, catching their breath. 'We're going to the planet,' Lorrent told him. 'My whole family.'

Franz didn't know what to say. He literally didn't have a clue. *My mom was the leader of the revolutionary movement that created two societies for planetfall. You know, the leapers and the squatters.* He knew well enough not to say that. Keep thinking, Mr Oort. Keep thinking. Franz supposed that if he ever did live on HD-40307g, he'd miss lots of things about Shipworld. Maybe she was the same way, even though she was a girl.

He asked: 'Do you think you're gonna miss stuff?'

'Everything,' she said, without hesitation.

Again, clueless. He nodded like an idiot and they both picked up their knees and started jumping higher and higher. They were out of sync now; when he bounced up, she dropped down, and vice-versa. In two weeks, Franz knew, Shipworld would come out of the Oort Cloud, named for his great-times-ninety-nine grandfather who discovered the sol system Oort Cloud without actually seeing it, which made no sense – yeah, yeah, keep thinking, radial velocity, star wobbles, dark energy, all that junk – and then they'd go through bow-shock territory, which sounded cool, and the heliosphere, which is space all choppy with both solar and interstellar winds. A few weeks later they'd get a good look at the planet through the big telescope. Then the final braking manoeuvre into orbit. It had to be done just right otherwise they'd skip past or burn to a cinder. After that, the landers would fill up and leave. More than half of all the people in the world, gone.

Some folks would be happy about it. After forty years of population growth, things had become pretty crowded with the Mess Hall serving meals constantly and families doubled up in apartments. But all that was normal to Franz, and it was normal, too, to hear through open roofs and windows women screaming as they gave birth. His mother said she'd cried with joy when he scrambled out, which secretly pleased Franz. According to the last survey, out of 951 shipworldmates, 503 were going down the gravity well, a one-way trip, honestly, because nobody knew when the New Pioneers would build a rocket to come back. Nobody knew if they'd even want to. The rest, 448 and counting, including a few bridgers, were staying onboard to bring back former glory. If that was possible. It seemed to Franz that the really good parts in history didn't repeat much. Better to try for new glory.

They bounced up and down, Franz and Lorrent. With five minutes left, he realised that he'd forgotten to make any videos. At almost that same moment, he landed on his ankle funny and twisted it. Franz just sat there, annoyed. A couple of robo-gulls roamed high above; none of the birds came near the *phligsparrfner*, maybe because flying humans freaked them out. Anyway, the session was almost over, and Lorrent scooted over on her butt.

'I have to tell you something,' she said.

'OK,' he replied.

'I heard my dads arguing. Tommy said he's not sure he wants to go to the planet anymore. But Riku said they have to go, that the ship's gonna fall apart even with the Loop, and also they promised to take me, they had an agreement with my mom.'

It was a lot to process. Of course she had a mom – a biological mom. But Franz wasn't so sure about the ship falling apart, although the whole idea of the Loop recycling everything perfectly had always seemed iffy. There had to be something lost in the molecular bonds, because people get old, don't they, they get old and die even with the Correction. But that wasn't why Lorrent was telling him this. Not why she was staring at him, looking frightened, waiting. Her eyes were brown, he realised. Her hair was shiny and straight, hanging almost to her elbows, and when she'd been jumping, even higher than he did, it had furled out like a cape.

Maybe Lorrent was worried about having one dad onboard and one on the planet. About leaving one behind. Just like he couldn't even *start* to think about his mom here on Shipworld while Teyben was on the planet. Until now, that is.

'Do you know your mom?'

'No, but they said I could meet her if I wanted to. I wish they'd just tell me what to do,' said Lorrent. She scratched a freckle on her chin; it didn't go anywhere. 'In the olden days, I bet parents told children what to do.'

Franz wished that, too. When it was time to tell his mother, soon, but not too soon, that he'd decided to go with Teyben to HD-40307g and become a New Pioneer, he wished that she'd simply tell him, go. Go, and I will miss you with all my heart. Or go, and I promise to follow you someday, when I'm done here. Or he wished that she'd forbid it. Say no, absolutely not, you're staying here, young man, and that's that. Any of those outcomes would be fine. But please, don't leave it all up to him.

A whistle blew and they had to get off the *phligsparrfner* for the next group eager to defy, and then give into, gravity.

✦

From the outside, to Kartuan, her home looked like the loneliest, most cryptic object in creation. That hardened cocoon, that spinning speck might as well be a grain of space dust in comparison to the black endlessness all around. Her co-pilot, Teyben, as if reading her mind, reached out his thumb and blotted it away. He was a smart young man, not overly cocky, perhaps even a bit of a dreamer, and she was glad to be his mentor in the pilot training programme. Now he pulled the landing craft, the *Marcus Marte*, within a kilometre of Shipworld. Three spacewalkers came into view, performing upgrades at a suite of remote sensing instruments. The planet colonists – check that, all talk of colonisation and its exploitative mindset had been nixed, see Earthworld's bloody history – the New Pioneers would rely on precise, orbital readings for landing-zone identification. Drop down in the wrong location – harsh desert, mid-ocean, volcano's mouth – and you're done for.

The spacewalkers' tethers quivered in response to the smallest movements. They looked, thought Kartuan, as if they were breaking into Shipworld, trying to crack the space egg and steal its secrets. Then she turned her attention back to ship systems – fuel efficiency, life support, navigation – and noted a slight variance between the video capture and their actual position. That's what shakedown cruises were for, to find glitches. She adjusted the wobbly shoulder-strap on her seat and tugged at the tight collar of her flight suit. A stray Allen wrench floated by; she grabbed and stashed it, no sweat.

'I think that's my fault,' said Teyben, laughing.

'Try a roll,' Kartuan suggested, and he set the boat spinning, once, twice – towards the ship, then the planet, ship, planet – and on the third spin he levelled out.

'Why do one if you can do three,' she joked.

'It's kind of a miracle,' he said, gesturing at Shipworld.

'Or maybe it's ordinary.'

'Remains to be seen,' he replied, steering them closer to home. All the while, Kartuan kept her eyes peeled for the docking port, which came around *now*, and mark, she aligned the landing craft in a corkscrewing approach vector. The nav-computer chimed approval.

'Did you ever wonder,' asked Teyben, 'what would have happened with a different group of Pioneers? I mean, if we did it a thousand times with a thousand different crews, would we get a thousand different histories? Or would things turn out pretty much the same? You know, destiny.'

'I haven't thought about it,' said Kartuan, 'but I'm pretty sure we make our own destiny. Maybe we'd have exploded half the time. Or there wouldn't have been an Encounter.'

'Only ten people are still alive from that. They were kids, so they hardly remember.'

'The birds were there,' she offered.

'Yeah, well, who knows what goes on in their heads,' said Teyben. 'I heard that a bunch of them are going to the planet. They'd be pretty good scouts.'

'Chickadee told me – *what the hell?*'

Something white streaked by – one of the spacewalkers – arms spread wide, tether trailing behind like an elongated tail. Teyben whispered a word in Orphanic, *jalanjay*, slang that evoked all the ways the world can go wrong, while Kartuan contacted the repair team, who were breathing heavily and barely able to speak. Something had exploded during a parts transfer, a man explained, severing the tether and sending Orchido flying. His radio was out and he wasn't operating thrusters. Then Kartuan linked with the bridge, where an officer said that the spacewalker's life signs weren't registering.

'What's the protocol here?' asked Teyben, his voice shaky. Kartuan looked at him as he stared at the white receding figure. She knew that Orchido was an Oort family friend, one of the Olmec Lunchers who'd forced through the Second Mission protocols.

‘He might be alive,’ said Teyben. ‘His physio unit could be shot.’

‘This ship isn’t outfitted for rescue,’ said Kartuan ‘Besides, it takes hours to depressurise and we don’t have helmets or—’

‘We can manually open the hatch,’ he interrupted.

‘It’s too dangerous,’ replied Kartuan, not for a moment unsure of her assessment, based on a dozen reasons related to the brute realities of spaceflight. She wasn’t going to take any crazy risks, certainly not with Teyben alongside, this almost-boy who was engaged to marry Aponi, an orphan-tall materials engineer seven months’ pregnant with their child. Nonetheless, Kartuan hated being the voice that said slow down, cut your losses. Give up.

‘Look,’ she said. ‘The spacewalker – your friend – he’s likely dead. I’m sorry.’

‘Continue docking procedure,’ advised the disembodied voice of the bridge officer inside Shipworld, which Kartuan glimpsed out the side portal.

‘We have a grappling arm,’ said Teyben, struggling to keep his voice level. ‘Permission to retrieve body.’

‘All right,’ said Kartuan. ‘External retrieval only. Repeat back the order, Teyben.’

‘External retrieval only,’ he said. Then he disengaged from the docking vector, reversed course and pulsed thrusters towards Orchido, who turned slowly on a diagonal axis. Teyben’s hands shook, though, and the *Marcus Marte* sailed past its target and had to make a long, looping U-turn. As the pilots worked together on the complicated aerial task of externally retrieving the spacewalker, on the specific challenge of grasping a rotating projectile with a robotic appendage, Kartuan observed that Teyben gradually became more focused and sure-handed, that his professionalism pushed aside his grief. She found herself, however, having to fight back tears, hot and ominous, gathering behind her eyes.

When their task was completed, they turned back towards Shipworld. The grappling arm held Orchido in front of the landing craft like some kind of macabre prize. From a certain angle, it looked as if he was steering them home.

'If we did this a thousand times,' Teyben asked, his voice firm, 'would it happen a thousand different ways?'

'Watch your approach, Teyben.'

'He could have gotten a stomachache and stayed in bed. Or someone could have noticed whatever caused the explosion, right?'

She made no reply, but kept thinking along this dreadful path. And not just regarding the myriad, torturing todays. When he was young, someone could have made a snide comment, or offered some praise, words that led Orchido to become an artist or farmer or Loop worker. If that had happened, then this horrible history wouldn't have come to pass. If Janelle Oort had never gone crazy. If Brenz hadn't written his soul-aching theses and signed them with his own blood, if Franika hadn't opposed him and become a tragic icon of courage, if Object X had just passed on by, if Parsons had failed to become tremendously rich back on Earthworld because his teacher, Marcus Marte, had not befriended him, if Kartuan had only...

The memorial service was held next to the Olmec Head; once more, daisies sprung from his torn brain. Standing amid flowering potato plants, Mona spoke to all of Shipworld. She praised her old friend's sense of humour and enduring loyalty. Then she declared: 'Our extended family has lost one member, one out of 950. The family will survive, with heavy hearts. But we are more than a family; we are also an entire world. On a world with billions, it would be as if millions of souls had perished.'

She paused; Chickadee lighted on her shoulder for a moment, then flew back to a railing where scores of robo-songbirds perched in a row.

'Very soon,' continued Mona, 'our family will be cleaved apart. There will be tears, just like today, but let us take comfort in knowing that two human families will be the result. Two human families facing the dangers of space travel and exploration. The Mission, as it is now defined, is to survive and thrive wherever we go. And to never forget each other.'

She walked from the potato patch. A low swell of applause, feeding upon itself, grew into a torrent. Teyben slipped forward and hugged his mother, followed by Orchido's grown daughter. Franz stood stiffly, staring at the Head. And in the following days and weeks the fusion engines kept firing, the braking continued. Shipworld slowed, slowed, slowed down to an interstellar crawl. Through the telescope, HD-40307g came further into focus. The object of intragalactic yearning, accompanied by two shy moons, displayed itself.

Its cloud cover, for one thing, was a big surprise, much thicker than the atmosphere of Earthworld. Carbon dioxide levels were also unexpectedly high, at 490 parts per million. That might be normal for a super-Earth, for this unique planet with its unknown geology and history, but it was eerily similar to CO_2 levels on the day the Pioneers had launched themselves from a certain planet where *Homo sapiens* had asserted industrial dominion.

Meanwhile, in her off-hours, Kartuan continued to stare through the maintenance engineer's rear window, hoping to see HD-40307g with her own eyes. One day, the planet simply appeared, a tiny dot of light. She experienced a moment of mingled joy and relief, but it faded quickly and once again the phrase 'external retrieval only' swam through her thoughts. Almost surely, Orchido had been dead when she gave that order to Teyben and made him repeat it. Considering the situation, she'd been absolutely in the right.

So why, she asked herself, am I so angry?

I had loving parents. I've achieved my career goals. Lorrent appears to be thriving, happy. And the great challenge of planetfall, the culmination of my life's journey, awaits, right there, in my eyeline. Sure, I've had ups and downs, sorrows, but that happens to everyone. People die, that's life. And I've *chosen* to stay single, to take lovers and drop them when they get clingy, possessive, as they always do; there's nothing wrong with that, establishing my own terms. There's nothing wrong with being competitive either. It's human nature, it pushes us forward. And so – why am I so incredibly angry?

Kartuan raised her right hand to the window. She pulled in her fingers, feeling her nails prick her palm, and deployed a fist. The fist covered HD-40307g. The thick glass pane in front of her, shock-resistant and thermally imperturbable, would barely register bone covered in skin driven by unleashed muscle, but nonetheless she struck her fist against it, moderately hard, once, twice, three times. She pummelled the window and the resultant shocks radiated up her arm to her neck – there, a shiver of pain – and dissipated about her head. Then she uncurled her tingling fingers and let the hand drop. She located the planet again.

Why, she wondered, did the anger flow so hotly within her – a subterranean river that seemed too deep, too explosive, to have resulted from her own experiences. She wouldn't come to the engineer's window anymore, decided Kartuan, but instead she'd focus on the bridge window pointed back to Earthworld, to the ancestral home where the nine billion inhabitants had been consumed with anger and outrage. Where they couldn't put aside their rivalries, even to stop befouling their shared nest. Where anger intensified in a tech-driven, negative feedback loop as civilisation collapsed, and who's to say we've escaped that? That it isn't ground into our genes, that killer instinct, that suicidal abandon – who's to say that Kartuan herself wasn't a carrier of that terrible anger, a dark seed waiting to be planted on HD-40307g. She wondered, too, with horror, if her worst impulses coursed within Lorrent.

A week after the funeral, Teyben married Aponi in a ten-minute ceremony by the Olmec Head. Franz was his best man. When not in school, the boy helped provision the landing crafts with equipment and food; fortunately, the final harvest had brought a bounty. Franz enjoyed the task's logistics, stacking this box here, that gizmo there, making a puzzle out of the things of the world – but he spoke nothing of his plans. He put off telling his mom that he wanted to leave for the planet. He kicked the can, as the saying goes, and then began to wonder why. Was he really so sure?

Three times Franz signed up for one last *phligsparrfner* bounce with Lorrent. After the third bounce they went for mint shakes and walked down Pictor Boulevard together. She held his hand, firmly, as if to anchor them both if a big wind welled up – of course, the only winds on Shipworld were fake ones to make sure the corn grew. But HD-40307g might be full of tornadoes and hurricanes, according to this kid in Franz's class whose uncle saw the meteorological scans. Not that he believed the kid, who had one of those long-distance relationships with the truth. And what was truth, anyway, but a bloated word people used to get what they wanted. At the same time, he knew that was a mean thought, an excuse for being negative, and he didn't want to be that kind of person. He wanted to be like Teyben, full of enthusiasm, and like his mom, so strong, so dependable. Such were a few of Franz's jangled, runaway thoughts as he blushed with pleasure walking down the boulevard with Lorrent, bouncy Lorrent, slurping her mint shake, as they held hands tightly just in case, *whoosh*, some rogue wind tried to separate them.

In the months preceding the Second Launch, a committee was convened to address potential issues related to living on the planet. Any person of any age or occupation was invited to serve on the *Committee to Establish Protocols for Engaging HD-40307g.*

At the first meeting, twenty-seven people showed up. We're here, said the chairperson, a retired member of the Psych Advisory Panel, to share ideas from multiple perspectives. Participants agreed that the matter of how to respect and caretake a new planet had been largely ignored in lieu of surviving the journey. Totally ignored, actually. It was, someone said, a can kicked *all the way* down the road and over the cliff. Now the time had come, better late than never, to establish guidelines for exploring and sustainably existing on HD-40307g, with or without the planet's cooperation.

Little else is known about this initiative, except for a tersely worded 'executive summary' of the one and only meeting of the Engagement Protocols Committee:

Meeting began with discussion of human contamination of target planet. Participants generally objected to classification of humans as contaminants. The term 'invasive species' also disputed. Scenario discussed in which sentient beings native to target planet request evacuation of New Pioneers. Commitment to settlement based on generational sacrifices invoked by several participants. Discussion ensued regarding compatibility of thirty trillion bacterial, fungal and viral cells living in human gut and skin with HD-40307g. Protective capabilities of the Correction *debated. Scenario in which sentient beings native to target planet imprison and/or consume humans offered for vigorous debate.*

Fifteen-minute break. Sandwiches served.

Meeting continued with proposed slate of planetary protection protocols (PPPs). General agreement. Shipworld sustainability practices proposed as template for PPPs. General agreement.

Proposal for mandatory oath based on PPPs soundly rejected. Individual censored for use of pejorative term 'squatters'. Proposal made establishing respect for all alien life. Proposal made for employment of fishing and trapping activities if caloric intake of Pioneers fails to exceed recommended minimum level. Meeting concluded with injunction by youngest participant to take action steps on target planet based on the inverse of historically documented treatment of former, abandoned planet.

✦

The achievement of orbit around HD-40307g involved turning Shipworld around after a decade of flying backwards, much to Kartuan's relief.

They settled into a stable orbit, eight hundred kilometres above the planet's surface, going west to east at a slight inclination above the equator. From that orientation, HD-40307g loomed every twenty-four seconds in the voracious eye of the Viewing Portal: a huge sphere mostly shrouded in swirling clouds with glimmers of oceanic blue and, less frequently, brown land. Crowds stared in wonderment, and people yelled out 'Water!' or 'Land, a strip of land!' whenever the clouds parted. Birds flew past to get a quick, wary look. On her way back and forth to the bridge, Kartuan often found herself gaping, but also watching the people consume the planet with expectant eyes, with the eyes, you might imagine, of every shipworldmate who had come before.

One day, at the Portal, an elderly man on a walker approached Kartuan. He reached out a shaky arm, patted Kartuan on the shoulder and said, 'Thank you'. There it was again – a burst of anger, rippling up her neck. Why, for being *thanked*? The man added that he wasn't going down the gravity well, as he'd entered very old age and didn't want to be a burden. But he appreciated everyone who'd helped them get this far, and when he closed his eyes at night, perhaps for the last time, he tried to dream of the planet, to see its beauty, to feel its promise. He turned before Kartuan could respond and patted someone else, an irrigation specialist, and said, 'Thank you'. They talked, exchanged a laugh.

The remote sensing division pierced HD-40307g's cloud cover and found two polar regions – shrinking or growing in size, it was impossible to tell – as well as an equatorial volcanic eruption and a wildfire around the northern pole. The fire's volume seemed low, however, so perhaps some kind of peatland, not forest, was burning. (Here one could make an unnerving parallel with the smouldering Siberian peatlands of Earthworld, a climate feedback loop that roared out of control in the decade before launch. Or the fires could be normal for this ecosystem.) Spectrographic readings confirmed the atmosphere as breathable at seventy-six per cent nitrogen, twenty per cent oxygen and four per cent trace gases. Not to mention a few novel concoctions in ultra-trace portions, likely the exhalations of exotic bacteria. Also confirmed: no bright lights shining in the darkness. No large-scale signs of civilisation as we know it.

Launch Day fell just three days before the landers were scheduled to leave. The usual celebration devolved into a muted affair. Mona set up next to the Olmec Head, and from a giant pot she ladled bowls of Veggie Galactic Chowder. Two musicians sat nearby, playing 'My Blue Heaven' on flutes. A woman named Rosemary, distantly related to the Rosemary who ran the library before the Brenzian Revolt, attached a microphone to a pole. She and a few colleagues read aloud the names of every person who'd lived and died on Shipworld. They started with Marcus Marte and sixteen hours later, three thousand three hundred and twenty-one names later, ended with Orchido.

Kartuan listened for a while. It was mesmerising and strangely soothing. She imagined that the names, no, something more basic, the *sounds* of the names ascended like stray neutrinos into the zero-grav centre point where Franika, the supposed Saviour, had lain in a coma during the Dark Era. (These days, Franika was seen by many as a narrow-minded fanatic for the status quo.) Of course, the bridge officer didn't share these flights of fancy with anyone. Her darker musings – unpredictable, stalking her – also remained a personal secret. If only such feelings could be Looped and turned into something useful, a screw or a microscope. Or that bowl on that table, next to the pot of chowder.

The smell beckoned; she went over.

'Greetings, Kartuan,' said Mona. 'Happy Launch Day.'

'Greetings,' she replied, startled at the friendliness from Remarque's daughter, who she usually avoided. Who, in fact, was nothing like Remarque, but still.

Mona ladled a bowl. Kartuan tasted it, nodded approval. The flutes stopped playing. Another name, *Jamison Kosenkee*, was read in a neutral, incantatory tone. Just then Franz ran up to the table and got chowder from his mother – and moments later Lorrent, in a cornflower yellow dress, followed behind. Kartuan stumbled as she stepped back, always stepping back from her child, and she heard Mona proclaim, 'Happy Launch Day, Lorrent!' and watched her hand the beautiful girl a bowl of chowder. 'Extra crackers, please,' the girl replied, and she received them. The kids hurried off.

'Is that your son?' asked Kartuan.

'Last I checked,' said Mona. 'I keep telling myself that he's too young to be in love. It's just a crush, that's what I tell myself.'

Kartuan looked at the curve in the path, near a wall-rack of berries, where the boy and the girl, possibly in love, had disappeared from view. That bend in space shimmered, briefly, and then filled with people coming and going and yakking away.

'Do you know Lorrent?' Mona asked. A logical question, nothing more. Kartuan looked at the woman's tired, lined face. The answer was obvious. No, she didn't know the girl, not really. Not in the slightest, actually. How could she?

'My older son Teyben is a pilot,' said Mona. 'Maybe you…'

'Yes, we've flown together. You should be proud.'

'Thank you. He's going down to the planet, of course, but Franz was supposed to stay. He's just *thirteen*. Now he says he's not sure, that he hasn't been for a long time. I wonder, what's a long time to a boy that age?'

'I don't know,' said Kartuan, who was rapidly trying to process what she'd just seen and heard. Another name, *Daniella Argova*, flowed from vocal cords to microphone to air and rose into the untrammelled space around the Tube. One thing was obvious, even from a moment's observation: Lorrent and Franz wanted to be together. Here or down there, it didn't matter. They wanted to be together.

'You might think this ironic, coming from the woman who ripped Shipworld in two,' continued Mona, 'but I don't think I can handle losing both of my boys.'

Kartuan found herself no longer breathing; then she took a deep, gulping breath.

'Are you OK?' asked Mona.

All Kartuan could do was shake her head. Mona stepped forward and touched her on the shoulder, much like the old man at the Viewing Portal, and enveloped her in a hug. She held Kartuan tightly, for several moments.

'I was so jealous of you, when I was young,' said Mona, stepping back. 'Forty years ago, it's so silly!'

Kartuan stared at Mona. Not as she was then, the coach's snotty, jealous daughter, but as she was now, today. 'I'll fix this,' Kartuan said, 'I have to fix this,' and she turned from the confused woman and rushed in a smothering panic down the path where Lorrent and Franz had disappeared minutes ago. Another name, *Robert Sim-Lubanz*, dissolved into particles and flew up to the refuge of zero gravity. External retrieval only – sometimes that's the best you can do. But not this time, not on her watch.

She sought out Riku, one of Lorrent's fathers. For the first time in as long as she could remember, she cried in front of another person. Only a few tears rolled off her cheeks onto her hands, but to Kartuan it felt like a total loss of control, an embarrassing display of blubbering. Remarque had once called her an 'artist at managing pain' – what a joke that had become. There was no containing this angry, unloosed longing, no harnessing it as competitive fuel. The fear of losing Lorrent, her child who she had not spoken to or touched in twelve years, engulfed her in pain, and her only defence was to desperately explain her motivations to Riku. And to herself, really. This unburdening further disturbed Kartuan, the paragon bridge officer, but she couldn't stop talking or push beyond the raw feelings, either. Riku took her damp, shaking hands into his. He told her, emphatically, that even though his husband Tommy had wavered, they were still committed to HD-40307g. Lorrent would go with them, regardless of her infatuation.

'But what if she won't listen?' asked Kartuan. 'What if she wants to stay?'

'Too bad,' said Riku.

The next morning, after surrendering herself to a dreamless sleep, an unsettling oblivion, Kartuan talked with Teyben. Without a single tear, she expressed her concerns for Mona, for her happiness, and for Franz, who just happened to have fallen for a young girl, her daughter, who damn well was going down to the planet. 'I didn't know any of this,' replied Teyben, who appeared more than a little shocked at what roiled beneath the surface of people's lives, at the intricate, intersecting orbits of their desires. His little brother, in love? Yes, Teyben promised, he'd help, and later that same day he and Kartuan met Franz after school – classes continued until the day before planetfall – at the Mess Hall table by the terraced sugar pumpkins. Most of them had been picked and made into filling for tarts.

Carefully, in a measured tone, Teyben asked Franz to remain on Shipworld and take care of their mother. She wouldn't make such a request herself, of course, because she believed strongly in the rights of individuals to chart the trajectories of their own lives.

So, he was asking. Please, stay, for her.

Kartuan spoke next. She told Franz, with all the gentleness that she could scrape from her sixty-two years of ungentle living, that they'd devised a special plan, one that hinged on his agreement. In this plan, Kartuan arranges for Franz to train with the remaining bridge officers. He can become a pilot, she promises, just like Teyben. He can even help build a new lander. And when he turns twenty-one – yes, it might seem like forever, but it'll come quickly – he can fly that lander and join them on the planet.

'Who knows,' Teyben joked. 'By then even Mom might come along.'

Not likely, thought Franz. Not ever.

'Lorrent's going down?' he asked.

Teyben and Kartuan nodded.

'And Shipworld's not falling apart?'

'No, of course not,' said Kartuan.

'Well, maybe a little,' said Teyben. 'But it's got at least a hundred years left in it.'

They sat quietly for a while. Franz looked across the wide space where he'd eaten a million meals, his eyes flickering. This is what he'd dreaded, having to make the decision himself. And yet, he also knew that he was being pushed in the direction of staying without Lorrent. He was being manipulated and that was OK, sorta; that cleared a path for him to walk down – if he chose to do so. Choice, what a funny thing. No one on Shipworld had chosen to live here. And you couldn't choose your parents, your siblings or your classmates, either. The things that excited you – bouncing on the *phligsparrfner*, loading up the landers with the right gear in the right places – it was like they chose you. Even the epic, intergenerational enterprise of Shipworld, taught in school as absolutely inevitable, a necessity, that was a choice, too, and maybe a stupid one. Why didn't they stay on Earthworld and fix things? Was it really that far gone? And down on that clouded-over planet, HD-40307g, who says we won't make all the same mistakes? Or new ones.

'I agree,' said Franz, sitting up straight in his chair. 'I'll do it.'

'Thank you,' whispered Kartuan.

Teyben tousled his brother's hair. Kartuan took off her white bridge officer's cap and slid it across the table to Franz. 'Just a souvenir,' she said, letting go, and she imagined the grim Earthworld anger that she carried also sloughing away, along the Tube and through the soil and water enfolding all life here and past the impregnable hull seals into the vacuum.

Two days later, more than 500 people boarded seven landing craft ready to transport them to HD-40307g. Lorrent, lingering at the bottom of a loading ramp, hugged Franz and gave him a kiss. Her lips pressed his, and then brushed them in receding. His first kiss, a goodbye kiss. A sad kiss, alone and unbracketed by others. And a promise-kiss, too, for there could be more in certain versions of the future. He promised her that he'd fly down to be with her, someday, and she said that if he didn't she'd be really pissed off.

Soon the landers emerged into outer space, a seemingly effortless birth, an exodus long in the making, but they didn't go directly to the planet. First, they spread out and made a slow procession around Shipworld, three orbits timed to match the velocity of its tireless spin, and for the ones who'd stayed onboard and stared up/down through the floor-windows and the Viewing Portal it was an awesome, sundering sight that they'd remember in the turbulent moments before death, and for those who'd gone, for most of them, it was akin to the Revelation of old, for they finally saw Shipworld with their own eyes.

7

Planetfall

Their former home reduced to a pinprick as the little flotilla assumed a V formation and conducted simultaneous deorbit burns. Five minutes later, the seven landing crafts shut down engines and glided towards the atmosphere. Teyben, pilot of the *Marcus Marte*, didn't look back once; there were too many systems to check, too many details to fuss over.

A new life had begun. A new world awaited.

In the passenger section, Aponi sat next to an elderly passenger, Hiram, the former councillor whose rash action against the Olmec Lunchers triggered the Fence Riot. The old man, still in his trademark orange sneakers, the white laces faded to grey, had been jittery and muttering since launch, tapping on the dead data/tracking panel in his forearm. Aponi, her jet-black hair cut at a sharp angle, adjusted her pregnant body against a rolled-up pillow and told Hiram a story passed down in her family about a great herd of caribou back on Earthworld.

Caribou, she explained in her soft, steady voice, are a kind of deer – four-legged creatures – with scraggly hair and bone branches called antlers growing out of their heads. These caribou lived in the frigid north country and were named for the Porcupine River where they gave birth, and no, she didn't know what porcupine meant. So, as the seasons changed, as the snow flew, the Porcupine Herd of over two hundred thousand caribou, just imagine, migrated several hundred miles every year, back and forth from winter to summer grounds, an endless cycle. They migrated for food and maybe for adventure, too, or exercise, or to elude predators, such as grizzlies, golden eagles and the wolfpack. Perhaps their migrations started when the temperature dipped, or rose, when the ground became harder, or softer, when the wind blowing through their fur felt wetter, or drier. Who knows, perhaps minute fluctuations in Earthworld's electromagnetic field compelled the caribou to set forth, via blood and bone compass needles in their brains. Whatever the case, they moved in a leave-and-return loop for millions and millions of years, evolving stronger adaptations against extreme cold and catastrophe, and they did it long before the ancestors of man dropped from trees and stood semi-upright. In the industrial era, luckily for the Porcupine Herd, their migration route took place inside a conservation zone. They were safe from man, at least up to the chaotic years before Shipworld's launch.

'I wonder,' said Aponi, 'if we'll encounter animal herds on HD-40307g. I wonder if my child will see anything like a caribou.'

Hiram's head bobbed as he listened. His wife and child had stayed behind on Shipworld. 'Why,' he asked, 'didn't they learn to speak?'

'I don't know,' said Aponi. 'I suppose they just didn't need to. The same reason why they didn't evolve to use tools.'

'Tools are honest,' said Hiram, the former Loop worker. 'Words lie.'

A few metres away, Chickadee and seven skittery grackles perched on a rail. These robo-birds had augmented their wings to serve as solar panels. In that way, they'd make less demands on the energy reserves of the New Pioneers and enjoy greater independence.

'Tell this story again,' chirped Chickadee. 'Tell us about the caribou.' Two of the grackles chimed in, simultaneously: 'Yes, yes, we want to hear.'

Soon after the second telling, augmented with details about caribou smelling lichen deep beneath the snow and being able to hear tendons snapping in ankles far away, the landing crafts hit the atmosphere. Teyben used the steering jets to maintain altitude. An orange mist of hot, ionised gases enveloped the ship, as if it was being hardened for the trials ahead. The trip through the upper atmosphere was bumpy, but didn't take long, and soon the landing crafts slowed to the speed of sound, producing sonic booms, seven in all, like drum claps, to be heard or not heard on the planet's surface.

They emerged into lighter cloud cover and reassembled into a flying V. Kilometres below stretched nothing but water, an alien ocean rippling with turquoise waves. The plan was to head north towards a sliver of land spied from orbit, maybe an island or promontory or coastline. They'd brought fishing equipment as well as desalination gear. Teyben glanced repeatedly at the water, hoping to spot a boat or creature leaping up. Franz, he recalled, had wanted to learn to swim. He'd probably do it on Shipworld, now that they were gone.

Twenty minutes later, they reached a slanted, rocky outcropping. Teyben's co-pilot, DeYulia, whooped, and from the passenger section came hollering and raucous chirps. The ground soon flattened and Teyben followed protocol by deploying emergency parachutes, which for obvious reasons had never been adequately tested. Three of the four chutes opened, slowing the craft's glide. The fourth chute became twisted in knots, whipping back and forth violently, and DeYulia jettisoned it. As the craft descended, Teyben searched for a landing space, a place without boulders or trees. In fact, he realised, he hadn't seen any trees at all, but couldn't be sure because he'd only heard about the old ficus and studied aerial photos of Earthworld forests. Then DeYulia pointed – there, there! Teyben steered the craft towards a tan area, perhaps desert, a ragged strip where nothing seemed to grow.

This is it, he decided. This will have to be it.

Minutes later, in fulfilment of a dream shepherded for generations, Teyben Oort brought the *Marcus Marte* to a bumpy landing on the surface of HD-40307g. Five other craft, including Kartuan's, also skidded to a halt without major incident. The *Neyjay-Usah*, however, experienced complete failure of the parachute system and overshot the target zone, slamming into a cliff several kilometres away. All souls aboard, eighty-three New Pioneers, died in the crash. They arrived but for an instant and then were gone.

✦

The lander door opened. Immediately, as if uncorked, one of the grackles flew out and came to rest on bare, dusty ground pocked with small stones. Iridescent purples and blues rippled across the robo-bird's head as it pecked at the windblown dirt and looked into the daytime sky. The other grackles flew out, too, and gathered around their hero. Then a set of stairs unfurled and Teyben started down. Minutes before, the young pilot had sent a message to Shipworld signalling their safe arrival. He was also aware that the *Neyjay-Usah* had run into difficulty and lost its comms. Now, he took a deep breath in, let the air out. He breathed in again and the wind gusted suddenly and nearly knocked him over, as if a giant, invisible hand had tried to brush him aside.

Teyben moved to the bottom step. He looked out – flat land, vast distances, limitless sky – and felt a spasm of dizziness and nausea, understandable for someone who'd spent almost his entire life inside a spinning egg. He stared down at his feet and waited for the disorientation to subside, for the world to slip back into sync. Then he looked out again, this time only several metres along the ground, and saw the strutting grackles who seemed at home already. He closed his eyes and raised his chin. His face registered warmth; rays from the planet's orange sun infiltrated his cheeks and forehead. The skin tingled as the warmth spread – but he didn't open his eyes.

Was he supposed to say something profound here, do something special? As far as Teyben knew, human beings had travelled to the Earthworld moon, Mars, a couple of asteroids, and that was it. This was an important moment, stepping onto a far-flung, habitable planet after such a long, long ride. An historic occurrence, with potentially vast ramifications, and yet he'd been so preoccupied with the difficulties of leaving home and the precise execution of the landing manoeuvre that he'd prepared nothing. No, that was an excuse; he'd avoided thinking about this final step in the journey, the instant when feet touched ground. After all, he was just Teyben Oort, one human being among the one hundred and twenty billion, give or take, who'd ever lived. The other pilots, and Kartuan certainly, weren't frozen by the epic nature of their tasks. They were eagerly jumping down, he suspected, unhindered by thoughts about everything left behind or hidden ahead.

'Teyben?'

He swivelled around. Aponi stood in the doorway. About once a day, as he gazed at her, he simply couldn't believe how pregnant his wife had become, how very swollen she was with a mysterious human being. He couldn't believe that he'd been a catalysing agent for such a momentous event. This was one of those times.

'Is there a problem?' she asked. 'We're ready to get out.'

He shook his head, then stepped onto the surface. The footprint he made was soon scuffed by other footprints, and all those mingled marks were later blown away in scouring, overnight winds. Teyben stepped onto HD-40307g and said through a sigh, 'It's about time,' and Aponi laughed. The chickadee, who had respectfully waited, now flew from the lander, and maybe, thought Teyben, that's not such a bad remark for this monumental day, it's about time. Or, more accurately, time is about us, about our movement through a universe of exploding supernovas and silent cell division, of stray noises and neutrinos in the night. Time is how we measure ourselves, ultimately, as we grow into ourselves and string our brief lives together. At any rate, he thought, let's save the philosophising for later. It's time to take more steps.

'Careful looking out,' he warned, but too late. Several New Pioneers who'd followed him were bent over with dizziness. One had fallen to his knees and was retching, anointing the surface of HD-40307g with gastric juices and strings of saliva laced with bacteria, proteins and antibodies that had evolved on another planet. But not Aponi. She stood tall, one hand on her curving belly, the other shielding her eyes.

8

Year 1: A New Era Begins

When the clouds parted, at just the right time of day, Shipworld appeared as a tiny, orbiting star in the planet's sky.

Lorrent imagined her former shipworldmates amid the strangely static stars. In a way, she could see them. But they couldn't see her, not unless they turned the big telescope away from some globular cluster and aimed it through a cloud-gap onto a hill where she happened to be standing. Then they could see her, waving. Hey, Franz. Hey, sweetie. After that, back to work. Four months since planetfall, it was so much work that school hadn't started, which Lorrent proclaimed a big mistake unless they wanted HD-40307g humans to be stupider than Earthworld humans, or the people who'd supposedly lived on this planet and then, maybe, made themselves extinct. She also thought the settlement needed a chronicler like Marcus Marte or Tender Remarque and that could be her – after all, a kid's view of the world is just as important as anyone else's, and maybe more honest – which meant going to school and improving her writing instead of weaving rope, making soap and gutting fish.

Marcus Marte hated gutting fish, and so did Lorrent. She'd read *The Chronicler's Journal* about fifty times and even remembered the red brick of the patio where boy-Marcus kneeled and the newspaper onto which he plopped fish guts: *The Register-Guard*. Just like him, she kept an eye open for treasure – minnow, pearl, gold ring, plastic doohickey – in slit-open fish bellies. So far, nothing, except for green slime that smelled bad on your fingertips.

Sunsets. If she were the Third Chronicler, that's what she'd write about. Every night, hundreds of people got together for sunset. They stood in clumps, a dozen here, a dozen there, on a promontory with this wide view of the ocean, all green and blue. Lorrent found herself drawn to the people's wide-open faces; some laughed out loud and others cried or let their mouths fall open as if they wanted to eat the setting sun.

'I never knew,' one old lady said every time. 'I never knew.' That's the way it is, decided Lorrent, we take for granted the beauty we grow up with, like a tasselled field of corn sweeping the curve of Shipworld, but when we're thrown into something new and beautiful it's kind of sad, too, because we've gone so long without. We don't know how to see it. We've got to learn, and night after night people came to the promontory (although fewer, over time), and their eyes squinched as the sun-colours oozed purply yellow and fusion-red through clouds and rolling fog that rarely brought moisture to land. And the old lady said, 'I never knew,' a raspy-voiced incantation that Lorrent loved to hear.

Overall, she guessed, things were going OK. The heavier gravity was bearable, even though Lorrent had to keep pulling her head up. Enough solar rays got through the clouds to power the fusion generator that sputtered on and off, and the desalination rig produced water for drinking and the hydro-gardens. Everyone celebrated when the first baby was born, to Aponi and Teyben. They named her Endive for this bitter lettuce leaf, but she looked kind of sweet, thought Lorrent, like Franz around her calm, green eyes. Then Hiram, the old man who scowled at the sky, died a few days later in his sleep, as if to make room for the baby. Somebody said that he went downhill fast, that the

Correction was nullified in this place. Lorrent sure hoped not. Somebody else said it was probably just his time. Lorrent mulled that over and decided it meant nothing. A cliché, a word husk.

At night, windstorms lashed the settlement. The heat could be pretty intense, too, but Lorrent liked the feel of her pores opening, a million springs flowing. What she didn't like was the radiation that HD-40307g's dense atmosphere had blocked from orbital detection. Gamma radiation levels were way above normal, in air and soil, but probably not high enough to cause serious illness. Very comforting, mumbled Lorrent, as she listened to her dads talk about how the people here might have dropped nuclear bombs on each other, hundreds of years ago, and now the land was barren because red-hot blast waves had vaporised everything and caused horrific wildfires. Or they'd let gamma radiation loose because they were ignorant or careless or for whatever reason your mind prefers in its dark, twisty corridors.

The first clues about the planet people – if they were people, wondered Lorrent, and not rotating balls of light – were discovered near the seventh-ship burial plots in ruins that looked like pipes sticking out of the ground. Lorrent dropped a pebble down one pipe, as she did so thinking about that awful day when they buried the remains of the people of the *Neyjay-Usah* in hard, unyielding ground, and it took five seconds before it went *ping*! She also spent time walking among the graves, but didn't know why. To make sure they were still there? OK, that was ridiculous, but so was the blue sheet lightning, bam, goodbye slate-grey sky, hello bright blue. Like a flipped switch, she thought, like everything true suddenly wasn't, and don't forget the only animals they'd found, these little snaky-ratty things – dirt devils, DDs for short – all brown with horns that spit burning liquid. They sure weren't on Shipworld anymore.

Adults were always talking about the ruins. Especially at night, around a fire. For instance, according to DeYulia, the ruins indicated that sentient life is *ubiquitous* (nice word, full of u's). Somebody else said that the ruins could have been a geothermal energy facility. Kartuan speculated that the pipes were a sad attempt at sucking carbon dioxide out of the air because, face it, they had a runaway climate change problem here. Lorrent considered Kartuan awesome for the way she stated things. Face it, folks. Let's not fool ourselves. Then Tommy threw in that space travellers had probably left the contraption behind. Galactic litter. Or maybe it was monitoring them. Look, weirdos have landed.

Others said, forget the ruins. The planet is huge and might contain primitive peoples, pre-technological, and either way after three hundred and sixty years it's time to finally finalise the contact protocols, *blah, blah, blah*. Shipworld had detected evidence of a young forest to the north, so it was agreed that humans and birds should go scouting over the mountain, and soon. Then Kartuan asserted that industrial pollution caused the planet's warming – the structure they'd found underwater, a sure sign of sea-level rise – and someone else said maybe but warming can be caused by volcanoes, and DeYulia said no, there would be more sulphur in the atmosphere. Tommy added that high radiation levels proved the nuclear theory and Teyben refuted that – *refuted*, another good word, decided Third Chronicler Lorrent – saying there could be natural reasons for high radiation, and Aponi proclaimed that it didn't matter because we're here, and it's a miracle. We've got a second chance. Then Riku said yes, true enough, but we have to learn from history. As if history has ever made sense, countered Lorrent, silently, we might as well learn from the future, or our dream of it. And on, and on.

'It's kind of disappointing,' said Tommy, one night. 'We came all this way and what do we find but…'

He sighed, a big fill-in-the-blank. The fire made a spitting sound.

'Well,' Tommy continued, 'it's not like I thought we were unique in the universe. I was just hoping we were uniquely foolish.'

Nervous laughter trickled around the ring of fire-lit faces, and right away Teyben changed the subject to this slippery fish he almost caught with his bare hands. He knew exactly when to speak up, Lorrent noted, when to make it fun. Just a few days later, real casual-like, she asked her dads if her mother was on the planet. *Alive* on the planet, she added, and she started to tremble because of course that's why she went to the graves of the *Neyjay-Usah*, she couldn't even admit it to herself. Tommy hugged her and apologised. Yes, she's alive, he said, we should have told you, we're such idiots, and Riku asked her if she wanted finally to meet her mom. Lorrent paused, then shook her head.

Three times a day, for twenty minutes, Shipworld came into radio contact. The transmission sounded staticky, like people talking from the bottom of a well. Demand was high to speak to old friends and relatives, so Lorrent had only spoken to Franz twice. He talked about school, which made her jealous, and about looking through the infrared telescope at the Eye of God Nebula with its cometary knots, like eyebrows, and how he'd also seen two silvery galaxies streaming through each without touching spiral arms. She told him about the windstorms and sunsets and then, just like she'd rehearsed, she said she missed him, and the line went silent. One second, two, three, and in a soft voice he said he missed her, too, and she yearned, another great word, she *yearned* to reach up through the gravity well and touch his face. Franz added, 'Say hi to Teyben for me.' Then time's up, put the next person on.

Soon, they started school for three hours a day. And two hours of play were mandated for children. Some kids created jumping dance routines using human catapults and others, plus a bunch of adults, learned to body surf on frothing waves that crested near a cove. Survival was paramount, explained Riku, but it was time for them to live their values. 'It wasn't your nagging,' he told Lorrent before she could grab credit.

During play time, Lorrent hiked out to the ruins with her friend Maribelle and her little brother Hernan. They pretended to be archaeologists. Lorrent pounded her shovel into the gravelly ground while Hernan messed around with a bent spoon, banging on pipes, and Maribelle measured the site with big strides and took notes in a logbook. Once Lorrent disturbed a nest of the dirt devils, causing four babies to scatter, and she wondered if she'd ruined their home. Her pinkie finger was bleeding – had a baby DD nipped her? She watched the blood gather at the finger's tip into a tiny drop and, suddenly, fall to the ground.

Today, Lorrent dug straight down and hit a black blob. It was hard and crumbly, not exactly a rock. Maribelle drew a picture of the blob and Hernan jabbed his spoon at it. A bit of yellow clung to its edge – paint, fungus? The next day, Lorrent dug another half metre and the ground smelled acrid and burnt. Then something flashed. She grabbed it: a round piece of metal, about three centimetres in diameter, pressed flat, with a hole in the centre. She rubbed off some dirt; it felt cold to the touch. Each side had embossed swirly designs, as well as slashed lines, and embedded along the edges were tiny, silvery flecks, like mica. Lorrent showed Maribelle and they jumped up and down like crazy, to heck with the grouchy gravity, and took tons of notes in the logbook. They even let Hernan touch it.

Back at the settlement, no one knew what it was. Jewellery? A medallion or game piece? Or a coin, someone said, indicating a currency-based economic system with the good and bad that comes with that. The archaeological trio received due praise, but Tommy and Riku were not pleased with the strange smell on their daughter. They scraped brown gunk, with the same burnt smell, from beneath her fingernails.

'It could be toxic,' said Tommy. 'You're not going back there.'

'Dad, no way!'

'Not without an adult,' added Riku. 'It's not safe, we don't know what we're dealing with here.' Then Kartuan, on the edge of the group, suggested that the 'artefact' should undergo tests; they had some basic instruments, nothing like Shipworld, but it would have to do. She stepped forward and put out her hand. Lorrent gave up the metal piece, reluctantly, dropping it in Kartuan's palm with a bit of an attitude.

'It's not fair,' she grumbled. 'I found it.'

Kartuan's face remained blank, while Riku shot her a stern look. Lorrent knew that she was acting selfish and entitled – a terrible way for a New Pioneer to behave – so she did some quick thinking and proceeded to appear totally onboard with her dads' concerns. *Super valid* concerns, she stated. Riku chuckled, but Tommy blew her a kiss.

The next day a supply pod arrived with food, clothing, medicine and two pairs of binoculars. There wouldn't be more deliveries for a while, or regular radio transmissions, because the shipworldmates had decided to explore the fifth planet in the system, HD-40307f, which was a lot like Neptune in the sol system. The plan was to scoop hydrogen and deuterium from its atmosphere and send a probe down to the icy surface. Then they'd gravity-assist around it and be back in a few months. Also, they'd finished rebuilding the river, making it wider this time. The Orchido River, they called it. And they were putting on a play that sprawled across Shipworld and would be video-recorded for the future.

Lorrent walked down to the shore that evening. She waded barefoot and enjoyed the warm, acidic tide splashing on her shins. Salty winds ran their fingers through her hair as a cardinal arrived and perched on her shoulder. 'Hi,' said Lorrent. The robo-bird replied 'Hi, hi' and made a shy, jittery bow, its solar wings catching the late-day photons. Then it brushed her neck. They waded together, and overhead a star-like blip appeared through the clouds. Lorrent wondered: was it Shipworld? Did it really matter? Whatever she saw, it was the past. If it was a star, it was a star of a million-million years ago, its past self, a ghost. And if it was Shipworld, ever-changing and off on its own adventure, it was hers only in the past. It didn't belong to her anymore.

This planet, so strange and flat – was it hers now? She didn't feel *at home* here, whatever that meant. To belong to a planet, did it have to be where your ancestors had evolved from apes and fish and amoebas and, forever before that, proteins huddled in a volcanic pool? How, she asked herself, do you make an alien place your own? You dig into it, sure, you bleed on it and wade into it, you pee on it and pull on it and think about how it works, you even try to leave it alone sometimes, but none of that seemed enough for Lorrent. Maybe you had to take a planet from someone else, from the people or creatures who already lived there, for it to feel like yours, for real. But that didn't seem fair, either. That felt like something awful rising inside of her.

The cardinal brushed her neck again, ruffled its carbon composite wings.

On Shipworld, they'd named their river after the dead spacewalker. It's time, she thought, to give this planet – her feet in its water, her toes in its sand – a name that's *prodigiously* better than HD-40307g. Not some code from a star list, but a name born from their lives, a name that means humans crossed the galaxy to do it right this time. A few people had made suggestions – such as Erica's Planet, for the girl who died in the Encounter – but an actual naming would become this big process with every adult providing input and endless feedback. So Lorrent decided to name the planet herself, secretly, and just making the decision to do so caused her to smile, to feel a little more at home.

Then, as if a lid had popped off, the name came to her. It sounded so beautiful as she whispered it. But she wouldn't tell, not a soul, not yet.

Lorrent imagined Franz floating on a raft on the Orchido River. Around and around the inner circumference of the ship he flowed, with his big feet trailing in the water and that funny, mind-churning expression of his. Was he thinking of her? Probably not, and Lorrent dashed such thoughts away – she was getting good at that, *dash*, gone, flick of the hand – and hurried back to her quarters, with her bird friend flying loops beside her. Immediately, she started packing for the scouting mission planned for tomorrow. She included her Parsifal blocks, extra socks and a journal for writing down everything new, which was everything.

Time to grow up. They had a world to discover down here.

✦

On the morning of the scouting mission, Teyben rose early and took a wandering walk over ground baked hard by drought. Maybe this landscape hadn't changed for a million years. Or, he hoped, great rains would come in a few weeks, activating wildflower seeds and bringing forth buried life. It was possible. On Shipworld, what you saw was pretty much what you got; horizons ran up, over and into themselves, not to faraway vanishing points, and the vacuum of space was always just metres away. Here, on HD-40307g, it still felt a bit odd to move through flattened-out terrain, bounded only by the limits of his senses, the reach of his legs. A world, surely, that had barely revealed itself. The long-view dizziness and nausea that he'd experienced upon planetfall had mercifully faded, but sometimes, just for a moment, the young explorer still missed his previous life within a bordered space.

Teyben noticed the scrabbly footprints of a dirt devil. He kneeled down and examined one. Six-toed, equal-sized. The print was deeper up front, meaning, perhaps, that the creature had been moving fast. Chasing something, being chased, running for the joy of it. Or some reason he couldn't imagine, and he thought of the mysterious medallion from the ruins.

According to spectrographic analysis, it was an amalgam of iron, copper and a ceramic compound. The slashes and swirls were machine-applied with deft precision, stated the materials report co-authored by Aponi. The silvery flecks happened to be microchips, each containing twenty billion transistors or so, with each transistor one nanometer (two atoms) across – much smaller than anything in Shipworld's computers. The mega-narrow connections betwixt and between transistors resembled ruthenium, which prevents quantum tunnelling effects from gumming up the on/off functions, or something like that. Teyben didn't pretend to understand it. These defunct chips, concluded the report in a flourish that sounded like his wife, may have been added to the medallion for decorative or totemic effect. Totemic, thought Teyben, as in glorification? As in prophecy? If so, he'd like to know what had been predicted.

Up ahead squatted a low formation of boulders. Teyben moved towards it, listening to his feet hitting the ground, his lungs sifting breath and his sweat evaporating into the planet's atmosphere. Nothing else stirred. He saw two robo-birds among the boulders, grackles, long-tailed and iridescent, with those tiny black eyes circled in yellow. Small heads, sleek beaks. One grackle was on top of the other from behind, as though they were mating.

He looked away, then back again. No, he decided, it was probably some kind of repair activity. Or an attempt at improvement, at mechanical evolution. The top grackle shifted its weight, exposing a zigzagging underwing tool that glowed burnt orange. It pressed the tool, gently, carefully, into the dorsal region of the bottom bird, who stared blankly at a rockface a half metre away.

'Excuse me,' said Teyben.

The grackle looked at him; it didn't retract the instrument.

'Hello, Teyben,' it said. Then, as if reading his mind, or his face, it explained that they were trying to counteract the effects of electromagnetic surges that triggered the blue lightning and, subsequently, produced navigational difficulties for the birds. So far, they'd only achieved partial remediation.

It was a lot to process. The blue sheet lightning on this slash of coastal land occurred at midday, two or three times a week for maybe ten minutes at a time. Nothing momentous happened before or after, no burning smell or temperature shift or cloud rumble. HD-40307g didn't shudder. Teyben hadn't observed changes in bird behaviour, either, so he'd assumed, incorrectly, that they didn't sense it, or didn't care.

'You're still able to fly?' he asked.

'Yes, but there are problems,' the grackle replied.

'Where do the electromagnetic surges come from?'

'From the planetary poles.'

'We didn't detect that.' It occurred to Teyben that the robobirds' science might be very different, and sometimes superior.

'We will share our data,' said the grackle.

'Thank you. Do you think it's dangerous for humans?'

The grackle stayed still for several seconds. 'We don't know,' it finally responded, and it withdrew the zigzagging tool, which continued to burn orange. Then the bird adjusted its position on top of the bottom grackle and resumed its tender ministrations. Teyben watched for a few more moments, with a lingering sense of impropriety, before turning about. He took a direct route home, observing the human settlement as it appeared in the distance and grew steadily with his approach. He walked into his dormitory, which had been constructed from the *Marcus Marte* landing craft.

Aponi, with four-month-old Endive strapped to her chest, was cinching a strap on a backpack.

'What's going on?' he asked.

'We're coming,' she said. 'Can't let you have all the fun.'

'But you didn't want to – you said it was too risky.'

'Changed my mind,' she replied, as she stuffed one more diaper into a pocket, then turned to him. 'Earthquake, tsunami, volcanic eruption – who knows what might happen here. Our little girl might sit up all by herself – you wouldn't want to miss that, would you?' Endive batted the air as her mother grabbed the backpack and hoisted it aloft.

'It's best to stay together, and keep moving,' she said, and departed the dormitory.

Teyben sat down on his family's double-cot. Was she angry at him? And why did she wait until the last minute to say anything? Nonetheless, he felt immensely glad about her reversal, and he took a deep breath, and another, and looked across the way at a small painting hanging on a nail pounded into the wall/hull: Dürer's self-portrait. The frame, he realised, was quite beautiful. Wooden, with gold trim and an inset panel decorated with white flowers and curlicues that echoed Dürer's eyes and sinuous hair. Mona had given the masterpiece to Teyben and Aponi, with the admonition to pass it along, someday, to her grandchild. He was tempted to take it on the expedition.

Several metres away, Zeritz arranged his hair into a ponytail. One of the lander pilots, he'd had a hard time since the crash of the *Neyjay-Usah*. His girlfriend and her family had been aboard, and for weeks afterwards he'd accosted himself in raw, guilt-fuelled tirades for allowing them to fly in a different ship. Aponi had managed to comfort Zeritz a bit, and Teyben had approached him, without success, to go bodysurfing. 'You'd really like it,' he'd said. 'Catching a wave, it's almost like being a pilot.' Now Teyben tried to connect again, walking over and asking Zeritz if he'd keep an eye on the painting while they were away; he even said that he'd be in the man's debt.

'Sure,' he replied, tying a string at the end of the long hairstalk, not making eye contact. Had he even heard?

'Just so you know,' said Teyben, 'it was a great treasure on Earthworld.'

Zeritz gave it a quick look, shrugged.

'Albrecht Dürer – first person ever to paint himself straight on,' continued Teyben. 'Looking right back, this is me. It was considered an act of bravery.'

'OK,' the pilot said. 'But isn't that all they did on Earthworld – look at themselves in the mirror?'

The image of the interlocked grackles reappeared to Teyben. Two birds among boulders in the desolation, conducting an intimate act, and now the top grackle disengaged from his flockmate and displayed a brush for an underwing tool. What might it dare to paint on the nearby rockface? Itself, *yes, me*, staring back? Other robo-birds? The humans, the lurching creatures who Svonne had supposedly taught them to respect? Or something ungraspable, heedless of human perceptions of time and space?

Zeritz placed a scrap of hair string on top of an object, a book, by his bedroll. Teyben had never seen a paper-and-ink book. It was thick and had a black cover. The visible edges of the pages were gold, as if the contents were of great value.

'What's that?' he asked.

'The book? It's been handed down in my family,' Zeritz replied, matter-of-factly. 'My triple-great Aunt Anat read it to the last Pioneer. The language is strange, but there are some good stories. Especially this King David guy.'

Teyben looked at Zeritz more closely. The short sleeves of his shirt were rolled up, exposing in full his biceps, bulged from work and push-ups, and he'd draped his ponytail over one shoulder. Vanity, perhaps, worthy of Dürer. Or just someone grasping at rituals, anything to keep the weight of grief from dragging him under.

'Hey, do you want to come along?' asked Teyben. 'We could use a few more people.'

'I don't think so,' said Zeritz, looking squarely at Teyben for the first time. 'There's lots to take care of here.' He paused, as if considering whether to say more. 'Some of us figured out how to make bricks. We found a clay deposit, and there's lots of sand. We're going to put up a monument to the *Neyjay-Usah*.'

'That's good,' said Teyben. He'd heard nothing about this project. 'It's a really important thing to do.'

'And a brick shelter, too, against the wind,' Zeritz continued. 'By the time you get back there'll be a whole city. Better than Earthworld.'

In that moment, he reminded Teyben of his mother. Something in the sharp, blue eyes, the casual manner disguising a turbulent spirit. Lately, Teyben had been missing Mona more than ever, for a very particular reason. He missed the way she looked at him with pride. Yes, he knew that was foolish, and needy, and of course she was still proud of him from afar, from away, but it wasn't the same as seeing the pride in her face. And if he never saw her again, which was likely, wasn't that a lot like her being dead? Teyben supposed that he was now like one of Marcus Marte's ancestors, the ones who chiselled the gravestones around his wife's grave, the ones who'd fled across oceans in coffin ships and never returned to their homelands. The ones who were gone.

'Is the story of Jonah in there?' he asked, pointing at the book. 'You know, from *The Chronicler's Journal.*'

'Yeah,' said Zeritz. 'Jonah thought he had choices, but he didn't.'

Teyben nodded. The idea of facing false choices, of being a pawn unaware of the moving hand, intensely bothered him. He didn't like being in the dark, as he'd been about Franz, Lorrent and Kartuan, about Orchido's random death in space, about Aponi's decision just five minutes ago – as he'd always been about his biological father, the man behind the blob of sperm randomly selected by his mother, the man who might be dead or alive, down here or up there. As he was about the birds and the blue lightning and every last thing on HD-40307g. Such thoughts, however, were best not voiced by a pilot, he told himself, by a leader of the New Pioneers. Teyben again thanked Zeritz, who was busy giving Dürer a long look, then finished packing his gear and headed outside.

Reflexively, he gazed up to connect with Shipworld, their lifeline, but of course it had gone. Good for them, and in his mind's future-eye his brother Franz, concocted from the same stubborn mother but a different mystery sperm-blob, was grown up and wearing Kartuan's bridger's cap as he steered the old rust bucket not just to the system's other planets and moons but past its Oort Cloud and towards a nearby star, and still with that sleepy-wild look in his eye.

Franz might turn his back even more. Teyben envisioned him taking ageing, ageless Shipworld in a return-arc across trillions of miles, and the distance between the brothers would grow greater and ever greater, yawning to infinity, and ultimately Franz and his descendants and their descendants, an unbreakable line of Oorts, would complete a thousand-year migration back to Earthworld, to the beginning of things. Or the boy might stick to the plan and make planetfall. There was no way of knowing, and besides, Teyben had his own child to worry about down here. A growing, changing human being. He had to figure out, and soon, how to be a good father to her.

Quickly, Teyben proceeded to the embarkation point where twenty-five human volunteers, plus Chickadee, six starlings and the cardinal, were gathering. Teyben and Kartuan had been selected as co-leaders. On this, the first day, they hiked inland across rubbly desert pocked with grey, twisted bushes – deeply rooted, survivors. The robo-birds flew ahead, then returned with news of a flat area at the base of the mountain, several kilometres away, where they could camp for the night. Upon arrival, the humans yanked up a mass of stubborn ground vines. Piled in a crisscrossing pattern, the vines weren't bad for a campfire and gave off a pungent odour, a cross between mint and rosemary. The starlings, when not arguing among themselves, or so it seemed, careened about the fire in a raucous swirl.

Teyben slept heavily that night, weighed down by a dream of Earthworld.

In the dream he was Albrecht Dürer. He was running up a curling, stone stairway within a castle, and he felt Dürer's moustache on his upper lip, tickling, and heard his footfalls, *duum, duum, duum, duum*. He was Dürer, the stout man in his stylish brown coat with the ripped arms revealing the silk shirt beneath, the coat an ostentatious frame for the silk, and as he ran, green countryside and blue sky flashed through cuts in the stone, vertical slits for firing arrows at one's enemies. Up he curled and burst into his studio. There, on an easel, his self-portrait stared back. His eyes wide, his palm open. The dream rebooted at this point, over and over, up the stone stairway and into the studio. He was Dürer, the first to proclaim *yes, me*, and finally Teyben/Dürer felt the knife in his hand. Its blade carried slashes and swirled patterns, like comets gone crazy chasing their own tails. Silver flecks trailed from shaft to tip. Teyben/Dürer rushed at the self-portrait, blade raised, and plunged it into the man's heart – then he awoke.

His heart beat rapidly, as if he'd really been running. A bitter scent filled his nostrils. Teyben sat up, next to his sleeping wife and child, and watched them as he calmed down in the near-morning cusp between darkness and light. Endive lay flat, arms tossed behind her head in an unnatural manner, and her father was much relieved to see a little finger twitch. Next to her, in a foetal curl, Aponi betrayed not the slightest motion. Gently, Teyben touched her back beneath the shoulder blade, a valley that his hand found when they made love, and there he detected the rise and fall of her lungs. All was well. Then he looked up into the undarkening sky where a few stars remained between clouds, and for a moment he understood how his distant ancestors, from dozens of light-years away, may have felt at the leading edge of day as they set out into new lands. For a quicksilver moment he wondered, as they had wondered, what lay beyond the seeking eye.

That day, they started the ascent. It was a slow, uneven climb, and Teyben and Aponi shared carrying their infant in a sling. There were no animals or bio-birds in sight, no flowers and no bugs to pollinate them, not even a DD diving into its hiding hole. Gaining altitude, strangely, made the air hotter, clingier. When the scouting party made camp, they couldn't find any vines for burning, so they sat around a lantern and ate dried fish in tomatillo sauce. The clouds above shrouded the starry rupture that is the trailing arm of the Milky Way – the inheritance of the people below, for they had traversed it.

It was the history they carried.

After dinner, Aponi stood and read aloud entries from *The Second Chronicler's Journal*. Lorrent, who'd regained the artefact and wore it on a necklace, listened raptly as Tender Remarque described concocting a cloud for her daughter. Then Kartuan called for Teyben to act out the founder's role in *Discovery/ Recovery* – yes, do it, hollered the lamplit New Pioneers – and so he stood and recited with typical Teyben flair, streaking comet-like from visionary young Parsons to scheming middle-aged Parsons to cantankerous old Parsons, who knows if any of them came close to the actual man, and then he returned to his public self and stated that there's no evidence of a Chinese ark ship. Hibernation technology remains a fantasy. And unfrozen Thaddeus Parsons, he joked, won't be jumping from behind a rock. Even as he said this, as laughter rolled around the circle, he wasn't entirely sure.

On the third day, the scouting party approached the mountain's summit. Then blue lightning hit and everyone stopped and looked up. Kartuan and Lorrent, instead, sat together under the sudden sky, talking and laughing and weaving a new world between them. The birds grounded themselves. Teyben turned his eyes to the peak, bordered in blue, and recalled the lullaby that his mother sang to him at bedtime. A silly song, she called it, and also a growing-up song, the same one that her parents had sung to her, and back it all rolled, from generation to generation, across forty-five light-years. Cecilia Oort had sung it to her wild daughter Janelle, who'd been haunted by fears of the beyond, of what's real and what's not.

The bear went over the mountain, the bear went over the mountain,
the bear went over the mountain to see what she could see.
But all that she could see, all that she could see,
Was the other side of the mountain, the other side of the mountain…

Other verses had the Bear – a family name? some kind of animal? – prowling through the solar system and the Oort Cloud and across the great void of the galaxy and finally into the prickly embrace of HD-40307g. As a child, Teyben had preferred the lone mountain in the first verse, perhaps because he'd never seen a mountain with his own eyes, never made the trek up a rugged slope. Snug in his Shipworld bed, he'd always been fascinated and annoyed by the song's elusive third line, *but all that she could see, all that she could see*, which made him wonder if they'd find grave disappointment at the end of their travels, on the other side of the mountain.

The blue lightning flicked off and they resumed hiking. Teyben, out front, began singing the lullaby out loud. Aponi picked it up and Endive burbled a few notes, and Riku and Tommy held hands as they sang, verse after verse, and soon every member of this motley group of climbing humans and swooping birds joined in, whether they knew the lyrics or not.

...the other side of the mountain, the other side of the...

Just below the summit, the scouting party negotiated stone slabs marked with scrapes and gouges – reminiscent, thought Teyben, of the tortured flanks of the Olmec Head. Then they made the peak and stood, out of breath, on ragged rocks interrupted by a few shallow pools of water. To the east, in the far distance, stretched mountain after mountain, brown and forbidding, the tallest ones crowned with snow. A nearby rock jumble looked like Parsifal blocks, if you relaxed your eyes. A few people twirled about, arms extended, and someone took photos while others set up the radio to report back to the settlement.

Lorrent called out, 'Over here, over here!'

Teyben and Aponi, with the sleeping Endive, joined her as she pointed at several deep markings at the base of a three-metre-high slab. 'They match it,' she said, pulling the necklace from under her shirt. The cardinal gibbered, 'What, what, what?', and Tommy and Riku came over and kneeled down, first examining the rock markings and then the object cradled in Lorrent's palm. Each displayed an artful maelstrom of swirls and slashes.

'Look at this,' said Kartuan, on the other side of the rock. Her fingers touched a brownish green splotch in a crack, rough to the touch. 'I think it's organic. Maybe some kind of fungus.' A few minutes later, a little boy discovered a scraggly bush with black berries that, when crushed, smelled sharp and spicy. No, he was told, they can't be tasted until they're analysed. Meanwhile, Chickadee and the starlings executed a sweeping flight away from the mountaintop, scouting the area and soaking up sun rays. Suddenly, the little bird U-turned and rushed back to the group, landing on Kartuan's shoulder.

'Something's moving, something's moving,' it chirped and whistled. Beak pointing east: 'That way, that way!'

Teyben brought the binoculars to his eyes.

About two kilometres away, across the valley, he saw a dark red object on a slope. Red fur? Red coat? Red skin? Was it a live being, or some kind of puppet? A greeting? A warning, a snare? Teyben blinked; his mouth became dry. The thing he saw through the magnifying lenses appeared to have four limbs and it seemed to move, or be moved, in a shambling manner, dipping its maybe-head to the ground, swivelling this way and that, and there were small protuberances, horns or beaks or sensors or tufts of hair. Utterly strange, and strangely familiar. It turned towards Teyben, as though looking at him, and then away.

'Is it caribou?' asked Chickadee.

'I don't see antlers,' said Teyben. He handed the binoculars to Kartuan, who looked through them for a couple of seconds. Then she gave the binocs back to Teyben and said nothing. She took a few steps away. Strange, he thought, her silence. A cryptic silence, a message in itself. As co-leaders, they had to agree on what to do next, and he was counting on her to have a definite opinion. Either full speed ahead because why else have we come all this way, or stop right here, no further for now. But Kartuan said nothing.

What, he asked himself, should Teyben Oort – descendant of the first Jan Oort, who divined the Oort Cloud from celestial clues – learn from today's phenomena, from blue lightning and rock markings, from fungus, berries and now this apparition, this lone chimera across the gap? A faraway smudge seen with his own eyes; a captivating, ambiguous image through the binoculars; and up close, perhaps something else entirely. Here Teyben stood at the distillation point of the journey out from Earthworld, from Shipworld, from their toehold on HD-40307g. What, in this dizzying moment, does the future hold?

Slowly, he gazed around at his companions' faces, some guarded, some churning with anticipation. His people, his tribe, and above them the robo-birds spiralled, chattering to themselves. Yes, Teyben decided, let's meet the beyond. Let's make contact, or make pursuit, and follow it to somewhere green and wet, an oasis bursting with trees and mossy vines, with life. A new shoot on a planet beginning to heal.

He felt an ancestral wind at his back. Yes, let's give in to hope, again.

That's what he'd say, if it was up to him alone. He walked over to Kartuan, who now balanced the robo-bird in her palm. 'What do you think, Chickadee?' Teyben asked. 'Should we keep going?' It ruffled its feathers and dug its talons in, as if destabilised by the question that had arrived like a clap of blue lightning.

'What do you think?' Teyben repeated.

'It is the human decision,' Chickadee said.

'No, it's our decision,' he replied. 'All of us.'

He looked again to Kartuan. In a voice that didn't sound quite like hers, she counselled caution. She counselled humility. If they keep going, she said, they should make every effort to communicate and cooperate, for they were the strangers here. They should try to see themselves in others – which is damn hard, she knew that – and see others in themselves. And while they can't predict the consequences of their actions, she told him in a voice so quiet and strong that it sounded, Teyben realised, like his mother's, they should try, always, to consider Endive and Lorrent and their children and their children's children, and all the generations as far out as they can imagine.

'There's a lot riding on this,' she said. Then, smiling: 'I say go.'

'We go,' said Chickadee.

'All right,' said Teyben. 'Go.'

Aponi, with Endive slumped across her shoulder, gave her husband a kiss on the cheek. She shifted the child, who had a way of becoming heavier as she burrowed deeper into sleep, as the infant's dreamworld, never to be revealed, came into rapturous being.

'Hey, maybe it's not interested in us,' said Tommy, peering across the valley. Next to him, Riku chuckled and muttered, 'Not yet.' He gripped a rock in one hand.

'Is it the bear?' asked Lorrent.

'No, silly,' said Kartuan. 'We're the bear.'

Her daughter stroked the cardinal nestled into the crook of her neck. 'We're the bear,' she repeated. 'The future shines in our eyes.'

It was time to go. The humans tightened their shoelaces, shouldered their backpacks and migrated down the other side of the mountain. The robo-birds stretched their wings and went aloft. Struggling to keep upright over steep, rocky terrain, and flying ahead but doubling back, together they moved towards the distant inhabitant of HD-40307g who loitered on its hillside beneath the alien sky.

ACKNOWLEDGEMENTS

I would like to thank Simone Caroti for his excellent book *The Generation Starship in Science Fiction*, which helped me grasp the amazing arc of this genre. There's so much to enjoy, from Don Wilcox's pathbreaking 1940 short story 'The Voyage that Lasted 600 Years', to Caroline M. Yoachim's short-short story 'Goat Milk Cheese, Three Trillion Miles from Earth' (2015), to epic novels such as Kim Stanley Robinson's *Aurora* (2016).

With thanks to my fabulous agent, Sara O'Keeffe, and her colleagues at Andrew Nurnberg Associates in London; my inspiring editors, Stephanie Rathbone and Elisabeth Denison, and their colleagues at Bloomsbury Publishing in London; insightful reader Leah Rugen – may her memory be a blessing – who commented on an early draft of the novel even as she was undergoing chemotherapy; my daughter, Kelsey, for our many wonderful conversations about all things sci-fi; and my wife, Elahna, for her loving encouragement.

A NOTE ON THE AUTHOR

Hal LaCroix has worked as an instructor at Boston University, a communications specialist with environmental and biomedical research non-profits, and a journalist for newspapers in New England. He is the author of the non-fiction book *Journey Out of Darkness*, and lives outside Boston with his wife, Elahna. *Here and Beyond* is his first novel.

A NOTE ON THE TYPE

The text of this book is set in Fournier. Fournier is derived from the *romain du roi*, which was created towards the end of the seventeenth century from designs made by a committee of the Académie of Sciences for the exclusive use of the Imprimerie Royale. The original Fournier types were cut by the famous Paris founder Pierre Simon Fournier in about 1742. These types were some of the most influential designs of the eight and are counted among the earliest examples of the 'transitional' style of typeface. This Monotype version dates from 1924. Fournier is a light, clear face whose distinctive features are capital letters that are quite tall and bold in relation to the lower-case letters, and *decorative italics, which show the influence of the calligraphy of Fournier's time.*